OF
CAVERNS
AND
CASTERS

Published in the United States

First Printing, 2018

ISBN 9781718156654

avadelauthors@gmail.com

Laine
For Jesus Christ my Savior, whose mercy astounds me.
For Mom, who made me write *something* every day.
And for Dad, who taught me that great authors steal.

Aria
For God, without whom nothing is made that has been made.

May your skies stay
bright,

Laine Nichols

&

Aria Nichols

OF
CAVERNS
AND
CASTERS

THE LOST ROADS QUARTET
BOOK ONE

Laine & Aria Nichols

Of caverns and casters
*   of whispers and daggers*
Of shadows and snow
*   of keys and lost roads*

The salvation of fate
*   finds its number in eight*
The realm stands condemned
*   less the stars bring them:*

A prince, a witch, a scientist
*   a seer, a child, a shade*
A girl of untamed magic
*   and a twin of no one's age*

Of caverns, two come
*   of casters, six are*
Of whispers, one cast out
*   of daggers, one bears scars*

Of shadows, one born
*   of snow, one lost*
Of keys, one given
*   of lost roads, all tossed.*

- The Wyrd of the Shadesnare's End

Chapter 1

LEAVI

When I was three, I wanted to be a princess. But there are no princesses in the High Valleys. Everyone knows that's only in fairytales.

Just a few months ago, I wanted to work as a scientist in Erreliah, my home and the shining capital of the world of research. Instead, my mother sent me to the city of Karsix.

Now, all I want is to stay alive.

It's curfew in Karsix, and the underground city wears a darkness so thick, I can feel it. It renders my pale skin invisible, and my long black hair blends into the solid shadows. As I finish shoving my tunics and leather pants into my satchel, my hands shake. Taking a deep breath, I wipe them up and down the side of my leg, as if that will somehow steady them. *Focus, Leavi. Panicking is pointless.*

I have a plan.

I will make it out.

I will not get caught.

Snapping back to my task, I grope for the cloth-wrapped instruments I stole from the laboratory earlier that day. One falls, and I start at the glass piece's muted *tink!* In the silence of my empty dormitory, it feels like a million alarms announcing my escape.

Every possible way this could go wrong flashes through my mind.

Crossbows click in unison as I race for the exit. "Ready… On my mark… Fire!" Agony runs through my back as the bolt pierces my skin. I fall to the ground, screaming out. They call, "Stay back! She could be infected!" Blood drains onto the ground, slipping from my dying body like hope slipping from my foolish plan—

Or, instead, I'm alone in a tunnel, darkness swallowing my plague-ridden body. Blisters cover me inside and out, pressing on my lungs as I rasp in my last breaths—

Or maybe snow frosts over me, the numbing cold of a topside winter lulling me to a final sleep—

I shove the thoughts away. That won't happen.

I have a plan.

I will make it out.

I will not get caught.

I stoop to recover the fallen test tube. My fingers flutter over its sides, searching for cracks. *Please, please, please don't be broken…*

My pent-up breath escapes in a relieved sigh. The piece is whole.

I gingerly wrap it back up, placing it on top of everything else. With my hands empty of a task, I stare at the bag through the dark. Despite the blackness, I feel like I can see it.

1

I've memorized every inch of the crisp leather, down to the tiny scratch from the journey here. I don't mind the flaw; my mother is the one who fretted over what my new luggage would look like when I arrived in Karsix, not me. I memorized that bag for a different reason.

Before the move here, it mocked me across my old room, representing everything I didn't want to travel toward and everything I didn't want to leave. Now that I need it, though, I've fixed on it, a single light of hope in the obsidian tunnels surrounding the city.

As I sling it over my shoulder, the panic bleeds away for a moment, leaving a cold stone of truth settling in my gut.

This is it. Everything that represents me is here; every scrap of paper, every leather-bound book, every testing instrument, everything I've ever known all jammed into one paltry bag. I even stuffed in my favorite book and the now pointless lab coat. They take up too much space, but I can't bear to leave them.

The future I imagined for myself is disappearing like ashes sinking into a river. I'm throwing myself into the unknown, risking my life to get topside in the winter, a choice that might kill me as easily as the Blistering Death could here. My hand pauses on the doorknob, the metal cool against my sweating skin. What *am* I doing? I should play it safe, keep in the quarantined areas, listen to the authorities, bide my time. I should do what any rational, mild-mannered citizen would. Behave.

I swing the door open. My foot crosses the threshold, and I resist the impulse to look back. It wouldn't do any good: the path behind is just as obscured by darkness as the path ahead.

A deathly hush pervades the dormitory building. My colleagues are shut up in their rooms, almost as though the quarantine curfew fades them into the corpses they so desperately wish not to become. One among thousands, they whimper that the odds must be in their favor, cowering in the hopes the disease won't touch them. But I refuse to leave my fate up to odds.

I have a plan.

I will make it out.

I will not get caught.

I slip out the back door onto a street just as morgue-like as the building I left. Cat-footing my way down the alley, I run through my plan one last time. *Over the wall separating me from the residential area, then west out of the research quarter. South down Butcher's Avenue. Then the Dead District will be all that's left between me and the Lesser West Tunnel.*

"All," I scoff. But that tunnel is the only one that won't be guarded. After all, infected cadavers should be sentinels enough.

The air is too still out here. The atmosphere presses in on me, and I tug at my jacket collar. In the darkness, imagination reigns, and I can almost see the contagion in the air, invading my lungs with every breath. Unconsciously, my foot takes a step back toward the safety of my dormitory.

Irritated with myself, I surge forward. *I'm not in the Dead District yet*, I scold myself. *I'm safe... as safe as I can be anymore.* Even so, I tug my muffler up over my mouth and nose because that supposed safety isn't going to last for long.

I've heard the horror stories. The slums fell to the Blistering Death first. By the time responders realized what was going on, other places were getting infected and resources were stretched thin. Keeping the sick elsewhere alive—and contained—became more important than burying the dead. Now a whole neighborhood is filled with corpses.

My hand skates along the rough stone wall, my only guide in the dark. The toe of my boot rams into the metal garbage bin at the end of the alley. I bite back a curse.

Shifting my bag to my back, I clamber onto the lid, which shrieks in protest under the strain. I cringe at the noise but reach for the lip of the alley wall. Stone scrapes my hand as I drop onto the other side of an empty street, stumbling a few paces before I catch my balance.

On this side of the alley, soft white light emanates from the brass planters of glow-moss that line most streets in Karsix. The city has yet to make the switch to the brighter oil lamps like Erreliah has—a fact I'm for once grateful for, considering the council would switch them off during curfew, plunging the city into solid black.

All down the row, the houses of prominent politicians and scientists loom in the ghostly light. The shuttered bronze-framed windows are empty eyes that trail after me, and the sculpted door-knockers, faces that usually offer a cheerful grin, have mutated into snarling monsters. I shudder and hurry along.

In the research quarter, the buildings stretch taller, clawing toward the cavern ceiling before melting into the gloom. They tower over me like expectant executioners, my pounding heartbeat their drum. In the quiet, my steps rap flat against the pavement.

As I turn a corner, my eyes can't help but wander toward the one stocky, gray stone building on the street, out of place against the surrounding glass giants. A small bronze plaque quietly announces the building as *Trifexer's Private Institute for Research and the Sciences.*

My workplace for the last three months.

I wonder what my colleagues will think when I don't show up tomorrow morning. Some will think it's odd; I've never missed a day, even when all this broke out two months ago. Some won't know, having holed themselves up in their dorms for weeks. Some will worry I caught it but be will be too scared to come check on me. And my partner, the great and almighty Sean Rahkifellar?

I doubt he'll even notice.

Why do you care? the stony face of the institute accuses. *You're the one abandoning them.*

In my unease, my fingers creep up to the tarnished chain of the necklace my father gave me.

No explanation, no goodbye, the building sneers. *You've stolen their tools and are running off in the dead of night. You'd think you were a common thief rather than a scientist.*

Guilt prickles in my stomach. We're hardly more than acquaintances, yet the scientists at Trifexer's are the closest thing to friends I have in Karsix. They at least deserve to know where I disappeared to.

Scooping up a loose pebble, I hurry to the entryway of the institute. The rock makes an awkward writing tool, but the scratched white letters show up on the stone wall clearly enough.

I'm healthy. Escaping through DD, LW Tunnel, and heading topside.
- Leavi Riveirre

3

I pause, then on impulse, add a single line.

May your skies stay bright.

It's an old blessing, back from when our civilization had always lived above ground. I suppose it's something strange for undergrounders to say now, but it seems fitting for some reason. Hopeful.

As I step back onto the sidewalk, I'm hyper-aware of the silence, no longer covered by the scratch of stone on stone or steps on pavement. The lack of noise almost feels like an entity unto itself, like all the sound is being sucked out of the world and gathered to form something malevolent. Streets should never be this empty. Cities are hubbubs of glittering light, flamboyant attire, loud crowds. Not this pressing, weighty, dead emptiness waiting to devour everything it surrounds.

Smothering anxiety rises in my chest, and I break into a sprint, desperate to release the pressure. The echoes of my footsteps chase me, a relentless *pap-pap-pap*. My arms pump, keeping time with my quickening breaths. A shadow in motion, my hair streams behind me.

Finally running out of breath, I skid to a stop on Butcher's Avenue.

The buildings here are smaller, various little one-story shops. Wares hang in windows: blown-glass trinkets, glassy-eyed windup toys, ticking timepieces. Inside the butcher's, strung-up hunks of meat swing beside glinting knives.

At the end of the avenue, a street-cleaner boy's broom swipes against the pavement. Our eyes meet at the same time, bodies going rigid. He swallows.

The kid's infected. As soon as the possibility flashes through my mind, I shove it away. There's no reason for him to sneak out to do his job during curfew if he's sick. More than likely, he's here right now to avoid the throngs of people during the day who might be.

Apprehension still flutters in my chest. He looks me up and down, his thoughts likely running similar to mine.

After a tense second, I edge forward. Surely he won't turn me in. He'd have to have a death wish. If a patrolman catches us out during curfew, they'll drag us to quarantine. Then we're both certain to catch the Death.

Still keeping his eyes on me, he resumes his sweeping, shuffling closer to the sidewalk. I take another testing step forward. His shoulders are tense, body angled away from mine. *Shff, shff, shff.* He follows his broom, warily maintaining the distance between us. The only noises are his sweeping and my footsteps, discordant music for our hesitant dance around each other. We come level.

He takes off.

My heart jumps into my throat, and I rush to the corner. The alley twists, grime and darkness both growing thicker the further I travel. Rubbish crunches underfoot, and I press my palm to the wall for a guide.

A sticky, viscous substance clings to my fingers. I recoil, wiping my hand off on my clothes.

Unable to bring myself to set my hand back, I take a deep breath, forcing myself to calm down. The kid's running home. Must be. There's no way he's going to get a patrolman.

One careful step at a time, my feet navigate the path, toeing trash out of the way and feeling for rifts in the ground. My progress is slow but steady, and eventually, the black is penetrated by faint, grasping fingers of light. I hurry forward.

4

The alley empties into a run-down road lit by isolated pots of moss. A wooden barricade slices through the cracked pavement, circling to cut off the Dead District. Spikes threaten from wall tops. Rough guard towers break the violent line, and I shrink back into the shadows.

Everything's still, though, the post abandoned. There's no use guarding the city from corpses, and no one other than me would be crazy enough to want in. Dozens of flyers litter the ground, only a few still nailed to the wall. Their faded faces shout mutedly—TURN BACK! QUARANTINE AREA!

I stride across the street. My fingers dig in between the logs as I try to scale toward the tower. The rounded edges make awkward holds. I only make it up a couple feet, sliding down each time. Teeth gritted, I try once more. Five feet up, fingertips reaching for the top—

My foot slips. Nails claw at wood, and one tears, peeling back in half. My feet collide with the ground.

I call out in pain, frustrated, and bang my fist against the barricade. This *stupid* wall is all that stands between me and a straight stretch to the Lesser West Tunnel. I refuse to lose to a pile of wood. There's got to be a way over this.

I scan the street. My eyes light on one of the pots. It's about a foot and a half in diameter, four feet tall. That should get me a third of the way up.

I drop to my knees to push the pot to the barrier, but it doesn't move. It's heavier than I expected, a monolith of dirt weighing it down. My eyes scavenge the littered road.

There. A curved iron bar, broken off from the top of another pot, juts up among the debris. I snag it, shoving the point under my pot's base. The other half extends out, angled sharply, and I jump on it.

The pot tips over with a clang, dirt and glow-moss spilling out. Moist clumps squish underneath my fingernails as I excavate the soil, my torn one stinging like jabbing needles.

Fifty feet down the road, a thin beam divides the darkness. My head snaps up. Searching, the beam sweeps away. I redouble my work, scraping armful after armful of dirt from the pot.

I've been making too much noise. They know someone's out here. My gaze flicks to the alley I came from. That would be my safest bet. Disappear into the darkness.

But if they know someone is trying to leave through the Dead District, they'll start defending it. Then I'll never get out of Karsix.

The beam appears again, more concentrated. They're about to turn off an alley. The pot's hollowed out.

"It's now or never, Leavi," I mutter.

The patrolman turns the corner.

I launch to my feet, heaving the pot upright. Metal on stone shrieks as I drag it to the wall. The patrolman breaks into a run. My sweating fingers struggle to keep their grip. He's only thirty feet away now.

I push the pot flush to the wall and scramble atop it, catching myself against the wood as the pot wobbles beneath me. It's almost too light now.

Twenty feet.

My perch stabilizes. I stretch for the window of the tower. Mere inches separate my fingers from the top, a tiny and impossible distance.

5

Fifteen feet away, he stops running. He slings the crossbow off his shoulder. "Halt!"

I set my foot into a hold. I just need to be a little bit closer–

A bolt shoots past my leg, slicing my trousers. I flinch, almost losing my balance. He's cranking his weapon to reload it. I don't have time to climb, I need to be in that tower *now*–

The bolt hisses at it releases. This time, he doesn't miss.

Chapter 2
Aster

My veins are acid. Blood drips out my burning nose, down my lip, and onto the wooden floor beneath me. My arms curl around my body as I shrink into a rocking ball, back and forth, back and forth. The pressure building in me increases as the magic shrieks for me to free it, but I cannot complete the spell.

I knew it was too complicated.

A scream echoes through the room, and distantly I realize it's my own. It's taken the place of the ancient words of power that I should be speaking. Now I'm drowning in agonizing incompetence, unable to release myself from this prison of pain.

Suddenly, the pain and pressure begin to drain away, slowly at first, then faster and faster until I'm nothing but a broken shell, a failure of a caster. Empty.

The tall magician crouching beside me removes his hand from my shoulder and stands, turning to face me.

As if it will shield me from the backlash of the failed spell, I stay slumped over, aching body limp. Blood still trickles from my nose, leaving my head light and thoughts slow.

"Aster!" he reprimands.

My head jerks up, dizziness washing across my mind and feeding the black spots dancing through my vision.

He looks at me for a moment, derision and disapproval filling out his sharp features. His cloak sweeps behind him as he paces the austere room.

"You've failed again," he finally growls.

I force myself to straighten up from my kneeled position and sit cross-legged. Pulling a handkerchief from my cloak, I pinch my nose to staunch the bleeding. My gaze returns to my master.

"I'm sorry, Agraund. I *will* figure it ou-"

He whips around to face me again. The firelight from one of the ensconced torches flickers across one side of his face, twisting his features into a demonic glower.

"Aster!" he repeats.

I flinch.

"This is the third time you've tried this spell, the third time you've failed, the third time I've had to *save* you from it, and the third time you've made such a promise. What makes you think that the next time will be any different?"

"I- I-" I stumble around for words, apparently. The malaise in my thoughts isn't helping, and all I can think is how I want to tell him that although it might not be next time, I *will* get it right eventually. But I would never dare.

My spine tingles.

"Uncle, I'll do better! I'll work harde-"

7

"You shouldn't have to work for it at all! You're the upcoming Second Son, next commander of all magicians in Morineaux, Aster. You're an adult, seventeen, for Antium's sake. Magic is in your blood. Jacqueline is in your blood. This should come naturally to you. It comes naturally to me, it came naturally to the Second before me, and the one before him. It is your fate, boy, and you need to decide what exactly it is that's keeping you from it. You're supposed to be the greatest magician in all of Morineaux, but you can hardly cast! I don't want to keep hearing these apologies and excuses!"

He crouches mere inches from me. His voice drops. "I want you to be the caster you're supposed to be. One day, this country will rest heavily on your shoulders. The success of your queen, of your people, will be your responsibility. So get yourself together, quit apologizing, and do it!" He pushes up.

Frustration and hopelessness bubble up inside me, like water boiling into steam, desperately pressing at my lips in hopes of exploding out. I know I'm failing my country. I know the responsibility I'll be facing. But I don't know what to do differently than everything I already have been doing.

Agraund simply watches me, an eyebrow raised.

I straighten up, pulling the bloody handkerchief away from my face. Determination not to fail him and not to fail my country hardens the steam into cold resolve. "Show me the spell again, my lord."

* * *

It's midnight.

The rest of the castle sleeps. Here in my bedroom, moonlight streams around the warm, red curtains over my windows. It provides enough light to illuminate me, sitting cross-legged on the rug my ten-year-old self snuck out of my nursery when Agraund forced me to move to this room. It depicts the history of Jacqueline, a story I grew up believing, although many adults dismiss it as childish nonsense.

The six Stellries rise from the ashes of the Fallen Star. In the rug's center, Lady Jacqueline spreads her hands out wide. Balls of light float above her palms as she ascends with the rest of the ancient beings. At the bottom of the picture, where I'm sitting, supplicating hands reach toward her, waiting for her to grace them with the world's first taste of magic. The Lady's head is tilted back, eyes closed, a blissful smile spreading across her face. She held more power in that single smile than I've ever mustered in my twelve years of training.

"What am I doing wrong?" I murmur to the Lady. "And how do I fix it?" Hopelessness rises inside me. I bite my cheek. "I've done everything Agraund has ever asked of me. Every tome on magic theory in this castle, I've read, studied, memorized. Every endurance exercise, I've practiced until unconsciousness overtook me. Every technique, every trick, every old wives' tale, I've *tried* it. Why do I not have the same skill as former Seconds, Jacqueline? Why am I not powerful enough?"

Her image offers no answers.

"Morineaux needs to stay strong, and a Second Son like me is *not* strength."

Angry and disgusted with myself, I stand, running a hand through my mussed blond hair. "What happens when, Stellries forbid, Agraund dies? What happens

8

when the other countries find out that a puny excuse of a wizard is all that stands in the old Second Son's shoes?"

Echoing silence is the only response in the empty room. The image of Jacqueline lays there, nothing but a carpet. My hope for some supernatural solution dies.

I growl, dragging a hand down my face. "I've lost it. I'm talking to a rug. A rug!" My tired body sinks into a red armchair. "What am I going to do?"

Go to sleep, the weak part of me suggests. *You have a meeting to attend with Agraund tomorrow, lessons to go to, a mountain of paperwork that will keep you up as late tomorrow as it did tonight. And who knows what extra practices Agraund might devise. You'll need to be well-rested for that.*

The downy comforter of my four-poster bed reinforces that call, and I rise, tempted to give in. It is late. A proverb of Jeanna, my nursemaid, rings in my ears. *You can do more good with a good night's sleep than with two tired days.*

I'm not a child anymore, though. Agraund's words rattle my head.

Improvement doesn't come to those who simply wait for it.

I stride out of my bedroom into the attached living and dining area. Here, the embers of the fireplace cast a low light across the space. A bookshelf rests on one wall, filled with tomes on magic theory, histories of Morineaux, and textbooks on strategy. In this room, cream cushions rest on the couch and armchair. They surround an ornate silverglass coffee table that sits on a cream and silver thread rug. The walls are a dull neutral color in contrast to the warm burgundy of my bedroom.

I march to the books and slide off a leather-bound giant with gold lettering: *An Expansion of the Art of Casting*. Perhaps there's some secret buried here that I've missed in the past.

There's only one way I know of to improve my casting—cast more. So that's what I'll do. Yet I can't let anyone realize I'm so inept I must practice at absurd hours of the night, which forces me to sneak about in my own home. Agraund will be irate if he learns I'm not sleeping when I can. A knot of dread grows in the pit of my stomach, but my determination pushes me to ignore it.

My black caster's cloak awaits me on a stand carved like a twisting tree, and I swing it on. A twitch of my fingers throws the cowl up.

I sneak through the castle corridors to the hall of the first-tier wizards' training rooms. Upon reaching mine, I click the key into its lock and enter. A flash of flint and steel lights the blackened torch on the wall. Some of its illumination spills into the hallway, and I hurry to shut the door.

I turn to face the rest of the room. The shadows dance on a wall of drawers filled with casting materials, cavorting as though taunting the light to come and catch it. The torch crackles in frustration at its inability to banish the darkness completely.

From one of the many drawers embedded in the wall, I gather the components necessary for the spell I want to attempt.

I sit. Arcanum powder and casting knife at the ready, phrases memorized, and rituals in mind, I cast.

My nose bleeds as the hours pass, and my palm burns from multiple shallow cuts. I pay both only enough attention to keep the blood from dripping into my materials. Hunger gnaws in my stomach like a growing beast, weakening my movements and fuzzing my vision. Only when I know that one more spell would spiral me into unconsciousness do I wipe up the blood on the floor and creep back to my bedroom. Exhaustion drags my limbs like iron shackles. After unlocking the door, I slip in.

Something crinkles beneath my foot.

A little white envelope rests on the floor, completely featureless. Something about its anonymity sets off an alarm in the back of my mind. If this is official castle business, there would be a seal, some indication of who it comes from. This has nothing.

As if in a dream, my weary body and muddled mind ignore the warning, stooping to pick up the letter. Six scripted words greet me:

To the Esteemed Prince Aster Jacques

Chapter 3

LEAVI

There's a thud as the patrolman's bolt drives home—right where I used to be.

Hanging on the lip of the wall, I drag myself into the rudimentary tower. My heart races as I glance over my shoulder. The patrolman's hurrying forward now, readying another shot.

I vault out of the tower, dropping all twelve feet. My boots jolt against the ground, but I roll to let my momentum carry the impact. I scramble back to my feet and run.

The patrolman makes it to the tower much quicker than I did. His shots chase the ground behind me. One whistles over my head, and I dive to the pavement. I scramble up before he can reload, ducking into an alley. My breaths come quick and short, but I don't stop running. Hopefully he's not crazy enough to come after me. I'm not counting on it, though.

Minutes later, I slow, back on a main street. I glance around, trying to get my bearings. Faint mosslight illumes the derelict houses. From one window, jagged glass juts like a lamprey eel's fangs. Inside, the shadows silhouette a vague form. Curious, I take a step closer, peering into the gloom.

I recoil. It's not the first time I've seen a dead body. But it's the first time I've seen one bloated and blistered, pockets of popped pus swelling every inch of their skin.

The breeze shifts, and the stench knocks me to my knees. I tear the muffler from my mouth and vomit into a filth-filled gutter, hands pressed against the cold, gritty stone. In the lab in Erreliah, our cooling-machine jammed once, and the fifty cave toads we collected the Friday before were left decomposing the entire weekend. Walking into that room Monday morning, I swore decaying toad guts were the most putrid stench on Earth.

That was before I smelled hundreds of corpses rotting around me.

Wiping my mouth, I tie my muffler back and wobble onto shaky legs. My whole body feels like it's the epicenter of its own earthquake, but the world is eerily still. Even the air is dead.

A sound splits the silence. A scratch against cobblestone, a thud as metal falls against pavement, a startled yowl like a fork against glass magnified a million times.

I run. I run faster than my legs have ever carried me, flying, not even sure if my feet are touching the ground. I fly past the district edge, crossing into the empty expanse before the tunnel. My brain yells at me to keep going, to put as much distance between me and the city as possible, but my lungs are heaving for air, cells demanding oxygen, and my body can't keep up.

As I come to a stop, my hands lean against the cool, rough cavern wall, heart thrumming in my chest. I stand there, panting, trying to calm myself back down. *It's*

11

okay, I assure myself. *I made it out. I'm right near the Lesser West Tunnel. It's okay.* Mostly collected, I turn to find the tunnel entrance.

Movement catches my eye in the darkness, and my muscles flinch so hard it hurts. *No one's supposed to be patrolling out here!*

The figure hasn't seen me yet. I press myself against the wall, dark hair and clothes blending in with the inky world, broken only by sporadic clusters of moss.

He moves closer, maybe twenty feet to the left of where I exited the district. At a diagonal, he crosses the bare ground between the tunnel and the city, taking careful steps as he looks back, then forth. Once he's five feet away, my impatient nerves prod me to move, but I will myself to stay still. One step. Another. Each of his movements is purposeful, measured. One step closer, and—

I jerk forward, catching his arm to slam him into the wall I was just against. Both hands press against his neck in a desperate frenzy. I can knock him out. I *can.* If I can just find those arteries...

Suddenly, I'm spun around, and it's *me* against the wall, and it's *his* hands on my neck. I try to push him off, but I'm shaking, and my energy is draining away with my vision.

His hands drop, feet taking a step back. "Riveirre?" he asks, incredulous.

"Sean," I gasp, surprised, bent in half to catch my breath. My eyes start picking out his features through the dim light—sharp nose, narrowed eyes, carefully combed brown hair. A dozen chains peek out of the pockets of his trench coat, and a backpack rests on his shoulders.

"What are you doing here?" he demands.

"I could ask the same of you."

He opens his mouth to speak, then takes a half-step back. "You attacked me!"

"I didn't know who you were! And can you please lower your voice? I don't want to get caught by an *actual* patrolman." Neither of us is conversing above a harsh whisper, but in the still, it feels like we're shouting.

"I'm not being loud." He spreads his arm out toward the Dead District. "And it's unlikely anyone else is out this far."

The reminder sends a chill up my spine, but I don't let him see my unease. "I am."

He drops his arm, glaring. "You don't count."

"Oh? I don't?"

He looks at me like I'm an imbecile. "Obviously not. I said 'anyone *else.'* You were part of the conversation."

I glance back and forth, getting antsier the longer we wait here. "What *are* you doing out here, Sean?"

"Same thing as you I suppose. Avoiding being a corpse."

"So what's your plan?" I straighten. "Are you just going to hop to the next town? Carry the plague there?"

"No." He sounds indignant. "Why? Was that *your* plan?"

"Of course not!"

"Then why in the world would you assume it's mine?"

"If you're a carrier-"

"I'm not a carrier, Riveirre."

I throw my hands up. "How can you know that?"

12

He takes a step forward, lank frame towering over mine. "I'd imagine the same way you're going to. I'll test for it." He leans back, popping the collar of his trench coat. "Look, we can discuss how we're not going to kill everyone in the known world when we're standing somewhere other than a burial-free cemetery."

He starts off, but I catch his shoulder, twisting him back around. "'We'?" I echo.

He shrugs me off. "There's only one way out. So, yes. We." Once more, he gestures at the ruined district behind us. "Unless you plan on staying here?" Not waiting for an answer, he follows the perimeter of the cavern, searching for the tunnel entry.

I pause, not pleased with the turn of events but not sure what to do about it. Sean Rahkifellar is a pompous, arrogant, self-centered idiot. He's been my research partner for the last three months, and there hasn't been one conversation where I didn't feel like we were somehow keeping score, trying to carve one more tick-mark for ourselves on the slate between us.

But he's right. There's only one way out, and traveling with even him will be better than wandering alone in the darkness.

Behind me, air wheezes through the tight streets of the District like the moan of the dead. I shiver and catch up with Sean.

Chapter 4

SEAN

We're still walking through tunnels. It's been three days, and honestly, we should be going into quarantine so we can test for the Death. Unsurprisingly, though, Miss Jumpy-and-Violent is rushing from plague-town Karsix like it's going to eat her if she stays in place for too long.

Walking. Left foot, right foot. Left foot, right foot. My mind jumps back to the Dead District.

I was walking. Just like that. Left, right, left, right. Concentrate on the steps, I thought—get through this corpse town. Think—it's just like a morgue, only smellier. It's fine. Left, right, left, right.

It's fine.

I shove my hands into my pockets. No reason to consider that.

Or what happened after.

Once again, my gaze wanders over to my traveling partner. Frustrated this keeps happening, I try to tear my eyes away.

I fail.

Two pink, slender lips set in determination—probably trying not to be the one to break the silence.

Two chocolate eyes squinting in the half-light—probably not used to illumination only by lantern.

One nose—no, that's not quite good enough…

Two nostrils, flaring—

Ah. Probably because she just caught me staring again.

I glance away once more.

She's frustrating. The past two months working with her have been… well, frustrating. She's helpful and kind one moment, and then—out of the blue, seemingly—she snips, snaps, retorts.

I wonder how much equipment she even thought to bring. I mean, her bag jingles with every step, so I'd imagine she brought at least *something* useful, but part of me is curious how much of it's honestly important. It could be stuffed with anything from hematesters and crys-cases to nonsense like lipstick and rouge. I've yet to see her take out much other than food and her blanket, so I have no way of knowing for sure.

We stop for the night in a close-walled tunnel and set up camp. Out comes her blanket, a thin purple throw she stretches over the smooth rock floor. She's dumb not to have packed a normal woolen blanket like I did—hers takes up less space in her bag, but it's also less warm, which she'll regret when we make it topside.

From the side pocket of my backpack, I extract a pouch of coal, setting a single piece on the floor. It won't burn long, but at least it'll drive away the chilled air for a while. The closer we get to topside, the colder it's getting.

14

I pull my flicker from my coat pocket, the metal cylinder cool and smooth against my hand. Leaning down, I hold it close to the coal and depress the delicate brass lever. A serpent's tongue of flame flicks out, smoldering into a small but intense blaze. The tunnel fills with the fire's crackling and the crinkle of paper as I unwrap my meal for the night.

Blackbread—about as tasty as rocks and only slightly softer, but at least it's filling. Three days of traveling and I've managed to limit myself to consuming only seventy-five percent of the loaf overall.

Riveirre tugs her jacket off and lays it flat, her long, moonlight arms bared in a short, puff-sleeved shirt. I'm shocked she didn't have sense enough to bring something warmer, but my gaze chases the shadows playing on her skin.

Her fingers slip into the jacket pocket, drawing out a handful of light grey mushrooms and sprinkling them over the garment. Her eyes are intense as she studies them. Sorting through the collection, she tosses discolored or crumbled ones to the side. Once she's satisfied, she snaps the stems off, setting them with her pile of trash. A strand of inky hair falls across her face, and she brushes it back as she straightens.

Reaching around the fire, she deposits five of the caps into my lap.

I look at her askew. "What are these for?" It's like she thinks I don't eat enough.

"I can take them back if you don't want them."

I scowl, thinking back to the lab.

We pulled an all-nighter. At least, I had. I wasn't sure if she'd stayed in the lab. I wasn't really paying attention to her.

But, at some point in the morning, she cocked her head at me. Didn't say anything, just looked. A few minutes later, she left.

When she came back, she dropped a biscuit on the counter beside me.

I glanced up. 'What's this?'

'Breakfast.'

Her hand holds steady over the fire, slowly rotating a mushroom skewered on a scalpel. The waves of her hair have crashed in around her face once more, but this time she leaves them be. The mushroom spins. Spins again.

I'm staring again. I glance away, searching for some piece of conversation to cover my blunder. "So do you usually carry random funguses in your pocket?"

Her eyes lift to meet mine, then drop back to her task. "Fungi. I harvested them while we were walking."

Her food has puffed out to look like some kind of angry monster. She pops it off her improvised skewer and into her mouth. Preparing the next one, she maintains her downward gaze, eyes fixed on her hands and clearly disinterested in me. "They taste better cooked."

Her brusque words remind me of the pile of food in my lap. I fumble for my pocket-knife, flick the blade out, impale a cap, and shove it over the fire. As I spin it, the space for words disappears.

It's silent. Just like the last two months. Better than bickering at least. She doesn't seem to know *how* to talk without arguing, sneaking in those little needles. Just because she got her masterate at sixteen doesn't make her anything special, or at least not as special as she thinks. After all, we're the same age, and I already have my doktorate.

15

My mushroom finishes cooking. The crisp, earthy taste breaks over my tongue in satisfying contrast to the blackbread I've been eating. I wonder if she'll pick more tomorrow.

I watch the sparks. Better than staring at her—again. I pop a mushroom into my mouth and stab another to start roasting it.

She puts her skewer away, and my gaze slips back to her. Done cooking, she stares at the wall like some hidden message lies there, waiting for her to decode it. The firm set of her delicate jaw is demanding in a way I feel would be surprising if a person had only ever seen her happy. I can't shake the notion that if she were to truly smile, her expression would light up completely, the grin transforming her face from the somber and businesslike girl that I know into a warm, enthusiastic person. Not that I have evidence to back that up.

Her gaze flicks to mine, just long enough to let me know I've been caught, then back to the wall. And we're back to where we started.

When she finishes eating, Mushroom Girl beds down, pulling her jacket close around her shoulders. She keeps her back to the fire—and me. After I eat my last fungus, I roll into my blanket and pretend to go to sleep. As I lay there, heat against my back, I try not to think so I can actually drift off.

It doesn't work. As usual.

Instead, in trying so desperately to ignore my thoughts, I end up rehashing everything. How the Blistering Death's sixty-one percent infection rate is shockingly high. How, in the slums alone, 9,000 are estimated to already be dead. How likely it is that less than a fifth of the city will survive.

How there's absolutely nothing I can do about it.

I tried. As much as I detest the little city that pretends to be a top-class research town, I tried to help. As a doktor—the penultimate level of education a scientist can earn—that specializes in neuro-alkemi, I had access to some of the few files they'd gathered on the Death. I was able to analyze the possible effects the sickness has on patients' brains and got to see how bad it is. How dangerous. With the resources at our disposal, there's little that can be done. For now, they can make the sick a little more comfortable. Do their best to keep them quarantined. That's what they're doing, but they can't save the ones already condemned. I wasn't going to stay there and let myself fall into the numbers of the dead.

I want to get back to my topside hometown, Xela. Admittedly, it has a lot less technology than the steam-thick cities below-ground, but I think Xela is a good goal. At least I'd know people there.

But first, I have to get out of these tunnels, and to do that, I have to make sure I'm not a carrier.

I was walking. Left, right, left, right. Tap, tap, tap, tapping on the side of my leg. The stench, the sights, the occasional scramble of rats. Or something worse.

Tap, tap, tap, tapping. Turn the corner and—

Schlick*! I tripped.*

Bloated and blistered, a child's mutilated body laid on the cobblestone. A horde of flies burst from where my shoe collided with the corpse's gory side.

I retched.

Then I ran.

As soon as I exited the district itself, I yanked out the warm boots I was saving in my backpack for the winter above-ground and kicked off the bloody shoes I was wearing.

I shudder, forgetting that I was pretending to sleep. Oh, well. She's most likely asleep anyway.

I'll be out too. Eventually.

Chapter 5

Leavi

I stare at him from across the campfire. The flickering shadows conceal his expression, not that I'd be able to read it anyway. This is our third night trekking through the tunnels, and he has yet to say much beyond the minimum. I refuse to break the silence, though. For days, the only noises have been shuffling feet, breathy exhales, and crackling flames.

I drop the mushrooms into his lap. He doesn't thank me. Then again, I didn't really expect him to. Sean Rahkifellar's not a thank-you kind of guy. He clearly prefers clipped words, to-the-point sentences, and functionality over feeling.

That's what he'll get in return.

While we eat, my gaze shifts to the fluid patterns the fire paints on the wall, and I catch him looking me over. It's a habit he had in the lab as well, like he's trying to peel back my skin and read the meaning hidden in the tension of my muscles. I feel like a specimen on his dissection tray.

I don't let him know it bothers me, though. Instead, I slide my eyes to meet his. His gaze darts away, knowing he's been caught, and my attention returns to the wall.

Silence thickens into tension, and I tuck myself into my blankets as soon as I'm done with my food. Back turned to the fire, the dark maw of the tunnel is the only sight to greet me, but I prefer the darkness to Sean's prying eyes.

My cold fingers trail up to my necklace. The metal provides no warmth, but as I pull it out, a wavering smile tugs at my lips.

The charm dangles from a tarnished silver chain. The pendant itself, though, shines as if new, glittering with a sheen like clear oil on glass. It's sculpted to mimic an old-timey shield, the kind depicted in children's fairy-tales where brave warriors march into battle. Embossed in the center, a sparrow flies against the moon.

It'll protect you, my dad said when he drew the necklace out of its dusty, padded case. *And as long as you're away from home, it'll remind you where you come from.*

Knowing I was only going to be studying topside for a few months, I joked it off, but I was touched, and I ached to put the heirloom on. Its obvious age somehow enhanced its beauty and gave it an air of mystery.

But that was back when my only goals were earning my masterate in vitaliti, the study of living things, and getting an official, paying research job in Erreliah. The only step that still stood between me and that was a stint of field work above ground and a dissertation. At least, that's what I thought.

I slip the necklace back underneath my shirt, looking forward to sleep. Somehow, dreaming feels louder than the restrained hush does.

In the morning, the silent dance between me and Sean continues. We prepare for the day's hike, moving around each other without intersecting, observing without being observed, the empty communication between us almost more tangible than real conversation.

Sean's collapsible lantern is the only light source as we shuffle onward. Somehow, in my whirlwind of preparations, I forgot to bring light. Perhaps it's because for my entire life, it's been provided for me.

In Erreliah, light twinkles from a thousand windows and lamps shine on every street, making it feel like the glow emanates straight from the city's core. Most people have something that glows on their person—a timepiece backed with moss, a miniature lantern on a necklace, transparent shoes whose gears churn and spark as they walk. At the very least, I could always rely on the moss planted liberally throughout the city and its well-traveled tunnels. The small plant may not provide much light, but it's better than the endless layers of midnight curtains hovering in this small, low-traffic path.

Since Karsix's Lesser West Tunnel doesn't connect to any other underground cities, its sole travelers would be the occasional poor topside merchant and undercity criminal. The disuse shows. Here, the only light is natural, sporadic glow-moss clinging to the high ceiling like faint stars on a cloudy night topside.

Ahead, our tunnel splits in two.

I glance around. "Where are the guide signs?"

Sean keeps walking. "You do realize that there's upward of nine-hundred *known* underground routes in the High Valleys? Not all of them get signage. Especially the ones that lead out. Topsiders are the ones that put any effort into connecting below- and above-ground trade."

"What, are you a cartographer now?"

"No," he calls back. "I paid attention in my geography classes."

Not bothering to consult me, he strides right up to the left tunnel, steps quick and confident and—

Hesitates.

It's just an instant, a falter in his steps, a quick look at the other path. Then his lantern lifts higher, and he continues forward.

I catch up. "Hold on!"

He doesn't.

I grab the sleeve of his coat and yank. He spins around. "What?"

Deliberately, I ask, "How do you know that this is the right tunnel?" He's half a head taller than me, but I look him straight in the eyes.

His gaze breaks, flicking to the dark behind us, but his words affect nonchalance. "Because, unlike you it seems, I prepare before departing civilization. There's these things called maps, you know." Now he meets my eyes. "You can study them for free in any local library. It's the left tunnel."

"Where is that going to take us?"

"A little trading post. Good enough to restock rations and get directions. Now, are you done interrogating me?"

He starts to turn, but I catch his arm. "Are you *sure* about this, Sean?"

"Yes, I'm sure! What good does asking me about it do anyway? I say it's the left tunnel. You don't have any better intel. That closes the matter."

"If we get lost-"

"Skies, Riveirre, we're not going to get lost! If it makes you feel better, this tunnel is inclining. See?" He gestures with the lantern. "Aside from anything else, that means it's heading topside. Alright?"

He heads off. Since he has the only light, I'm forced to keep up. Unease flutters in my stomach, though. Just because the tunnel's going up right now doesn't mean it won't dead end. Mr. Paid-Attention-in-Geography should know that. He almost certainly *does* know that.

A burst of nervous energy tingles in my veins. He doesn't remember, I realize. He doesn't remember which way leads to the post, or at least he isn't certain. I'd bet the last one-cent stone-mark in my pocket on it.

"Sean."

His steps are crisp, snapping against the stone. "What?"

"Why don't we pull out the map and double-check? Just to be sure."

He pulls short, turns, and cocks his head. Slowly, he says, "I told you. The map is in the library."

I close my eyes, trying to process that. "You're saying you didn't bring the map you found? Weren't you lecturing me on being prepared two minutes ago?"

"You mean I didn't *steal* the map I found? Yeah. That's what I said." He reaches into a pocket, popping the lid on a timepiece, and scrutinizes it as he responds. "I may be many things, Riveirre, but a thief is not one of them. Although I'm curious about you now." He clicks the piece closed and continues down the tunnel.

Yet again, I follow.

A few hours of silence later, Sean shatters the air. "We'll stop here."

He's pointing to a five-foot wide opening in the rock. Beyond, a path curves, the vague edges of a chamber entrance visible at its end. Lit by the warm, dull orange of the lantern, the scene looks more like a faded oil painting than crisp reality.

It isn't even quite lunch yet. "Why?"

He turns around slowly, as if I'm not worth the effort it takes to address me promptly. The lantern swings with the motion, sending the shadows skittering across the walls. "Because," he draws out, "personally, I don't feel like killing the known world today. It's contrary to your opinions of me, I know," he says, holding up his free hand, "but for some reason, mass homicide wasn't on my to-do list for this week." His eyes darken, serious now. He turns back and starts through the side-tunnel.

"What?" I call. "Are you planning on quarantining here? It's only-"

"Four days out from Karsix?" he finishes. "Yeah." He draws the word out, as if I'm a simple child. "And we're getting close to being topside. Haven't you been checking your barometer?" He smirks at me. "Or are you scared someone from Karsix is going to run all the way out here," he pantomimes mockingly with his fingers, "and cough on you?"

I draw myself taut. "I've been checking it. I simply think we can afford to keep moving. More distance between us and Karsix isn't going to hurt."

In reality, I have no idea how close we are to the surface. I brought a barometer, but I haven't bothered looking at it. At least in some small way, Sean's right. I am afraid we're too close to Karsix. If we made it out, that means others might be able to as well. If someone infected catches up with us, that's it. We're dead. After all, there's no cure, and there haven't been any survivors. So he can mock me all he likes. I'm not going to get this far and die now.

He has the gall to laugh at me. "You are such a liar. You haven't pulled any barometer out."

"You haven't either." If he had, surely I would have seen it.

He holds up a chain around his neck, a hollow glass pendant the shape of a U dangling below. Inside, quicksilver fills from the top of the left side to halfway up the right. He's right; we are close to the surface. In Karsix, the quicksilver would be compressed to about the middle. The higher we go, the more the U will fill up.

"Happy?" A cocky smile curls his lips, and one brow is raised.

I cross my arms, looking back the way we came. *Four days out, Leavi. Four days out, through the Dead District, past a tunnel split, hidden in a side passage. No one's going to make it that far. No one's going to find us. Surely.*

"Fine," I say, still looking off.

Sean nods, knowing he's won, and moves into the side tunnel.

As we wind through the passage, the sound of trickling water falls against my ears. I wonder if Sean noticed it when he picked this spot to stop or if he just got lucky. We'll need to hole up here for at least forty-eight hours to complete the quarantine, and since we'll be stationary, we'll need running water. Plus, where there's water, there's moss.

When we get into the room, I signal Sean to put his lantern away. He doesn't argue, whether because he agrees or because he was going to do it anyway, I'm not sure. Probably the latter.

The room is lit with a white fairy-glow. Moss blankets the sides of the whispering stream, and the dancing water glints as though winking at us. In the rill, I'm surprised to see fish with functioning eyes rather than the blind types that usually alone thread their way through underground streams.

In puddles against the bank, cave frogs squat, casting their own tiny green glow. Water moths dart above the waves, their shimmery white pattern helping them to blend into the mossglow. Here and there, a pink tongue flicks out or a fish darts up from the water, and a moth disappears, its natural camouflage having failed it.

One rock toward the end of the room creates a barrier the stream gently waterfalls over, forming a slightly calmer pool before the water narrows back out and flows away. Hanging over the pool, tiny cavefisher crustaceans dangle the bobbing antenna they use as bait, hoping to catch an unlucky minnow.

Entranced, I step forward. Even at only sixteen, I've traveled more than the common undergrounder, studying the life forms of the High Valleys and its caves. However, I've never seen a haven so rich with life in an area so devoid of sunlight. This cave is like a whole world unto itself.

Suddenly, I'm grateful Sean forced the stop. That I could have walked by and completely missed this is unthinkable.

I collect myself, though. Out loud, all I give him is an even, "This is a good place to stop."

In return, he nods, and we set up camp. It's going to be a long two days.

Chapter 6

SEAN

Despite the gurgling water and the low lights that would lull most people straight to REM, I'm still awake. At this point, I've given up maintaining the pretense of slumber since *she's* asleep.

Instead, back to the wall, facing the opening to this little room, I've pulled out three notebooks, one typifier, and one presswrite. My thoughts wander as I type, fingers dancing over the keys.

Left. I took the left path. Left was the right way to go. I know it. That's what the map said.

Or was it?

Of course it was. Left. It was definitely left. I wouldn't forget; I'm not a 'forgetting' person. I know that, I know what I'm doing, and randomly forgetting the directions that I made *sure* to memorize is not something I would do.

I don't just forget things.

I still remember word for word an entire Chemistry of Addictions lecture; I still remember line for line the first brain diagram I had to study; and I still remember shade for shade the pattern of the wood-grain on my year-two desk at my primary.

I don't just forget things.

So it must have been the left. I know it's the left. I wouldn't have gone that way if it wasn't.

I confidently return to my typing. *Clack, clack, clack, clack.* The sound bounces between the cavern walls.

Squi-plat!

I start and look at the stream. A lizard with frills and gills around its neck is sliding back under the water, twitching frog legs protruding from its mouth. Shaking my head, I turn back to the presswrite. *Clack, clack.* Deep breath in. *Clack, clack.* Let it back out.

Way to let a weird lizard startle you, Sean.

Alternately referencing my notes and typing, I manage to fill the next few hours. For the fun of it, I take a sample of stream-water with the typifier, a cube-shaped device for identifying elements.

Using an eyedropper, I put four droplets onto its finely perforated grate. They sink through, and I wait. After three minutes and twenty-one seconds—according to my timepiece—six of the nine vials begin to glow. Orange, green, blue, white, and purple. Absynium, Stygan, Vistia, Wyneall, and Gren.

The Absynium and Wyneall, of course, make up most of the water itself, the Vistia is common in places with plants, and the Gren and Stygan is what you'd expect in an area so full of animals.

But black also shows. Unknown.

My brow furrows. This is one of the most advanced versions of typifiers there are. What could be in this water that it wouldn't include?

A few feet away, there's a rustle as my quarantine mate rolls over, slightly humming as she comes to. Out of the corner of my eye, I see her sit up and squint against the glow of the typifier. "What're you *doing*, Sean?"

I glance up from the device. "Figuring out what's in this water." What does it look like I'm doing?

"In the middle of the night?" she asks, incredulous.

I shrug, looking back to it.

Breaking into my thoughts once again, she says, "It looks more like you're glaring at it than figuring anything out."

"I'm sorry my methods don't please you," I drawl, stealing a sidelong glance at her.

A piece of hair falls into her face, and she swipes her part to the other side. "You're having such a hard time reading it that all you can accomplish is a dedicated stare?"

Of course she assumes that me thinking something over is me not knowing what I'm doing. What kind of a scientist does she think I am exactly?

Judging by her pointless questions, not much of one.

"Yes, Riveirre, I have absolutely no idea how to operate this terribly complex item. I just thought it'd be fun to *fiddle* with it." I quirk an eyebrow.

Adopting false tones of concern, she says, "Well, don't hurt yourself. Alkemi instruments can be dangerous." Dropping the act, she raises her eyebrows back at me.

"What?" I demand, cross.

She lays down. "Nothing," she says to the ceiling. "I guess if you want to spend your life pondering over a glass cylinder, I've got no right to intervene." She stays reclined like that with her eyes closed and hands folded over her stomach, seemingly relaxed.

Slightly annoyed now, I reply, "I never asked you to."

She simply *hmm*s, as if I'm not worth her time.

Shaking my head, I return to analyzing the typifier.

Her soft breaths mingle with the murmur of the stream. She's obviously not asleep, though. The breathing pattern's all wrong, too fast, too uneven.

After scribbling down the data from the previous test, I reset the typifier and try another sample. When it's ready, I see the same composition as before, including the black 'unknown' glow.

"Curious." I scavenge my bag and pull out a tox-strip. Removing the grate-plate on top of the typifier, I extract the black-filled tube. I rinse my eyedropper in a little clean water and drop a couple dots of the dark liquid onto the strip.

When the spots of solution on the paper declare the fluid safe by not changing color, I pull the vial to my face and sniff. A sharp scent fills my nose, and my brow furrows. I record my observation. Putting a bead of the black liquid on my finger, I lift it to my mouth.

Suddenly, Miss Safety Patrolman sits bolt upright. "What are you doing, you idiot?"

I pause. Raise an eyebrow at her. She sits there watching me, eyes wide, messy hair haloing her head.

"What exactly woke you up, Riveirre? You were so sound asleep a couple of seconds ago." I smirk. "And I'm not being an idiot."

A voice echoes through my head. *'You'll never make it anywhere, you idiot, failure-'*

No.

"You're not?" Riveirre asks. "You're attempting to consume unknown substances. As though *that* doesn't break any safety regulations."

Disdain permeates my voice. "It's definitely not like I used a tox-strip." I eye her steadily to drive my point home.

She scowls. "Those don't detect everything. Besides, how did you get ahold of something like that? Do you even know how to use it?"

What does she mean, 'do I know how to use it?' Do I know how to use something that's a fundamental tool in alkemi? Seriously?

"Of course not," I reply, irked. "I'm just an idiot, remember?"

"Well, you were going to use your *mouth* as a scientific instrument, so…" She tilts her hand side to side in a so-so gesture, but there's something hard in her eyes. Determination. No. Concern? Probably not.

"'When all else fails," I begin to recite, "in the identification of an alkemitic substanstance-"

"You eat it?" she interrupts.

"'- and the substance has been shown to be safe-"

"Supposedly."

"'- especially with the use of a tox-strip, test the substance with one's olfactory and/or gustatory senses.' Rulebook of Alkemitic Discoveries, Vol. Two, Chapter Three, Rule Number Five."

She narrows her eyes. Then she sighs. "I always did think alkemists were halfwits."

"So very sorry you don't understand our genius."

Arching her eyebrows, she says, "You mean your insanity?"

My jaw clenches, but surely in the low light, she doesn't notice. "Well, if that's the way you want to see it," I growl. More lightly, I add, "But if you're so disinterested, perhaps you simply wish to return to your faux slumber?" I look back to my finger and move the dot toward my tongue.

"No," she says, snatching the digit away from my mouth. "I need you to register as good and healthy two days from now. If you insist on consuming mysterious substances, you're going to ruin my test."

"Look," I snap. I twist my wrist out of her grasp. "This is standard procedure. Plus, in the crazy off-chance that it isn't safe, I'm consuming literally less than a milliliter of this 'mysterious substance.' And," I draw out, "like I mentioned before—this is in our drinking water. If it's not safe, I figure it's better to identify it now rather than later, after we've had more than our fill." My glare hardens.

She presses her lips together. Deliberately, she returns, "Not necessarily. In the stream, whatever you're dealing with is diluted. Therefore, in water, it might not be dangerous. Concentrated, however, might be a different case. And I, for one, don't want to have to wait any longer for us to screen clear than we have to."

"Yes, Riveirre, it's completely possible that it could be more dangerous concentrated, *if* it's dangerous at all. However, at such a low amount, even if that

24

were the case, it would be highly unlikely it would do any sort of significant damage. And if it did, it would probably fade quickly. You seem to forget that alkemi is what I have my *doktorate* in."

Her lips press together as she takes that in. She gathers herself. "It's not about the amount. It's about the concentration."

"A concentration that the tox-paper counted as not," my eyes narrow, "harmful."

Her speech is steady and gains confidence as she continues to argue her faulty logic. I know what I'm talking about, though, and no matter what arguments she poses about solution concentration and possible contamination, I know the quantity isn't enough to hurt me. I know more about this topic than she does, yet she's treating me like a child.

Finally fed up with her stubbornness, I bite, "And why, exactly, do you care? I'm just that idiot you're stuck with, right? The one you didn't even want to travel with in the first place. What's it to you if I get hurt or killed? It's not like you need *me* to do the screening on yourself. Right?"

She leans back, looking struck.

"So—what?" I press. "Why would it matter if this doesn't go well? Because," I slightly shrug, simmering, "at least then you'd know it wasn't safe. Right?" I smile, a fake, sour, venomous twist of my lips.

Her mouth tightens. She levelly restates her argument, adding on, "As to why I care—I can't leave until we both pass our screenings. I'm stuck here as long as you are."

"How do you figure? You don't have to stick with me. You don't have to bother with that—you obviously disagree with the kinds of decisions I make; you've questioned every one of them. Why not just split? But," I add on a fake, brighter note, "I'm sure you, with your masterate in biology, know so much more about this subject than I do."

"I know more than you think I do, Sean."

"That's beside the point. The point is whether you know more than *I* do. And I'm pretty sure I know what I'm doing."

"It's that fraction of doubt that has me worried."

"Excuse me?" Who does she think she is? Just because she's from high-class Erreliah doesn't mean she knows everything.

"You're 'pretty' sure. You're not a hundred percent sure. You're not confident. You admit you could be making a mistake. Rationally, I don't see any reason to risk it."

My thoughts flick to another argument, another time, another person. *'You don't know* anything, *and you never will! You think you're so smart, but you're just a little boy with an arrogance issue,'* he raged at me.

I'm not. I'm not. I know what I'm doing.

Or do I? my mind whispers.

Of course I do. I've studied for years. I've put everything I can into alkemi.

'You're never going to get anywhere in life,' he said. *'You're going to be stuck in this place, making your mother cater to you for the rest of your life. You're just an insane little smart-aleck.'*

No! I am successful. I am capable. I am informed about this situation.

I know what I'm doing.

But if I'm wrong…

If I'm wrong, I'm risking my health over little more than my curiosity. Risking that this could hurt me because my immune system might be low due to the plague. Risking that this could weaken my immune system and give the plague the opportunity it needs to destroy me.

'You. Are. Nothing.'

I set my jaw. But none of that is going to happen. I know this is safe. I know what I'm doing. This substance is in a tiny quantity, tox-paper declared it safe, and it doesn't smell putrid or overly sweet or sour. It's safe, and if it's not, it's too small an amount to matter.

I know what I'm doing, and some vitalitist that wants to pretend to know alkemi isn't going to make me think otherwise.

My eyes narrow at her. "I'm 'certain' someone who's been studying the subject as long as I have knows how to deal with unknown substances. It's standard procedure."

"Well, maybe you need to get a rulebook that uses logic."

My jaw clenches, nostrils flare, and this time, I honestly don't care if she sees. "Right, Riveirre," I finally draw out.

'What are you thinking? You can't do anything. You're gonna be here forever, you little worthless-'

I push the memory away.

She gives a soft, exasperated huff. "Just—wait till the screening's over," she repeats tiredly.

I glare. "Fine. Whatever. Remind me not to try and look out for dangerous things in the future." With that, I shove my things back into my bag and roll into my blanket once more.

I don't have high hopes for sleep tonight.

Chapter 7

ASTER

The glow of the candle-lit chandeliers floods the opulent dining hall like an angelic mirage; it smooths out the cracks that whisper of flaws lying beneath the calm, kind demeanors of the room's occupants.

My mother sits at the head of the room's long, pristine table. My father is in one of the two slightly less extravagant chairs beside her at the top of the table. She smiles at him and laughs. The corners of his lips lift in return, and he brushes an invisible hair from her cheek. The courtiers smile at the sweet scene, but my mother's fake joy and father's feigned care stir no admiration in me.

Agraund rests comfortably on her other side. Around the corner from Father sits Sela. Her high cheekbones, a characteristic common in our family, are lightly dusted with rouge, and her lips are artfully painted. Beside Sela, our brother, Ren, slides into his seat. His formal military uniform is one that I'll thankfully never have to wear; the careful art of casting far surpasses the brutality of his whack-and-bash principles.

I pass the seated Ladies of my mother's court, the army officials under my father, and the top-tier wizards commanded by Agraund. Tinkling laughter and hearty conversation glide through the air around me as I take my place around the corner from my uncle.

Agraund, straight-faced as ever, remarks, "You were almost late."

I glance over to where Ren is still settling into his seat. *Not really.* "Yes, my lord," I return evenly.

A serving-maid leans around me to fill my wine glass.

I glance up at her, offering a quick smile. "Thank you, Alena."

She smiles back and flits away to fulfill some other duty.

Agraund demands my attention once more. "It's not polite to speak familiarly with servants when there is more dignified company in the room."

My fingers press harder than necessary into the napkin I'm unfolding. "Yes, my lord."

"Do you even know her?"

I place the napkin in my lap. "Only well enough to know her name, my lord."

"Well, then. Perhaps you should refrain from conversing with unknown help when there are more important things going on. Aster, I know how you like to associate with the lower classes, but someday you're going to have focus on reality. Your fantasies won't help you when it comes to the world of politics."

I smooth out the napkin. "Of course, my lord. I understand."

"Good." He nods. "Now, enjoy the meal. There are a lot of important people here tonight." He smiles encouragingly.

I offer a smile back, but he's already turned his attention away from me. He laughs as the Queen mutters something to him. I follow their gazes to one of the Ladies. I can't remember her name, but I do know she has a long history of being as

27

self-centered as she is empty-headed. The only reason she's even on the court is her family's old money. Mother can't afford to gain the bad favor of an influential line.

The Lady's ensemble seems to be what they're ridiculing. It appears as if she attempted to morph into a peacock; feather earrings dangle from her ears, feathered clips jut from her hair, and her bodice is bedecked in blue, green, and brown beads. Honestly, if it had been done with a little more grace and a little less pompous enthusiasm, it would look rather stately. As it is, she looks more like a peacock-costumed goose amidst glittering doves.

Mother could have pulled it off.

Her already swan-like neck would be the perfect dais for the large, cock-colored stones the woman is wearing, her dark-blonde hair the ideal bed for the clips. Her large brown eyes would be a flawless match for the dress' beads, and her honeyed skin optimal for the sweeps of blue and green shadow beneath the woman's brow.

The country adores her, their dear Queen Diane Jacqueline. They know her as benevolent and sweet but still firm and powerful. They never see her careful manipulation, how the kindness is merely a mask and the doting a charade.

They never see her as the woman incapable of loving even her own husband.

Across the table, light diverts my attention as it catches Sela's elegant silver choker. She chuckles softly at something Ren must have said.

Four years older than me, Sela looks remarkably like Mother and hardly anything like our father. After all, his face is all angles, strong and sharp, rather than the curving grace of Sela and the Queen.

"Good evening, Aster," Sela says, catching my gaze.

I smile politely, a pang in my chest. *So formal.* "Evening, Princesse."

Her lips turn up in kind, but her heart clearly isn't in it. While perhaps passable to most, I know that smile is nothing like the genuine, mischievous grins she used to flash me. "How are you?"

Only a handful of years ago, you would already know. We'd have been around each other all day.

"I'm good, thank you. And you?" I remember a dinner similar to this back when I was ten, her fourteen. Like this time, our conversation had started because I saw her chuckling at Ren. Like this time, she turned to me to speak. There the similarities end. Because, then, she relayed the witticism Ren had imparted on her, about how some piece of food on her plate looked exactly like Agraund. We'd laughed hard, enjoying ourselves much more in that moment than either of us likely will throughout this entire conversation.

I doubt there will be much, if any, genuine laughter tonight, at least from me. This kind of event is always long and dull, dry and full of posturing and double-speak.

"Wonderful," she says. "How has your instruction been going?"

"Ah. Good, thank you. Yours?" Despite the words rolling smoothly off my tongue, I feel awkward, like this is somehow a perversion of how our conversation should really be going.

I'm rescued from what once would have been the best conversation of the night by the peacock woman calling to Sela. "What's your opinion, Princesse?"

She turns to answer, our exchange forgotten.

An elbow almost knocks my plate; I follow it up to see my uncle's second sitting beside me. His lank, yellowing hair is pulled back into a ponytail at the nape of his neck. He sits erect with his face pinched, as if he has a stick for a spine, leaving him both ramrod and uncomfortable. "I thought Agraund would have taught you better, Prince."

My gaze snaps up to his face. He still faces forward, fork raised lightly to his lips. "Taught me better than what, Mage Solus?"

"Than to stare."

Heat rises in my cheeks, and I'm grateful my almond skin covers it. "I was only admiring your comportment. No one holds themselves as you, sir."

He grunts but gives a self-satisfied smile.

Relieved at avoiding a confrontation there, I return to my own food. Hopefully no one else will bother me. Dread rises in me at the idea of having to talk to any more of them; I'd rather not be repeatedly and creatively condescended, mocked, and manipulated. I'd rather not engage in any more hidden verbal sparring tonight.

I would much prefer to spend the coming hours locked away in my training room, pushing my body and mind to their limits, fighting for every inch of improvement I can get.

I have another option, I remember, *than wearing myself away with practice.*

The note.

It's from an academy in Draó, at least a month's travel north, that specializes in instructing magicians. They've offered me a chance to study there. I can't seem to keep it off my mind for long, but I know that my family would never agree to let me go. I *want* to become a more talented caster, but my place is here, not gallivanting about in foreign countries. Which means I keep finding myself faced with one painful question:

Am I really willing to abandon my country to become the caster it needs?

Chapter 8

SEAN

I can't fall asleep, and my fingers are jittering too much to type properly. I either keep hitting the wrong button or hitting the right button with the wrong rhythm.

The paper in my presswrite currently reads, 'Upo n noting that the ttpefier could mnot isdentify the substanceee, it wass testred by smell. The testtt yieldedd a dsharp scent, but wasstill unidentifiedd.'

Tomorrow, we test for the plague.

My fingers err again, and I smack the buttons with my palm—a string of nonsense letters clutter my paper. I set the machine aside.

I can't seem to concentrate. *What if I made a mistake in telling her she should travel with me?* I could be infected. And if that's the case, then I've killed her too.

I try to push the thought away. No. I'm not showing any symptoms, I never came in direct contact with the gore...

I tripped.

Schlick*! My shoe was covered with the pus and blood from the child's side. The flies burst from the hole I created in her body.*

No, no, no. I shouldn't think about it. I shouldn't worry about it. What's done is done, there's no going back. I just need to quit worrying, quit thinking about it. Worrying about things that can't be controlled has never done anyone any good. No, it's not going to do any good, it's not going to help anything—

I tripped.

Schlick*! My shoe was covered with the pus and blood...*

"Stop it!" I hiss. I cringe and cast a glance at Riveirre, hoping I haven't woken her. Unease tightens my throat at the idea.

I don't know if I could handle an argument with her right now. I'm not sure what stupid things I would say if I had to.

I don't know if I'm going to be clear of the plague. I'm not sure what I can do if I'm not.

My shaky fingers bounce against my leg while I sit here. I want to pace, but this stupid cavern is too small to take more than a step or two without tripping over Riveirre.

I tripped.

Schlick*! My shoe was covered with the pus and blood—*

My eyes and fists clench, tight, fingernails pressing hard into skin.

"Calm down!" It's out of my hands.

I drag a deep breath in through my nose. Raggedly release it through my barely parted lips. Repeat.

I open my hands, spreading my fingers across my leg. My eyelids relax.

'Everything will work out, sugar,' my mother's voice whispered. 'It always does, one way or another. Just breathe, Sean. In and out. In and out, sugar.'

In and out.

30

Chapter 9
LEAVI

The cavern walls rise up around me. My entire body is so tight, I feel like a constrictor snake is wrapping around my muscles and squeezing as if its life depends on me becoming its next meal. As the snake twists my stomach, anxiety rises to fill me, a toxin climbing toward my throat.

I betray none of this apprehension to Sean. My hands stay steady as I draw his blood with a syringe. We've been in such close proximity the last six days that if either of us are infected, we're both dead.

Taking out my hematester, I carefully drip the blood from my syringe's needle into the glass tube. Inside the device, several miniscule, mineral-coated nets separate the fluid into its constituent parts. The thick liquid laboriously trickles through the layers, adding a drop to my anxiety with every slow drip. Once I empty the syringe, I cap the hematester and shake it up and down, careful to keep it straight. That helps speed the process up.

A few long minutes later, the device has done its work. "Hold this," I order, handing the tube to Sean. He complies, allowing me to pull out my magnifier. To a layman, the tool probably looks like a trinket someone might put on their keyring. Ten thin, teardrop-shaped crystal lenses clink together on an iron loop. Reclaiming the hematester with one hand, I pull a magnifier lens to the top of the ring and peer through.

Adjust the distance, I instruct myself. *Better. Flip the next crystal. Now, adjust the distance. No, not quite. A little closer—too close. Back one millimeter, two, two and a half... Good. Flip the next crystal. Adjust the distance...*

"This lighting is terrible," I mutter, pulling more crystals up one by one. Now that I'm staring through all ten, the blood in the tube transforms from a homogenous red liquid to millions of tiny but distinct shapes. Being sure to keep it the same distance away from my magnifier, I raise the tube increment by increment, examining its length. If I change its proximity in any way, I have to start back at the first crystal.

Sean's lantern flares to life behind me. My eyes relax their squint, the light bright enough to allow them to focus.

But they don't. Instead, my gaze turns back to three days ago, staring into a gutter swimming with dirty bandages and overflow sewage. My hands press against the street, grit clinging to my skin. My lungs drag in the filthy air. Contamination is everywhere here. The trash, the ground, the atmosphere. It wouldn't be that hard for it to transfer to my skin, my nose, my cells. It wouldn't be that hard to get infected, to have infected Sean.

In fact, it would be far too easy.

The soft tinking of Sean's nail on the glass of the lantern pulls me into the present. *Focus, Leavi.* If one of us caught it, there's nothing to do about it now.

31

Instead of comforting me, the thought allows the constrictor one final squeeze, spilling toxic anxiety into my veins. My eyes wander back to the crystals, and I force myself to concentrate. *Let's get this over with.*

Layer One—Clean.

Layer Two—The blood cells swirl before my eyes, one perfect circle after another, no foreign proteins bound to them. Clean.

Layer Three and Four—Is clean.

Layer Five—

My hand is trembling slightly; I can't get a good picture. *Stay still!* The first four layers were clean, so the last one is most likely—

My hand stays. "Clean," I sigh. Behind me, I sense Sean relax, the muted *tinks* ending.

Now for me.

I clean the hematester of Sean's blood, use the flame of his lantern to sanitize the syringe's needle, and draw my own sample. As the blood steadily rises in the syringe, I have the irrational thought that the pulse of my heart is a solemn drum, announcing each step closer to my execution.

I force the thought away. I *will* stay calm, and I *will* do this right.

I prepare the hematester and begin flipping lenses.

Layer One—Clean

Two—Clean

Three—

As I move the tube, my magnifier blurs. *Come on, Leavi. You can do better than this.* After all, I've run hundreds of tests like this before. Usually, I can whiz through a dozen samples in five minutes flat. My mind is buzzing, though, and my lenses aren't the only thing I'm having a hard time focusing. My breaths come short and shallow. Every piece inside of me feels like it's trembling.

Calm down, I scold myself. *Be professional. It's one sample like any other. You're just looking for irregularities. This is normal.*

Yet it isn't. The results of this test condemn or free two lives, and once we know the verdict, we can't pretend everything's okay. We can't wish for the best. If we're judged guilty, there's no hope of pardon. There's a gallows, a stage, and a long, painful way down.

Another hand draws the tube from my own. Startled, I turn to see Sean holding another magnifier, beginning the process of flipping through the lenses. "What am I looking for?"

Embarrassed anger waters down relief. "I can do that, Sean."

"So can I. What am I looking for?"

I hug my jacket closer to me, disguising the hands that have lost their resolve. Words shivering in the air, I respond, "You know the normal structure of a red blood cell?"

"Yes."

"Any abnormalities in that." That would show that plague had altered the cell, the first step it takes in infecting a person. For some reason, the explanation doesn't come out of my mouth, but Sean doesn't ask for it. He just steadily scans the tube.

After a minute of study, he declares, "You're clean."

"Are you positive? It's easy to miss something, and we can't afford-"

"It's just as important to me as it is to you, Riveirre," he interrupts. "Yes, I'm positive."

The tension drains out of my body. Mentally berating myself for not having been able to pull it together, I nod. "Thanks." I busy myself cleaning my other instruments and packing everything up, ignoring Sean's watchful eyes. He hands me back the hematester, and I clean and stow it away. "We should get going."

He nods, and we leave. I can't help but take one glance back at the stream's little paradise. I wonder if we'll ever find something like it again.

By the end of that day, we haven't quite made it to the surface, but the barometer shows we're close. The ground has started sloping more precipitously, and if Sean was to turn off his lantern, I fancy I could faintly see the halo of the moon creeping down the tunnel's mouth.

My lips tip a smile to my cloudy-headed daydreams. They used to get me in trouble when I was at my primary. Now, with nothing better to focus on, it's nice indulging, letting reality and imagination blur together.

Tonight, the air between me and Sean is lighter, empty, like someone filled balloons with all our animosity and set them free to fly away. It's not friendly, but neither is it dangerous. When I catch him staring, I don't let him know. I just gaze contentedly at the shadows on the wall, imagining them to be flitting fairies.

We're healthy. We're going to make it out. The detached realization makes me faintly giddy the way that lack of oxygen does. My tiny smile gradually morphs into a full, carefree grin.

I roll out my blanket, and glance over at Sean. "What do you think it'll be like where we come out?"

He pauses, staring at my face, eyes momentarily lingering on the curved corners of my mouth. He seems surprised that I addressed him. "Sunnier than here." Though his words have a sarcastic ring, there's no bite in them.

"Fantastic deduction, doktor," I mock. But the smile is still on my face, and he doesn't seem to take offense.

"Most topside trade posts are just small, halfway points. Other than that, I guess we'll know in a few days."

I nod, tucking myself in. "I suppose we will."

As I turn away, I hear him lay down. The fire crackles between us. A few empty seconds pass.

"Night," I offer belatedly.

"Night, Riveirre."

Chapter 10
ASTER

The candles are extinguished, and my curtains are drawn. My hands hesitate on the open travel bag on my bed, filled with my changes of clothes, casting materials, and rations.

If I get caught leaving... I'm terrified to imagine what Mother will have to say. What Agraund will do.

I shiver. Being late autumn, the castle is drafty, only adding to my chill.

If I leave, I'll be counted as a traitor. Sela will have to admit her once-dear brother has abandoned his country. Ren will have his justification in thinking me a weak coward. Father will finish forgetting my existence. Mother will be more worried about spinning my disappearance into a story that paints her in a positive light than my actual wellbeing.

And Agraund... He'll search for me and not give up until he finds me. When he does manage to drag me back, he'll be the one in charge of delivering the proper recompense.

My skin crawls at the thought.

But no matter what they think, I won't be abandoning or betraying them. Morineaux is the embodiment of everything I stand for, everything I love. No country will ever be her equal or deserve my loyalty more.

No *thing* will ever deserve my loyalty more.

"I need to improve," I say to the empty room, "and I will not let myself fail my country."

My life is owed to this land, to the people that inhabit it. They trust the line of Jacqueline to wisely and lovingly lead them. They trust *me* to lead them. As Second Son, I'll be responsible for all the country's wizards. I'll be the one everyone turns to when some non-military plight ravages the nation. I'll be the one they expect to foresee disasters, to find magical solutions to impossible problems. If some upstart nation is to ever threaten our borders, I'll be the one everyone looks to for intelligence. When the army makes a mistake, I'll be the one they expect a miracle from. When all else fails, I'll be the one sent with a dagger and a spell book to protect our country's secrets.

If I cannot, there is no one to take my spot. So I have to go. I don't have a choice. My Morineaux needs me, and I can't let her down. My attempts here to improve clearly aren't cutting it. Perhaps this academy holds some secret I've not yet found, some trick to help me unlock what's been hidden to me for so long.

So I have to go, no matter the consequences, no matter what punishment I'll face; if there's even a chance I can become stronger, I have to take it.

I snap shut the button on my bag. "It's my duty to my country to do everything I can to be the best I can."

Worry and fear congeal into resolve. I'm going to do this. I'm going to improve. For Morineaux.

For that cause, I know I must do whatever I can.

I sling my bag over my shoulder and, for the last time until I'm the caster Morineaux needs me to be, stride out of my bedroom. I drop a note to my family on the coffee table, and on comes my cloak.

I leave.

Cowl up, I slip through corridors I've known my whole life. I've only ever left N'veauvia, the capitol of Morineaux, for exercises with Agraund. I've only ever left in hopes of serving Morineaux; that's still my aim.

I can't leave through the front doors or the castle gate, though. The guards will have too many questions, things I can't answer in a way they'll understand.

So instead, I make my way toward one of the servants' exits. No one should be walking through there at this time of night. The minutes pass slowly as I cat-foot through corridors rarely traveled by the nobles of the castle. In these passages, sporadic torches leave the darkness mostly untouched.

Nearby, the clank of a night guard's armor echoes from a hall, and icy nerves shoot through me. His footsteps thud closer, and I glance around for cover. There's nothing but a long, empty hall and a stretching side table.

The glow of his torch seeps into the darkness of the corridor.

Heart racing and feet making only the ghost of a whisper against the stone floor, I slip through the supports of the table and fold over. My caster's cloak flows shapelessly around me, blending into the darkness. As flush to the wall as possible, I slowly pull in one, long breath and hold it. My body goes still.

Light floods the hall as the guard marches through. He's ten paces away. Only the faintest light comes near.

Five paces. The safety-ensuring darkness scatters from the torch. I can only hope the shadow cast by the tabletop is deep enough and wide enough to cover me.

He's directly beside me. My burning lungs beg to release the breath I've so carefully pent, but I refuse to let go. If I move now, it's over.

He keeps walking, but I hold my position. I can't afford to relax now only for him to turn and catch me.

Only feet away, he pauses. Panic claws my thoughts. *Why is he stopping? Did I make some sound? Did I move?* My protesting muscles assure me that I haven't. They tremble lightly as my body urges me to take a breath.

I steel myself; I'm not going to let him notice me.

He resumes walking. My head becomes light, heart rapidly thumping.

I hold still.

Reaching the end of the hall, he turns, the light leaving with him. Still afraid of making some slight noise, I let the air out slowly. Then my lungs greedily drag back in what I deprived them of. Only when I can no longer hear his footsteps do I let myself unfold from my hiding place.

Still jittery from the close call, I ghost toward my goal. The proud stone walls stand tall around me. I can't decide if they're judging my choices or kindly condoning them. The floors have switched to worn-down wood.

A flight of servant's stairs rises before me as I turn another hall. I crouch on the lowest step, digging my nails into a small gap between the base of the stairs and the floor. My fingers work around the thin trapdoor, and I pull up.

Dust showers from the edges, and a creak echoes up the stairs. I dart a glance over my shoulder. Someone probably heard that.

I hasten to lift the trapdoor. Beneath, a short, cobwebbed staircase lies. I hurry down, pulling the hatch closed above me. The low-ceilinged corridor forces me to stoop, and cobwebs trail against my face. I brush them away.

When I was a boy, this corridor stayed clean; I walked it almost every day. The Great Records Fire of centuries ago fascinated me, and I had the fanciful idea I'd be the one to recover all the hidden passageways we lost record of in the blaze. I wanted to impress my family with my dedication and success.

A bittersweet smile tugs my lips. That was back when I believed blood was thicker than water and marriages were made for love.

I never did tell them. Originally, I wanted to reveal it all in one fell swoop, but I quickly realized that none of them would care; they only wanted my dedication and success at magic. So I kept the secret halls as they were and stopped pretending that my unrequited affection would change my family's opinion of me.

I travel the maze of hidden servant passages until I'm under a hall that leads out of the castle. I rest my ear against the hatch. If someone's up there when I come out of the tunnel, I'm caught.

It won't take Agraund long to find out about it after that.

Only silence greets me, though, and I push the platform up. The hall's empty. Surrounded by tall stone walls and the last fizzling reaches of torchlight, I can finally stand up straight. After closing the trapdoor, I quickly exit the castle.

Outside, the chilled air plays with the edges of my cloak, and I tug my cowl closer around my face. In the expansive grounds, I suddenly feel exposed. Before I can leave, though, I need a horse. In the trek facing me, walking could take up to half a year. Even on horse it'll be about a month.

Crossing through the shadows of the castle grounds, I make my way to the stables and lead a black mare out of its stall to saddle it. It whinnies softly, and I stroke its nose, shushing it.

Motion stirs in the corner of my eye. I spin that way, fingers automatically digging for arcanum powder.

From atop a pile of straw, a boy scrambles up. He pushes his too-big hat out of his eyes. "Hey! You can't take that. Horse thief!" he calls to the air around. "H-"

I shove my hood back. "Hey, hey, calm down, Collin. It's me. It's Aster."

Eyes wide, mouth gaping, he stops shouting. Then, look turning skeptical, he takes a step forward and inspects me.

I kneel, smiling. "Hi, there."

Seeming to be satisfied I'm not some vagabond, he stands up straight and smiles back. "Hi!"

Heart racing and hoping that somehow no one heard him, I say, "What're you doing here tonight, Collin?"

"Oh! Well, Mirá cracked a hoof yesterday, so Mister Thamas told me to stay here with her." His brows draw together and eyes squint. "Wait… why're *you* here, Prince? I mean, it still looks like you were thiefing Calista."

I laugh softly. "Why would I need to steal a horse? I just didn't expect anyone to be here."

36

He nods, brown eyes wide and voice excited. "Yeah, that makes sense. But why do you *need* a horse? It's the middle of the night!"

If he keeps being this loud, someone's going to hear him, but I don't know how to quieten him without sounding any more suspicious than I already do. "I'm on a mission," I whisper. Perhaps he'll follow in kind.

He leans forward. "Yeah?" His voice drops.

I relax slightly. "Yeah. You see, Prince Agraund needs me to go…" I trail off, desperately thinking of an excuse. "He needs me to take a very important message to a town very far away."

"Really? Why?"

"It's a secret." His mouth 'o's at the seriousness I imbue into my voice. "But I'm going to be gone for a few months."

"Oh, no!" he breathes.

I nod sadly. "It's very important, and I'll be back as soon as I can. When Thamas asks you tomorrow why Calista is missing, though, you can tell him that I took her, needing to go serve Morineaux. Okay?"

He nods enthusiastically. "Okay!"

Relieved, I smile at him and set to readying the mare. Somehow, despite already having talked myself out of a problem with Collin and dodged a guard, and despite having resolved to leave and packed my bag, preparing this horse makes it seem real.

My chest tightens. I'm leaving. Only for a short time, and only to improve myself for my Morineaux, but I'm leaving nonetheless.

I walk Calista to the wall that surrounds the castle grounds, stepping from shadow to shadow. When I reach it, I search for the spot I'll exit from, marked by a small rune carved into one of the stones.

My eyes catch it; it's about a quarter of the wall away from the gate. I'm suddenly thankful that the guards only watch for intruders, not people leaving. Out here, with only the thin darkness for cover, I feel like I'm going to be spotted any second.

I pull a singed and yellowed paper from one of the many pockets of my cloak and unfold it. Straining my eyes to search its faded instructions for the ancient phrase, I breathe, "*Airesë asjault erræ!*"

My horse dances nervously when a low rumble echoes from the wall. As I back away, I glance at the gate. Surely, it was too quiet for them to hear that far away.

I hope.

Bits of moss and crumbling rock fall as a portion of the wall begins to separate, swinging open on some invisible hinge. The city street lies beyond, inviting me to leave.

I pause.

This is it. This is my last chance to turn back, to stay home, where it's safe, where I won't be taking a risk. This is my last chance to not attend the academy before I'm counted a traitor.

But the importance of my duty outweighs the importance of my image. If I've improved, they'll learn to forgive me when I return.

I walk Calista through the opening, then speak the words to close the section. It swings back into the space, still quietly protesting. I turn to the street behind me, relaxing slightly.

I've made it out of the castle. Now I just need out of N'veauvia. I should be in the clear after that, unless they scry me.

Wait. They can just scry me to find where I am.

All that stands in the way of them seeing where I am, at any time, is a blackwood bowl, a pinch of arcanum powder, and the will to cast the spell. Agraund has access to all of that before he even rolls out of bed.

Worry shoots up in me again, and I scramble onto the horse. I need to find out how to stop them from scrying me, but I can't do anything until I'm in a more secure position.

The brightly painted faces of healthy businesses and wealthy houses blur as I ride past, every clack of the horse's hooves feeling like the crack of a breaking blade.

Halfway through this sector of the city, I turn onto a side alley. As I tug my small Book from my cloak, whispers fill the air around me.

"Hello, Prince…" the myriad Voices of the Book breathe, each out of sync with the next.

"Hello," I murmur, glancing around. "How do I keep someone from scrying me? It's important."

"Hm," they consider. *"Yes, we suppose it is."*

My brow furrows. I'm unsure why they agree; usually, I have to convince them of something before they help me.

The Voices quieten, as if pulling away and turning to one another to converse, excluding me. After a moment, they increase in volume again.

"We agree that this path will align with the best outcomes…" They trail off, almost a guilty tone to their last word, like they feel they've given away too much. *"But that is beside the point, young prince. Here."*

Knowing the only questions they answer are ones concerning magic, I stay silent. The pages of the Book flip, opening to a sheet covered in black scrawl. I envy the occasional legendary wizard that can understand the language of magic but take comfort that I can speak the words without knowing what they mean.

"What will it do?" I mutter, slipping off my horse.

"It makes it impossible for the focus of the spell to be directly scryed. It is relatively easy to put into place but must be renewed daily. However, if you're around someone else that gets scryed, the view will still show you."

"Thank you." This is exactly what I need. Unease rattles within me that they're being so cooperative; they must be leaving something out. But I have to trust them. I have no other choice.

The Book whispers the instructions of the spell, and the words glow gold as I speak them.

I swing onto my horse when done. I'm slightly lightheaded, but not enough to impair my riding. I'm beginning to think there somehow isn't a catch; maybe the Voices have a reason I don't understand. Either way, I doubt I'll find out any time soon.

Cowl up, I canter through the city, my horse's hooves first rapping sharp against cobblestone, then dully thudding against the dirt road of the outer parts of the city.

It smells like rain.

* * *

It's quiet. I walk through a small field, tracking footprints, the waning moon the only light. I pass a small cottage, the house of my quarry. But I know that's not where he is tonight.

A creak splits the air. I spin.

He couldn't be behind me, could he? Could he? Who is that—what do I do—they're coming closer—I can't fail Agraund—

They're practically right on top of me, why haven't I done anything yet? I cast hastily, the only thing I know to end it, end it now. They scream, long, tortured. They fall.

Behind them, somehow, somehow, there's another, and I cast again, anything to get this over with, anything.

They scream. Agonized, endless. Endless.

I snap awake, shove up, walk, and lean against a tree.

Breathe.

Breathe.

It's over.

Taking one more deep, shaky breath, I turn from the tree and gaze at the dirt road, a three days' ride from home. The sun's hesitant rays are creeping onto it like a terrified servant easing into their tyrant Lady's room.

I shake my head, bending to gather my things. I'm not getting back to sleep, so I might as well take advantage of the daylight. Upon resaddling the horse, I swing on and urge her to the road. I ride.

The skies break open.

Chapter 11

LEAVI

On the third afternoon since our quarantine, birdsong echoes down the tunnel. Their high chirps convey a freedom that electrifies me. In all my study for my chosen focus—*aehrixi*, the group of animals that fly—birds have always fascinated me the most. They're independent, graceful, free-willed, but no matter where they fly, they find their way back home.

In Erreliah, I used to wander for hours through the menagerie's aviary. Here, though, the notes make me want to run off, to burst into the open, to leave the death and darkness behind, yet at the same time, they send a pang of homesickness through me.

Right now, despite its surrounding darkness, my Erreliah shines bright in a cavern far below me, as though the architects stole a million stars and sprinkled them through the streets. Nostalgia creeps up in my throat, but I swallow it. I'll be home eventually. Once we make it topside, I can get directions and make the trek back east, past Karsix and on to home.

The first rays of sunlight filter through the mouth of the tunnel. Before, with Sean's lantern, every image was yellowed, fuzzed at the edge. But in the white, natural light, I can finally see. I can see the glitter of the tunnel walls' variegated granite. I can see the dirt caked on my arms, the pebbles strewn across the dry, dusty floor, the shimmer of water as a tiny stream threads into a crack in the rock. I can see the blue sky like I never have before, filling the entire cave mouth. I rush past Sean and into the open air.

The cutting cold snaps my enthusiasm. Wind tears at my hair, greedy fingers combing, tossing, tangling the long, dark strands. Grey grass scatters the ten square feet of flat land in front of us, then drops away with the ground into a rocky, sixty-degree slope. One barren, snow-dusted tree thrusts through the earth like a skeleton grasping at the sky. Thankfully, it's early winter yet, the snow accumulation not having reached the several feet-high mounds I've heard that reckless travelers die among.

Opposite us, thirty-thousand feet tall mountains jut against every inch of the horizon. All three times I've seen them, something hollow has rattled within me. There's an unsettled quiver at my core as my brain struggles to comprehend their monstrous size and strange beauty. The behemoths simultaneously command an attraction and a primal fear. Their powerful presence forces me to realize just how insignificant I am in comparison.

You mortals keep on scurrying about your frivolous lives, the mountain wind hisses. *We have been here from the beginning and will be here until the end.*

Sean catches up to me. His eyes close, nostrils flaring as he breathes in the crisp air. He looks oddly content standing there, shoulders relaxed, sharp features momentarily softened.

Despite the towering mountains and bitter wind, there's something calming about being out in the open, fully surrounded by nature. No harsh human monuments litter the landscape around us.

Wait.

My eyes sweep the area, panic mounting. *No, no, no, no, no.* "Sean? We have a problem."

His eyes snap open. "What?"

I swipe my hand toward the barren plateau. "Where in the world is the trading post?"

"It's—it's right here." He rakes a hand through his hair, searching. "It's supposed to be right here."

"It's not."

"They must have moved it-"

"Moved it?" My satchel hits the ground with a thud as I sling it off. "Sean, this place is too small for a building, let alone a whole post! Where have you brought us?"

"It was the map, the map must have been wrong-"

"Or maybe your memory's not as great as you think it is."

"Riveirre, I have a nearly eidetic memory. It's not like I just," his hand gestures in frustrated circles, "forgot!" He shakes his head, shoving his hands into his pockets. "It had to be the map."

There's a strange frenzy to his movements that makes me feel bad for him and uncomfortable at the same time. I bite my lip, glancing away. He's not going to admit to forgetting, and there's nothing to be gained by forcing him to. "Well, whatever it was, we're lost now. So what's our next move?"

In my peripheral vision, I can see him pacing. "It's simple. We head back the way we came and take the other tunnel."

"That's a three-day trip. And that doesn't include making it all the way through the other tunnel and up to the post. I'm almost out of rations, Sean." I turn to face him. "Aren't you?"

His pace falters for a moment. Then he spins on his heel, talking over his shoulder. "Get more of those mushrooms."

"I'm not some sort of presto food dispenser! Those don't grow this close topside. I might be able to harvest some edibles from the chamber we quarantined in, but again, that's three days away."

He turns back toward me, but his gaze is on his steps. "Humans can survive for three weeks without food."

"Depends on the person, and that's not considering energy expenditure and metabolism. Or the fact that your muscles start cannibalizing themselves after a while. But even allowing that we make it back to the quarantine chamber, you know what humans can't survive, Sean? The Blistering Death, and we can't be sure no one's traveling these tunnels behind us. I don't want to meet up with them halfway."

He skids to a stop. "Then what *do* you want to do, Riveirre? Because so far, you've done nothing but shoot down my ideas."

"I…" What should have been a sentence trails off into nothingness. The mountains stare down at me, knowing I don't have an answer.

"Haven't actually thought about it yet?" he finishes for me, brow raised.

"No! I-" The wind splays my hair into my face. Frustrated and needing something to do with my hands, I twist it into a bun. "I'm getting there. Give me a minute."

Sean's jaw clenches, and he goes back to pacing. I lean against the skeleton tree, and a crow caws in the branches above.

I know it's irrational, but my thoughts keep circling back to my original goal. "I'd like to go back to Erreliah," I tell him. "We could travel overland-"

Sean scoffs, interrupting me. "Whatever you'd 'like,' Riveirre, that's not a plan. Even if we got unreasonably lucky and found a way there, what do you expect them to do? Welcome two plague survivors with open arms? They'll be checking everyone's passports at the cavern entrances. And since yours is marked 'Karsix'..." He mimes a patrolman firing a crossbow.

I throw my hands up. "What then? You want to winter in some topside, backwards hovel of a town? How would we even find one?"

Only after the words come out do I remember the rumor that those 'backwards hovels' are where he grew up. But what I said is true all the same. They're farmers. They can't *spell* science, and I seriously doubt their ability to differentiate between a laboratory beaker and a vase for their wildflowers.

"Beats getting shot." He pulls one of the chains out of his pocket, pops the device's lid, and studies its face. "You got a better idea?"

My eyes search the imposing, cold slopes of the mountains for answers I know I won't like. Danger waits in the tunnels. Death waits in Erreliah.

Wintering topside is our only option.

A flash of movement interrupts my thoughts. In the valley far below, a colorful contingent of carts, horses, and humans roll among the pine hills. "What is that?"

Not bothering to look, he nods in mock appreciation. "Nice change of subject."

"Seriously, Sean. What *is* that?"

Chapter 12

SEAN

The breeze changes direction, flooding my senses with the familiar scent of mintgrass.

Mama laughed, pushing her hair out of her face. Beaming, she grabbed my hand. 'Come on, silly boy.' She ran with me through the town park, air whipping her long hair into my face.

We broke through the trees into a small field, a magnificent view of the mountains rising up around us.

I gasped, pointing at the rolling waves of blue-green. 'Mama, wha's that?'

She grinned. 'Mintgrass, sugar. Here.' She bent and gracefully plucked three strands from the ground. 'Oh, wait.' Correcting herself, she grabbed one more and handed all four to me. 'There you go, sugar.'

I stared at them. 'Whaddo I do with 'em?'

'Like this,' she smiled. After pulling two pieces for herself, she tore off a bit from the bottom of each and placed them on her tongue. 'You suck on it.'

I repeated her actions, and a bright spice of sharp flavor hit my tongue. My eyes widened. 'Wow...'

The bright smell fades as the wind shifts again.

That's what showed up as black in my typifier. Though common where I lived topside nine years ago, mintgrass doesn't grow in the caves. Whatever undergrounder designed the device wouldn't have made it to test for any unique alkemitic substance the plant contains. But when I tasted it after the wannabe alkemist was asleep, I realized immediately—mintgrass.

I thought then that this bluff would be covered in it, and I was right. The plant grows abundantly around the cave mouth, a small stream running through a patch and into the mountain.

Near the plateau edge, Riveirre's pointing at the distant outskirts of the valley, where a fair-sized band of Traders—southern peddlers, judging by the tattered black and gold flags—wind along. Odd that they're up this far north this late in the year.

"Are those people?" she asks, shielding her eyes against the declining sun.

"Marauders."

Her head snaps toward me, smug mouth jumping into a shocked 'o.'

I struggle to hide my smirk. "Let's go say hi."

I head toward the slope, but she grabs my arm. Despite the cold, her hand warms my skin through the jacket fabric. "I'm not just going to go mingle with a group of topside criminals! Are you trying to get us killed?"

"Nah. Just you." Her eyes darken, and I laugh. "Your glare might be trying to kill me, though. Have a bit more faith, Riveirre. I know what I'm doing."

"Just like you knew which tunnel to take?"

I close the distance between us in one step. My voice lowers. "What's done is done, Riveirre. But these guys?" I point. "They're our ticket back to civilization. So let's cash it in before we lose it."

When she's angry, there's a sharpness to her features I'm not comfortable studying. I focus on the Traders below us.

She lets me go, and I head down the slope.

Chapter 13

LEAVI

The jagged path of disconnected ledges descends at a sixty-degree angle, forcing me into a crabbed combination of walking sideways and hugging the wall of the mountain, my view limited to the craggy dirt facing me. Even worse, frost dusts some of the stones, slicking the handholds I rely on for balance. I never was a good hiker, even after doing the topside fieldwork for my masterate. Instead, I relied on my sturdy leather boots to keep me from slipping and the better instinct of my professor to pick and keep a path. Luckily, I brought the same boots and Sean seems strangely confident making his way down the mountainside. Either he's more familiar with this type of terrain or his natural cockiness is leading us down to our doom.

Marauders. He wants to bet our survival on people who make a living preying off topsiders, and idiot me is following him. Again.

A frozen chunk of rock breaks under my foot, and I cling to the mountainside, cheek pressed against stone, breaths hard. My heartbeat thumps in my ears as the pebbles I dislodged rattle down the slope.

Sean glances over. He's upright, as if staring a hundred feet down a mountain with nothing to hold onto is as comfortable as walking down a flight of stairs. "You know, this would be easier for you if you walked like a normal person."

"Easier for me to fall, maybe." I'm still afraid to move, not sure I can trust my footing anymore. In front me, a spider crawls down the rocks, a thread of web anchoring it. "Why didn't we bring rope?"

"Rope's heavy, and you're making a bigger deal of this than it is, Riveirre. There's a stable spot about five inches to your left. Keep up." Then he's ten feet further down, hopping ledge to ledge with the surety and disgruntled frown of a mountain goat.

I grit my teeth. "Thanks, Sean," I grumble, glancing down at this supposed spot.

The world swirls beneath my feet as my eyes take in the distant ground. The tops of the trees look like moss floating in a pond, and the group we're trying to reach is further down still, a tessellation formed of carts and colors. Nausea creeps into my stomach, and I sway, simultaneously weightless and terrified of gravity.

Sean's voice breaks through my floaty hysteria. "Don't look down, Riveirre."

Irritated with myself, I snap my head back up. The vertigo that flooded my body drains away to leave behind only a knot of dread. "Not exactly new advice, Sean."

"If it's so obvious, how come you weren't following it?"

"How exactly am I supposed to find whatever spot you mentioned without looking down?"

Annoyance edges his voice. "Feel for it. You act like you've never been topside before, Riveirre."

"Two full months! And two visits before that. That's more than most undergrounders." *I've just never enjoyed this part of it.*

"Well, then, you must be an expert. A whole two months. I deeply apologize for critiquing your mastery."

Irritation overriding fear, I peek down to scowl at him.

I gasp.

He's mid-air, trench coat flaring out. His feet connect with a ledge in a solid landing, knees bending to absorb the impact. He steps onto the next shelf. "Hurry up, or the plague's going to have died out before we even manage to catch up with the Traders."

I swallow, hoping I'll be able to ease down that jump. *Show-off.*

Gingerly, I reach out with my foot for the hold Sean mentioned. It's a few inches too far to reach, and my burning arm stretches for a close, snow-dusted stone. My muscles are tensed, probably more than they should be. Though the incline is at a diagonal, it might as well be straight down for all I'm concerned.

Closer now, I tiptoe for the foothold. My toes slide into a pocket of stone, testing it. Satisfied it'll hold my weight, I ease over.

Now to do that about a thousand more times.

I look for something to distract myself. "Did you just say these people are traders? I thought you called them marauders earlier."

"You bought that?" he calls up. "And they're not just any old 'traders.' They're *the* Traders. Like, the people. How do you not recognize them?"

"Wait. You lied to me?" Angry, I glance down at him and instantly regret it as it makes me question my balance. Tightening my grip, I focus on lowering myself to the next ledge.

"Yes, and you bought it. Good recap. Now—how come you don't know who they are?"

My toes brush the landing, and I make sure my feet are flat before releasing my handholds. "I've never even heard of them."

That's misleading. I do vaguely recollect them from my *High Valley History and Theories of the Outerlands* class, but I spent most of my time in there working on *Advanced Cellular Structures* homework. Anything not directly related to a scientific advance was a footnote in my education. If I was to keep up with the science courses my mother expected me to take, I didn't have time to waste on every random name and date.

"They come to the topside towns regularly," he explains. "This group should be headed south, down to the valley villages for winter." He trails off, and I suppress the urge to examine the group in question again.

Feeling for the next foothold, I ask, "Why?"

"You're going to have to be more specific than 'why,' Riveirre."

A short, exasperated breath escapes me. My hand brushes a rock, and a shower of scree tumbles past, startling me. I stay silent for a minute, concentrating on following Sean down.

It doesn't take him long to lose his patience. "Well?"

"Well what, Sean?"

"Aren't you going to ask your question?"

"I'm focusing on the task at hand. Don't you think that's a little more important than our conversation?"

His footsteps pause as if waiting for me to catch up. "Can't move your mouth and your feet at the same time, Riveirre?"

I scoff, indignant, but after a moment, give in. "Why do they travel between the topside towns so much?"

Even five feet below me, I can feel his smirk. "I'll give you a hint—they're the Traders."

My cheeks flame red. Buying time to form a retort, I lower myself down to the next ledge, Sean on one a few feet below.

"Wait, Rivei-!"

There's a sharp crack underneath me, rock falling away from my foot, and suddenly gravity is more than an equation I've memorized. I'm sliding, dropping, desperately scrabbling at the wall in a useless attempt to find something, anything to grab hold of. I fall past Sean, and his hand darts out, catching my jacket sleeve. Our gazes snap together. Dread and apology flood through his eyes, and mine reflect his like a pool of water. We both instinctively know the same thing.

My momentum is too much.

The leather wrenches through Sean's weak grasp. A scream tears from my lips as I skid, scraped, cut, banged, bruised by the protruding rocks. I crash into one, and my body rebounds. I fall through the air.

My feet smash into a jutting lip of the cliff. My knees buckle, and I crumple sideways to the ground. I don't move.

Sean calls out above, and I hear him scramble down to join me. "Are you injured?"

Breathe, Leavi. My cheek is flush with the cold stone, and there's something strangely comforting about its solid stillness.

"Riveirre?"

Breathe.

His hand's on my shoulder. "Riveirre?"

I drag air into my body, then cough, frozen lungs churning back to life.

He hovers above me. "Are you okay?"

"Of course, Sean," I groan. "I fell down a cliff, and I'm fine."

"Be serious, Riveirre." Carefully, he rolls me onto my back. I stifle a moan. My body protests in a million places, but it's a dull ache rather than searing agony. *Please let that mean I didn't break anything.*

Sean's hands dart over me, pressing and prodding. I weakly swat him away. "Quit that!"

He draws back.

Annoyed, I push up, finishing the check by myself. Ulna, radius, tibia, ribs... My probing fingers detect no fractures. A swipe of my forehead comes away damp, a small cut stinging.

I glance at Sean. His initial concern has melted into impatience. His foot taps, eyes following the Traders' progress. I spot the broken ledge I fell from and realize it's only fifteen feet up.

I shove to my feet, determined not to slow us down any more than I already have. Pain shoots up my left ankle, and I glance away, trying to hide my wince from Sean. My boot already acts as the best support we have at hand for a sprain.

Looking me over, he nods once. "Perhaps you *can't* move your mouth and feet at the same time."

My jaw drops. He's already starting back down the mountain, though.

Under my breath, I say, "You fish-gutted, guano-filled, inconsiderate-"

"Can't hear you, Riveirre," Sean calls.

"That was the point," I mutter. Gathering my nerve, I find my next hold.

* * *

The temperature drops rapidly as the sun sets over the white-topped horizon. We've made it into the valley, the cliff to the cave entrance a few miles behind us. The ground rolls with hills, and pines rise up around. Underneath the shadows of the trees' branches, patches of unmelted snow lay. I shiver, pulling my jacket tighter. "Sean, I think we need to find shelter for the night."

Barely ahead of me, he shakes his head. He's hunched into his trench coat, a wary tortoise barely sticking its head out of its shell. "They're just over the next rise."

"You can't know that for sure. And it could be another hour before we top that! We need to find someplace to keep from freezing to death while it's still light. We can't afford to trudge up there only to find out once it's dark that you were wrong."

He whirls back on me. "So what do you want to do, Riveirre? Miss them tomorrow when they've moved on?"

I adjust my satchel on my shoulder. "We'll catch up. They're a big group; they can't be that fast."

He barks a humorless laugh. "They pack up camp faster than I bet you packed up your bag there. Traders know how to book it. If we don't catch up tonight, we won't at all." His eyes blaze a challenge, daring me to disagree. Deliberately, almost desperately, he repeats, "They're just over the next rise."

I consider him for a second. Framed by the snowy hill ahead and setting sun, he cuts an imposing figure. A tired but confident figure. A figure willing to risk his life on his ability to memorize the topography and keep track of how far we've come.

The safest bet is to find a place to sleep, out of the wind, where we can start a fire, lay out our blankets and stay dry. But if we do that and lose these people, we might wander these mountains forever.

He's right. We need to keep moving. We'll just have to hope he's also right about where they are.

I press my lips together and nod. He offers me a curt one in return. Then we're off again.

With every foot we climb, we gain a sliver of the sun, but with every minute, we lose a slice. My feet ache, and I can feel my ankle swollen against the leather of my boot. The cold burns my fingers and bites my face. My toes are going numb, and my skin stings where the rocks cut me.

When the sky finally goes black, icy knives of wind slash our skin, but we still trudge upward, always upward, one frozen foot after another, until the ground levels out, and Sean turns to me with that smug smile I hate but can find the room to love just now because he was right.

The Traders' camp is right here.

The land in front of us is a world of flickering lights and colored fabrics flowing in the wind. Before, I was too focused on putting one foot in front of the other to notice the warm hubbub of voices floating from the camp, the braying of animals, the jangle of wind chimes, but now my senses drink in every detail, reveling in relief.

They really are here.

Together, we hurry forward, exhausted but excited. On the edge of the camp, a woman feeds a mule out of one hand, rubbing behind his ears with the other. Her back is turned, attention focused on the animal.

I approach her. "Excuse me, ma'am?"

She turns, startled, and her brows draw together. She spits out some question, but it sounds like gibberish.

Sean steps past me. He answers the woman, enunciation crisp enough that this time I recognize the words as the topside Common. I had to take a couple years of it in secondary school, but beyond that, I never paid it any attention. Being the language the topside towns use, I thought I'd never have any use for the simplistic, guttural tongue beyond the phrases I needed for my topside studies.

The woman regards us warily and shakes her head.

Sean sighs, passing her a few stone-marks from his belt, and asks her a single-word question. She eyes the money in her palm, mouth twisted in thought. Despite her hesitation, she snaps her fist closed, shoving the marks into the folds of her clothing. She turns and leads us further into camp.

We pass tents full of curious eyes and people scurrying around, taking care of last minute business before sleep. A smile creeps to my tired lips as a pair of giggling children scamper away from their harried mother.

Our guide takes us to an elaborate tent two or three times the size of the others. A black pennant with a golden owl embroidered in the middle cracks once in the wind. The woman steps forward and hesitantly calls to someone inside. There's a pause.

A massive figure pushes back the tent flaps. Covered in thick pelts and fur boots, he fills up the full entrance of the tent. Stone beads hang all though his wild beard and hair, both of which come halfway down his chest. Between a bushy brow and a wide, crooked nose, a pair of dark eyes examine us.

Wordlessly, he shoulders into the clearing. Sean holds his ground, but I unconsciously step back. The man's eyes follow my movement, raking over my figure. I hold his gaze, refusing to be cowed. The corner of his lip twitches up before his attention shifts.

The man jerks his chin toward Sean. "*Ach escherisch?*" His voice is harsh, aggressive.

Sean answers the behemoth's question in his usual self-sure tone. They jab sentences back and forth like street fighters throwing punches. I'm hopelessly lost. I can understand Sean a little better than the man—his accent's not as guttural—but I'm only catching words here and there. Their tone implies a fight for dominance, but their anger is measured, like they're waiting for the right opportunity to press their attack. A couple minutes into their spar, I tap Sean's elbow, hissing, "What's going on?" He waves me away irritatedly and keeps talking.

As the man's scowl deepens, Sean argues more and more insistently. Finally, the man shakes his head. He makes a wide, disgusted gesture with his arm, dismissing Sean, and calls to a couple of men nearby. Behind me, someone grabs my arms.

Panic tightens my chest, and I thrust my elbow back, connecting with someone's stomach. My offender grunts, but his grip tightens, drawing me to his chest.

"Let me go!"

Sean's head snaps toward me. He throws an arm in the air, yelling at the leader. With his other hand, he digs for something in his pockets.

The man holding me drags me back. I try to wrench out of his vice, but he jerks me to the side and backhands me. I stagger. Still gripping my left arm, he yanks me back, dragging me away again.

"Sean!" I scream.

"Give me a minute!"

My feet kick wildly, spraying snow. I catch my captor on the shin, and he growls, digging his fingers into my flesh. He hauls me another couple feet, my resistance burdening him no more than if I were a child.

Sean thrusts an object overhead. The moss-backed compass shines through the dark. It twirls on the silver chain hanging from Sean's fist, strangely beautiful amidst the violent commotion.

The leader raises a hand. He walks forward, one slow, ponderous step at a time. He stops in front of Sean, putting his hand beneath the compass.

Sean lets it dangle, meeting the man's eyes. He poses a careful demand.

The leader grunts, but Sean repeats his terms.

A huff of breath escapes from the man's nostrils and fogs in the cold air. Sean holds his gaze.

The leader gives a decisive nod, and Sean drops the compass into his palm. The man stands there, examining it, seemingly entranced.

Sean clears his throat. The man looks up, gesturing lazily at the guy holding me. My captor shoves me away. I spin on my heel and glare at him, and he sneers at me. Brushing off his furs, he saunters to the leader's side. Out of the corner of my eye, I see the woman who brought us here hurry away.

As I turn, Sean grabs hold of my elbow. I jerk from his grip. "What do you think you're doing?"

"Shut up and go along with it," he hisses.

Taking my arm again, he marches me off. We head back the direction we came, attracting odd looks, but Sean offers me not a word of explanation. Finally, he stops in front of the tent with the lady's mule outside. Right now, the animal has bundles piled on his back instead of just his blanket. I stare, confused for a moment, until I see the woman come out with an armful of belongings.

She pauses momentarily to glare at Sean but places her load on her animal. She gestures at the tent angrily, as though to say, *It's all yours. Happy?*

Paying her no attention, Sean pulls me into the structure. Inside the thick hide walls, it's noticeably warmer. He releases me.

I turn on him, only one word on my lips. "Explain."

He shrugs his bag and coat off. "Women are second-class citizens here."

I spread my hands, incredulous. "What does that have to do with anything?"

He stares at me like he doesn't understand how his random fact was not an explanation. Delayed, he blatantly states, "The Ufir thinks you're my slave."

"The *who*?"

"The Ufir. Their leader. They-"

I cut him off, realization kicking in. "Wait. Did you *tell* him that?"

"No. I simply didn't confuse him."

I gawk, unsure how else to handle him. "You didn't correct him?"

He tips his head, considering me with one eye. "I just said that."

For once, I don't have any reply. Despite understanding each word, I feel as if we're speaking two different languages.

After a minute of bewildered silence, Sean sighs. "Look, here's what happened. I told them to take us to Xela, my hometown, and I would pay them. He liked the look of you," he continues, ignoring my indignant protest, "and offered to take you and the money as payment. We argued. He decided to take you and leave me here. I gave him the compass instead of you. The end."

Sean's blunt explanation does nothing to end my speechlessness, but he doesn't seem to notice. He's too busy looking around our new quarters. After giving one satisfied nod, he begins to lay out his blankets.

Several moments later, he notices me staring at him. "What?" he asks obliviously.

"I-" *I'm not sure whether to be furious or thankful.*

My answer not forthcoming, he turns back to his pallet. "I don't know about you, but I'm beat. I'll see you in the morning." Just like that, he rolls into his blankets and goes to sleep.

Chapter 14

SEAN

I claimed to be going to sleep more to keep her from venting her frustration at me than because I was actually tired. I mean, I'm not much happier about matters than she is, but complaining about them's not going to do any good.

I don't understand the Traders' view of women. Males and females have, on average, equivalent mental capacities. That's all that matters. Such primitive people. Fitting, perhaps, that they should be the ones to return me home, bring us to that backwards town I never thought I'd have to set foot in again. But even going back to everything I ran from so long ago is better than dying out in the cold.

And even the Traders thinking Riveirre is my slave is better than us wandering the mountains forever.

* * *

A wad of something large and soft drops on to my face. Forcefully.

Annoyed, I shove the woven stuff-sack off and stand, spotting the woman from the night before in the flap to the tent.

"What?" I ask, cross.

"We're moving in thirty minutes. Pack up." Her accent is rough and guttural, nothing like the casual tones of Xela or the flowy, run-together voice of my mother.

"I take it we missed breakfast?"

She narrows her eyes and tosses a small package at me. "Day's meals." Then she turns and ducks back out.

I peek into the bag. Dried fruit, some nuts, and jerky—meager, but enough.

I start gathering my stuff. "Riveirre. Wake up."

She sighs, shifting. The corners of her lips are slightly upturned, as if dreaming of some pleasant world. Her long, dark lashes flutter faintly. Otherwise, she remains still.

My eyes search her face. The gentle curve of her jaw, much kinder in sleep than in her conversations with me. The light catching her cheekbones, high and elegant. The messy spill of her dark hair across the pillow, wavy and somehow meticulous despite her sleep. The vibrancy in her skin, pale and smooth, cheeks tinted with a light natural blush.

The clamor from outside tugs me back to my senses, and I nudge her with my toe. "Riveirre. Wake up."

She hums and stretches, and I swing my bag over my shoulder. She doesn't seem in any hurry, or even like she's fully realized our surroundings, so I announce, "We're leaving in twenty-seven minutes."

"What?" Now her eyes open. "Why didn't you wake me up before now? How long have you been awake? Did I miss breakfast?" She scrambles up and swats me on the shoulder. "Why didn't you wake me up?" she accuses again.

52

I smirk, letting her believe what she wants about how long I've been up, and reply, "Well, I tried, but you just sighed at me and didn't move."

She glares and gathers her things.

"Here," I say when she's done. "Breakfast."

Surprised, she takes the proffered piece of jerky. "Where did you get this?"

"The kind donkey-woman." I jerk my thumb behind me, biting into my own share.

She laughs, shifting her satchel on her shoulder. "Are you talking about the one from last night? With the mule?"

A mule? Isn't that just a less-ridiculous-sounding term for a donkey?

I maintain, "It's not a horse, it *is* a pack animal, and it sounds like a donkey. It's a donkey."

"No, it's not, but it doesn't matter." She pulls her hair back, twisting it into a bun. "Didn't you say we were supposed to be somewhere?" She finishes securing her hair with a leather band. A single strand falls to brush her cheek, and she frowns at it, tucking the piece behind her ear.

I turn to leave the tent. "Yeah. Help me pull this down. We've got a lot of walking ahead of us."

Chapter 15
LEAVI

It snows steadily on us, sky dropping wet, slushy flakes that melt and drench us as soon as they hit our clothes. I'd rather have rain. At least that wouldn't have an icy bite as it struck our skin, like the stings of tiny vindictive insects.

I'm not the only one who's miserable. Between the narrow pass walls, the women and children trudge through the mud, their frowns bundled beneath an assortment of fur scraps, woven blankets, and colorful rags. It doesn't matter, though; it's barely noon, and the snow has already soaked through their hodge-podge defenses. Ahead, the men seem fine, most of them riding, all of them in sturdy shoes and heavy fur coats.

I turn to Sean to see if he's noticed the disparity, but his gaze is on a metal trinket he's pulled from his pocket. He turns a knob on the side, frowns, and continues fiddling with it. I shake my head, deciding not to bother him. He'd probably just say something like, "I already told you it'd be like that," and that would be the end of the conversation.

As we walk, the wall to my right drops away, and I gasp. Every single stinging snowflake suddenly becomes worth this view. Far below me, a thick forest sprawls, dusted with white flakes and kissed by silver ice. In the open sky, the snow spins and twirls like airy dancers in practiced concert. It's ancient and magical, something I thought I'd only ever see drawn in story books.

From behind, someone taps my elbow. I shake back to reality and realize the group ahead has moved on while I was standing entranced. I glance back, looking for whoever wanted my attention. A little girl, no older than seven, stands there, scraps of cloth serving as her poor excuse for a coat. Her tangled blonde curls frame an angular face, a streak of dirt swiping her forehead.

I kneel in front of her, nearly blocking the narrow path. Stones scrape against the ground where people begin to shift impatiently, but surprisingly, no one moves to prod the girl forward or take her hand and pull her along. I glance at the jagged line of people, but no attentive eyes claim her. Rather, each woman's irritated stance and disinterested attitude say that the girl is someone else's problem.

My gaze flicks back to her, and she stands there wide-eyed. She probably tapped me as a cautious reminder to keep moving, not out of any expectation of attention. No. I doubt she gets much of that.

"Where are your parents, sweetie?" I ask. I have a feeling I already know the answer, but the question passes my lips anyway.

Her head tilts, not understanding, and I suddenly remember that no one here speaks my language.

In the waiting crowd, someone calls out impatiently, probably demanding we start moving again. I cast a look over my shoulder and see the rest of the group getting farther and farther away. About thirty feet from us, Sean's finally realized I stopped and has turned around to catch back up with me.

As I return my focus on the girl, I realize that people have started trickling through the five-foot gap between me and the precipice. The girl fidgets nervously, but her curious eyes remain on me, probably wondering why I'm still here. I shrug my jacket off, trying to hurry so that we don't get any further behind. Her already wide eyes turn into miniature moons as I press the fabric into her hand.

"Keep it," I encourage, even though she can't understand.

She chatters at me in reply, but a sudden clatter to our side pulls our attention away. A wagon teeters on the cliff; the front left wheel hovers in the air, its diagonal counterpart hanging off, the other two grabbing for purchase. Some impatient driver must have tried to make it past me and the girl. Now that woman scrambles up. She reaches the edge of her seat, tilting the balance of the cart. Its front wheel slams onto the ground.

Her foot is mid-step down, and horrific realization hits me. I vault up. "Stop!"

But the woman can't understand my words, and if anything, the urgency in my voice only propels her.

She jumps onto solid ground.

Groaning, the back of the cart slips. The mule pulling it brays, a panicked, grating sound. With the animal still bridled, the doomed vehicle drags the creature toward the cliff, no matter how wildly he strains against the weight.

I surge forward, my cold fingers desperately scrabbling against the knots chaining the animal to the wagon. The cart lurches, and I'm jerked forward. I stumble into the mule, and the hysterical creature brays again, swinging his snout. He swipes my shoulder, knocking me to the stone.

A crack resounds as part of the cliff crumbles underneath the back-left wheel. Pops echo as wood splinters, and the ledge breaks away.

The mule's calls are hurried and haunting as he shakes his head, mouth frothing, hooves slipping against the gravel.

Everyone watches, frozen and shocked, as the poor animal and a whole cart of supplies simply slip over the edge.

Shakily, I clamber to my feet. The mule's cries carry as he falls, and the eerie notion that he's already dead infects my imagination. I sense Sean come stand next to me more than see him. Everyone's still focused on the spot of the disaster, as though if we all stare long enough, everything will reappear. The incident feels unreal, too quick in life and yet strangely stretched out in memory.

I'm not sure how long we stand there, snowflakes piling in our hair and dusting our skin. All the sudden, though, hoofbeats break our vigil, and the Ufir swings off his horse. He doesn't even wait till his feet are on the ground to start yelling for an explanation.

Slowly, fingers begin pointing at me, quiet, condemning things that tremble from cold and fear. No one dares speak up but simply slides all the blame onto my account with a silent gesture.

From the corner of my eye, I notice a leather jacket ghost into the crowd, avoiding the trouble. The wagon driver is also conveniently invisible.

I square my shoulders, ready to face whatever's coming. It's not as if I can argue my case, and even if I could, what good would it do? As if anyone would ever believe the foreign girl over their own people.

The Ufir comes forward quickly, and I hold my ground. But it's not me he strikes.

It's Sean.

He stumbles, shocked. As he straightens, the Ufir shouts at him, gestures large, wild, and angry. For the first time since we ran across the Traders, I'm glad I don't truly understand their language.

Sean stands there, eyes ablaze for a moment. However, as the Ufir continues his torrent of abuse, the fire begins to dwindle, then withers away completely, leaving only dead embers and ashes. His previously clenched fingers become a group of nervous drummers tapping a distracted tattoo.

He's not going to stand up for himself, I realize. And I'm not going to let this keep on.

Without thinking, I move in front of Sean, shoving the Ufir's chest with the flat of my hands. "He didn't have anything to do with this!" I call.

He simply swats me away. His casual blow is powerful, and I stagger into the mountain wall. Ignoring me, he continues yelling at Sean. I gather myself, then with quick, determined steps, advance to slap the Ufir across the cheek, the same way he did Sean.

He pauses mid-sentence and stares at me, as if incredulous that I had the audacity to attack him not once, but twice.

I stand tall under his gaze. "I said, he had nothing to do with it."

He might not be able to translate my words, but tone is a language even a savage like him can understand. His arm snaps out, and he grabs my face with one massive hand. He drags me toward him, pulling me close enough to feel his hot breath across my cheeks. Jaw clenched, he studies my features and finds nothing but defiance and disdain. Despite that, a dark hunger lights in his eyes. Sickened and unsettled, I try to jerk away, but his vise is iron.

My brain searches my memories, looking for one of the few words I know in this brute's language.

After a drawn-out moment, my tongue spits the answer. "Pig."

He stares at me for a moment. Then, unexpectedly, he pushes me away and throws his head back, laughter roaring out from him. After a moment, he recovers, still chuckling slightly. He swings onto his horse and wheels it around. Tossing some command over his shoulder, he rides off to join the other half of the group. His horse disappears around a bend.

The greasy imprint of his fingers lingers on my cheeks.

Sean's still standing in the middle of the path, tense, fingers jittering at his side. His chest falls in irregular patterns as white plumes tint the air from his mouth. His eyes are cold, glassy coal now, seeming to focus on some distant reality.

I set a hand on his shoulder. "Sean?" I try. Around us, people are starting to move again, and I've already learned my mistake. "Hey, Sean. Sean, we need to go. Okay?"

No response. "Okay, you're not talking to me. That's fine. Let's just get going then, alright?" I glance around, but no one's really paying any attention to us, and we're losing time. "Alright." I start walking, guiding Sean by his elbow. Thankfully, he follows me.

We never stop for lunch that day. I have a feeling they normally do, though, based on the grumbling of the group around me. I wonder if it's because of the lost cart or the wasted time or something else entirely. I would ask, but even if I could remember the words to, I wouldn't understand the response. Besides, by the generous bubble of space around me, I'm fairly sure I've just become the latest social pariah. No one's going to chance their leader's disfavor by talking to me.

At some point before that, Sean shrugged off my grip, but doesn't ever say anything to me. I keep my silence in return.

We just walk.

Chapter 16

SEAN

His palm flies against my cheek.

My head snaps to the side.

The Traders stare at us.

The snow dribbles down my face.

The Ufir's shouts rip through me.

And there's nothing I can do about it. I bristle, angry, at the man accusing me, insulting me for something not my fault, something I could do nothing about.

But I have no control.

Tears ran down my face.

'Mama, please, I need to.'

'Sugar, I don't understand.' She stood in the doorway of my bedroom.

'Let me, let me, please!' On top of my desk, I knew the floor was just far enough.

'Sugar, this isn't healthy. This isn't right. You need to just—just stay there, okay? Let me come to you, sugar.'

'I don't know how I can not do this, Mama! I'm—I'm scared,' I sobbed.

The Ufir is screaming at me for not keeping control of Riveirre, not stopping the cart. Screaming about something I had nothing to do with. Screaming just to make himself feel better, higher, stronger, more powerful.

'What's wrong with you?' he screeched. Mama set a hand on his shoulder, but he shrugged her off. 'Why can't you do anything right?'

'I'm trying, I'm trying...' My fingers twitched a constant, comforting beat on my leg.

'You're such an idiot! You're all,' he gestured angrily, 'messed up! Why are you so stupid?'

I feel my tense posture relaxing. Now I'm just standing there. The only defense against a loss of control.

They laughed.

'How did you end up here? You're too small to be with us.' One of the older kids shoved me against the classroom wall. 'Go back to the toddler school.'

'I'm not a toddler!'

They laughed.

'Whatever.'

'Get out of here.'

I stood there, resolute, and they continued to yell. Insult. Push.

But then I realized something.

They can't hurt a shell.

So I stand. I take it. If I block it out and ignore it, it can't bother me. It doesn't mean anything.

But then Riveirre pushes forward, hitting the Ufir, yelling at him. He shoves her. Ignores her. Keeps yelling at me.

None of it matters, all of it's distant. I don't have to care. It doesn't affect me; there's nothing I can do anyway.

She comes into view again, slamming her palms against his chest. He grabs her face.

She says something to him.

A timeless pause. Every moment stretches as the man glares at her, just watching.

A peal of sharp, harsh, mocking laughter escapes his lips, and he drops her.

He wheels back around.

Another, smaller pause as the spectators process the events. The Trader women begin to drip around us.

Riveirre turns back to me.

None of this matters. I don't need to do anything.

The drip becomes a thin stream.

She says something.

Just ignore it all. I only need to be a shell.

The stream becomes a lazy river.

She repeats herself, more definitively.

Leave me alone.

The river becomes a flood.

She takes my arm, pulling me along.

I'm just a shell. I just need to do what I'm told. It's the best defense.

We mix into the water, pretending we fit, match, belong. We pretend not to be oil.

* * *

Nobody's yelling, nobody's angry, and the last person I ever expected to stand up for me is leading me along like I've taken a vacation from reality.

I'm not broken.

I shrug her off.

Chapter 17

LEAVI

Frozen fingers struggle to tie tent poles to each other. I've put tents up before, but those were more sophisticated, with premade loops that stretched over pegs and metal poles that unbent and snapped together. Instead, unwieldy wooden rods and bulky strips of hide compose the building materials for the Traders' tents. As the sun drops behind the mountains and campfires wink to life around us—the Traders having long finished setting up their tents—I begin to wonder if I should have gotten my degree in architecture rather than vitaliti.

Eventually, a little boy, no older than eight, takes pity on us. His tiny hands whiz over knots before driving the stakes into the ground by stomping on them. Brushing his shock of blonde hair out of his eyes, he turns and asks Sean something.

Sean frowns, but before he can respond, a woman's voice calls out. The boy's head snaps behind him. I follow his gaze. A woman with white-blonde hair and a baby on her hip waves the little boy over. His shoulders sag, but he glances back at Sean.

Sean rolls his eyes and flips him a one-cent stone-mark. The boy runs off, brandishing his mark to the blonde woman like he found a hidden treasure chest.

Sean ducks into the tent, and I follow him into its warmth. After digging for the throw in my satchel, I sit, soft fabric wrapped around my arms. "What was that about?" I ask Sean.

"With the kid?"

I nod.

He strips his wet coat off in favor of the dry blanket in his leather bag. "Told me he'd set our tent up for us every night if we paid him a cent each time."

I eye him, a confused smile making my words light. "Then why did you act upset?"

He scowls as he pulls his shoes off. "Because we just got shown up by a child."

I laugh, leaning back onto the ground. Despite my exhaustion—or maybe because of it—I'm strangely giddy.

Sean watches me, eyebrows drawn together as though trying to decide if I've lost it. His mild befuddlement just makes me laugh harder. My merriment is cut short by someone calling Sean's name outside the tent. The giggles fade into hiccups of breath as Sean opens the tent flap.

A man with curly brown hair, ruddy cheeks, and a snowfox pelt hanging around his shoulders shifts nervously in the opening. His eyes flick to me, and the already red tone of his face deepens.

Oddly embarrassed, I sit, combing my fingers through my hair, and the man's gaze hurriedly moves away. He clasps a fist to his chest, dipping his head in some sort of greeting to Sean. Head still down, he extends his other hand, proffering a string of stone beads coiled in his palm.

An exchange passes between them, and Sean takes the string. The man makes the strange gesture again and starts to leave. He pauses before Sean closes the tent flap, though, and hesitantly says something else. They talk a second longer, the man's feet shifting more as they speak, his fingers playing nervously with the fox's fur. Eventually, Sean raises a hand in parting, and the man, looking relieved, walks off.

Sean considers the beads in his hand, letting the tent flap drop closed.

"That was strange," I remark.

He glances at me. "Yeah." Kneeling, he hooks the string to his backpack.

"Care to explain?" I scoot closer to study the beads. Foreign designs carved in tiny and intricate strokes swirl through each one.

Sean tugs his bag closer to him, digging for something inside. "They seem to think I'm a magic-man or some such."

I look at him askew. "Because you just radiate mystery and power." I roll my eyes. "So, what, they not only buy into some kind of supernatural hogwash but think you have it? How dumb are these people?"

He shrugs. "I've seen it happen before. Some topsider tries to peddle a bit of below-ground tech to a Trader, and they get greedy, curious, and nervous all at the same time."

"So you're saying when you gave them the glowmoss compass, they thought it was-"

"Some sort of relic? Yeah. Our visitor was a messenger from the Ufir. Apparently, the beads are a peace offering so I don't curse him for striking me. I accepted." He smirks. "It was rather magnanimous of me."

"You're so full of it." For someone who all but regressed into a walking corpse before, he's oddly casual about it now.

He doesn't bother replying, finally pulling out the notebook he must have been looking for. After lighting his lamp, he settles his presswrite into his lap.

"So that was it? He dropped by a string of beads in hopes you wouldn't rain down your non-existent magical fury and left?"

"No. He also politely requested we stay in our tent tonight."

I draw my necklace out, playing with the chain. "Why?"

His head's down, focused on his typing. "Apparently they're having some sort of tribe meeting. No outsiders."

"Hold on. They're having a secret meeting and your plan is to kindly do as asked and stay in?"

"Where it's quiet and warm? Yes, it sounded like quite a good plan to me." His fingers tap dance over the keys.

"You ever think the fact they don't want us there is exactly the reason we should go?"

"You ever think to keep your nose in your own business?"

I snatch his presswrite.

"Hey! What was that for?"

"Sean, listen." I force him to meet my eyes, my voice earnest. "Whatever they're talking about tonight could be important, especially since we're more or less at their mercy—aside from whatever weird privilege your supposed powers give you."

61

"No matter what they say at their meeting, Riveirre, it's not as though you can do anything about it. We might as well stay in here and out of their way." He pries the presswrite from my grip.

"Are you serious?"

He ignores me, tapping resolutely at the keys. Each unconcerned peck adds to my irritation. Frustrated fingers tug loose my waves of black hair before pulling it into a tighter bun. He didn't even bother thinking the situation over. I never thought Sean Rahkifellar would be so devoted to holing himself up in ignorance.

Knowledge is power. My mother's favorite saying. *And ignorance is a weapon waiting to be used against you.*

"Well." I stand, letting my blanket fall to the ground. "If you're not going to go listen to them, I'll at least go watch."

"What?" His typing stops, attention fixed on me. "You can't even understand them!"

"Some information's better than none. You can come with me if you like, but either way, I'm going."

I barely pull the flap back, peeking outside. Other tents spread out around, but in this area, all's quiet. Everyone has either gone to their bed or to the meeting.

A hand grabs my elbow, pulling me back inside. I yank from Sean's grasp. "Let go of me! What? Are you afraid your little 'slave' is going to get you into trouble?"

"As though you haven't already!"

Drawing back, I say, "I gave a jacket to a little kid in *rags*, Sean, not-"

"You caused a whole cart to go over the mountainside!" His hands spread out wide. "You killed one of their pack animals!"

I shake my head, angry. "Don't put all this on me. I didn't notice you standing up for yourself."

"Their Ufir's twice my size!"

"So is that it then? You're scared? That's fine. You just stay cozy in here. I'll go make sure they're not getting ready to roast us on a spit or anything." I push out of the tent.

"Riveirre," Sean growls.

As I ghost through the night's shadows, I hear his heavy steps behind me. A strange mix of annoyance and relief surges through me. Just by listening to his footfalls, I can tell he's terrible at sneaking, but at least I'm not alone. Plus, with him along to translate, we have a better chance at getting some useful information.

He catches up as I pause in the shadow of a tent. I grab his sleeve to keep him from bumbling ahead. "Can you be any louder?" I hiss. "Here's a tip: the goal is to *avoid* the dead wood and loose stones."

He flushes, angry.

My fingers drop their grip. "Just step where I step. Okay?"

I move off, darting between tents and keeping away from the scattered campfires. Most of the camp seems abandoned, though.

Voices rise in the distance, and I follow them. Once I figure I'm close enough to see—but hopefully far enough away that no one will see me—I peek around a tent's edge.

About thirty feet away, a group of at least fifty gathers. Most of them are men, but a handful of women are present as well with a few children scattered throughout. A sparking fire highlights the group's anxious expressions. In the center, commanding everyone's attention, stands one giant of a man.

The Ufir.

Chapter 18

S EAN

I don't understand why Riveirre can't just lay low, keep to herself. Especially since she's already screwed up once by going against the grain. She doesn't understand, not just the language, which she should have known anyway, but also the world she's been thrown into.

And she'll never understand me—she clearly struggles with even simple logic sometimes. But it doesn't matter; we can coexist for as long as we need to, and then we'll go our separate ways.

I just have to hope she isn't running around, asking for trouble that she doesn't need the *entire* time I have to deal with her.

I catch up with her as she ducks back around a tent, out of sight of the Traders. Before I can ask what she saw, the wind carries the Ufir's booming words to my ears. I peer around the tent.

"...can't keep on like this, brothers! Winter hit earlier than we've seen in generations, and the season can only get harsher. We're not prepared!" He stalks back and forth across the clearing, eyeing the crowd. "The cart that fell today is the third we've lost this month! First the landslide, then the bear, and now the foreign girl! The gods of the mountains are against us." He sweeps his arm in a wide gesture. "Look at the rags of our women and children, listen to the growls of your stomachs, feel the weary ache of your feet, and tell me it is not so!"

"But what can we do?" someone cries.

His answer is immediate. "We leave the High Valleys."

Murmurs of discontent ripple through the group. Hidden in the crowd, a single voice yells, "That's madness!"

The Ufir's eyes scan the crowd, but he seems unable to find the source. "It's our only choice. It's not the first time our people have done it when we've hit hard times. Eight Ufirs before me, we traveled from these mountains, down into the Outerlands. We are still here."

"What's in the Outerlands?" a woman's voice shouts.

"Warmer temperatures." The Ufir radiates confidence, despite talking of something he can't possibly know anything about. "Plentiful game. No snow."

His gilded promises create a few hopeful rustles among the crowd.

"Are there people?"

"No."

Whispers of worry spread in the crowd.

"But we can't trade anything else this season anyway!" the Ufir continues. "We need all we have for ourselves, and villages won't bargain with their essentials this time of year. The Outerlands are our only hope."

The thick clouds above open up, dropping a heavy snow.

"We march for the Outerlands!" the Ufir says. "Aye?"

People in the crowd shiver. The snow melts wet and cold against my skin.

"Aye?" he repeats louder.

Quiet agreements course through the group until they build into a resounding chorus. "Aye!"

The Ufir keeps talking, but my attention's elsewhere. On the fringes of the group, people have begun peeling away.

I curse under my breath and duck out of sight. "We need to go."

"What? Why? He's still talk-"

Rather than explain, I grab her wrist and hurry away.

She jerks out of my grasp. To my relief, she keeps pace, though.

Tired and worried voices rise behind us. Riveirre yanks me around a tent and onto the ground. We lay facedown in grass, snow, and shadows.

We wait, my heart pounding in my ears.

Footsteps draw closer. My brain yells at me to run, but it's too late for that. I just have to trust that Riveirre's got half a clue about what she's doing.

Snow crunches right in front of us.

The offending pair of feet don't hesitate—they shuffle off, hurrying to get out of the elements.

Relief floods through me.

I can't hear their steps anymore. I go to get up, but Riveirre grabs my wrist, fingers digging into my skin, and I flatten. My breaths count the seconds. Eighteen breaths later, another group passes us. Seven breaths, one more person. Fifteen—

Riveirre taps my shoulder, offering me a hand up, and we're off and running from shadow to shadow.

We burst into our tent.

I lay flopped on the ground, recovering my breath as water rolls off my skin. Out of the corner of my eye, I see Riveirre wrapping up in her purple throw, hair pulled back down, pale nose and cheeks cherry red. She looks more like a little girl than a sixteen-year-old.

My heart gradually slows its hammering. I swear I've run more in this week than in the last 8 years of my life.

She sits cross-legged like a kid in their first-year classroom. "What was the Ufir saying?" Her dark, deep eyes watch me, waiting for answers.

I push up. "They're going to winter in the Outerlands."

Long lashes flutter in confusion. "Aren't the Outerlands a myth?" Her fingers peek out from her blanket to play with that chain she always wears around her neck.

"They don't seem to think so." My shirt is clinging to me where it's wet. I tug it off.

Riveirre looks away, cherry cheeks turning beet. "They also think magic is real. There's nothing outside of the mountains of the High Valleys. What would that even look like?"

"Flat, probably." I pull another shirt on.

"A whole expanse of land can't just be flat, Sean. Even if the Outerlands are real, they've got to have-" A fisted hand tightens her blanket's embrace. "Something. A different mountain range. Hills maybe. Besides, if it did exist, wouldn't we know? Someone would have gone and come back by now."

I snort. "Undergrounders are too interested in finding new caves to worry about anything that might lay beyond the mountains. Topsiders are too poor. Traders would be the ones to know, and as you pointed out, they're not the most reliable source."

The fiddling fingers at her neck grow more agitated. "How are we supposed to get to Xela now?"

"They'll still take us there. It should be on the way. They already think the 'gods of the mountains' are against them; they're not going to risk me cursing them and making it worse."

"You can't do that, though."

"They don't know that." Her head's still turned. I go ahead and change into a dry pair of pants as well. "I figure they'll drop us off along the way."

"You're sure?"

No. How can I be? "We'll be fine, Riveirre. Get some sleep." Tomorrow will be just as grueling as today.

Chapter 19
ASTER

The town hosts a deathly hush. Though sunlight seeps into every crack in the dried dirt road, a darkness hangs in the houses, whispering of some catastrophe. Dust on the windows obscures the contents of the buildings.

A week into Draó, a lonely copse of trees constitutes a forest, and anything with more than one main road is considered a city. Tragedy comes in many forms, though.

As Calista walks down the road, I see doors no one bothered to close swinging with the breeze and wildlife bones no one's moved resting in the shade of houses.

No sounds of chatter drift down the street; no peals of laughter ring from the houses. The only noise is horse hooves thumping against the dirt.

The town is abandoned. It looks like it has been for a while. The whole place echoes with the kind of emptiness only accomplished by the complete lack of people and the silence of animals.

I've heard of towns like this before, where some disaster strikes, and everyone flees. Whether because some warlord takes over or because some famine or drought strikes, broken towns like this lay scattered all throughout the war-ravaged and poorly cared-for land of Draó. Terror or calamity falls upon the people, and they run from what was likely their only home in search of some place a little better.

In the quiet, and knowing some disaster had to have caused this, I feel like it would be irreverent to speed through this shell of civilization. I walk Calista down the road, silently regretting whatever happened to the people here.

If Draó was as organized as some of its lordships claim it is, this wouldn't happen, at least not nearly so much. They would have programs, plans, for when something goes wrong and would be prepared to combat it. The towns that face constant attack from upcoming warlords wouldn't be defenseless and would have soldiers provided for them by their leader.

Instead, they pretend and connive in order to get towns to trust them, just so the warlord can claim taxes and larger borders. They do nothing to help the people.

Before she became my nursemaid, Jeanna lived in a Draón town just outside of Morineaux's border. She used to tell me about the stories people would carry into her town, stories of danger and despair. The peoples' old towns had been taken over by some tyrant, or bandits had ransacked their homes and left nothing but the buildings for the townsfolk. She'd talk about how the warlords wouldn't send help because of their greed or distance from the town it happened in.

Then she'd remind me how, when I grew, it would be my job to help predict, prevent, and resolve the tragedies in Morineaux. She would tell me how Morineaux takes care of her people and how the riches and privilege I am gifted with are only compensation for the hard work I'll be doing—that I shouldn't abuse it.

A sardonic smile lifts my lips. Eating only trail rations and sleeping in ditches, I am fairly certain I'm not abusing my privilege.

I make it out of the town and urge Calista faster. A lone, large tree graces the horizon, breaking up the flatland. I angle the horse toward it. If I'm lucky, I can reach it before nightfall. Then again, I haven't been graced much travel luck so far. Rain that seemed like it would never end and terrain I despaired I'd ever conquer have hindered my progress considerably. Plus, I can only imagine the conditions will worsen as I move further into Draó.

I rub Calista's neck. "We've got a hard ride ahead of us, girl."

Chapter 20
LEAVI

Two months.

Two months marching along narrow passes and treacherous ledges.

Two months of bone-chilling cold and exhaustion.

Two months among foreigners.

Two months with a near-silent Sean.

I never knew two months could be an entire lifetime. But, somehow, these have been.

It's as though someone plucked me out of my home and dropped me in another dimension. The language is different, the culture is different, the entire rules of survival are different. There's never enough food to go around, and I spend any meal we eat just praying their appetite never outweighs their superstition. As long as they stay scared of Sean, we'll survive on what scarce rations they parcel out.

I've never gone hungry before. Never even considered it. I've passed beggar upon beggar in the streets of Erreliah, and the thought never struck me, "That could be me. That could be me begging, me sitting on the cold curb in my rags, my skeletal fingers holding a cracked tea cup to passers-by."

But here, I ache for that woman on the curb. I *am* that woman on the curb, reliant on the grudging generosity of strangers looking on me with contempt. Here, my skin is ice, my clothes are grime, and my stomach is insatiable.

Here, endurance is key.

Before, surrounded by scientists, the only thing my strength was useful for was popping the seal on jars of formaldehyde. Instead, in this world of endless marching, my intelligence is what holds all that triviality. The sole thing it's done so far is let me decode a little more of their language.

Other than that, the only learning I accomplish is physical. The cotton-top boy stops showing up, and my hands learn to tie the tent knots. Rations decrease to one meager noonday meal, and my stomach learns to appreciate whatever it gets. Marches lengthen, and my feet learn to walk no matter how much they ache. My nerves learn to ignore the blisters.

We'll be in Xela soon, I tell myself. *Just a little longer, and this will all be over.*

At least the traveling has gotten easier as we've gone on. The Traders led us down into a valley. Its flat land stretches so far I can't even see the mountains that must be waiting for us beyond the horizon. It's warmer here, more autumn than winter weather. Drizzling rain replaces biting snow. It's not as pretty, but it's easier to cope with. There's no more narrow paths or steep drops to navigate, just even terrain.

All of it's a needed relief, and I don't question it. Just like they have been, my feet keep moving, relishing the small respite. Just like it has been, when my head hits my blankets, I fall straight asleep, never stopping to consider anything. And just like they have been, my thoughts stay mechanical, fixed on moving one foot in front of the other.

Which is why it takes me two days to realize—

The flat land we're in? It's not a valley. How in the world could we be in a valley if there are *no mountains* around?

This thought blasts into my head as I'm drifting off to sleep, and my eyes snap open. "Leavi, you idiot!" Fire sparking in my veins, I throw off my blankets and shove to my feet.

Sean calls out behind me. "Riveirre, where are you going?"

But I'm already storming across camp, eyes locked on only one thing: the massive tent in camp's center. When I get there, that savage is going to spend the rest of his life regretting the day he ever dared to cross Eleaviara Rivei-

A hand grabs my wrist, and I spin around swinging.

Sean ducks my punch. "What the blazes?" He straightens, startled eyes looking me over. "What's gotten into you, Riveirre?"

I try to pull my wrist loose, but Sean's grip stays tight. For a second, anger poisons my mouth, numbing my tongue. My head shakes, short, sharp motions, and the anger spews out. "They *lied* to us, Sean. They betrayed us. They-"

"Hey, hey, calm down there. What are you talking about?"

I try to still myself and look him straight in the eye, but outrage quivers through my body. Deliberately, I repeat, "They *lied* to us, Sean."

He just stares at me, gaze even.

"They told us they'd take us to Xela, right?" He pauses, then gives a single curt nod, and I continue. "This," I gesture wildly with my other arm at the vast nothingness of land, "is not Xela. I don't even think it's the High Valleys, Sean." A heavy, expanding dread climbs its way from my stomach to my throat, and my voice tightens, furious and despairing. "Look at it! There are no mountains. When in your life have you not been able to see mountains?" I break off, shaking my head in those quick, violent bobs again. "They've taken us from our home, Sean. They've taken us from our home, and we have *no* way to get back." My hand slices diagonally through the air, emphasizing my point.

My breathing's escalated, soaring to dizzying heights. I gulp in a breath, striving to compose myself. The anger plays anesthetic to my lips, and I try to talk around it. "Who-" My tongue trips, but I continue. "Who the *blazes* do they think they are? What makes them think they have the, th-" I pull ragged air through my lungs. "The *right* to drag us out to this wretched, backwards, empty place of-" My hand spikes up toward my face, looking for the right word. "Nothing!" I spit out. My gaze swings back to Sean's, daring him to defend them.

He pauses, a long one, two, three full seconds, blinking at me. "You didn't know we weren't in the High Valleys?"

My jaw creeps open, words frozen.

I explode, shoving his shoulder. "You knew?" Shocked, he lets go of my wrist, and I advance, pushing him again. "You *knew*? Why didn't you tell me?"

Fire lights in his eyes akin to the moment when the Ufir first hit him all that time ago, and he bites back, "I didn't realize you were stupid enough to need telling."

I stare at him, stunned and hurt.

"What?" he presses, his single word twisted into a sharp and jagged weapon.

"I-" *I'm broken. I was red-hot glass, ready to burn the world, and you dropped me in a pail of ice-cold water, and I shattered. That, Sean Rahkifellar, is what.*

70

Beneath that, a small voice whispers, *I just want to go home.*

I blink back blurry eyes. My lips numb again, but this time for a different reason. I swallow, then dare to meet his eyes. "Nothing, Sean."

I push around him. The full moon watches me hurry back into the tent. My bare feet are cold and dirty, and I hastily wipe them clean before burying myself in my pallet. Hot tears leak out of my eyes, and I press my face into the blankets to hide them. Sean Rahkifellar will not see me cry.

The tent flap rustles as he enters. He crosses to his side of the structure, sitting to tug his boots off. Soon, a steady rhythm of clacks fills the dead air. The noise simultaneously comforts me and sends a sickening twist through my stomach. My dad had awful handwriting, so he always used a presswrite. It sat on the great bronze desk in his library. When I was a kid, I would sneak in during evenings and curl up in the armchair by the fire. He always saw me come in, but he'd pretend not to. He never asked why I wasn't studying or what I was doing with a silly chapter book. He just kept typing. When the tap of his fingers against the keys eventually lulled me to sleep, he'd slip the novel from my hands and toss a blanket around my shoulders. Then he'd scoop me up, tuck me into bed, and hide the book under my pillow.

I'll probably never sit in that armchair again. I'll never watch the flames crackling in the hearth, never catch his ink and leather scent, never feel his arms wrapped around me. I'll never run my hand along the wood-paneled walls of our hallways, dig my toes into my bedroom carpet, watch the firelight play off the crystal coffee table in our living room. My window seat will stay conspicuously empty, the smudges of my nose against the glass wiped away by the woman who comes to clean once a week. The stuffed animals on my shelf will stare vacant, gathering dust, and the pages of the books I hid from my mother will yellow and crumble.

We're in the Outerlands now, a place that's supposed to be no more real than magic or monsters under the bed. It's a children's story, and any scientist worth their degree knows there's no such thing as truly flat land. The world is mountains, and the mountains don't end. Somehow, though, they did, and somehow, we're outside of them.

I don't know the way back. Even if I somehow found my way to my mountains, I'd still be wandering through the wilderness. I'm hopelessly lost, and my only chance at getting home is sticking with people who look at me more and more suspiciously each day.

"Would you *please* put that thing away?" My voice is thick as I tug my throw closer around my face. "I'm trying to sleep."

The tapping peters off.

The silence I thought would be comforting sounds eerily like death.

A sob wracks my chest, and I try to muffle it. Though I might stop the sound, I can't stop the tears. I cry for my home, my Erreliah, the home that was, that might never be again. The home that could so easily be touched and swallowed by the plague. The home I didn't bother to wait for news of.

The Blistering Death isn't the first plague to creep through the caves of the High Valleys. School children sing chants about the last one, the one that ended less than a hundred years ago. That epidemic began in an average city, just like Karsix, finally infecting what was then the capitol, a full week's journey away from ground zero. Less than five percent of the old capitol's population survived.

What used to be only a cold fact now sends tremors through my body, because I know that my Erreliah has every potential to become that doomed capitol. But rather than stay to learn its fate, rather than try and fail—but at least *try*—to help find a cure, I left. I broke quarantine. I ran.

Just like the coward I am.

I abandoned my family, my colleagues, my friends, and now I cry because I *miss* them. I ran away from Karsix, and now I mourn because I've left my homeland.

I don't deserve these tears.

But I'm in the Outerlands. I've left the realm of reality and entered a lonely world I know nothing about. A world with no mountains. A world with a flat, dead horizon.

I don't deserve these tears. I cry anyway. I'm tired. Aching. Scared. And I miss home.

Chapter 21
ASTER

I draw to a stop beside a low, natural overhang formed by a hill. Though no thunderheads have filled the sky for the last two months, if another extended storm decides to attack, the overhang should provide enough shelter from rain. Swinging off Calista, I ready camp for the night.

The overhang offers welcoming shadows, and I slip into them. Calista lays down, just outside the shallow shelter of the hill. Between us, I light a fire. The hill and the horse should block most of the light from passers-by, and it's likely too dark for anyone to make out the smoke.

This far into Draó, I'm no longer worried about castle soldiers finding me. Instead, I take these precautions against whatever dangerous bandits roam the area. The past few nights, I haven't lit a fire at all, but the further north I go and the more time I somehow manage to lose, the quicker autumn spins itself into winter.

My breath frosts the air, and I rub my hands together close to the flames. They lick at the air as if they've been aching to breathe. They're longing for power, always trying to extend their reach.

"Me too," I mutter.

I pull out a pinch of powder and renew the anti-scrying spell, just as I have every night since leaving. Gratitude rises in me that I was able to bring so much powder. Two full bags hide in the pockets of my cloak, and another half-used bag is tied to my belt loops. It doesn't typically take much arcanum powder to cast, but when I was packing, I had no idea what I might end up facing. Plus, casting at least a spell a day drains resources.

Despite that, the terrain, and the weather delays, I know I'll make it to the academy. No matter what happens, I'll do what I need to. I'll train, I'll learn, and I'll come back to the castle a successful caster. I'll come back someone they can depend on.

I eat yet another meal of jerky and dried fruit, then roll into my blankets.

* * *

A scream tears unbidden from my lips. Firelight stretches out my shadow into a grotesque and cruel figure. I fall to my knees, the stone floor cold beneath my hands.

Sharp pain slices against my back, attempting to pry another screech from me. My jaw is clenched tight, though. I won't yell again, I won't, I won't.

Another lash. My skin is burning, each new stripe searing fire.

'Get up,' someone growls.

Shakily, I crawl to my feet, but make the mistake of not turning around.

Agony grips me yet again, and—

I jerk awake, the ghost of a sensation burning my back. My breaths come ragged. I sit up, and the air bites my skin, returning my back to its usual numb state.

Calista whuffles in her sleep, and my eyes dart to her, my breathing still too fast. She seems calm.

The fire pops, and my gaze wanders to it. In the hours that I slept, it dimmed and died some. The sky is still dark. Resolute to get more sleep tonight, I poke the fire back to life.

"Not giving up on me, are you?" I whisper to it. "I still need you tonight."

It flares up, and I lay down once more. I watch the flames until their hypnotic dance lulls me back to sleep.

Chapter 22

LEAVI

Rain follows us the next day, my mind hanging in its clouds. The numbing repetition of travel continues, and perhaps a little too eagerly, I slip into its haze.

By afternoon, the rain drizzles away, leaving behind a golden streaked sunset. For the first time in two days, I really look at what's laid out in front of me. The sun is so large, so frighteningly big set against an open, even skyline. The High Valleys' mountains always cut the sun to ribbons.

Presented with this new, sweeping view, my dread battles my awe, each pressing for dominance. This sunset is *wrong*, just like every aspect about this place. Everything in the Outerlands is subtly off, real but impossible, similar but skewed. Unsettling. Yet something is entrancing about it, beautiful even though it hurts to see.

A view like this wasn't supposed to exist. But I'm here, this imaginary place is real, and my world is so very, very flat. I feel free to move but like I can never leave, as though the land goes on forever. I'm exposed and yet safe because I can see anything coming for miles. The flatness is inherently wrong, and yet it exists, so in some way, it must not be.

"Amura," I mutter. Experiencing two conflicting emotions at the same time so that the brain registers them as pain rather than deciding which to believe. My mother, the zealous mentaliti professor that she was, lectured me on it more times than I can count. I never thought I'd feel it this way, though, this strongly, in every single, simple sight I take in.

Amura. The first sign of a breaking mind, she said. A mind too weak to reconcile its own perceptions, to process its own stimuli. Instead of work, it cripples itself.

Amura.

A bird dips across the sunset. Brown and golden feathers flash as it lands, talons outstretched to catch the branch of a solitary tree. It's a hawk. Specifically, a Northern-slopes Hawk, according to the coloring. It spends summers in the northern stretches of the High Valleys and migrates south during winters.

I take a step forward, hand shielding my eyes, double-checking. But no, that's definitely it. This is so much farther south than we ever predicted it could fly, though. Farther than we could have even *imagined* it flying. A High Valley bird wintering in the Outerlands. Madness.

I step back, realization clicking in my head. "If it can get back," I mutter, "so can I."

Sean pulls the tent out of the stuff-sack, everyone around also us in the process of setting up camp. "You planning on helping me, or are you just going to keep glaring at the horizon?"

I grab Sean's wrist and drag him away from the group.

"What the blazes, Riveirre?"

When we reach the hawk's tree, out of earshot of the others, I let him go. "You have to talk to the Ufir."

He scowls, straightening his coat sleeve. "Why the blazes would I do that? And about what?"

"He has to take us back to the High Valleys. Now, before we get any farther out."

He laughs, a harsh, mocking noise. "Any farther out, Riveirre? You realize we left the High Valleys about two days ago? You make it sound like we passed up the corner store."

"We didn't 'leave,' Sean. They," I point at the group, "tricked us into coming here. They lied to us. You need to tell them to take us back, get us to Xela, like we agreed on in the first place."

"Simple as that?" His eyebrow creeps up.

"Yes, Sean, simple as that." I cross my arms over myself. Suddenly unable to meet his gaze, I look off at the horizon.

He sighs. "They're not going to do that."

My gaze snaps back. "Well, you're the magic-man, the guy who's going to abracadabra a curse on anyone who doesn't do what you say. Use it."

"Oh, come on, Riveirre. You know that's not how that works."

"And why not?" I demand.

He shakes his head and leans against the tree, hands tucked in his pockets. His gaze is fixed on the Traders as they pitch their tents. Close by, one group of children huddle near a fire, fighting off the damp chill the rain left behind.

"They were brave," he says, "or desperate enough to drag us out here in the first place. They only fear what I might do, but they *knew* what was going to happen if they stayed in those mountains. They're not going back any time soon."

"You told me they'd drop us off at Xela!"

"I thought they would! They were going south. Must have taken a different route, something quicker, so they could get out of the mountains faster."

"Then-" My hopes are crumbling faster than I thought possible. The air in my lungs trembles, and angry at myself, I close my eyes to recollect. "Then they can give us a map."

"They don't do maps, Riveirre!" He pushes off the tree. "Why do you think I didn't ask for one before? And even if they gave us directions, what do you want to do? Die of starvation as we wander through the wilderness with our non-existent rations? It's not like we're just two days from civilization—*that's* over a month away, back through all those valley passes and far up the mountains."

Wind musses my hair, and I rake a hand through the mess, frustrated and desperate. "I just want to go home, Sean!"

"Well, that's nice." He steps forward, lank frame casting me in shadow. My nerves set on edge. "But that's not the reality of the situation. It's time you got your head out of the clouds and realized that. We're here now. We're in the Outerlands. And we're not getting back home." His eyes force me to meet their gaze, holding me in their harsh conviction.

My voice threatens to break. "How are you so ready to give up?"

His gaze softens. "I'm not giving up, Riveirre. I'm analyzing our circumstances as honestly as I can. They're running out of food, and they've yet to run into the 'plentiful game' their Ufir promised them. I don't know if you noticed, but more and more people are acting shifty around us. Uncomfortable. We're a drain on their resources, and they know it. I don't think it's going to be much longer before they say screw the curse and decide to kick us out. Our only chance to make it back to the High Valleys would be sticking out the winter with them, but I sincerely doubt we make it that long. Part of me doubts *they* will make it that long."

The wind blows across the plain, rippling the grass like a clowder of snow cats creeping through the stalks. The air breaks cool against my skin, and I shiver. "Then what can we do?"

Half-turning, he follows my gaze. He's quiet for a long time.

Finally, he answers, "We wait. We see what opportunity allows."

I swallow, a mix of emotions threatening to close my throat. My eyes flick up to Sean's. He still stares at the never-ending stretch of land before us and its foreign horizon.

I wet my lips, preparing to pose my last question. Even though it doesn't matter, even though it can't change anything, something in me still has to know. "Sean?"

He turns back to me. "Yeah?"

I swallow. "Don't you care about getting home?"

He looks away, gaze turning distant. The setting sun outlines his profile, casting half of his sharp face into stark shadow. The contrast darkens his brown hair to midnight, and the wind catches it, teasing ripples out of the short locks like air over water.

He looks back at me, stuffing his hands in his pockets. "I left home a long time ago, Riveirre. You learn to get by." He jerks his head toward the Traders. "Come on. Let's go get our tent set up before dark."

* * *

By lunch the following day, the air is surprisingly muggy. The sun beats down on us as if in revenge for being held prisoner by the rain. Though I'd almost prefer the chill over this sticky humidity, the Traders seem encouraged by it. Their voices raise with their spirits, and the hubbub of conversation rings all around.

Despite being back-stabbing barbarians, Traders tell good stories. I suppose when you spend your life traveling, you acquire a few interesting ones, and in the long hours of boredom, you might as well come up with ways to wildly exaggerate them.

A few feet away, a man is spinning such a tale. I can't understand everything he says, but between the gestures and what words I do know, I'm fairly certain he's talking about killing a ten-foot tall mountain lion with nothing but a fallen tree branch. Or maybe nothing but a river fish. I'm not listening closely enough to be quite sure.

He's on his feet, arms out wide in sweeping gestures. His companions are rowdy, hollering as if right there in the story with him, urging him on. Five feet outside their group, I look away, jaw clenched. It irks me that they're so at ease.

I bite my tongue, reminding myself not to do something stupid, and return to my food. Beside me, Sean's finishing his rations, oblivious to it all.

I try to find something else to focus on. Today, we've finally stopped at the edge of a red and yellow forest, breaking up the endless skyline. The sea of grass laps at the edge of the trees, calming some of my unease.

A chance hush reigns, the laughter and cheers dying down for a moment. In the relative quiet sounds a gentle and hauntingly familiar *ta-twill, ta-twill, ta-twill.*

No. Surely not.

Grabbing my bag, I stand, listening for it. The cry rings out again. Its simple notes stir some chord deep inside me, and I can't help but take a step forward. In this alien world, those high, free notes sound like the one thing Sean says I'll never get a taste of again—home.

More certain of the direction now, I stride toward the forest, following the chirps. When I've all but reached the trees, Sean catches up with me, belongings in hand. "What are you doing?"

Not slowing and hardly paying attention, I answer, "Looking for a bird."

His footsteps pause. "A bird."

I cast him a distracted glance. "Yes. If it's-" *Ta-twill.* I hold up my hand.

"I wasn't talking," he protests.

"Shhh!"

The bird repeats its cry, and I shift direction.

After a moment, I continue. "If it's the bird I think it is, I need to see it."

"And why's that?" he asks, somehow sarcastic and disinterested at the same time.

I flash him a glare. I can't tell him why I'm really chasing after it, though. If he's right and we never make it back home, this bird will be the last thing from the High Valley's I'll probably ever see, the closest to home I'll ever be again. He wouldn't understand that. So I give him the reason of the scientist, the researcher.

"This particular bird is supposed to be extinct. It's called a snowfire. A lot of-" I listen for it, then pick back up. "A lot of High Valley home remedies claim the red feathers have restorative properties, even though I've never seen any study back that up. Anyway, they disappeared in the High Valleys a few years ago. We thought they'd all been hunt-" The *ta-twills* chime much louder, and I look up.

There he sits, feathers ruffled and wings slightly extended as though he's not yet sure if he wants to take off or settle down. The little bird is mostly white, only a few red feathers gracing his crown. His beak shines black with a red gloss. Bright golden eyes peer down at us curiously. Apparently deciding to get comfortable, he assumes a more restful stance on the branch.

"Oh, aren't you a beauty," I murmur, pulling out my journal to sketch him.

The book's binding crinkles as I open it, and the bird cocks his head. I freeze.

He tears off the branch.

"No, no, no!" I shove the journal into my satchel and take off.

"Riveirre-" Cutting himself off, Sean growls and chases after me.

The snowfire darts through the treetops. Within seconds, the thick vegetation renders him invisible. I crash through the undergrowth, following his shrill warning cries. He whizzes back into view, then out again, cutting left and right, a flash of white, a flit of red, here, gone.

I follow him, pausing only when I have to listen. I run hard and fast, run until my legs are wobbly rubber, and then keep running, spurred on by the bird's calls.

My tired foot trips over a root. I fly forward, chin slamming against the soil. My head rings as I catch my breath. The bird's cries drop off.

I lost him.

Regret sweeps through me, simultaneously hollow and filling. My cheek leans against the dirt, and my mother's voice scolds me. *Pathetic, Eleaviara. It's just an animal. Get up. You're making a fool of yourself.*

"You plan on lying there all day, Riveirre?"

I glance to see Sean jog up, panting as he joins me. I'm about to bite off some retort when I notice something more important in the branches above him.

Thirty feet up, the snowfire rests in a nest, small, bobbing head pruning his feathers. Gently, I push up, sneaking beneath its tree and sliding my journal out again. I take care opening it this time.

Sean must recognize my intent expression because he keeps quiet rather than popping off another snarky comment. I sketch the snowfire's picture, taking in every line, every feather, every color. Then I write down every note I can think of, from the surrounding vegetation to his nest materials to his preening behavior. I want to keep this moment.

Finally finished, I close my book. Almost as though the bird realizes his job is done, he calls out and flits way. I smile after him, bittersweetness tainting the curve of my lips.

Then again, perhaps not so bitter. After all, this little bird was forced out of its home as well, but it's survived. Even made a new one, it seems. Maybe, somehow, I will too.

Still smiling, I slip my book into my bag. From canopy to ground, the world lingers in blissful silence. It suddenly occurs to me the deep booming laughter of the Traders is absent. We must have gone farther out than I thought.

I rise, turning to face Sean. "Which way's back?"

In return, he delivers a pained but irritated glare. Finally, he draws out, "I thought you were paying attention to that."

My eyes widen. "I was looking for the bird!" I defend. "What were *you* doing?"

Exasperated, he throws his hands up. "Well, I suppose just making sure you weren't lost *and* alone."

My heart plunges. Looking back, I can barely even tell where I fell; beyond that, everything looks the same.

We're lost.

In the Outerlands.

I turn my face up, taking in the canopy of red leaves spread above us. A soft murmur escapes my lips. "What do we do now?"

Chapter 23

SEAN

We've been walking in this stupid forest so long, my legs feel numb.

My stomach growls. I hadn't finished eating yet when crazy-bird-girl dragged me away from what few resources we had and the only people that gave us any chance of making it back home. Thanks for that, Riveirre.

Now we're wandering through foreign land, with no knowledge of what's out here and absolutely no safety net if we fail. Nothing to save us from dying except whatever meager survival skills we have.

So we're walking. Maybe we'll find some sort of resource, some shelter. Maybe we're destined to walk until we can't anymore, until we're skeletons sitting against a tree, just waiting for some other poor soul to wander upon us centuries from now.

One hour passes.

Two.

Four hours.

Seven.

The light of the dying sun turns murky, dripping through fall leaves and barren branches. The air is hazing into liquid amber, like we're specimens in some vitalitist's jar of formaldehyde. In the silence, the dry crack of our footsteps against deadwood makes an eerie echo.

The wind creaks against the trees, cutting colder with each minute. Riveirre shivers, hugging her arms closer to her chest.

I glance away. "It was colder in the Valleys."

She glares. As though trying to cover her reaction, she looks away, dropping her arms. "I know."

"Skies, Riveirre, I wasn't making fun of you." I shove my hands into my pockets. "I was just saying that we shouldn't freeze to death."

She's uncharacteristically quiet, the steadily rising wind speaking for her instead. "Shouldn't," she finally says, "is a lot different than won't."

Her level, weighted words give me pause. I stop walking. "What are you saying?"

She keeps moving. "Standing there isn't going to find us shelter."

"Hey." I catch her arm. "What are you talking about?"

She turns to me, her serious brown eyes staring into mine. "A storm's coming, Sean. So I'd suggest you let go and help me find somewhere safe."

Her arm drops from my grip, and she keeps walking. In spite of her collected tone, the tension in her shoulders betrays her apprehension. She glances left and right, searching but not seeing.

I can't even see the sky through this canopy, much less make out a storm cloud. "And how do you know?"

Now she pauses, facing me again. The air whips her hair in swirling rings around her head, and the evening shadows shroud her gaze. "There are no birds in the trees, Sean."

A dark colored blur flies between us, and I start. The darting bird buries itself beneath a bush.

"They've been doing that for a while now. Have you not noticed?" she asks.

Night finally falls as I try to reinstitute a regular rhythm to my breathing. "So what? Dive-bombing birds equal our impending doom?"

I pull my lantern out just in time to see her eyes spark. "You know, Sean, sometimes animals are smarter than humans. Especially certain ones." She stares at me pointedly. "Birds hide before a storm. If we had half the sense they do, we would too."

"Well I'm not the one who dragged us away from our guides and tent!"

"You followed me! Don't blame me for your decisi-" Lightning flashes above us as thunder cracks in the sky. Our gazes slowly lower as the thunder rumbles away.

She rubs the charm of her necklace. "That wasn't far."

A dark form slinks at the edge of my peripheral vision. I freeze. "Hey, Riveirre? You think there's any big predators in these woods?"

Something in my forced calm tone seems to set her on edge. Her eyes sweep the area. "Probably bears. Some wolves, maybe lynxes. Why? What did you see?"

The undergrowth rustles, and I swing my lantern around. A pair of glowing yellow eyes track us low in the bushes. My fingers fumble for my pocket knife, and I flip it open. Riveirre edges closer to me. The leaves shake again, moving around the creature as it steps into the open.

Riveirre laughs. "A cat, Sean? You were scared of a cat?"

"What, and you weren't? Besides, it could still have rabies or whatever, couldn't it?"

The fat white fuzzball regards us, then plops down and rolls onto its back, as though wanting to be petted.

Thunder cracks the sky again. Riveirre flinches, but the cat only gives a mild meow, like the thunderstorm is an irritating neighbor ruining its plans for the night. When we don't oblige it, it wriggles back onto its feet and starts moving the way it came.

A few steps away, it stops and turns, head cocked, sulfur eyes staring at us in a weirdly dead manner. I shake my head. "Come on, Riveirre. We've wasted enough time here."

"Wait! Aren't we going to follow it?"

I look over my shoulder and raise an eyebrow. "You want us to follow the cat?"

The first drops of rain ping against my head, cold and sharp.

"I don't know if you noticed, but it seems rather… well-fed to say the least."

"So?"

"So someone must be taking care of it, Sean!"

The wind drives the rain across my cheek, drops coming thicker and faster. We need to find shelter, soon, and Riveirre wants to go on a wild goose chase. "There's no people in the Outerlands."

"A month ago, I would have told you there was no Outerlands! We don't know anything about this place."

Hardly believing my luck getting stuck with an animal-following crazy person, all I can do is repeat, "You want to follow the cat."

Water glistens on her face. "Look, Sean, if you want to stay out here, get drenched, and die of hypothermia, feel free. But I'm getting out of this storm."

The cat meows indignantly at the rain. Its whole body jiggles as it tries to shake away the drops. Realizing that strategy isn't working for it, it meows again and starts plodding away.

Riveirre spreads her hands. "I'm leaving, Sean. Come if you want." She tucks her arms to her chest, ducks her head against the rain, and hurries after the cat.

"You don't have any light!" I protest.

"Then come with me!"

"Riveirre..." I growl and hurry after her for the second time today.

Rain punches through the air in sheets, falling thicker every minute. Shadows twist around us, half-formed shapes that rise in the swinging lantern light and disappear behind the deluge. The cat weaves through the forest, dipping left and right surprisingly quickly for its size. Booming thunder rolls through the sky, chasing us as we stumble to keep up with our guide. Water soaks my clothes and streams down my skin, freezing my bones. The air seems more liquid than gas, like we're swimming in an ice river rather than running.

We burst into a clearing.

Ivy crawls up a pink-paneled house with chipped paint, candles flickering in the windows. A faded, golden-lettered sign informs us that we've arrived at the "Kuddly Kitten." Through the murk and water, an amateur cat caricature scowls from the sign. The real cat struggles up the steps and bumps its head repeatedly into the powder blue door. Riveirre and I hurry under the porch awning, exchanging looks of disbelief.

In a strange brogue—but definitely my language—a voice calls from inside, "Hold on, my precious!" A few seconds later, a middle-aged, round-faced woman opens the door. Atop her head, a failure of a bun frizzes out around her face.

The woman picks up the cat, returning to a living room inside, and places the spoiled feline in her lap. She coos at it in a voice people usually reserve for infants. "Oh, my precious little baby! You're all wet! Where have you been, you sweet little thing? Why, you've been out wandering the forests again, haven't you?" She grabs a throw blanket from her couch, wrapping it around the cat. "Haven't you? And you brought me new people."

Here she flicks her eyes up at us, smiling, and I decide that's enough invitation to get out of the weather. Stripping my shoes and soaked jacket, I stride inside. Riveirre's eyes are wide as she peers into the building. I look back and forth between her and the room, trying to hurry her in.

She takes the hint, hurriedly wringing out her hair on the deck before following. The door shuts, muting some of the storm's noise. Inside, the air is warm, but my chilled limbs still shake.

The woman must not have gotten enough time with her 'precious baby,' though, because she ignores us and returns her attention to it. "Why, you must be tired! Going all that way out there in the rain! Here, baby, you need a treat."

She fishes three blocks of cheese out of an apron pocket. The cat lazily laps them out of her hand. "Can't have my little baby getting all exhausted, can I?" That taken care of, she finally finds her way to the land of adults. "What can I do for you two?" she beams.

82

My eyes rove the room, taking in the soft sofas and warm fireplace. "This is an inn," I realize dully. That's what the sign was about. An inn in the Outerlands. The enormity of everything I don't know about this place settles hard in my chest.

The woman takes my quiet statement as a question. "Why, yes it is! Are you looking for rooms?" Without waiting for an answer, she calls to another part of the house, "Bukki, we have people looking for rooms!"

"What, dear?" a man's voice calls out.

"We have-" she starts to yell, then shakes her head. "Oh, never mind."

"What, dear?" he repeats.

"Never mind!"

"You know, how about I just come in there?" On 'there,' a stick of a man wanders around the corner, still yelling. "Oh. Sorry," he says, lowering his voice. A pair of outdated spectacles perch low on his prominent nose. He brushes his unkempt hair out of his eyes. "Dear, why didn't you tell me we had visitors?"

I look at my fellow cat-chaser and raise my eyebrows. Beside me, she mouths in Errelian, *Crazy?* A questioning look fills her eyes, mixing with the doubt and fear already there.

"Yeah, I'm out of here," I reply quietly, beginning to turn back the way we came.

She grabs my wrist. "Where else are we going to go?"

"I don't know, Riveirre!" I hiss. "But I'd rather not be stuck with two nutjobs and their cat in the middle of nowhere."

"You don't have another choice!" she whispers.

"What are you saying, dears?" the woman inquires innocently, having finished straightening everything out with her husband.

My eyes slide to her, misgiving still heavy in my mind. "I was going to say goodbye." I turn again.

"Oh, no!" She sounds honestly dismayed. "Where are you going to go? It's pouring! Look, if money's an issue, that's perfectly alright."

"Money's not the problem," I interrupt. Your questionable sanity is.

"Splendid. How's a copper a night sound?"

My brow furrows. "What do you mean 'a copper'?" A blank look is all I receive in return.

Riveirre pulls out her bag of stone-marks and presses a few into the woman's hand. "Here."

The woman inspects them, a puzzled frown creasing her lips. "Why, these are just rocks with some sort of weird design on them. They're not copper at all." She passes the marks back to Riveirre. "I'm not sure which strange lordship uses these, but they won't pass in this area. You two are welcome to stay, though, as long as you need. Just… reimburse me whenever you can afford it. How's that sound? Plus, there's dinner. Well, and breakfast and lunch. But right now, dinner." The brightness of her smile could give the sun some serious competition.

As if on cue, my stomach growls.

"Oh, see, we can't have that. Come on. I've got everything in the oven." She rises, laying the cat on the coffee table.

I grimace at the furry blob settled next to a bowl of mints.

"Bukki, go get them some dry clothes. Jacin should have some that'll fit Mr…" She glances at me. "What did you say your name was, dear?"

These people aren't even supposed to be out here, and she wants something as trivial as my name? She acts as if this is all normal, understandable, rather than a crazy, impossible, confusing mess.

We're not getting back to the Valleys. Any tiny hope of that is as washed away as the path back to the Traders. And this lady thinks us being here is *normal*.

"Rahkifellar. Sean Rahkifellar."

"Mr. Rahkifellar," she finishes, "and the girl will just have to do with something of mine." She returns her attention to us, smiling. "Well, what are you doing just standing there? Go dry off by the fire."

With that, she flits off to another room, not a care in the world.

Chapter 24
LEAVI

I've forgotten what it's like to be in a house—the cozy heat of a fireplace, the sensation of bare feet against wooden floors, a towel to dry off with, clean clothes against my skin. Though the living room fire is small, the floor snags, the towel is rough, and the clothes drape on me like I'm a little girl who's stolen her father's nightshirt, at least we're in a house. We're safe inside a solid building that doesn't rock with the wind. Tomorrow, we won't break it down and pack it up. It will stay here, whether or not we do. That knowledge anchors my thoughts, grounding me in reality. It's refreshingly normal, refreshingly human.

People are not meant to be herded like animals.

A quilt wraps around my shoulders as I sit in the floor before the fire, reviving heat dispelling the chill of my wet hair. Sean sits beside me, brooding eyes focused on the flames. I scoot closer to him, voice low. "Who are these people?"

He glances over at me, then slides his gaze back to the fire. "How am I supposed to know?"

"But where could they have come from? Are there more of them? And why-"

"Riveirre!"

I start.

He looks me dead in the eye. "I. Don't. Know. Okay?"

I press my lips together, angry and embarrassed, but nod, sliding back to where I sat before.

The fire crackles in the silence.

A few minutes later, our hostess returns. "Are you two dry now?" The woman's accent is thick, making her Common harder for me to understand. However, at least my months with the Traders produced some fruit since I can, in fact, understand her. At least I won't be completely lost, like I was at the beginning of this journey.

"Yes. Thanks," Sean answers.

"Of course! Couldn't leave you out there in the rain, could I?" She smiles. "Come along." She ushers us into the dining room, where a pot of soup waits on the table. As soon as its savory scent hits my nose, my mouth starts watering. It looks like simple fare, but I've never wanted to try a food so badly.

Picking up a silver bell from the table, she raises it above her head, ringing it repeatedly. The jangling tones stab my ear, and I wince.

"Dinner!" she calls.

I hope she's calling other inhabitants of the house and not her somewhat deaf husband standing right behind her.

Apparently, he has the same fear. "I'm right here, dear," he informs her at a decibel just above a comfortable level. "No need to raise your voice."

She gently swats him. "I wasn't calling for you, silly." Ringing the bell as though daring it to break, she shouts again, "Dinner!"

I have the sudden thought that maybe she's the reason her husband lost his hearing.

Little feet pad excitedly down the hallway, and a seven-year-old bursts into the room, grinning. Behind her, a deep voice calls, "No running inside, Zena." He enters as she clambers into her seat. He's stocky and I'd guess in his mid-twenties, about a decade older than me.

Zena pushes to her knees in her chair, hands braced against the table. Her ash-blonde hair falls into her face, and she blows it out of the way, annoyed. "Who are you two?"

Ignoring her, Sean offers his hand to the man. "Sean Rahkifellar."

The man gives Sean one strong shake. "Markus Delroy." He turns to me. "And you are?"

Embarrassment washes over me. My brain scrambles to offer a proper introduction, settling on an awkward, "Ah... Leavi." Understanding much more of the Trader's language than I can speak, I've spent the last three months avoiding dialogue. I suppose I'm paying for that now.

Markus' hand hovers in the air, waiting for me to shake, and I hurry to accept it. He takes his seat next to Zena, and I tuck a piece of hair behind my ear, suddenly self-conscious.

Behind me, the door pushes open, and I turn to see a boy maybe a few years older than me saunter in. "Marcí, that smells exquisite!" A simple copper chain peeks from beneath the neck of his white tunic. His sleeves are rolled up to his elbows. Roguish, inky hair wisps above lightning-blue eyes. They light on me.

"Hello." He greets me as though we're old friends, his tone easy and smile bright. "Mrs. Marcí," he scolds playfully, calling around me. "Why didn't you tell me we'd gotten such a beautiful new guest?" Turning back, he clasps my hand in both of his. "Jacin."

"Leavi," I answer, more confident this time.

His grin stretches wider. "It's very nice to meet you." Releasing my hand, he pulls out a chair and gestures at me. "After you, miss."

I blush, sitting, and he takes the spot beside me. Marcí settles on my other side, her husband next to her, leaving Sean at the far end of the table. While Marcí passes out plates, she quickly reintroduces everyone. "This is Markus," she starts. "Me and him are cousins. And this is his darling little daughter, Zena."

She pushes up on the table again. "I'm not little!"

Markus shushes her, gently pushing her back into her chair.

"Of course you're not, dear." Marcí winks at us conspiratorially. "Anyway, that's Jacin Jazere. He just started boarding with us, oh, what was it? Three months ago?"

Jacin sips from the wooden water cup. "I think that's about right."

Marcí says something else, but I miss it, beginning to get lost in the rush of conversation. She speaks as though she's afraid her words are going to run away from her if she doesn't use them quickly enough.

My confusion must be obvious because Jacin passes me a sympathetic glance. His gaze darts to Marcí, whose back is turned as she volleys a new barrage of words at Sean. Affecting overly wide eyes and an over-the-top smile, he mouths along to her bubbly monologue. I stifle a laugh with my hand, and he drops the act, giving me a genuine grin.

He leans over to whisper in my ear. "You'll get used to her eventually."

My attention snaps back to the conversation as Sean says, "That'd be appreciated."

"Oh, good!" Marcí exclaims. "And what about you, Leavi?"

"Ah..." Marcí stares at me, wide-eyed and expecting. *Please stop looking at me and ramble about something else instead.* But her eyes stay fixed. "I, uh... I sorry? No... hear?" *Terrific, Leavi. Way to sound like an idiot.*

Marcí's friendly face suddenly adopts a pitying look. "Oh, dear," she says to Sean regretfully. "Is she not very..." She taps her temple, unwilling to say it.

My jaw drops. Sean smirks, not bothering to correct her.

Jacin is the one who comes to my rescue. "No, no, Marcí. She's just not from around here. They've both got an accent, hear?"

"Oh." She smiles, patting my hand. "Well, then, I know the perfect job for you. They were looking for a girl who wouldn't talk too much anyhow."

"Excuse me?" I manage, indignant but still stumbling over the words.

"Oh. Right." Opening her mouth wide and projecting her voice, she says slowly, "A jo-ob. Wo-ork. You. Need. Yes?"

I actually have a harder time understanding her like that. I fist the over-large fabric of my skirt. *She means well,* I try to convince myself. *I sound like a foreigner to her. A dumb foreigner. She means well.*

In Errelian, Sean prompts, "And now you say yes to the generous ditz, Riveirre."

My jaw tightens.

Marcí blinks at him. "What, dear?"

Switching back to their language, Sean says, "I'm just translating for her." He meets my eyes, smug smile glued in place.

"Oh, good! So she'll take the job?"

He waves at me with his fork. "I'm sure she can answer for herself." He leans forward, one elbow on the table, waiting for my response.

Marcí's attentive eyes focus back on me.

I swallow. "Yes. Thank you."

"Great! I. Can. Get. For. You." She beams and returns to her food.

Jacin's eyes offer a subtle apology, but Sean looks like he's trying to keep from snickering. My look turns black, and his smile creeps wider, the gloat of a self-satisfied fox. I look away.

Marcí keeps up cheerful chatter all through dinner. Despite my efforts, though, my tired mind refuses to keep up. The thrumming rain plays on the roof like music, its simplicity distractingly enticing. The drops are drums, the wind a pipe, the thunder crashing cymbals. No words, no expectations. The noise is hypnotic.

Eventually Marcí claps her hands together, and I start back to reality.

"Oh, dear me!" She places a hand on my shoulder. "Is she normally this skittish, Mr. Rahkifellar?"

I lean forward on the table, upsetting Marcí's hand, and hiss in my language, "Sean if you tell her yes, I swear I will-"

"Oh, we've got her all worked up." Turning me toward her, she leans in close enough our noses almost touch. Over-enunciating, her lips contort as she purses each word in slow motion. "It is okay. I did not mean to frighten you."

Anger swells within me, sick of being underestimated, by her, by the Traders, by Sean. Too tired to bother tempering my actions, I shoot to my feet, causing Marcí to jerk back. "I am not *'frightened.'*"

A shocked silence stretches through the room. I stand there, quivering from frustration and fatigue. The stress of the last two months is slowly crashing in on me, making my head simultaneously fuzzy and strangely electric. "Just exhausted," I whisper in Errelian.

Sean makes the switch with me. "Riveirre, you're overreacting. Calm down before the crazy landlady decides she doesn't want to host us after all."

My eyes flash to his. Angry tears well in my eyes against my will, and his gaze softens. "We're here now, Riveirre. No more wandering. Even if she is crazy, even if this is improbable, at least we're *somewhere* now."

I turn my head.

"I think it's been a long day," Jacin interrupts. "Especially for those of us who had to travel to get here." I can feel him staring at me, but I resolutely keep my eyes on the wall above Markus's head. "Perhaps it's time we retire."

Marcí mutters, "Well, if they're going to be rude, I'm not sure I-"

"Marcí." Bukki sets a hand over his wife's. "Jacin's right. The girl's just tired. Why don't you show them their rooms?"

His kind eyes hold hers until she relaxes, nodding. "Alright. Come along." She stands and strides from the room. Sean grabs his bag from beside his chair and follows her. I hesitate, but the promise of a bed tugs at me, and I come. She takes us up a flight of stairs and opens the doors to two opposing rooms, gesturing for me to enter the one on the right.

A candle in a tin holder dimly illuminates the space. Gaudy flower prints cover everything: the comforter, the rug, the runner over the bedside table. They're even painted on the walls and carved into the foot chest and headboard. Lacy curtains line the two windows on either side of the bed and ridiculous frilly pillows dominate it.

Nothing's ever seemed more inviting.

"Let me know if you need anything, dear. Oh, and here's the key."

She presses it into my hand.

I stare at her, knowing how generous this all is. I could be in the rain right now, wandering in search of shelter, but instead, I'm here, warm and safe. Though we have nothing to offer her, though I've been less than polite to her, she's helping us.

"Thank you," I say warmly.

My accent apparently reminds her that she has to talk to me like I'm three. Too loudly, she answers, "You. Are. Welcome!" She smiles at me, then leaves, closing the door behind her.

I drop my bag and collapse onto the bed, sinking into the luxury of a mattress. It cradles my body, much more forgiving than the hard ground. I slip underneath the heavy comforter, nestling into the mountain of pillows.

When I close my eyes, I can almost pretend I'm home.

A silent sob pulses through my body at the thought, and I pull the blanket closer. My heart is so heavy, so full, it seems like it should rupture. Instead, tears leak from my eyes, and I cry myself into sleep for the second time since leaving Karsix.

Chapter 25

SEAN

I'm tired, and the clothes I've borrowed shift awkwardly as I walk up the stairs. I'm out of my element, reduced to using my intelligence for little more than snappy comebacks.

Nearly useless.

But I also have a stable roof over my head. A bed. A weird but generous landlady. A full stomach.

Things I haven't had in over two months.

And even though I know that I'm not getting back to the Valleys, back to 'normal,' I think that I can survive here.

They said that guy our age just showed up a few months ago, which means he must have come from somewhere. Besides, this is an inn—who has an inn in the middle of nowhere? No one, so there's definitely more to this strange place than a crazy couple and their cat.

I'm not going to let it beat me down. I've made it past everything that's been thrown at me—risen above and thrived. I won't let this trip be the thing to destroy me.

Sean Rahkifellar will not go down that easily.

Finding courage in my resolve, I examine my new room. Everything's a glaring orange.

Four marigold curtains on one carrot-framed window. Two dreamsicle-and-cream rugs. One cantaloupe bedspread. Nine tangerine throw pillows. I move one pillow to the floor, behind the bed and out of sight. Make that eight tangerine throw pillows.

This room looks like an orange alkemitic mixture exploded all over it.

I drop my bag on the bed and pull out my presswrite. Climbing onto the mattress, I slide beneath the plushy blankets. They're soft, but not smooth and crisp like the ones back home.

"Home," I scoff. "And where exactly is that?"

I left Xela too long ago for it to still truly be home. Besides, there's nothing left there for me.

I was too distant, too purposely detached in the underground city that I obtained my doktorate in to call it home.

I didn't go to Karsix of my own will in the first place, and I stayed there for much too short a time for that to be it.

So I'll put it all behind me. Remember the lessons and forget anything that'll get in the way of forging my new path in the world.

The sound of glass breaking shattered the air. I scrambled beneath my bed. There was nothing I could do, nothing I could do—

The sound of yelling spilled into the air. I shoved my hands against my ears. I didn't want to know what he was mad about this time, didn't want to k—

The sound of a strike rang through the air. I flipped open a textbook. Life will fade in the face of facts, fade in the facts...

Put it all behind me.

Chapter 26

ASTER

I'm drained. The rigorous nature of my travel through war-torn Draó has left me in less than prime condition—dirty, lacking rest, and ready to do something more than sit in the saddle all day. I practice what spells I can as I ride or break for meals, but that's not the most productive way to hone my ability.

My excursions with Agraund never lasted this long, and they were never through territory this bad. The stony, overgrown paths that count as roads in Draó would be considered little more than wilderness in Morineaux. It's taken me much too long to reach my destination, not accounting for the time I'll spend at the academy or on the journey back.

My mind flicks once more to the consequences awaiting me in N'veauvia.

I urge Calista faster. No use worrying about it right now. I'll train dedicatedly, and I *will* improve. Nothing else is acceptable. Nothing else matters.

In front of me, blocky silhouettes of houses stand, somber sentinels in the dark. Something about the tiny village raises the hair on my neck, even though the invitation told me I was coming here. Still, some misgiving lingers in my mind, and I pull the letter out of my pocket to reference. The night presses around me, attempting to smother my vision, but the full, silver disk suspended in the sky pushes back against it, lending me just enough light to read by.

Prince Aster Jacques S'Pierre S'Diane,

Second Son of Morineaux

You have been cordially invited to attend a private casting academy in northern Draó. We, the faculty and administration of the Arcanum Academy, would be honored to have a hand in your instruction and development as a high-class magician. If you feel you do not need our assistance, we request that you come to impart some of your vast knowledge upon our students and staff. For you, my lord, attendance would be perfectly free, as your presence would be such a privilege.

Thank you for your time,
Arcanum Academy

Post Script: If you choose to come, travel first to the large town of Dellaby, near the center of Draó. Follow the north-eastern road to Crystys. Then travel due north until you reach the hamlet of Niv. There will be a northern trail that will lead you to our establishment. If you have any problem along the way, most citizens know of these landmarks and will likely be willing to help. Vini veagiann!

Why the Academy, being in northern Draó and most closely bordering Kadran, ended the letter with 'good travels' in Bedeveirian, the language of the country farthest from it, I am not sure. Then again, considering the mongrel nature of Draó, perhaps it's not too surprising.

I skirt the town in hopes of not attracting too much attention from the likely completely innocent townsfolk. Then, finding the dark trail from the note, I move into the woods. The bare limbs hang around me, as if reaching to snatch me away.

"Stop it," I hiss at myself. "The dark has made you into a child."

A clearing opens up, and I peer through the silver-edged darkness at what must be the Academy. The ornate architecture and marble arches give it a powerful and official air. It's not as extravagant as the Morineause castle, of course, but compared to the vast swathes of war ravaged land I've traveled though in this country, it's impressive. An iron-bar fence surrounds the land, but the gate is open. Still irrationally disconcerted, I ride up near the door of the building to dismount, tethering my horse under a large tree. Gravel crunches under my feet as I approach the vaulted entrance. I knock.

As if waiting for me, the large stone door swings open. Inside, eerie silence resides in a black that, this time, even the moon can't banish. I lean forward slightly, hoping to catch a glimpse of someone.

There isn't a soul in sight.

Heart in my throat, I take a few steps in and call, "Hello? It's Prince Aster Jacques..." A shiver travels its way up my spine at the whisper of stone against stone—the door falling back into its place. I spin around.

From the corridor behind me, a high voice greets me. "How kind of you to join us."

Chapter 27

LEAVI

When I wake up, I don't open my eyes. Faint light filters through my lids, and I pretend it's the Errelian street lamps reaching full brightness, announcing the new day. The boring beige walls that my mother never let me paint over stare at me, willing me to wake up and go to university. The desk in the corner holds the two textbooks I'll need today—*The Study of Class Aehrixi* and *The Anatomy and Physiology of Wings in Nature*. Any minute now, my mother will yell from downstairs, "Eleaviara Riveirre, if you don't get your butt out this door in the next five minutes, the professor's going to lock you out!"—though I've never been tardy to a class in my life. Then the door will slam as she hurries out, always on the brink of running late herself. Dad will have already left for his lab, slipping out early to avoid my mother. If I'm lucky, though, he might have left me some hotcakes in the oven—

Maroon flower print greets my opening eyes and marks the death of my fantasy. Disappointment and frustration at my overactive imagination mix into anger.

I push up, throwing off the covers and dragging my bag onto the bed. I rifle through it, digging out my brush. "Skies, Leavi." The bristles tug my hair, yanking at the knots. "What, did you think you were going to wish your way back home? Get your head out of the clouds."

The hairbrush battles another knot, and this time, it loses, getting stuck in the tangles. Fed up, I extract the brush and toss it back in the bag. My involuntary soaking yesterday is the closest I've come to a chance to wash in at least a week. Plus, 'wash' might be an exaggeration considering I haven't seen soap since leaving Karsix. I'm disgusting; I feel like my hair and skin are covered with an invisible layer of grime that paltry damp cloths and rain showers can't wash away. I know I can't be that bad since the other boarders didn't screw up their faces and run the other direction yesterday. I know it's probably mostly in my head. All the same, I feel like the bed sheets should be grey where I laid.

I need a wash, a *proper* wash. Steaming shower, real soap, warm towel. I want to scrub the last two months from my skin.

Grabbing my least dirty change of clothes, I head into the hallway. Past mine and Sean's rooms are two more pairs of parallel doors, with one more capping the hall. Guessing the others are more dormitories, I open the door to the last room.

The faint smell of urine mixes with the floral scent of wilted purple primroses drooping in the vase atop a wooden stand. Neatly folded towels nestle in the stand's shelves. Beside it, a half-full basin rests on a narrow plinth, a wet washcloth draped over its side, a mirror hanging above. To the back of the room is an orange, tin bathtub, an alternating ring of cats and flowers crudely painted along its side. A metal bucket with a lid sits in the corner.

That's it. No toilet. No sink. No faucets. It's more like a powder room sporting a confused tub than a bathroom. How in the world do they get water in here?

I start to go to find someone to ask, but my reflection moves in the mirror, catching my attention.

I expect to see normal me. Me with the paper-white skin from a life spent underground. Me with the clean face and clean hands, pristine hair, pressed clothes. Me with the slightly rounded-out cheeks, the arched eyebrows, the clear brown eyes, the smooth, pink lips shining from a touch of gloss.

Instead, I'm greeted by a travel-worn stranger. Her skin's mostly the same tone, but faded streaks spot her once polished complexion. Her cheeks are thinned out, bones sharper. There's something darker in her eyes; a quiet sadness, tiredness maybe. Or perhaps the new angles of her face simply make them seem like that.

My fingers brush the silvered glass, my reflection reaching to match. The image echoes in me, the hollow repetition of a sound, like when bats call to each other in a cave but only the edges of noise are audible. This girl is not Mastera Eleaviara Riveirre. This is a ghost, a simple outline of what once was.

Or maybe the haughty mastera is the empty one, and the girl staring in the mirror is, in fact, more complete.

The image in the mirror stares steadily, daring me to dismiss it. *I am you*, it claims. *And you will become me. Don't you remember your vitaliti lessons, Miss Scientist? All organisms...*

"All organisms are in a constant state of adaptation and change," I mutter. "Any organism not changing is dying." The first rule of vitaliti.

The reflection holds my gaze, driving her point home. *It's time to adapt, Leavi, and to stop holding onto the past. You've got the chance to explore a whole new world. Take it and stop looking back.*

I press my lips together. "You're rather bossy for a reflection, aren't you?" But even as much as I want to get back to the High Valleys—if that's even possible—I can't deny the tug of intrigue at the mirror's idea. Maybe it's right.

"You okay there?"

I whirl around.

Jacin leans against the doorway, a sideways smile splayed across his face.

An embarrassed half-laugh escapes my lips. "Yes." Just talking to my reflection like some kind of mental. At least he couldn't translate what I was saying. I wonder how long he's been standing there.

"Do you need help with something? You look a little lost."

"Oh." I glance around, trying not to meet his eyes. My gaze lands on the bathtub, reminding me why I came in here in the first place. "Where is the water?"

He tilts his head at me. "You mean the well? Come on. I'll show you." He pushes off the wall, smile encouraging me to follow.

I hesitate, confused why they would keep the water someplace other than the bathroom. It seems counterintuitive, but Jacin's halfway down the hallway. I catch up.

He pads downstairs and moves through the house to go out the backdoor. I follow him into the crisp morning air. The sun hangs low, the dew still wet on the grass as it slides against my bare feet. A mossy stone structure stands alone in the clearing, sides open, roof pointing to the sky like some prehistoric temple. In the middle of the tiny building, a wooden bucket dangles crookedly from a rope.

94

A well. Even the tiny topside town my field-group visited briefly at least had a pump. This thing is something out of a fairytale. Part of me expects some sort of magical creature to spring out and make us solve a riddle before we can drink from it.

But Jacin lowers the rope down and no mystical being challenges him. I rest my arms on the cool lip of the well, watching the bucket descend. *Mother always said reading those novels would do funny things to my head.*

He heaves the bucket back up and dumps the water into a large container at the base of the well. As he lowers it again, I take my time to form my question. Once I'm sure my words are right, I ask carefully, "You have to do this each time you want to wash?"

He glances at me, a teasing smile dimpling his cheek. "What else would you do? Will it to appear?"

"No, I-" Blushing, I turn to stare at the treeline. How am I supposed to answer him? *Well, in a normal society, water is filtered and piped to all the buildings. The only people that use wells are wax figures in history museums.*

"You know, Leavi, if it wasn't for your complexion, I'd think you were one of those snooty Morineause."

Not entirely sure what he said, I can't quite tell if it was an insult or a joke. I turn back and catch his wide grin. Joke, then.

I smile back, and he finishes pulling up and dumping out the bucket. As he resets it, he says, "Did you know Marcí was originally from Morineaux? Not the Draón border that tells itself it's Morineaux either, but actual, proper Morineaux. Or at least that's what she claims. Not sure why they'd come so far up north if that's the case, but it makes a lot of sense at least."

I don't know what these places he's mentioning are, but considering the way he's talking about them, I get the feeling that if I asked, he'd look at me like I was crazy. "Why?" I say instead.

"It'd account for her better-than-thou attitude," he winks.

I have the uncanny sensation that there's a joke there somewhere and I'm missing it. I smile like I know what he's talking about.

"You know, she actually told us once that when she was a kid, water would magically appear in the bathroom and kitchen when you needed it. Wish they'd share that kind of magic with the rest of the world, right?" He laughs. Pouring his latest haul into the receptacle, he wipes his brow and leaves the bucket hanging. "Come on. This should fill the tub about halfway. That'll be enough for you, right?"

I nod but set a hand on his shoulder as he moves to grab the receptacle. He stops.

"You say 'the rest of the world'?" I ask.

Confusion seeps across his face. "Yeah?"

I pull my hand back. I'm still worried he's going to think I'm crazy for asking this, but I have to know. "How—how *many* people are," I look for the right word, ending with an uncertain, "here?"

"In the village?"

"In the world."

He whistles. "I think you'd have to ask one of those Morineause scholars for that. And even then, I doubt they'd actually know."

My mind whirs, translating and trying to sift meaning from his words. "There is... many, then?" *How could a 'mythical' Outerland hold so many people that they can't even be counted?*

"Well, Leavi," he chuckles, "there's five countries. I'm no mathematician, but I'd say that's 'many.'" He smiles.

"Countries?" My tongue tests the Common word, unfamiliar with it.

"A group of lots and lots of villages." His face screws up. "That was a terrible explanation. What language do you speak? Maybe I know enough to translate."

"Errelian?" I offer hopefully.

He shakes his head, and my heart falls. *Of course he doesn't know*, the reasonable part of me reminds. *He's already heard you speak it and never seemed to understand.*

"What part of Draó are you from, exactly, Leavi?"

"What is Draó?"

He laughs. "Surely they haven't renamed it in your language. Avadelian might not be your native tongue, but usually the country names translate."

"This... language. You call it 'Avadelian'?" I pronounce the word carefully.

He nods. "Why? Your Errelian have a different name for it?"

I nod. "Common."

He shrugs. "Suppose that's as good a name as any considering the Morineause are about the only ones who might turn up their nose at learning it. You can get just about anywhere in Draó with a good grasp on Avadelian, and I figure most places in the rest of Avadel too. But I get the feeling you haven't traveled much, have you?"

I shake my head.

"That's alright. I hadn't left my village until a couple of years ago myself. Been traveling ever since. You'll catch on." He winks. "Now, let's get this upstairs for you." He grabs one end of the receptacle, and we carry the container to empty it into the tub. Jacin dries his hands on his pants. "There you go. Now to go fill up another for Marcí's kitchen."

"Oh. I did not mean to... bother-"

He waves it away. "Don't worry about it. Gotta earn my keep somehow, right?" He smiles. "See you around, Leavi." He picks up the container and leaves, closing the door for me.

I drag Marcí's clothes off me, dropping them into a pile on the floor. As I sink into the tub, cold makes my skin prickle, but I refuse to flinch. For the first time in months, I'm in clean, pure water, and I'm going to savor every second if it. I dunk my head below the surface, scrubbing at my hair, running my fingers through the wet tangles. The freezing water is refreshing, and I welcome its bite as it rolls over my skin.

My lungs call for oxygen, and I sit, water streaming from my hair. Using a washcloth, I rub at my skin, washing away the long marches, the trails and the dust, the Traders and every lie that came out of their mouths. Like a butterfly emerging from its chrysalis, I shed the dirt and the dead skin.

I lean back, relaxing. The tips of my hair float around my shoulders while foreign words float around my head.

Morineaux. Draó. Avadel.

And the topside Common. They call it Avadelian.

How could so many people be in the supposedly empty, supposedly *fake* Outerlands?

The Outerlands—or Avadel, as they seem to say—is a world unto itself. A world we never knew existed. Until now.

My mind works to piece it all together. These people don't seem to know anything about the High Valleys, which would make sense considering that we don't know anything about them. We're in a—a country, he said—named Draó. There are five of these countries in Avadel. Morineaux is another, and Jacin seems to think everyone from there is an entitled jerk. I suppose it's the same way the topsiders think of people from Erreliah.

Which means Morineaux is likely Avadel's hub of intellect.

I'm still musing on that as I rise. Water dripping down my skin, I quickly dry off and step out. I reach for my clothes but hesitate. My things rest on the towel shelf, grime encrusted on the fabric. I grimace. There's no way I'm putting those back on.

Snatching them, I drop them into the tub and scrub. After the dirt loosens and comes free, I wring the articles out as much as possible. They'll be damp, but at least it won't feel like I'm wearing caked dirt.

Finally dressed and presentable, I head for the kitchen. The house is quiet, and the sound of Sean's presswrite echoes down the hall. As I turn the corner, I find him at a wooden island, munching on an apple with one hand while typing with the other.

He glances at me, fingers still in motion. "You're wet."

"Really?" I spread my arms out, examining myself. "What an excellent observation, doktor."

Shaking his head, he returns his attention to his work.

A glance over my shoulder reveals the house is quiet and still. I push onto the counter beside Sean's presswrite.

"You're blocking my light," he says, eyes down.

"Does it even matter? Listen-"

"It matters to me."

Something between a growl and a sigh bursts from my lips. "Would you pay attention to me and stop messing with that stupid machine?"

He looks up sharply. "Attempting to further my knowledge is not stupid."

"What knowledge are you furthering?" I exclaim. "What data have you collected to analyze? We're not in your laboratory, Sean, and we have more important things going on here."

"Few things are more important than the advancement of one's self."

"You're impossible."

He smirks.

I snag the paper out of his presswrite, ignoring his protest. "Would you like to find out what I've learned, or do you prefer to bury yourself in nonexistent work?"

He throws his hand up. "You didn't tell me you'd learned anything! All you did was stroll in here and start mocking me."

I roll my eyes. "Because it's my life's goal to degrade you, Sean. Look, I don't know if you've noticed, but unless there's something important to discuss, I don't go out of my way to deal with you. You're hard enough to handle when I actually have something to say."

"And there you go again with the insults." He turns in his seat toward me. "What do you want, Riveirre?"

"I thought I'd provide you with relevant information about, I don't know, this foreign world we've wandered into?" My hand sweeps a gesture at the inn. "But you seem to be busy." I push off the counter.

"I was giving you my attention!" he explodes incredulously. "I don't understand you, Riveirre. You're not happy when I'm not focusing on you, and you're still angry when I am! What do you want from me?"

I want you to act like what I have to say matters. I want you stop staring at that presswrite all the time. I want you to take me seriously.

I turn my gaze to the fall forest outside the kitchen window. A robin swoops onto the sill. It cocks its head at me and then flies off again. *Let it go, Leavi. He's not going to do any of that, so stop expecting it and make do with what you have.*

"Know what?" I retake my seat on the counter, offering him a small, tight smile. "It doesn't matter. So, you want to hear what I've found out?"

He stares at me for a solid five seconds, gaze a mix of frustration and bewilderment. I bite my tongue, trying to keep from saying something I'll regret.

Finally, though, he pushes a slow breath out and says, "Yeah. What've you got?"

"You haven't been talking to the people here, have you?"

"Not unless you count the brief conversation with Marcí about jobs last night. That woman hardly lets you get a word in edgewise."

"Alright. Well, I was talking to Jacin-"

"The creep with the necklace?"

I look at him askew. "He's not a creep. But yeah. Him. Sean, some of the things he said-"

"Just spit it out already."

I glare, but then collect myself. "If what he told me is true, these people here aren't some random group of Outerlands survivors. The Outerlands—this place is a whole society. Its own little world. And we don't know anything about it, and they don't seem to know anything about the High Valleys either."

He nods, seeming strangely unsurprised. "I figured there'd be more people, but its own world?"

"Yes," I affirm earnestly.

"How do they speak Common?"

"I'm not sure. They call it Avadelian though. Maybe-" The memory of the supposedly extinct snowfire hits me, and I clear the counter, pushing Sean's presswrite and a bowl of apples to the side. "What if, a long time ago, humankind started here," I point to the top of the counter, "in the High Valleys. And some disaster happened: a plague, like why we left, or a drought, a flood, a war, something. Something big. So some people migrated, and they came down here," I drag my finger to the middle of the table, "to the Outerlands. What they call Avadel. The rest stayed in the High Valleys. Either it happened so long ago no one remembers, or the disaster was so catastrophic it wiped out any records we might have had."

A thoughtful expression fills his face. Then he tsks and shakes his head. "That doesn't work. Why would they be at a different level of technology than we are?"

I press my lips together, considering. "Different access to materials maybe? And necessity's the mother of invention, right? We live underground; we've had to adapt to and overcome our environment. Maybe they haven't had to do that as much."

He nods, the idea seeming to catch on. "The topside towns aren't that much more advanced than this, either."

"And there's always the chance," I point out, "that we're in a less developed part of the world. Jacin talked about somewhere else called Morineaux. He seemed to think they were more advanced. Well, actually, he thought they had magic, but you know how that is."

Sean considers. "So that's where we'll want to head then."

My chest tightens. I push out a breath, trying to relieve the tension. "So we're giving up on getting home, then?"

He sighs softly. "Riveirre, if you want to leave and try to track down the Traders in the hope that they'll take you back to the Valleys, I'm not going to stop you. But they're half-a-day's march past where we last saw them. They could have gone anywhere. And like I said, I don't think *they're* going to make it through the winter, much less make it back up to the Valleys. But, again—it's your choice."

"And if I did decide to leave?" My heart thrums in my chest.

He pauses, pointers drumming a short beat on the counter, then gently says, "I'm not coming with you, if that's what you're asking."

My heart falls. I know home is long out of reach, and I know Sean's too logical to chase an unpredictable, risky ticket back. But for some reason, I still feel like I've lost something.

"I can't, Riveirre," he continues. "I don't have anything back there. You obviously do, but I've tried to tell you before—sticking with the Traders will be dangerous. The day before yesterday, you asked me what we could do, and I told you we'd have to see what opportunity allowed. Maybe this is our opportunity. Mine, at least." His gaze flits away, suddenly intent on the neglected apple in his hand. He takes a distracted bite.

For some reason, his insistence to stay makes me want to leave even more. "If we don't go after the Traders now, Sean, we'll never get back home."

"I already told you I'm not worried about that."

"Maybe I am." My fingers wander back up to my necklace, feeling lost and angry.

He rubs at a spot on the apple. "Then leave. But odds are, you're going to end up dead before you ever hit the Valleys."

I feel he just socked me in the gut. "Well, then. Thanks for the warm concern."

He looks up. "I'm only being honest, Riveirre."

Marcí bustles into the kitchen, humming.

I shift to face her, arms crossed loosely, my back to Sean.

"Oh, hello, dears!" she says. "Early risers. That's good. I do dislike a layabout." She rifles through cabinets, pulling ingredients out and setting them on the counter. "I'll bake some muffins for breakfast, and then it's off to work for the two of you!" The brilliance of her grin is making my head hurt. I've never seen anyone be this chipper this early in the morning.

"You already have a job lined up for us?" Sean asks.

"Well, I have a letter of reference written up, and that should be just as good. Shouldn't have any trouble. Now, what is that strange contraption and what's it doing on my island?" She points at Sean's presswrite with a mixing spoon. "Off it goes. Otherwise I won't have room to make breakfast." She turns, opening a cabinet door. "Now, where *did* that flour go?"

Sean watches her, faint amusement flickering across his face. He folds his presswrite closed, pulling it off the counter.

After we finish eating, Marcí spouts out directions but speaks so quickly that I only catch every other word. Then she bustles out of the kitchen, no longer concerned with us.

I turn to Sean. "Did you get that?"

"What, you didn't?"

I scowl.

"Yeah, I got it." Out of the corner of my eye, I see him look me up and down. "I guess you're as dry as you're going to get. Come on. Let's go see where the mad woman has sent us." He heads out the door.

Chapter 28

SEAN

Fake. Pretty, but fake.

From far away, it would almost fool me. The smooth granite facing, the glittering gold gates, the shining marble arches.

Then we get closer to our potential new workplace. With a glance, I see that the arch is actually made of mrablin, a cheap, easily deteriorated rock that only looks like marble. And something about the way that the gold gleams strikes me as strange. As we pass one of the gate doors, my hand brushes the metal. Like I expected, a small amount of the color rubs off on my fingers. Flecks of paint.

I shake my head. This was too easy to figure out.

Riveirre gives me a questioning look, glancing between me and the gate. I stuff my hands into my pockets and ignore her.

We walk up to the entrance and knock on the door. It swings open on well-oiled hinges.

A man stands there in a pressed uniform. "Business?" he inquires imperiously.

"Here for a job. Marcí said you had an opening. Sent this." I lift the letter.

"Mrs. Marcí Dae?"

"Are there a lot of Marcí's in your fantastically large hamlet?"

He narrows his eyes and takes the letter. Giving a single glance to the envelope, he hands it back. "I don't deal with personnel. You'll have to find the steward for that."

"Well, where's the steward then?"

Slightly behind, Riveirre prods me in the ribs. "Quit being rude!" she hisses in Errelian.

"What? I'm just asking where the steward is."

The butler clears his throat. "I doubt the likes of you are going to last long here, but it'll be fun to watch you get fired at least. The steward's in the council hall, getting things organized for tomorrow's meeting." He steps back, letting us in. "Through that door, two halls down, third room on the left."

I start off.

Back in Xela, there was a fair every year where a bunch of people dressed up like they were from the town's history. A lot of them dressed as simple folk—pioneers, farmers, blacksmiths—but some dressed like they were the people that were going to oversee the place. Crisp cotton suits, tailed jackets, intricately carved wooden buttons.

This is what I think of when I see the man evidently in charge of whether we get a job. His outfit bares enough likeness, and with his fair hair slicked back and the self-important, smug smile he sports, he's like a carbon copy of those fair-goers. He stands in the center of the large room, directing a flurry of people. "Those chairs need to be in *line*, Emmrick, not zig-zagging back and forth like some drunkard."

He turns, focusing on two men carrying a large potted plant onto a dais that faces the chairs. "What addle-brain told you two to bring that monster in here? With it and the podium, where do you expect the councilmen to stand? Ankle-deep in soil? Get that out of here!"

A servant boy hurries up to him, a folder tucked under his arm. "Sir?"

He spins on him. "What now?"

"Lady Veradeaux says she wants you to handle these reception arrangements."

"Reception? We've never had a reception before. I swear, every year she makes these things more and more over-the-top. We're stretched thin as is." He snatches the folder from the boy's outstretched hand. Pulling out a pen, he flips through the pages, scribbling notes as the work continues around him.

Considering that interrupting him when he's writing is probably better than when he's mid-yell, I stride up to him. "You're the steward, right?"

He glances at me. "Scat."

"I'm going to take that as a yes." I drop the letter onto his stack of papers. "Recommendation from Marcí Dae."

His head turns sharply. "Who exactly do you think you are?"

"Your soon-to-be employee," I smile.

He scowls. "Wipe that smirk off your face and get out, or I'll call the guards."

Smirk? That wasn't a smirk. As I open my mouth to argue, Riveirre steps around me. "Sir?"

An exasperated growl escapes through his teeth. "What?"

She freezes. Great, Riveirre. Way to lose us our chance at this job.

Then she speaks, slow yet purposeful. "You seem busy."

He coughs out a strangled laugh. "That's an understatement."

"We can help," she finishes.

"Oh?" he sneers, amusement shining in his eyes. "You think you can oversee this lot of idiots, deal with all the paltry paperwork pushed at me, *and* see to Lady Veradeaux's growing list of demands while we don't have manpower enough to deal with them? That's what you think you can help me with?"

She hesitates. "No."

The corner of his thin lips quirks up. "Well, then." He starts to turn, and something catches his attention. "You idiots! I told you to take that stupid pot out of here, not drag another one in. Where are you even getting these? Take them out!"

The men shuffle out of the room with their burden.

The steward glances back at us. "As the young lady so eloquently said, I am busy. So, once again, leave or I'll have the guards escort you out."

"Wait," I say. "Didn't you just say you don't have enough people?"

He sighs, calling to a servant, "Go get some guards."

One of the workers nods, setting down the chair he had been carrying, and hurries off. The steward returns to his paperwork, moving the letter to the back of his folder, and walks toward the dais.

I circle in front of him. "Hold on a second! You're *shorthanded*. Then hire us, and for the sake of all that is logical in this world, stop trying to throw us out! We'll tackle anything you can throw at us. At the very least, we can't do any worse than the idiots already working for you."

His eyes continue skimming the words on the page. A sly smile curls his lips. He meets my gaze. "You know what? You're right. And I have just the job for you. Emmrick!" A servant's head snaps up. "Show this man to Master Heizer. He's been requesting a new worker for ages."

The guy hurries over to me, gesturing toward the door we came in. "It's this way."

"Hold on. What about her?" My thumb jerks toward Riveirre.

"She'll be in the reception hall. Emmrick, can you drop her off on the way?"

"Yes, sir."

We head off.

He leads us through the manor, leaving Riveirre in a ballroom. He offers a quick explanation to a woman leading a troop of maids in through another door, then takes me outside.

I glance back as we walk across the grounds. "Um, the manor's that way. In case you got turned around."

My sarcasm is lost on him. "I know. You're not working in the manor."

"Then where in skies' name are you taking me?"

"To Master Heizer," he answers simply.

I roll my eyes. "That much was obvious."

He doesn't reply, and I don't waste breath asking him more questions since he's obviously too obtuse or contrary to answer. As we make it behind the manor, a fence comes into view. Along with a long wooden building, it blocks off an open field.

Full of horses.

No. This can't be where he's taking me. There's got to be another building, somewhere beyond, and we just have to pass this one. Sean Rahkifellar is not a—

"I brought you a new stablehand, Master Heizer!" Emmrick calls, pulling the building's door open. Inside, the air is a musty mix of animal, wet wood, and defecation.

It smells like everything I hated about home.

From one of the stalls, a deep voice grunts, "Did ya now?" A shovel tosses a pile of manure into a wheelbarrow outside the stall. Two more shovelfuls follow before a man lumbers into view, pushing the cart out of the way. Broad shouldered, he stands with his feet apart, a confident hand resting atop his shovel's shaft. "Let's have a look at you."

I hold my ground. If he expects me to spin around like some sort of model, he's going to be standing there for a long time.

He studies me. "You got any experience in stable work?"

"No."

"Horses?"

My jaw clenches. "No." Why couldn't Leavi have gotten the animal job, and me the cushy one inside?

Shaking his head, he hooks a thumb through his belt loop. He glances at my guide. "Boy, you go back and tell that addle-brain of a steward to quit sending me hands that can't tell one horse's mouth from another's arse."

"I—um. I can't tell him that, sir."

Heizer snorts. "Get on out of here."

103

Emmrick scrambles.

The stable master tosses his shovel at me, and I fumble to catch it. "Come on, boy. We've got work to do."

He hastily gives me instructions for cleaning out the stalls and ambles away. Grimacing, I slide the shovel under a clump of manure. It squelches as it comes up. "Skies." I try to take shallow breaths; the smell is so strong, I can taste it. I sling the shovel over the wheelbarrow and dump the load.

Now I only have to do that a thousand more times.

Swallowing my distaste, I set to the work. Despite the cool temperature, a sweat builds at my brow. I struggle to keep a grip on the shovel.

When I'm almost finished with the first stall, the stable master shoulders back into it, moving past me. A frown creases his tanned face as he studies my work. "You're doin' it wrong."

I jam the shovel's head into the ground. "Then how do you want me to be doing it?"

He glares. "With less of a mouth on you."

"What mouth?" I spread my arms out wide. "All I did was ask a question!"

He narrows his eyes. Then he shoves me.

I careen backwards, tripping into the wheelbarrow. Cold, squishy muck and wet hay press against my back, and I shudder, trying not to gag. Skies, I'm *sitting* in it.

Heizer stands over me. "Boy, I don't care who you think you are, but I am in charge here, and you will respect me. I done told you how to do it—you only throw out the wet hay, you have to search for hidden manure, and you *don't* cover up wet patches. You, on the other hand, have wasted most of my hay, yet somehow managed to leave bits of dung *and* cover up the wet spots. That's talent, that." He shakes his head, irritated. "Get up."

I extricate myself from the wheelbarrow. The back of my shirt clings to my skin. I grimace.

"If you ain't gonna do a proper job, then you ain't gonna have a job. I don't care what the steward says." Grabbing the handle of the wheelbarrow, he flips its contents back into the stall. "Do it again. And right this time."

I only half-listen to him. Disgust coats my face as I try to move as little as possible.

"Oh, you bothered by the manure, boy? Let me help you." Grabbing my shoulder, he shoves me down. I fall front first into the pile he poured out. The smell suffocates my nose. Bile rises in my throat, and I desperately swallow it down.

He pushed her. Grabbed her shoulder and shoved. She fell back to the floor hard, head smacking the table. Blood in her hair.

'Get up!' he yelled.

"Maybe now you'll do a better job," Heizer says, "not afraid to get your hands dirty." A chuckle rumbles out of him. "Now, get up and get to work."

Gingerly, I pull up. I refuse to look at myself, but I can feel it, all over me. I'm covered in feces. My skin crawls. "Is there not somewhere I can clean up?" I call as he's leaving. My fingers tap at my leg. *One, two beats, three, four beats. One, two beats, three, four beats.*

"Clean up when you get home," he growls. "And you can go home when you get the job done." Then he's down the aisle and walking out the stable.

104

I pause. Swallow.
And do it again.

Chapter 29

LEAVI

My fingers are red and raw, flimsy coverings for aching bones. A hot, tingling anesthesia burns in my arms. They drag themselves back with the brush, then forward, heavy and mechanical. My entire world is one white, four-foot tile, my sole enemy the smudges of dirt sullying its surface. They hold out against the bristles of my brush like rioters resisting arrest, but I can't stop to until I conquer them.

Forward. Back. Forward. Back. My body rocks with the strokes. My thighs shake. The uniform the maids' manager gave me stretches tight across my chest and pinches under my arms, wet, itching, and too short to protect my throbbing knees from the hard floor.

I could have left hours ago. I suppose I still can. But I won't. If the work has one benefit, it's that it allowed me time to think. As much as I hate to admit it, Sean's right. Rationally, I've known he was right for days, but the emotional, fantastical part of my mind—the part my mother used to so condemn—dared to hope he might be wrong, that something might change. But nothing changes unless someone changes it, and I can't afford to rely on the Traders. Even assuming I could find them, they've already burned me once.

So Morineaux it is.

The way Jacin talked, they must have running water there. If they have that, they'll have other technology as well. Something more like the Valleys, maybe. Like a real civilization. Maybe I'll be able to put together some kind of home there.

And say goodbye to everything I've ever known.

I push the thought away. If I want to get there, to Morineaux, I'm going to need money. Their kind of money. Which means a job. *This* job. I keep scrubbing.

Half an hour later, a pair of hands clap twice. I glance over my shoulder. The maids' manager, a rounded woman with neatly braided hair, stands in the doorway. "Alrighty, girls. Good job today. A little touching up tomorrow, and I'm sure this place'll be right good for even Lady Veradeaux's tastes. Now, let's pick up and get home."

Around me, the other maids grab their buckets and brushes, murmurs of complaint filling the room as they rise. My knees crack as I get up, and my tired muscles are slow to relax enough for me to stand straight.

I follow the others as they leave and put away their cleaning materials. We head to a changing room to retrieve our things, and the girls start to revive some. Tired laughs titter around me, questions about what they're each doing tonight, if they want to come over, and by the way, did they know that so-and-so was dating someone else now? My ears filter the details out, but the simple triviality of it brings a smile to my lips. I wonder how the girls in Erreliah are doing.

My chest tightens, and I clench my jaw, angry for even thinking it.

They're fine. They have to be fine. Probably doing their makeup right now, getting ready for a date or a party at the Docks. Entertaining any other idea is unacceptable. The plague can't have spread that far.

The blue skin of the Dead District corpse flashes to mind.

I slam the door to the cupboard they let me keep my clothes in. That was Karsix. Not Erreliah. They're *fine*.

I struggle to pull the too-small uniform off over my head. A seam pops, but the dress comes off, and I drop it to the ground. My clothes, damp this morning, are dry now, and the leather of my pants is comfortingly smooth against my skin.

After shrugging on my shirt and lacing up my boots, I grab my uniform and leave the room, the other maids still chatting behind me. In the halls, people trickle toward the exit, other employees heading home for the night. Together, we walk to the manor's gate, the chill fall air whispering at us to hurry home.

The others do, passing through the gilded bars and down the path back to their village. Instead, I lean back against the cold gate bars, arms wrapped around myself as I wait for Sean.

A gust sweeps through the manicured grass, and I shiver. From behind the manor, a tall figure trudges across the grounds, silhouetted against the setting sun. His head's down, shoulders hunched, posture dedicated to studying his feet.

"Sean!" My voice surprises me by cracking, and I realize that's the first word I've spoken in hours.

Sean's gaze stays on the ground. The glare of the sun against his profile disappears as he gets closer, revealing what I couldn't see before. Chin-down, he's been shellacked in thick, pungent, brown... Skies, I hope that's mud. I ease forward, just enough to get a whiff of him.

The wind shifts, slamming me with the scent of manure. I gag, caught off guard. Sean walks past me like I don't exist, following the path. We pass up the fork to the village, letting us avoid the crowd.

Neither one of us speaks as we plod our way back home through the forest. When we get to the house, Sean doesn't bother going in. Instead, he heads straight to the well, draws the bucket up, and promptly upends it over his head. Water streams down his body, sloughing off the horse dung. He repeats the process again, and yet again. By the fourth time, every inch of him is dripping, all the excrement possible to remove this way already washed off with the last bucketful.

"Sean." He glances back to look at me, hair plastered to his forehead. "I think that's enough."

"I was just putting it up." He moves to wipe the water from his face, then pauses, staring distrustfully at his hand. His upper lip curls. Turning, he strides toward the house.

I move to cut him off. "I don't think Marcí is going to be happy if you flood her house." I look him up and down.

His jaw clenches, irritated. "How else am I supposed to get dry clothes?"

"Just," I sigh, surveying him. "Stay here." I start to head inside.

"Well, I'm not going to stand out here and drip dry!"

I glance back, rolling my eyes. "Well, skies, Sean. That was my entire plan. How ever are you to get dry now?" I pin him with a gaze. He hesitates, and before he can find something else to argue about, I go in.

107

I climb the stairs, head down, worn-out muscles protesting every step.

"Hey there." I glance up to see Jacin at the top of the steps. A smile brightens his face, and he pads down to meet me halfway. "You getting ready for the party?"

I look at him, confused. "Party?" A tangle from my failing bun spills onto my face.

He shrugs. "Yeah. Marcí is throwing one tonight. A sort of welcome for you. She did it when I showed up too, but it was smaller. She had me running invitations for hours today. I think I ended up passing them out to half the town."

"For us?"

"Well, she says it's for you. She's been complaining about people not being social enough for the last few weeks, so I think it's more of an excuse than anything. But," he shrugs, "it'll be lively at least. So you'll come?"

Right now, attending a party is the last thing I want to do, especially one thrown by Marcí. Her version of the perfect party is probably a quiet quartet, girls wearing dresses they can't breathe in, and hours of small talk that numb any intelligent brain to mush. I'd rather curl up in bed than spend hours at an event that sounds dangerously close to being even more boring than the work functions my mother used to drag me to. I can imagine her in her pearls now, fluffing her hair in front of the mirror. *You want to get ahead in this world, Eleaviara, you talk to the people that are already there.*

Jacin's bright eyes watch me expectantly.

I bite my lip, hesitant to let him down but not knowing how to get around it. "No."

His face falls.

"Sorry," I add quickly. "I am... I am only tired." *'Only' tired, Leavi? Get your words straight.* I look away, embarrassed.

"Oh." His voice is flat. "Well, if you change your mind, your clothes are in the foot chest. They should be dry." He brushes past me.

I glance back at him, but he doesn't pause and disappears around the stairwell.

Once in my room, I open the lid to my foot chest. Inside, my two changes of clothes are neatly folded. Clean.

Jacin must have done this, and I just blew him off.

I snap the lid shut and sit heavily on the box, dragging a hand down my face. "Idiot." How much could it really cost me to go to this stupid party? A few hours of boredom and tired feet.

You need to get your priorities straight, Eleaviara, my mother used to say. *Relaxation is for failures and the dead. You want to get ahead—*

"You talk to the people that are already there." I stand, mind made up. I'll need to wash up, straighten my hair, change clothes—

Wait. Clothes.

"Sean."

Angry with myself for forgetting, I hurry to grab a towel and some clothes from his chest. He's pacing when I make it outside. I press the bundle into his hands. "Here."

He stares at the clothes.

I start to head inside but pause, glancing back at him. "There's going to be a party tonight." He looks up, as if surprised I'm talking to him. "I'm going. You probably should too. Half the town's supposed to be here apparently."

He nods, strangely quiet for once.

"Okay. Well. I guess I'll see you there."

As I head for the door, one quiet word hits my ear. "Thanks."

* * *

Music drifts from outside, a strange, upbeat twanging accompanied by the bright jangling of some sort of percussion instrument. The living room has transformed into a lounge, couches turned away from the fireplace, toward the open area. Adults mingle, sampling food from the spread laid out on the relocated dining table. Through the window, I see couples dancing, the girls' simple skirts swirling about their knees as they spin. I smooth out the wrinkles in my pants, suddenly self-conscious.

Oh, well. The closest thing to a dress I have here is my lab coat. I finish descending the stairs.

A couple of the women pass me odd looks, but I ignore them, opening the door and stepping out into the cool night air. Two musicians, a woman and a man, play on the porch. The man's fingers fly over an odd stringed instrument with a triangular body while the woman claps a ring of little metal pieces against her hand in time, broad smile on her face.

"Leavi!" Jacin catches my attention, padding up the steps to greet me. "I thought you weren't coming."

I shrug, smiling, and he takes my hand. "Dance with me?" he asks.

I *hmm* playfully, looking away, and he pulls me down the steps before I can refuse. We merge with the crowd, him following the steps with the rest of the group. Unfamiliar with the dance, I'm left struggling to keep up.

He extends his arms to push me back. I fumble to match the movement, and he laughs. "You don't know this one, do you?"

You have no idea, I think to say. "No," I admit, my accent thick.

"That's alright. You've got good rhythm at least. And you've yet to step on my toes, so you can't be doing too badly."

Me, step on your toes? Never. I've far too much grace and good sense for that. Half a laugh escapes my lips instead of the ridiculous words I don't know how to say.

"So where are you from?" he asks, twirling me.

I spin lightly, coming back to face him. "Very, very far away."

He tsks at me. "You can't stay mysterious forever, Leavi. Second time I've asked you this, and you dodged then too. Give me a hint, at least. East, west, or south?"

"No." I grin slyly.

"What do you mean 'no'?" He twirls me again. "How much farther up north can you get than this tiny town?"

I wink. "Far enough to say 'Common' and not 'Avadelian.'"

"Oh, you think you're clever, don't you?"

I shrug.

"That's okay. You don't have to be modest." He dips me, and for a moment, I can see flecks of green concealed near his iris. "I think you're pretty clever too," he whispers in my ear.

Air whooshes past me as he pulls me back upright. "Oh, I almost forgot. I found something for you." I tilt my head, the last notes of the song petering off. "That's perfect timing. Why don't we head inside, and I'll bring it down to you?"

I follow him in, and he hurries upstairs. While I wait, I wander around sampling food until a pleased clap catches my attention. Nearby, Marcí greets a woman in a voluminous scarlet dress. Pearl pins fasten back the lady's platinum blonde hair, and silver bracelets rest against her honeyed skin.

"I'm glad you could make it!" Marcí gushes.

The lady smiles. "Well, it's always good to visit a fellow Morineause woman."

"With the council meeting tomorrow, I was sure you'd be swamped! It seems no one can ever get ahold of you this time of year."

"Yes, well. All work and no play make this Veradeaux a dull, dull girl."

Marcí titters, and the woman—*Lady Veradeaux*, I realize—gathers her hair over one shoulder, a ruby ring catching the light. "Besides, my steward has everything under control. I left him seeing to the accommodations for my guest of honor."

Marcí's laugh falls away, confusion flickering across her face. "Guest of honor?"

"A visitor from the east. If everything goes well, this meeting could prove very lucrative indeed." A self-satisfied smile flits across her lips.

I edge closer, curiosity piqued. Marcí opens her mouth to speak.

Someone grabs my wrist from behind. Alarmed, I spin around swinging.

Jacin catches my fist. "Whoa, there! I startle you?"

He smiles, and a shaky laugh pushes out of my lungs. "Sorry." I pull my hand back.

"No harm done. Here. This is what I wanted to give you." He hands me a large, leather-bound book, its pages yellowed with age.

My fingers brush the cover, its weighty antiquity reminding me of the night my father gave me my necklace. "What is this?"

"A book of words. Found it up in old farmer Zairren's attic. Looked like it's been there a long time; the words are a little out-of-date. But I thought it still might help you. I mean, if you're wanting to learn more Avadelian."

Pages crinkle as I turn them. Word after word meets my eyes, each accompanied by short explanations. A dictionary, then. An old dictionary with faded letters and a creaky spine, but a dictionary all the same—and it's so much easier to read Avadelian than it is to listen to, even if I am a little rusty at it. I look up from the book to find Jacin's anxious eyes, and I remember that I've yet to tell him what I think of his gift.

"Thank you," I answer warmly. He relaxes. With a book, I can study. Anything I can study, I can learn. "This will help me."

A loose grin breaks out on his lips. "Good. I'm glad you like it."

A piece of his story sticks in my mind, though. "Doesn't 'old farmer Zairren' need it?"

"Oh, no. I forgot to tell you. He died a few days back. Marcí sent me out to his house yesterday to help some of the town's folk clean it out. Guy didn't have any family."

110

He stole from a dead man?

But then again, whoever oversaw the cleaning probably told people they could take things as a sort of payment. I don't know how to ask about it without offending Jacin, though, and I really do appreciate the gift. If this town is anything like the poor topside ones, he could have sold the book for a good bit of money despite its age. Instead, he gave it to me. Conscience more-or-less at ease, I thank Jacin again and take the book to my room.

When I come back down, Jacin's in conversation with a few other men in the room. I wander around, playing meet and greet with the townsfolk, until I spot Sean in the corner of the room. He's set so far back into his armchair, it's like he's trying to become a part of it. The steady *tap, tap, tap, tap* of his presswrite is in time with the beat of the music outside. I doubt he notices though. As always, he's focused on his work, dedicatedly ignoring the rest of society.

I suppose I can't really blame him, though. After all, I almost didn't even come.

Someone else catches my attention. I shake hands and learn names, but no matter who I'm talking to, my eyes keep drifting back to Sean.

Head down, his usually short hair dangles above his eyes. His shoulders are tense, but his fingers are in perfect time. With their unconscious dancing, I can't help but wonder how well he would do if he tried.

Outside, the music takes on a soft, almost haunting tone.

The people around me have wandered away. Suddenly ill-at-ease, I fiddle with my necklace. A humorless smile rises unbidden. Between the presswrite's percussion and the anxious rasp of my necklace, Sean and I could almost have our own band.

Enough waiting, Leavi. The song's not going to last forever.

Against my better instinct, my feet approach his chair. His eyes stay down, typing still rhythmic.

My fingers release their grip on the chain. "Sean?"

He glances up, still tip-tapping on his keyboard.

My stomach's in a nervous flight, but my hands stay steady. I gesture out the window, where the stars glisten over the dancers, a gentle wind mixing with the wistful music. "You know, it's an awful pretty night to be stuck inside all evening."

Tapping keys and hesitant eyes are all that answer me.

My heartbeat accelerates. *What is wrong with you, Leavi? It's just Sean.*

I extend a hand, a smile teasing my lips. "Would you honor me with a dance, Doktor Sean Rahkifellar?"

Chapter 30

SEAN

I'm not sure why Riveirre asked me to come to this party. She hasn't talked to me yet, and she probably won't. These people will only be here for a few hours; she could talk to me anytime.

Then again, she's already clearly stated that she tries to not talk to me unless she has to.

She slips past me and through the door, once more in her form-fitting leather pants and dark red top, collar high against her neck. She walks smoothly and confidently, unconsciously swaying to the music. Her long, wavy hair gently moves with her.

Through the window, I see Jacin approach her. A sly grin coats his face, dark joviality hiding in his eyes. I don't like how blatantly he hits on her—he's got to have something up his sleeve. Something about him just seems... off.

Of course, she doesn't notice. When he takes her hand, she beams and hurries down the steps with him, beginning to dance. I shake my head. Her admiration will not end well; I can just feel it.

I go back to typing, the beat from outside moving through me.

One, *two*, three, *four*. Tap, *tap*, tap, *tap*.

The music is hypnotic, lulling me into a trance; the world is nothing but the notes and the beat, me and my presswrite. Mindlessly, I work, time passing in immeasurable increments.

Someone approaches me. "Sean?"

I glance up at Riveirre but had just started a measure, so I don't stop typing.

"You know, it's an awful pretty night to be stuck inside all evening."

Is she just going to criticize my lack of sociability? I already came to the stupid party for her, and she's ignored me until now.

She extends a hand. "Would you honor me with a dance, Doktor Sean Rahkifellar?"

My fingers miss a beat. Mastera Eleaviara Riveirre actually wants me to do something with her that she doesn't *need* me for?

Riveirre wants me to dance.

But I haven't danced in years.

'See, sugar? Do you feel the beat?' She swayed back and forth, humming along to the music that was just right. It filled our living room. She took my hands, encouraging me to dance with her.

'Just back and forth, Mom?'

'If that's what you want, sugar. Or,' she grinned, 'we can do this!' She twirled me. I laughed.

'Do you want more cake, sugar?'

I smiled at her but shook my head. 'Not right now, Mom. This is goo-'

The door bangs open and—

Can't think about that night.

"No."

Her previously carefree attitude evaporates. She takes a half-step back, lost hand still hovering slightly in the air. It doesn't matter though—Jacin comes back over and hands her a drink. She starts talking to him again. She's fine.

I turn back to my work.

Chapter 31
ASTER

Distantly, footsteps ring down the hall. My eyes snap open, greeted only by the featureless stone that forms my empty cell. The darkness weighs heavy in this windowless, torchless room.

The approaching steps are lighter than those of the guards that fell upon me when I entered last night. They subdued me before I could even reach for powder, and immediately robbed me of my cloak and rapier belt, storing them in a room we passed as they dragged me here.

Now I'm sitting on the floor, against the wall, hands tied, wracking my brain as to why these people have imprisoned me. It's not like I have any political power yet; I'm only the Second Son to *come*. Even Agraund wouldn't listen to me.

Ransom's the only thing I can come up with, and even then, there's no way for them to be sure I didn't inform my family when I got the letter. For all these people know, everyone at the castle could be aware of exactly where I am.

The sound stops just outside the door. The shifting noise of metal being lifted off metal echoes through the space, and the door creaks as it opens.

Silhouetted in the entrance is a tall woman in a royal-blue evening gown, blonde hair cascading down her elegant shoulders. Her golden skin screams of my home nation, but I haven't even the beginning of an idea as to why a Morineause woman would imprison me.

A sly smile creeps onto her face. "Aster, Aster... It's been a long time. You've grown."

My eyes narrow. She brushes a hair from her face, and a ruby ring glints in the light.

Wait. That ring—

Chilled recognition shudders through me.

"Amarris," I murmur.

"*Lady*, dear. Lady Amarris."

I shake my head, nostrils flaring. "You forfeited that title the moment you left your home."

"Oh, don't be so harsh, Aster. I'm just on... let's call it vacation. A very, very rewarding vacation, in fact, if you can just answer a few questions for me." She paces forward, heels tapping the ground. The door clangs shut behind her.

"What do you want from me, traitor?" The rope bites my wrists. "I have nothing to offer you."

"Traitor, dear? Again, such harsh words, especially to a woman who knew you when you were just a baby. I'm no traitor."

I bark a short laugh. "Even if you weren't before, kidnapping and holding a member of the royal family is a federal crime. The only way Morineaux would want you is if you showed up for trial."

She closes the distance between us, crouching. Her fingers tilt my chin up. "Morineaux will never hold me in its court, Aster, unless it is as a Lady. Let's get that straight right now."

Her cold, steely eyes send chills through me, but I refuse to let her see she's unsettled me. Calmly, I reply, "All that needs straightened is your crooked morals, Amarris. You're nothing but a simple criminal."

She laughs, rising. "Still the little idealist you were at thirteen, Aster? Shame." She paces the room, skirts swishing behind her. "So, here's the heart of the matter. You're in *my* house, under *my* custody, and I would imagine you didn't bother telling your family where you were running off to. Wouldn't want to disappoint dear Uncle Agraund, now would we?" A snake's smile slithers to her lips as she waits for my response.

I consider lying to her, refuting her statement and promising that Agraund knows exactly where I am. But if that were true, I would have had a whole entourage traveling with me and wouldn't look like I've been sleeping in the open. She'd see right through me.

"What do you want, Amarris?" I ask instead.

"Why, just a few answers. If you cooperate, I might even help you get back home. Sound like a deal?"

"Ask away, *maedame.*" A dry smile twitches at my lips at my intended slight. Without my casting materials or weapon, my only defense is confidence. The moment I seem powerless is the moment she gets everything she wants from me.

The light in her eyes turns hard. "I said, my title is that of a lady, and while you are in my house, you will address me as such. Are we understood?"

"And my title is that of a prince, no matter *whose* house I am in." I hold her gaze.

She stands there, glaring at me, for once no condescending comeback at the ready. "Well, then," she clips. "To business, shall we?" She resumes her pacing. "How many troops are stationed in the capitol?"

I sigh and lean against the wall disinterestedly. "I'm not the First Son, Amarris. I don't have access to that kind of information. And why does it matter? If you want Morineaux to accept you again, fighting its army on your own isn't going to do it."

Her smile slides back into place. "Don't worry, dear. I know how to take care of my own business. Now, an estimate. You have to have some idea at least."

"There's enough that any attack is a suicide mission." At least, I think. There should be; Morineaux's the strongest country, which should mean that she has more than a formidable army within her capitol's gates. But even if there's not, there isn't a chance I'd tell Amarris that.

"Oh, I know you're proud of your country, but don't get cocky now."

"So you admit it's no longer your country?" A smirk plays at my mouth.

She sighs dramatically. "Too bad your brother has better sense than you do, or I would have lured him here instead."

I laugh. Ren is about as sensible as a potted plant unless he's talking battlefield strategy.

She faces me, countenance turning dark. "You're negotiating for your freedom here, Aster. Answer my questions."

I shrug. "I *have* answered you. For some reason, though, you don't seem to appreciate my efforts."

Her eyes narrow. "Battle casters, then. How many?"

"Every caster in the castle is a battle caster." Some of them are only amateurs in that respect, but still.

Her hand makes a dismissive gesture. "Throwing pebbles at the enemy with your mind doesn't count. How many are *trained* for battle?"

"All of them. I would have thought an interrogator would be better at listening."

"Aster, quit dodging my questions," she stops, stoops, and locks my gaze, her nose only inches from mine, "and answer me properly."

One second passes.

Two.

"No."

Fire flashes in her eyes, and she slaps me. My head snaps to the side, cheek stinging.

"Fine. You don't want to talk?" She smiles venomously. "That's okay, dear. You will soon enough."

She stands, sweeping out of the room. The door clangs shut behind her, and the sound of the bar dropping back to its place rings.

I just have to wait this out; eventually, Agraund will find me.

Because the anti-scrying spell isn't active anymore.

Chapter 32

LEAVI

The town council reception at Lady Veradeaux's manor is more like my parents' stuffy work functions than last night's party at Marcí's was. Ten council members parade through the space I spent all yesterday cleaning, spouses in tow and glasses of watered-down alcohol in hand. The men's tall, stiff collars force their necks into a perpetual stretch, a posture that reminds me of uncomfortable geese. Though the women fake smiles, they're surely not at ease either. After all, their corsets are so tight I'm shocked no one's fainted or popped a seam. With my back to the wall and uniform still too small, I'm not in much better shape. At least I'm not one of the active serving maids, though, winding their way through the crowd as guests snag food from trays while entirely ignoring the girls who bring it to them.

In the center of the room, Lady Veradeaux laughs and flips her hair, the only one here seeming comfortable. Chandelier candlelight reflects off her golden brocade, making her seem as though she's glowing.

Beside her stands the mysterious 'visitor from the east.' Billowing black robes swallow him, sleeves long enough to conceal his hands. A deep hood hangs against his back. I've never been a superstitious or religious person, but if he were to put the hood on, I swear he'd be what I met on the opposite side of death. He stands slightly too still, but his gaze flickers over everything like a bird of prey analyzing its victims. Lank, shoulder-length red hair gives his already pale skin a sickly pallor. Though he stands half a head shorter than Lady Veradeaux, his composure is just as confident.

Across the room, his dark eyes snap to mine. My stomach drops, hyper-aware he caught me staring. He holds my gaze for an unnerving amount of time.

Raising a single finger, he beckons me over. I freeze, not wanting to be any closer to him than I have to be. His eyes narrow, lips parting slightly. Despite being twenty feet away, his one-word command is as clear as if he'd spoken it directly in my ear.

"Come."

A cold tingling runs over my skin. Scared what will happen if I refuse, I force my leaden feet forward. He turns away from his group, toward me. I stop five feet from him, but that condemning finger raises again. Hesitantly, I close a few more feet.

He grabs my wrist, yanking me close, and tips my chin up, inspecting me. Before I can protest, he's released me. "You're not a Kadranian brat or you'd have better manners." His voice is gravelly, accusatory. "Where are you from?"

I lean back, heart hammering in my chest. For a second, my frazzled mind considers telling him the truth, but I doubt he'd believe it. Instead, I provide the lie Jacin seems to accept. "Draó."

A sardonic smile rises to his lips. "Convenient. You look like a mongrel, though, so I suppose it makes sense." He turns back to the group. "Lady Veradeaux, do you often make a habit of hiring insolent maids?"

Panic flickers briefly in her eyes, but she covers it, smoothing out nonexistent wrinkles in her dress. "Of course not. Why? Is that one giving you trouble?"

"Perhaps it is different in your land. However, in my country, lowly serving girls are taught to keep their eyes to their own affairs." His gaze rakes me down.

"If it's a problem," Lady Veradeaux offers, "she can always be dismissed."

He stares at me, and I hold his gaze. Looking in his eyes, though—there's something dark and cold there. Subtle but undeniably wrong. It unsettles me, and I glance down, breaking the connection.

"No," he concludes at length. "I believe she's learned her lesson."

He turns away, and I hurry back to my spot at the wall. Anger and humiliation burn in my chest, but a chilled disquiet tempers the flames. I keep my eyes down, only looking up if one of the guests summon me.

No matter what, my gaze stays off the Man from the East.

* * *

The manor halls echo.

"I haven't seen her in three days," a girl says, turning the corner onto my hall.
"I heard she got fired…"

It's the morning after the reception. Thirty feet down from me, the maids' gossip is as clear as if we were sitting side by side. I try to focus on my work, but with nothing besides varying patterns of dirt to distract me, it's impossible not to listen.

I glance out of the corner of my eye. The first girl who spoke has blonde hair and bright blue eyes round in worry. The second girl is plump with mousy brown hair.

"For what?" a lanky, carrot-topped girl asks. "I always thought she did good work."

The fourth and oldest one scoffs. Her wavy black locks slide over her shoulder with a casual toss of her head. "Maybe for that mouth on her."

The blonde maid shakes her head. "No. She was a good girl. She wouldn't have done anything stupid."

"Because she hasn't before?" the eldest retorts.

"I-" The younger girl gathers herself, then narrows her eyes. "I'm worried about her and all you can do is run your mouth off. You never did like her anyway, did you? You probably *do* hope something happened to her."

"That's not true!" Changing tack, the dark-haired girl narrows her eyes, words turning cloyingly sweet. "I'm just looking at the facts, sweetheart. And the facts are that she never liked keeping her mouth shut or falling in line. And those are the kinds of things that get you fired in a job like this."

"If she got fired, she would have told me," the blonde protests.

The other assumes a haughty expression. "Or maybe you two weren't quite the bosom buddies you thought you were."

"Something's wrong. I'm telling you it is!"

The older girl rolls her eyes and goes back to dusting.

After a second, the carrot-top takes pity on the blonde. "When did you say you last saw her?"

She sighs. "Three days ago. That morning. She told me she'd seen something weird in the north wing—"

118

The carrot-top recoils. "The north wing? What was she doing there?"

I find that odd myself. That was one of the first things my manager said when she gave me my assignment yesterday—don't speak unless spoken to, do what you're told, and keep out of the north wing. It's off-limits. Why, she wouldn't tell me.

The blonde shrugs. "I don't know. She wanted me to come look, but I made up some excuse. I didn't want to get caught, you know? But now I'm wondering if I should have gone with her."

The oldest maid, not even bothering to turn her head, snorts. "And then you'd be out of a job, too. You really can't put it together? She went where she wasn't supposed to, and she got fired for it. It's plain and simple, sweetheart."

The girl spins toward her. "That still doesn't explain why she hasn't talked to me!"

The brunette shakes her head.

Seeing the mystery solved, the carrot-top pats her on the shoulder, making some consolation, and gets back to her work. As if irritated by the condescension, the first maid declares, "I'm going to find her."

"Whatever you gotta do, sweetheart. It's your job. Just keep us out of it."

The girl huffs and stalks off.

The other three's conversation turns to who's dating who and the latest thing the manager has done to tick them off, and I tune them out, considering what I heard. I feel bad for the missing girl if she really did lose her job, but I think her friend is overreacting. Either way, it sounds like it was the girl's own fault.

I catch myself. *Skies, Leavi. Are you seriously analyzing the gossip? Just because you wear the uniform they do doesn't mean you have to adopt their IQ.*

Annoyed with myself, I finish the spot I've been cleaning and move on.

Chapter 33

ASTER

It's hard to keep track of time here. The lack of light alone makes the days and nights warp, but the lack of food makes it worse.

They give me bread crusts—occasionally. They let me have a little water with it, but it's hardly enough to wet my throat. I don't even think they bring it at regular intervals, so I still can't measure.

I think it's been three days.

My head aches, my hands shake, even tied as they are behind my back. I sleep and wake up, somehow still tired, somehow getting weaker by the hour.

Every moment stretches to a millennium, destroying what little sense of time I do have. The person that comes to feed me is the only one I've seen since Amarris, and he always refuses to speak. The only interesting thing he does is cast what looks like the anti-scrying spell on me.

Help is a much more distant dream now.

The door opens. Amarris stalks in, easy self-assurance radiating off her in venomous waves.

Inwardly, I curse my inattention; if I'd been listening better, I would've been able to prepare myself for her. Instead, I look exactly as she wants—starved, weak, and broken.

Since she's already here, though, I don't move. I relax, comfortable and indifferent. She will *not* have the pleasure of thinking me ready to grovel.

"Hello, dear. Do you feel a little more cooperative yet?"

I level my gaze. Silent.

She narrows her eyes. "Let's try a different line of questions. How many ways are there into the castle? There's got to be another entrance besides the gate."

A spike of fear runs through me as my mind darts to the secret door in the wall, but I stay quiet.

She purses her lips, perfectly manicured nails tip-tapping against her ring. "You *will* talk to me."

Nothing.

Sharply, she steps forward, heels clacking against the stone. "Speak, boy!"

I press my lips together, a smile tugging at them.

"Well," she spits, pacing the small room. "I suppose I shouldn't have expected you to be helpful—it's not like you're good for anything else." She barks out a laugh. "For goodness' sakes, all anyone would have to do to run Morineaux to the ground is kill that self-righteous idiot Agraund and put you in charge!"

My jaw clenches against my will. She catches it, turning to face me.

"Sensitive topic, dear?"

I don't reply.

"Well." She considers something. "Aster... Aster, Aster." Her voice turns soft, intimate. "I think I might be able to help you. I have many friends, you know.

120

Friends skilled with magic beyond your wildest dreams." She kneels in front of me. "They could teach you things, Aster. Things you could take back to Morineaux. Things that could make you the most powerful Second Son of all time. Agraund would be a *novice* compared to what you could do." She catches my gaze and holds it.

The desperation and frustration from all my failed lessons well up inside me, once again begging, screaming for a solution to my incompetence. I need to learn. I need something to show for this enormous mistake of a situation I've put myself in.

"All you have to do is answer a few easy questions. It's not going to do any harm." Her voice is gentle. "Just let me know a couple simple things, and you could have more power than you ever imagined. Just like that."

It *wouldn't* be that hard to answer her. They're not impossible questions. Estimates, that's all she'd asked for before. Estimates and an entrance.

My head throbs. If I cooperated, she'd give me proper meals. I could become the Second Son I need to be. I open my mouth.

She smiles warmly, but dread gnaws in my stomach. *This is treason.*

But no. I'm only telling her this to get better—*for* Morineaux. More powerful than Agraund... I could protect our country from anything.

Anyone.

At what cost?

"It's okay, Aster," she whispers. "It's okay. All I need is a few simple words from you. That's all. In return," her fingers brush my cheek. "You get unimaginable *power*. All the food you can eat. And I'll give you a better room, the one you deserve—comfortable, befitting a man of your station." Her gentle fingers catch my chin. "Just answer a few, simple questions."

I want to. The allure of her promises—food, power, comfort—it tugs at something deep within me, beating down my ability to resist. I *want* to answer.

But there's a hard knot inside me that knows she has no reason to go through with what she says; she has no incentive to truly relocate or empower me. Whatever she's planning, it won't be good for Morineaux.

That's all that matters.

Silent still, I close my eyes and settle against the wall. I won't keep listening to this viper's lies.

She waits for a moment. "Aster?"

I maintain a steady silence.

She slaps me. "Answer me!"

Cheek stinging, I ignore her, eyes still closed.

"Fine, then." Her voice is sharp, angry, but I hear her rise. Her gown sweeps across the floor as she crosses the room. The door creaks open and slams shut, the clacks of her footsteps receding down the hall.

I relax, tense energy leaving me. She's done with me for now, and if her interrogations don't change tack, I'll be fine.

I just have to hope Agraund somehow finds me before my hunger outweighs my sense.

* * *

121

Hours pass—days maybe. Probably not, though. They haven't fed me again, so it's probably not the next day.

There's a shakiness in my bones I can't dispel.

Steps. They're soft and swishing, coming closer to my door. The grate in the door jerks open, and—

There's nothing there. It slides shut.

I blink at the impossible sight. No. No, I am *not* hallucinating. I've not gone without food for that long.

Have I?

A chill runs through my body. The bar rings as it's lifted from the door, and Amarris stalks in. She's followed by a man in leather armor, glinting metal cylinders gripped tight in his fists.

So she is changing her method. I shiver, a strange, tingling coldness washing through me.

"This is your last chance the kind way, Aster. Do you agree to cooperate?"

I lift my eyes to meet her gaze and deliberately set my jaw. I won't be speaking today.

The man marches forward, fist flying against my mouth. My head jerks to the side, the weight of the striker in his hand transforming what would have already been a powerful punch into one that makes my head spin.

"Wrong answer, dear. Would you like to try again?"

I say nothing, and the man attacks me. I spit blood into the floor.

"If you would like this to end, I'm listening." Her nails tip-tap on her ring.

Silence.

"No? Well, then. I'll let my friend here work with you until you *do* have something to say."

The man mutters something to Amarris, and she nods. He leaves, returning only a moment later with a chair, and hauls me into it. I groan, this my first movement in who knows how long.

He pummels me. Punch after merciless punch, he batters my face. Every new injury to my head throbs, each one a separate, aching entity. Blow after ruthless blow, he attempts to tear away my resolve, my vow of silence.

What blunder have I wrought?

Still the furious bashing continues, knocking my head back and forth. My ears ring, my eyes swell shut. Another jab rocks my jaw, and my teeth clamp down on tongue, the taste of copper filling my mouth.

A blow to my gut sends me doubled over, blood trickling from my lips. Pressure hits my spine, and my back arches. He doesn't stop.

My mind slips into a haze. This doesn't matter, can't matter. The pain will only be temporary. *Temporary*, I promise myself. But my thoughts are fuzzing more and more with each new blow. I don't think I have the presence of mind to answer her questions even if I could abandon my country to.

I have no idea how long it lasts. All I know is that my weakened body aches with a million bruises, pressure cuts scattered across the black and blue. My head pounds like a dagger is fighting to carve its way out of my skull.

Finally, the man steps back. I'm limp in the chair, either unable or without enough will to move. I fear to test which.

"Now, dear—I'm sorry to have dealt with you so harshly, but I fear it *was* necessary. Are we ready to talk?"

Drained of everything else, my only focus is my silence. Nothing else matters. She waits.

Nothing else matters.

The man hefts me from the chair, dropping me like a heap of rags and bone back into my corner. They march out, dragging the chair with them. The pain dulls my thoughts and destroys my sense of anything around me.

Then it's gone. The agony disappears, and with it, the chill that has permeated my soul.

I drag in a deep breath, shocked at the sudden release of pain. I blink open unswollen eyes. No bruises darken my skin. No cuts mar it.

A shadow fills the open grate. It snaps shut, and darkness swallows the room once more.

Fearful goosebumps rise on my skin.

I shift, testing my body. Nothing. No aches, no bruises, no blood.

Was it a dream? I never went to sleep, though. It couldn't have been a hallucination, either. It made far too much sense for that. Which leaves only one option.

Amarris has an illusionist.

Chapter 34

LEAVI

Over a week working at the manor and I still haven't managed to figure out its layout. The place is massive, its estate likely a fourth the size of the village. Jacin says it was probably some old warlord's fortress. Now it's just an absurdly large building full of people who don't know how to give proper directions.

"Where is that stupid room?" I mutter to myself. My arms are starting to burn under the weight of a pastry tray.

The food's supposed to go to some meeting room I've never heard of, and the dumb supervisor who shoved the platter into my hands hurried off before I could ask for clarification. I tried to stop someone else, but around here, everyone's either busy or trying to look that way.

However, this part of the manor is strangely quiet, and I've about given up hoping to see anyone else when I hear voices. Relieved, I head that way. At this point, I don't care how busy or important they look. Risking bothering someone is better than wandering around for an hour.

Their words echo down the hall through a barely cracked black door. "You need better security down here, Miss Veradeaux." The low, gravelly voice is unmistakable. *The Man from the East.*

I freeze.

"My title is Lady Veradeaux, as I've told you before," my employer's voice clips. "I stopped being 'Miss' thirty years ago."

"And you stopped being 'Lady' when you fled your country. Yes. We know much more about your past, *Miss* Veradeaux, than you think. My master doesn't take on business lightly—especially not with traitors."

A furious silence fills the quiet.

"Now," the man continues. "As I was saying—security. Apparently a maid wandered into the wing." My heart jumps a beat, thinking for a second he's talking about me.

"They're not supposed to be down here," Lady Veradeaux protests.

"An order to steer clear is not a guard against prying eyes, Veradeaux! You need men, ones with tight lips, securing this sector. Otherwise, I will take our business into my own hands and you'll never be 'Lady' again. Do you understand me?"

Her words are ice. "Crystal clear." A short silence follows, broken by a pop of the lady's lips. "Whatever did you do with the... misplaced maid?"

"She's been taken care of." His tone sends a tingle down my spine. My skin prickles with danger, like I'm staring into darkness, knowing something's there but not knowing what it is.

Lady Veradeaux *hmm*s. There's a thoughtful second of silence, and then a rustling as if the pair is moving to stand. My eyes widen. I'm going to get caught eavesdropping, and I'm developing a sinking certainty that I'm exactly where I'm not supposed to be. I cast back the way I came, but the hall behind me stretches straight, long, and empty.

Lady Veradeaux's heels clack against the stone.

I swing back around. There. Just past the door, a twist in the corridor, somewhere they won't see me.

Clack, clack.

I hurry forward, trying to keep the tray from slipping.

Clack, clack.

I can make it, I can make it, just a few more steps…

Clack, clack, clack.

The door opens just as I press myself against the turn of the wall. My heart pounds, my hands shake, but I force my breath to still, terrified they'll hear me. I wait, every nerve-wracking moment dragged out to an agonizing millennium, praying they won't turn my way.

The footsteps fade down the hall.

I gasp, releasing my pent breath. I have to get out of here. But if I go the way I came, they might spot me. My only other option is to follow this side hall.

I glance around. This area of the manor doesn't look much different from anywhere else. A little dustier, perhaps, but that's about it. I can't help but wonder what they have hidden in here that's so important. I shudder, recalling what the man said. *She's been taken care of.* Words that could be so innocent. A tone that makes them so menacing.

There's got to be a way out of here.

Walking through these inner, stone hallways feels like navigating some ancient, torch-lit maze. The soft black slippers of my uniform whisper against the floor. Old, splintered doors along the passage monitor my progress, and I'm terrified one of them is going to open and reveal me.

The corridors continue to twist and turn with no end in sight. I'm about to give up on finding a different way out and take my chances with my original route when I spot something odd.

There's a door. Just a simple wooden door, identical to all the other doors in these halls. Well, identical but for two things.

No other door has a sliding hatch, right at eye level.

And no other door has an iron bar set across it.

Haltingly, I walk toward it. I lay the tray on the floor, eyes locked on the mystery. As I stand, my fingers run along the wood, and I reach up, gently sliding back the hatch.

The room inside is dark, visible only by the torch on the sconce behind me. At first, in the still black, the space looks empty. Then something moves, catching my attention, and my eyes widen.

A boy with ragged blonde hair and a gaunt, dirt-covered face lays against the wall, arms bound behind his back. Shockingly soft mahogany eyes plead with me, and when he speaks, his voice is a whispered rasp.

"Help me…"

Chapter 35

ASTER

I hear footsteps and cringe. The illusionist's interrogation was yesterday, I think, or the day before. It doesn't surprise me that they're back, but a cold dread still creeps up in me. I'm not sure I can handle another questioning like that.

The footsteps stop. A shaft of light pierces the shadows, and I squint against the foreign brightness. Slowly willing myself to look, I see curious chocolate eyes peeking through the grate.

This must be the illusionist.

She doesn't look at me, though. Instead, it seems as if she doesn't even know I'm here. The nerves that jumped into my throat shift into confusion with tinges of worry. She glances about the room, and her Kadranian-pale skin seems to glow in the relative darkness.

Who is this?

Her eyes fix on me, and she starts. I shift weakly. Taking a chance, I rasp in what I know of Avadelian, "Help me."

Her eyes soak in my pathetic state, and horror slowly seeps through her features. She breathes something in a foreign language, compassion and shock mingling in her words.

My rising hope for escape drains away. The first real person I've seen in weeks and she doesn't even speak Avadelian. My momentarily soaring soul drops like the blade of a guillotine. My mind is whirling, searching for some way to get her to understand me.

But this is Draó, I remember, and my hopes rise again. Just because her first language is a foreign one doesn't mean that she can't speak the common tongue too. "Can you understand me?"

Clarity slowly returns to her gaze. "Yes. Did-" She presses her lips together as if she can't wrap her mind around what she's seeing. "Did Lady Veradeaux do this to you?"

Confusion dominates my mind for a moment until realization clears it like sunlight dispelling mist. A wanted criminal, Amarris must have opted to go by her last name, rather than the one she was known by in the court. If I remember correctly, the great-grandmother she claimed as her line to nobility was a Veradeaux. "Yes. Please, help me."

Fear grips my heart, cold understanding washing through me. Amarris isn't going to let me go. She wouldn't want Morineaux to expect an attack, and she knows I'll tell Agraund everything that happened as soon as I get back. No matter if I answer her questions or not, I'm—

I'm dead.

Words trembling in the air, I whisper, "They're going to kill me."

Her lips press together, the shock in her eyes hardening into determination. "No, they're not," she promises. "I'll get you out. Okay?" The strange girl's accented words encourage hope, and her intent gaze promises sincerity. I don't know who this foreign stranger is, and I'm desperately hoping she's not an illusion.

The doorknob rattles. She hisses. "It's locked." She glances back and forth down the corridor. "I can't stay here for long. I'll come back. With keys. Here." Her face disappears from view. Then her hand reaches through the grate, and she tosses me two pastries that land on the floor.

Right now, they look like the epitome of high dining.

"I have to go now. I'll be back soon. Everything's going to be okay." She disappears.

Weak but spurred on by my hunger and hope for what's come, I lean and eat the pastries. If someone told me weeks ago I would be reduced to eating off the floor like a dog every time I'm given food, I would have laughed at them. At this point, though, it doesn't matter. Food is food, and I'll take what I can get.

I don't know how long passes, but the grate slides open again. Momentarily, I brighten, but a shudder runs through me, and the hole closes without having revealed anything past it. I swallow.

The illusionist is back.

Chapter 36

SEAN

I wonder what Leavi's doing. She was quiet all the way home. She's been quiet around me for the last week, so that's no shocker. But she hurried straight up to her room, didn't even stop to talk to her new best friend. She seemed impatient. Impassioned. The way she would get when we got handed a new assignment at Trifexer's.

But it doesn't matter. I don't even know why I care.

Actually, I *don't* care. We don't have anything to do with each other, and we don't need to. She gets her company with Jacin, and I don't need company. My papers, my equipment, my study. That's all I need.

Well, that and food, water, and shelter, which I also have. So, I'm good.

Sliding my bag onto my back, I push open the window and sit backwards on the sill. I might not be the most athletic person, but being able to work up on the roof where I don't have to deal with the chatter and clatter of the other house inhabitants is worth the effort.

I pull myself onto the roof, landing flopped over like a fish unceremoniously dropped onto dry land. After squirming onto the roof, I clear away a spot to work, pull my things out of my backpack, and begin.

Sometime later, an incredulous voice calls up from my bedroom. "Are you on the roof?"

I lean over on one elbow, looking over the edge, just in time to see Riveirre's head poke from the window. "Nope," I answer.

She glares. "Why?"

"Because I don't particularly care to deal with lots of avoidable noise while I work. Do you?"

"Hold on." She disappears back into the room. "I'm coming up there."

"Why?" More softly, I say, "I *just* said I liked working in the quiet."

"You know I can hear you," she grumbles, making her way up.

"So?"

She makes an annoyed sound.

Somehow she gets up here much more gracefully than I did and ends up crouching with one knee on the tiles.

"What do you want?" I ask.

She pushes up. Her hair hangs in long, loose waves around her shoulders. She pulls the midnight mess to one side, breath fogging in the air as she sighs. "I need your help."

I raise an eyebrow at her. "Really? And what, exactly, can the great and magnificent Mastera Eleaviara Riveirre not do that she needs *my* help with?"

She scowls. "Carry a man."

A startled "What?" escapes me before I can give a better response.

The snow crunches under her feet as she closes the distance in a few quick steps. Kneeling beside me, she pulls some papers from her pocket and spreads them out in my cleared area. "Look at these."

I glance down. "Incredible," I remark dryly. "It's a map." An incomplete one, at that. It sort of looks like it could be the manor, if the manor went through a major earthquake and lost random chunks of itself.

"Yes, it's a map. But it might have some things that you're not expecting." She points at a section at the left edge. "*This* is the forbidden north wing of the manor." She meets my gaze again, almost as if for dramatic effect.

Unimpressed, I ask, "So?"

"So, a few weeks ago, a maid went in there and never came back out."

"Oh no!" I feign terror. "An awful pit of doom must be concealed there! Or," I add, dropping the act, "she got fired for going somewhere she wasn't supposed to. I don't suppose you actually saw her not return?"

"No, but that's not the point. I thought the same thing you did. Until," once again, she pauses, "I ended up back there."

I drop my head into my hands. "Don't tell me you got fired," I mutter. "Please don't tell me you got fired." I look back up at her scowling face.

"No, you idiot! Do you think I'd come to you for help over a lost job? Look, I actually saw something back there, and if you're not going to take this seriously, I'll go find someone else who will." She starts to gather her papers.

"Aw, does that mean I was your first choice?" I turn back to my presswrite. "Okay, go ahead. Have fun trying to get people in on your conspiracy theory in broken Avadelian."

"Does it sound broken to you?" She's switched to Avadelian, accent still thick but words quick and clear. "Jacin gave me a dictionary. I've been studying."

She's a quick learner—I saw Jacin give her that only a week ago. Admiration rises in me, but I shove it down. Admiring an object that doesn't want your attention doesn't do any good. "Good for you." I turn back to my presswrite.

Frosty silence. Crouched beside me, she's close enough I can feel the faint heat of her presence. She stands. "Lady Veradeaux has a man imprisoned in her manor."

That's a little strange. I didn't know the manor served as the prison, but it's not like I've been *inside* it much. There's probably a lot I don't know about it. "Okay. So? What'd he do?"

She throws her hands wide. "What do you mean 'what did he do?'"

I reply slowly. "I mean that anyone that's been imprisoned by the local government probably has a reason to be." I assumed that was common sense.

"Do they have a reason to be starved to death too?" Her lips press firmly together, a hard, angry line.

"He's dead?"

"No, Sean, would you just-" She breaks off. "Would you just listen to me for once? How in skies' name can someone be imprisoned *and* dead?" She tugs her hair into a bun. Painfully calm, she starts over. "The subject in question shows evidence of extreme malnutrition and neglect."

I know she's serious now—she's brought out the science vocabulary. "And?" She seems frustrated that I'm not getting the point.

"And much more of this, he *will* be dead, Sean."

I pause. "Yeah... That's sad."

She's speechless for a moment, either the cold or anger painting her cheeks red. Finally, she says, "That's sad? That's *sad*? That's it? That's all you have to say?"

"Well, what do you want me to say, Riveirre?"

"That you'll help me!" she demands. "That's why I came up here after all."

"What, you want to go storming the manor, break this stranger out, and then lose your job?"

"No. I want to *sneak* into the manor, help someone who can't help themselves, and do what's right."

I hold up a finger. "You still didn't address the issue of losing your job."

"Look, we have this week's wages. If they suspect us, we move on, get a job somewhere else."

"You think we'll have that opportunity? If they're willing to kill through neglect, and whatever they may-or-may-not have done to that maid, you think we'll *know* they're onto us before they do something?"

"Then we'll leave. We'll just leave. You hate it here anyway."

"Yeah, well, we still need money, Riveirre."

"We *have* money. I just pointed that out."

"Sure. A whopping fourteen copper between the two of us, assuming neither of us has spent anything. What's that going to buy us? A week at an inn?"

"A week's enough to find jobs."

"Oh, and that was a week excluding your animal rescue project."

"It'll have to be enough."

"It doesn't *have* to be anything. Let it go, Riveirre."

"And let this guy die? Sean, you didn't see him. He's our age. He-"

I wave my hand to cut her off. "No, I didn't see him, and I don't want to. Better him alone than all three of us."

Her hands explode into the air. "You've got to be kidding me!"

I stand. "No, Riveirre, I'm not kidding. Besides, they've got him imprisoned for a reason. They must need him for something. Or, maybe he *is* some sort of criminal, like I said earlier, and deserves to be incarcerated. Either way, I doubt they're going to kill him. But if what you think about the maid is true, they will us."

"How can you be so cold?"

"How can you be so illogical?" She's going to get us killed if she keeps on like this.

"I guess because unlike you, I have a heart." Her deep, brown eyes hold steady with mine, as if waiting to see if I'll change my mind.

Simmering anger rises beneath my skin. I'm not emotionless. I'm just able to think things through before foolishly committing to them.

I glance away, jaw clenched.

She hesitates. Then, shaking her head, she turns to leave.

"Everyone has a heart, Riveirre."

Her steps pause.

"I'd just like to keep mine beating. What crime is there in that? You, on the other hand, are going to get yourself killed."

She whirls around. "Well, I'd rather die doing what I know is right than live with this on my conscience, Sean!"

130

"You mean like you did when you left Karsix?" She draws back, but I continue. "Sneaking out of a city under strict quarantine was the 'right' thing to do? No, and you know it. It was the logical thing. It was the way to survive. But it was not the 'right' thing."

My words hang in the air as hurt ripples through her features. Her voice dissolves into a pained, angry whisper. "How dare you."

"How dare I what, Riveirre? Analyze the situation? Tell the truth? What exactly have I done wrong?"

"You've compared two entirely different events! We couldn't *save* them, Sean. We were *powerless* to do anything but stay there and hope we didn't die. This is so, so different. This time, we have a choice; we have a chance. We can save this person. If you'll just help me."

"So then that's what this is about. You want to make up for what you couldn't do before. Save the criminal and atone for leaving behind the city you couldn't, right?"

"No! Sean-"

"Guess what, though. It's people like you—people who try to play the hero—that leave everyone else picking up the pieces. And you know what else?" I take a step closer. "When you get found out, and caught, and murdered, you know who they'll guess to be your accomplice? Me. So sure. Go ahead. Go fruitlessly die. And kill me in the process."

Something shimmers in her eyes. "Wow, Sean," she breathes after a moment. "I always thought you were a jerk, but now I guess you've finally proven it."

"Better a living jerk than a dead hero wannabe."

Suddenly raising her voice, she exclaims, "Maybe that's what's wrong with the world! There are too many people like you surviving and too many people dying because they couldn't get help. Survival of the fittest, huh? Sounds more like survival of the selfish." She turns.

"You're going to get yourself killed," I repeat calmly after she takes a step. "And you're not going to have changed anything."

A pause. Then, a simple, "At least I'll have tried."

She leaves.

I shake my head, exhaling softly. Nothing I say is going to change her mind. I move back to my spot and sit.

The click of my keys and the keen of the wind are the only sounds now.

What is she thinking? She's going to die. Pointlessly. What, does she think that she's just going to waltz—sorry, *sneak*—in there, open the cell, and walk out with him? No, because that's not the way things work! Life isn't a storybook.

"You're not going to be a hero, Leavi," I mutter to myself. "And being a martyr doesn't do anyone any good."

Leavi... you'll be dead. And no one will know what happened but me.

"No," I reprimand myself. I don't call her that, I never have, and I'm not starting now, not when she's about to die.

I'm not supposed to care, *Riveirre*, what happens to you. You're just another arrogant scientist with delusions of grandeur. You don't matter. You're not an equal, you're not important.

You. Are. Nothing.

Nothing to me, nothing to anyone. You're just Mastera Eleaviara Riveirre. You're not a person.

But you'll be dead soon.

My fingers rap sharp on the keys. It doesn't matter. It's not important. I don't have to do anything. I don't need to do anything. Everyone dies at some point.

But if that's true, why does it matter that *I* survive? Because I'm a person. She's just, she's just—just *her*.

So why was I trying to get her not to go? Because it was the logical thing for her not to.

But if she doesn't matter why was I wasting my time on her?

Because—

Because—

"Just because!"

Because she's a person, too.

"No!"

Yes! Not the "haughty Mastera," not "Riveirre," not just my "traveling partner," not "Mushroom Girl," not "Miss Safety Patrolman," "the vitalitist," the "animal-following crazy person," or anything else.

Leavi.

Her name.

She's a person.

I get up quickly, shove my things back into my bag, sling it over my shoulder, and swing into my bedroom. I rush into the hall after her.

Chapter 37
LEAVI

Self-centered. Selfish. Egotistical. Manipulative. I expect all of this. I mean, he is a scientist after all.

But when someone's life is in the balance?

Self-centered. Selfish. Egotistical. Manipulative. I'm these things, too, I suppose. All the intellectuals of the High Valleys are. But we're all still human. There are certain things we all know are wrong, we all know are right, that we would never do, or that we must do. Animals are the only organisms that act solely for self-preservation.

Or that's what I thought. In truth, it seems I've managed to meet the one person in the world that doesn't have any intrinsic humanity to him.

Facts and figures. Risk assessments. That's all that lays inside Sean Rahkifellar's head. He has more in common with a textbook than he does with a person. Somehow I've managed to be surprised. But it doesn't matter. I don't need him. I'm not even sure why I've bothered with him as long as I have.

I find tears blurring my vision, and I blink them away angrily. My feet thud against the wood floor, and I compose myself as I spot Jacin at the bottom of the stairs. Maybe I can convince him to help me.

But then another set of footfalls echoes behind me. "Leavi!" Sean calls. Shocked, I stop walking—he never calls me by my first name.

Jacin glances up and hurries up the steps. I turn back toward Sean, trying to hide my irritation. "What?"

He skids to a stop. "I-"

I raise my eyebrows at him, as if to say, *Well, get on with it.*

Jacin pads down the hallway. "Is everything okay here?" He's looking between us.

Sean practically glares at him. "Can we talk somewhere?" He looks back to me. "More private?" he adds pointedly.

"He can't understand us," I point out. "Whatever you need to say to me, I'm sure we can take care of here." I turn to Jacin. In Avadelian, I assure, "Everything is good. One second." I look back to Sean, prompting him to get this over with.

He taps the side of his leg, obviously frustrated. At length, he says, "Fine."

I stare at him for a moment, expecting him to continue. He doesn't, though, just stands there looking slightly put out. "Well? Go on."

He scowls. "What? What else do you want?"

I tilt my head, considering him perplexedly. Slowly, I respond, "Whatever it was that you came down here to tell me."

"I came to say, 'fine.'" He sounds irritated.

I blink, open my mouth to respond, and then close it, not sure what to even say. Opening it again, I finally settle on, "You came all the way down here just to tell me 'fine'?" My tone is even, but incredulity hides beneath its surface.

He's staring at me. "Yeah. Fine. Whatever. I won't, you know, let you sacrifice yourself alone, especially if your quest'll probably get me killed anyway. So, fine."

Now I'm speechless but for a different reason. Without thinking, I launch myself at him in a hug.

"Ach!" He shoves me away. "What was that?"

My jaw drops, and heat flushes my face, embarrassed. "Nothing," I manage after a moment. "Thanks, then. For your offer, I mean."

Jacin looks between us. He's been watching the interplay, but with only our body language to go off of, he must be lost. "Are you sure you're alright, Leavi?"

I turn back to him. "Yes," I answer in his language. "Thank you. I'll talk with you later?" Right now, I need to start planning with Sean.

"If you're sure…" He hesitates but takes his cue and leaves us alone.

When he's gone, Sean asks, "So what's the plan?

I press my lips together. "Well… come up with a plan."

He closes his eyes, jaw clenched. "Really, Leavi?"

"Look, it's not like I haven't done any work on it. I have a map-"

"A fraction of a map."

"And I've been to his cell. I know what we're dealing with, and understanding the problem is the first step to fixing it, right?"

He shakes his head slowly, eyes still closed. "What are we dealing with, then?"

I walk down the hall, pausing outside my room. "A locked door, a prisoner who probably doesn't have the strength to stand, and a watchful Lady Veradeaux."

He follows me, eyes open. "Guards?"

"Not yet."

I push open my door.

"Skies." Sean momentarily freezes in either shock or revulsion at the appearance of my room. Perhaps both. "Yours is worse than mine."

I spare him a glare as I lay the map out on the floor. He sits, and we begin.

Chapter 38

SEAN

It's my lunch break, and I stand nervously outside a servant's entrance to the manor. I attempt to lean casually on the wall to avoid looking suspicious.

I'm pretty sure I only look more uncomfortable.

Frustrated, I push off the wall and pace. Then I come to a stop and run a hand down my face. Pacing doesn't make me look any more innocent.

Innocent? I haven't done anything wrong.

Yet.

A frustrated noise escapes me. I need to calm down.

The door opens. I jump, giving a startled yelp.

The out-of-breath Leavi peeking from the door shoots me a glare. "What was that?" she hisses.

"Shut up. Do you have it?"

"Yeah." She digs a key from her dress' pocket. "Hurry, though. I still have to take it back, and I almost got caught nicking it."

"That's not my fault!" I take it. "Why do I have to pay for the mistake?"

An exasperated look fills her face. "Just *hurry*."

I nod, steadying my breathing, and walk back toward the stables, key in my pocket.

Pulling a fence gate closed, Master Heizer rumbles, "What're you doin' back so soon?"

Blazes. I need an excuse for coming back early, and quick. I can't afford him forcing me back to work. Leavi still needs this key.

"Um, forgot..." I point vaguely, "something." I know I look guilty but have no idea what to do about it.

He raises an eyebrow at me but thankfully doesn't question it. "Well, get movin'."

I nod once, grateful, and hurry behind the stable. I scoop up a shovel and head for a small pile of horse feces that I left out here. Using the shovel, I move an even smaller amount to a patch of sunlight and flatten it into a thick circle. I toss the shovel aside and kneel.

Cringing, I gently press the key into the muck, trying to keep it as even as possible. The key comes level with the surface of the circle, and I let go. From my pocket, I take a pair of tweezers and extract the key from the mold. A bit of the manure clings to the key, and I wash it off in a nearby water pail.

Now I just have to hope that Heizer doesn't see the mold and destroy it.

I tuck the key into my pocket and hurry back to Leavi. She's anxiously tapping her foot. "Why did that take so long?"

"It didn't. Now go away." I pass her the key. "Get that back where it came from. We'll have to wait for the mold to dry."

She takes a deep breath and nods. "Okay." She goes.

Tense at the situation and yet relieved that my part is done, I quickly eat lunch and walk back to the stables. When work's over, I hurry around back to retrieve the mold. I kneel by it and gently test the edge to see if it's hardened and sturdy enough to survive the trip to the inn.

It doesn't give, and I breathe a sigh of relief.

Carefully, I pick the disk up. If I break it, there's no way I can make another in time for the current plan.

Holding the mold beside my leg in hopes of blocking it from people's view, I head over to where I'll meet Leavi. She's already standing by the gate when I reach it. Rather than say anything, I nod at her and start off. She follows.

Once we've reached the forest, she says, "So have you got the key?"

"I've got the mold for the key."

She stops me. "Why in skies' name didn't you just make it back there? I don't want Marcí noticing-"

"She won't. I'll be in my room. But it takes too long to set to do it there."

She pulls her hair down from its bun, nervously combing out the tangles. "Alright."

When we get to the inn, I go straight to my room and set the disk on the bedside table. Out of my bag come two test tubes and a stir stick. Retrieving a cup of water from the pitcher downstairs and bit of white powder from one of my pockets, I begin the process of mixing together the two parts of what will go into the mold.

I sprinkle some of the powder into the bottom of the mold. The water's thankfully still cold, and I pour a small amount into one of the tubes. Into the other goes a larger amount, and that I hold with one hand over a candle flame. My other hand stirs almost all the rest of the powder into the cold tube. Once the water is boiling, I carefully pour both test tubes' contents into the mold.

When the hot water meets the mixture, they swirl together and congeal, the extra powder at the bottom catalyzing and insulating the process. With all the water inside the mold, I sprinkle the last bit of the powder over it. It fuses together, creating a shell around the gel within.

Now just to wait. Once it sets overnight, we'll have a hard, cloudy-colored key.

I smile. Maybe this won't be so bad.

* * *

Snap!

I freeze and wince. Leavi's head whips around toward me.

She glares, the shadow cast by the manor intensifying her features. "Can you be any louder?"

"I could be yelling."

Her glare darkens. "That's the sixth twig you've stepped on."

"It's only the fifth," I whisper. "And it's the groundskeeper's fault, really. There shouldn't be any twigs for me to step on."

"If there was anyone watching out here," she hisses, "you would have already been caught ten times over!"

"Then it's a good thing there aren't. Do you want my help or not? Let's get going."

I move to push past her, but she grabs my sleeve. "You are not leading." She lets go, shaking her head as she turns. "Step where I step."

Irritation buzzes in my head. When we planned this, she thought I was too incompetent to sneak back to the servant's entrance by myself—even though I made it here fine yesterday—so she left the manor earlier to fetch me from the stables and is leading me along like I'm some kid who can't find the way on his own. She's been weird all day, though. Snappy. Tense. Now, ten minutes before the manor closes for the night, she's keyed-up ten times worse.

My fingers drum against my leg.

We're beside the building now, walking as quietly as possible. The fading light throws the building's shadow out across the ground, grotesquely stretched out.

Leavi disappears into the building, and I slide in behind her. She slips up a stairwell. In the gathering darkness, her form is only visible when she moves. She reaches the top and glances left and right. In the distance, servants' voices echo as they leave for the day.

They're coming closer.

Leavi curses and grabs my wrist, yanking me into the shadowy hallway. She pulls me a few steps toward the far end of the hall. Ducking into a crouch, she tugs me down beside her.

"Wha-"

Her hand flies over my mouth, fingers warm and firm against my skin.

The voices raise as the group turns onto the hall. In the black, stone hallway, my eyes sense their movements more than see them.

"Why do they always keep these hallways so dark?" one girl whines.

"Oh, Kala. Stop being such a baby," another girl says. "Someone's got to lock up these side entrances, and it's worth getting out of cleanup a few minutes early to do it. Come on."

They make their way toward the doorway we just left, passing so close by, I could reach out and grab one of the girl's ankles.

I hold my breath, the speed of my tapping fingers increasing proportionally to my anxiety.

They tip-tap down the stairs. Below, the door bangs closed. The lock clicks.

Leavi's fingers peel away from my face, and my tension leaks away.

"So in all your planning," I whisper, "did you bother considering that we could get locked in here?"

She fishes in her pocket and holds up a metal key. "Snagged this from the changing room. They keep a board of them in there for the girls who lock up." She puts the key back in her pocket.

Silence fills the air, broken only by the occasional closed door and distant footsteps. We wait in the dark, pressed against the wall, minutes turning into hours. The manor falls quiet, but still we wait. We want the place to be nice and dead when we go skulking through its corridors. My fingers tap against my leg.

Hours later, when the silence is so thick it rings in my ears, Leavi rises. We turn a couple of dark halls, but navigating these straight, level passages is easy compared to the High Valleys' tunnels. Then, up ahead, there's a flicker of a torch, and she heads for it, taking us down what looks like a more well-travelled hall. She never hesitates, and I'm pleasantly surprised. She said she knew the path; I'm glad she wasn't mistaken.

She flattens me into a shadow.

"Ow!" I hiss.

"Shut up!"

Voices carry from around the corner. "...can't believe Veradeaux has us down here on night shift," a man complains. "I mean, I've got a bed and a bottle to get to."

My jaw clenches in disgust.

"Maybe if you didn't have quite so many bottles, you wouldn't have to take two shifts," another guy points out.

"Oh, shut it. Already hear enough of that from my wife. I don't need it from you, too-" He breaks off in a curse.

"What's the matter?"

"Forgot my truncheon back home."

"Seriously?"

Intense itching suddenly rises in my throat, and dread spikes through me. I'm going to sneeze. Right now. Fifteen feet from two guards, with nothing but a thin shadow as cover. My hand flies to my nose, and Leavi shoots me a look. I pull in a deep breath, desperately attempting to smother this.

I don't have high hopes.

The second man sighs. I must have missed a bit of their conversation. "Fine. I'll come with you."

A smothered, spittle-filled noise escapes me. Leavi looks like she wants to murder me.

Before they do, that is.

A pause in the footsteps. "Did you hear something?"

Tense silence reigns. Finally, the other says, "Sounds quiet to me. Come on. Let's get there and back before we're any later." The footsteps recede.

To my right, Leavi releases a pent-up breath. She whirls on me. "Are you *trying* to get us killed, Sean?"

"In case you weren't aware," I answer, "sneezing is an involuntary action." I wonder if she gets as vexed with other people as she does with me. If so, that's pretty impressive because right now she looks like she's about to explode. Unable to even manage words, lest she set off the blast, she snatches my wrist and drags me through the hallways. I quietly protest, but she ignores me. We turn off the main hall, and she lets go.

I rub my wrist pointedly, shooting her a look. She rolls her eyes, gesturing to a turn at the end of the hall. "That's it," she whispers. "That's the entrance to the hall they're keeping him on."

"Well, then, why are we just standing here?" I begin to creep that way, pulling out the copied key, and glance around the corner.

Two guards stand in front of a barred door, and I jerk back. Leavi opens her mouth to speak, but I raise an insistent finger to my lips. Please don't say anything, Leavi, and please don't have noticed me, guards.

I wait, heart pounding. Nothing happens. Relieved, I nod and drag Leavi back down the hall. "You said there wouldn't be any guards at his door," I hiss.

"There shouldn't be. There wasn't the day before yesterday." Apprehension suddenly shines in her eyes.

"Well there is now. Two of them."

She blows out a breath, eyes closed. "Lady Veradeaux got her security in place."

"Hold on. You knew this was going to happen?"

"I knew it might, but I was hoping we would get him out before-"

"You didn't bother telling me?"

"Would you have helped me if I had?"

Doubtfully. Her stubborn eyes pin me.

Probably.

"Look," she says, "we're in this far. Let's finish what we came here for."

"How, Riveirre? You expect me to take on two guards with this?" I flip out my pocket knife.

"No. I-" She huffs. "Come on, Sean! We're scientists. Problem-solvers. There's got to be a way to distract them. We just need to think."

"This is a really bad situation, Leavi."

"I'm not just giving up-"

"I didn't say you were giving up! Just—just give me a second." Distraction, a distraction... I pace. How do you get two people that aren't supposed to move to completely leave their post?

A torch pops, catching my attention. My eyes narrow.

"Hey, Riveirre? They have any lye around here?"

"In the cleaning closest. Why?"

"Show me."

"*Why*, Sean?"

A smile slips across my face. "Because I've got an idea."

Chapter 39
LEAVI

I lean through the closet doorway, peering over Sean's shoulder as he mixes lye and water in a wooden bucket.

"Are you planning on scrubbing the guards to death?" I ask.

"No," he clips. "You asked for a distraction. Here it is." He stands, snatching something from the shelves rising around us, then crouches back down to pour it into the bucket.

"What's that?"

"Do you want the explanation or the result, Leavi? Quiet, and let me work." He stands, scanning the shelves, and grabs something else to add to his mix. From his trench coat, he pulls out what looks like a normal timepiece. He clicks it open, revealing not a watch face, but black powder. A pinch goes into the bucket, and he snaps his metal container closed, tucking it back in his pocket.

The mixture bubbles ominously.

Sean jams the bucket's lid down into it, sealing it shut. "Ready to run?"

"What?" I exclaim.

Standing, he grabs my hand and takes off. I let him lead me, and we fly through the corridors.

Only a few hallways away, a booming *crack-THUD* reverberates through the building. The vibration pulses through the floor.

I stare slack-jawed at Sean. "That was you?"

He nods, putting a finger to his lips. "You think you can get us back to your charity case's cell?" he whispers.

Recovering, I dig my half-map out of my pocket, glancing over it. "Yeah. I think so."

"Let's go then. The back way. Hopefully, those guards will be headed here."

We wind through hallways, in and out of darkness and light. Making it back to the hall the boy's cell is on, I edge along the wall. Heart in mouth, I peek around the corner.

Empty.

I wave at Sean, and we hurry to the boy's door. Sean unlocks it while I pull the bar off. The door swings open.

The boy is sitting, leaned weakly against the wall, hair mussed, face gaunt, dirt caked to his skin and clothes. His eyes barely flutter open as we come in.

"You're here," he murmurs, voice slurred as though in a haze.

My heart twists. "Yes," I assure him. "We're here."

My eyes dart around the dark, dirty room he's been held in for skies knows how long now. "Everything's going to be okay." My lips press together. "Come on, Sean. Let's get him out of here."

We pick him up and hurry out of the room, not even bothering to close the door. The limp body between us is even lighter than I expected. His bones press into my arms, making me think more of a corpse than a living boy.

The air smells like smoke. Feet scuff the ground, and our shadows shift wildly on the walls, like ghosts scurrying to chase us. We turn onto the principal hallway, shouts echoing from further in the building. Close to Sean's bomb.

I pull us into an adjacent corridor. I'm not exactly sure where it leads, but I am sure that if we stay in the main way, we're going to get caught. We'll just have to find a different way out.

The boy stirs. His head turns back and forth, as though trying to take in the rushing walls. His breaths come loud and fast. "No," he moans. "No, I-"

"Shut him up," Sean hisses.

From the halls behind us, the shouting increases.

"No one's going to hear him."

The boy twists in our arms, his fevered gaze catching mine for an instant before he goes limp again. *He's delirious.* "Let's get him out of here."

"No! No, no-" He thrashes in our arms, movements surprisingly wild for someone so weak.

"What the blazes is wrong with him?" Sean exclaims.

I pause, struggling to keep from dropping the boy. "Set him down."

"What? We don't have time for this, Leavi! We need to be-"

"Set him down, Sean! We can't carry him like this."

The boy's arm jerks, smacking me in the mouth. I flinch away, and Sean all but drops the boy to the ground.

He calms some. Sucking on my lip, I crouch beside him. The guards' cries still ring in the background, and my heart's beating faster than it should.

"What's wrong?" I inquire gently.

The boy's eyes don't quite see me. "My cloak," he mutters. "My cloak. I need my cloak. I need my…"

"We need to get going, Leavi."

Sean moves to lift him back up, but the boy becomes frenzied again. "My cloak," he groans. "My cloak. My-"

Startlingly clear, a man yells, "Go get help!"

Anxiety is lightning in my blood. I hurriedly wave Sean back and take the boy's face in my hands, forcing him to focus on me. Deliberately, I ask, "Where is it?"

Faint light shines behind the haze in his eyes. "Black door. Black door," he murmurs to himself again.

I stare at him, confused. Most of the doors in the manor are brown. I don't remember ever seeing a black door except when—

"Leavi, come on." Sean grabs my shoulder, but I shrug him off. His voice is tight. "We need to get out of here. Now. If you'd prefer to do it with your head still attached, that is. Let's go."

"Stay here."

"What? Are you trying to get us killed?"

"No. I'm going to go get his cloak."

I steal toward the main hallway, but Sean cuts me off. "The guy's talking out of his head, Leavi!"

"And fighting us like a madman! We're not going to get him out of here like that. Now, *stay here.*" I push around him, heading down the hall.

"'Black door' isn't exactly a foolproof direction!"

I pad the last few steps to the hall's end. "It is to me."

Peeking around the corner, I peer down the long, main hallway. Near the end, smoke billows from the mouth of the cleaning closet's corridor. A guard runs out of another hall and into the smoke, hauling a bucket of water. I glance over my shoulder. "I'll be right back. Just stay quiet and out of sight."

He spreads his hands in outraged bafflement. "We're in the middle of an empty hallway! How do you expect us to stay out of sight?"

"Then just stay quiet." Before he can say anything else, I dart across the hall.

Smoke filters into my nose. I press my muffler to my face and hurry along the corridors, back the way we came.

There it is. The black door. The one I watched, frozen, waiting for its occupants to come out and catch me eavesdropping. The one that was slightly ajar and is now shut tight. I step forward to twist the handle.

Locked. Of course. I cast around for some way to open it, but just as before, the hall is empty.

Wait. "The bar," I mutter. *But that's halls away.*

Far off, a guard calls out. Sean's distraction won't keep them busy forever.

"I'd better hurry, then," I murmur, hastening through the halls.

There, lying discarded, is the iron bar that held the boy's cell closed. Hefting it over my shoulder, I hurry back to the black door, and before I can talk myself out of it, bring the rod down on the handle.

A metallic clang echoes down the hallway. The handle's still solid. In the distance, a fire crackles.

What did you do, Sean?

Adjusting my angle, I try again.

Loud noise, no result. "Come on!" I'm running out of time.

Another swing, and—

This time the ring is accompanied by a satisfying crack. The door swings open.

The room inside is dark, lit only by the torches in the hall. It's a study, bookshelves lining the walls, a small sitting area surrounding a cold fireplace. The back of the room hosts a large, raised worktable, reminiscent of the lab tables in Erreliah.

I hurry toward it.

There. A finely woven but plain black cloak. It's laid flat, items partially pulled out of dozens of pockets. Each item wears a little white tag labeled in tiny, neat handwriting, like someone was cataloging it all. Fingers fumbling, I shove everything back in and scoop the cloth up.

The smoke grows thicker as I run back toward the main hallway. I cough and tie the muffler around my mouth and nose. Holding my breath, I peer around the corner.

My jaw drops.

Fire rages through the main hallway, crawling its way up toward me. Guards scurry through the smoke and flames, shouting orders to each other and throwing

142

buckets of water on the blaze. The water evaporates to steam, fire never quenched. I tear my eyes away, sprinting to cross the hall before the flames reaches me.

I slide to a stop.

There, in the midst of the blaze, stands a figure in midnight robes. The deep hood swallows his face in darkness, but I can *feel* his eyes on me. The flames around don't touch him, clear in a circle as though afraid to draw near.

The Man from the East.

He raises his left arm, and behind him, a section of the fire dies. The right arm raises; a portion of inferno goes cold. He extends his hands out toward me. The flames flare up, licking closer with a dark, hungry intensity.

I turn and run.

When I skid into the hall, Sean's waiting with the boy. He looks up. "Leavi?"

"Pick him up!" I shout.

I throw the cloak over the boy's shoulder and grab his arm. "Let's go!"

Flames leap at the mouth of the hall. Sean glances back, eyes widening, and we get the boy back to his feet, racing for the exit. We twist through corridors, the fire chasing behind like a living beast. Smoke permeates the air. Sweat pours down my face. My lungs burn, eyes stinging. My body begs for me to stop, needing more oxygen than the toxic air gives it, but my brain screams to keep running. We need a way out, but I'm lost, and there's hallway after hallway, no exit, no way—

Recognition ignites in my brain. "This way!" I call to Sean over the fire's roar, ducking into the next hall.

We loop back to the servant's entrance. Stumble down the stairs.

Fire eats at the top of the steps.

I let go of the boy with one hand, desperately jangling the exit's handle.

"They locked it earlier, remember?" Sean shouts. "Where's your blazing key?"

I fumble through my pockets. The inferno burns hotter against my back. I glance over my shoulder. It's halfway down.

My fingers trip over metal, and I dig the key out. Fingers slick and shaking, I try to jam it into the lock.

I lose my grip. The key clatters to the ground.

The fire's so close, so hot, I swear it's melting my skin.

I drop to my knees, and Sean grunts, holding the weight of the boy on his own. Scrabbling across the ground, frantic fingers find the key.

The fire's at the landing, only five feet away. The heat and smoke suffocate me. My sight's a blurry haze.

I shove the key into the lock and try to turn it.

It sticks.

No, no, no, it has to turn, has to—

The roar of the fire is so loud I can hardly hear myself think.

I twist the key in the lock.

It turns.

I scramble to my feet, and we throw the door open, tumbling outside into the freezing night. Blustering snow flurries through the air, swallowing the manor grounds in white. The fire still roars behind us.

We run.

143

We make it to the front of the building, eyes fixed on the gate. We're cutting across the grounds diagonally when, halfway there, a voice behind us calls, "Halt!"

My head snaps back. Two guards—the ones that went back for the truncheon—stand at the entrance to the manor, half-turned toward us. Shock fills out their features.

I curse. Sean shoots off, and I'm tugged forward, almost losing my balance. Narrowly catching my footing, I run with him, and now it's nothing but a mad dash for escape, a race we can't hope to win but must try for anyway. The guards' feet pound behind us.

We make it to the gate, and Sean shoves the boy at me. I stumble back but manage to keep him upright. Sean struggles to lift the thick cross-piece barring the gate.

The guards are less than thirty feet away.

"Sean!"

"I know, I know!" His arms heave up and away from the gate. The bar clatters to the ground.

Together, we push through the gate, the boy dragging in the middle. The guards gain on us steadily as we run. Finding some reserve I didn't know I had left, my legs pump harder and harder, powering through their exhaustion. Somehow, Sean matches me.

We tear down the path, snow blurring our vision. The split's twenty feet ahead, and the last logical piece of my brain realizes that if we skirt the village, the guards will know we're staying at Marcí's.

I make a split-second decision. "This way!" I pull left, off the path and toward the forest. Sean follows. Behind us, the guards' feet slam against the ground, still in pursuit.

We dash for the woods, the boy's deadweight sagging between us. My feet drag through the snow, and I struggle not to trip. My legs burn, my arms numbing with strain, but still we press on. The moon disappears as we break through the treeline. Our feet become our eyes and our ears our catalyst, our only goal to lose the sound of the stomping steps behind us.

At some point, Sean stops, breaths coming heavy and fast. I wheeze, struggling to catch mine as well, and we wait there, straining to hear any noise behind us that might urge us onto deadened feet.

It's quiet. There's no sound but the calls of the night birds and the rustle of wind against dead branches.

Sean and I look at each other. Too terrified, tired, and relieved for a word to pass between us, we turn and head back home.

Chapter 40

SEAN

The boy is in my bed. I understand why it's necessary, but I have the sinking feeling that Leavi's going to continue to expect me to let him stay in here.

He's barely conscious, and Leavi's trying by candlelight to drip chicken broth she nabbed from downstairs past his chapped lips.

Snow flurries outside, the moonlight reflecting off the falling flakes.

"Leavi." I lean against the windowsill, a smile slipping onto my face.

She looks up.

"We're not dead." We made it and got this guy out. Without dying.

She laughs, in that giddy, not-quite-thinking way that she gets when she's tired or excited. "Yeah," she says, breathless. "We did."

"What now?"

A shadow falls over her face. "I'm not sure. I don't know if it's safe to go back."

I somber as well. "Do you think the guards saw us?"

"It was dark... I don't know. They could have. And," she pauses, setting down the bowl, "someone else might have seen me."

I tap. "Who? How?"

"When I was coming back from getting his cloak, he was there, in the hallway. In the fire." Her voice trails off, a spooked look filling her eyes.

"He *who*, Leavi?"

Her eyes refocus. "The Man from the East."

"Okay. Please, I ask, quit with the theatrics." Indignant offense flashes across her face, and I hold up a hand. "I know you're probably not doing it on purpose, but I need you to speak clearly, Leavi."

The anger in her expression hardens into remote, scientific interest. "Alright, Sean. What, precisely, would you like to know?" Her voice is crisp and cold.

A heavy sigh unconsciously forces its way from my lips. I wasn't trying to offend her. "Who is this person, why are they important, and how much influence do they have?"

"A guest of Lady Veradeaux. She listens to him—has to, it seems. I hypothesize that whoever he's working for is paying her to keep him," she gestures to the boy, "locked up."

"Okay. Thank you." I pause. "And why did you sound so scared of him?"

"I'm not scared, Sean." She bustles around, dishes clinking together as she puts up the soup. The boy's drifted back into unconsciousness.

"Now isn't the time for saving face, Leavi. What's up with him?"

She freezes for a moment, back to me. Then she busies herself again. "He's just an intimidating man with the resources to make our lives a lot harder. He, and Lady Veradeaux, are going to come looking for whoever did this. The question's just whether or not he knows it's us."

"Okay…" I can't shake the feeling that she's still hiding something, or at least playing it down, but I don't know what.

"I was wearing my muffler, though." She turns back to face me and pulls the cloth that was dangling around her neck to cover her mouth and nose. "Do you think he'd recognize me from just this?"

I pause. Only her eyes are revealed, deep brown and worriedly waiting.

But I can also see her midnight hair and moonlight skin. I still see the tiny scar just beneath her hairline and the single faint freckle beside her eyebrow. The muffler doesn't disguise her frame, tall and confident. It doesn't hide the girl I've studied long enough to recognize in the darkness of caves and the half-light of lanterns.

"Maybe." I hesitate. "How long was he looking at you? I mean, it might work for a stranger."

She pulls the fabric down, letting it hang around her neck again. "Only a few seconds, I guess. But it-" She cuts off, that troubled look filling her eyes again. Just as quickly, it fades. "Only a few seconds."

"'But it' what? Leavi, what aren't you telling me?"

Her mouth twists. "But it *feels* like he recognized me, Sean. Like he looked at me and *saw* me." She looks away, fiddling with the dishes again.

The people around here have light skin, but darker than Leavi's. They have blue eyes. Blonde, red, or light brown hair.

She looks little like them.

But it was also dark. She was only there for a moment. And just because most people look that way doesn't mean everyone does. There are outliers, just like in any set. Leavi's not the only option.

"I'm sure he wouldn't have had enough time or information to identify you. Fire's a tricky light source—you know that. And other than that, it was dark. And you had your muffler. I'm sure it's fine."

She glances back at me. "You think so?"

"Yeah." Uncertainty lifts my voice a bit.

She turns to face me, frustration and worry etching her expression. "Tell me the *truth*, Sean. Do you think he knows it was me or not?"

I throw my hands into the air. "I don't know, Leavi! *I* know what you look like, even with the muffler on, so I can't judge if others wouldn't. Okay? Besides, we probably have to operate like people know it's us anyway. If you plan for the worst-case scenario, then things hopefully go well, right?"

She closes her eyes, nodding. "Yeah." She looks back up at me. "You're right."

I run a hand over my face, trying to wipe away my anxiety. "Okay. So what now, then?"

"Well, we don't go back to work tomorrow for one. And," she sits down on the edge of the bed, "I guess we move on to another town. Like we said before, we have a little bit of money. We head in… whatever direction Morineaux is. Get work in between?" She looks up at me, as if waiting for my approval.

I nod. "I think that's the best idea. But we don't have food, any knowledge of the geography of this land, or really, anything to be camping out in this environment with."

"We can get directions. Jacin's traveled quite a bit; he might have some tips. And if the next city's not too far, we can buy a tent there." She must notice the reluctance and distaste on my face. "What?"

"I-" I lean on the bedpost. "I don't know. The library in town probably has a map, wouldn't it?"

"You think this place has a library?" she scoffs.

"The guy with the kid would know where the next town is right? That would surely have a map."

"You mean Markus?"

I wave it away. "Whatever."

She rolls her eyes. "Yeah, he might. But I'm still not convinced we're going to find a *library* anywhere near this area. These people are even more backwards than the topside towns." A strange look crosses her face. "I suppose these are topside too, but-"

"I know what you mean. But even if there isn't one, Markus probably knows just as much as Jacin."

"What does that matter, Sean?" She stands. "What do you have against Jacin anyway?"

"He's creepy!"

She throws her hands in the air.

"I don't know what you have *for* him," I say.

"He's been nothing but helpful to us since we got here."

"Maybe to you, but from an outside point of view he's obsessive and possessive."

"Where is this coming from?"

"What do you mean?"

She sits back down, shaking her head. "Look, I don't know what he's done to you, but it's beside the point. We get directions. Who from, I don't care-"

"I do. I don't trust him."

"Okay, Sean. You've made that clear." On the bed, the boy stirs. She turns and checks on him.

After a moment, she says, "When are we planning on leaving? I don't think he'll be ready to travel until at least the day after tomorrow."

"Whoa, whoa, whoa—he's coming *with* us?"

"Well, we're not just going to leave him in the same city he was captured in, are we? That's not much better than having left him in his cell!"

"Yes, it is! He's out of the manor, he's not going to be found, and he'll leave when he can. Besides, we don't know where he's headed. He'll be a drain on our already scarce resources."

"He's helpless, Sean. I'm not just leaving him here." She straightens the covers with one hand.

"I'm not saying we shouldn't make sure that he's okay. But once he can do for himself, I say that he gets lodgings here and provides for himself. I think we've done enough for him."

Her eyes widen. "He can't just lodge here, Sean. He's wanted by the local government."

"Then he can leave on his own and feed himself!"

"With what money?" she exclaims, shooting to her feet.

"That's what I'm asking about ourselves already!"

"We have enough. We have enough to provide for ourselves and at least get him to the next town with us. Okay?"

"No! Not okay. Leavi, we don't know how much our little bit of money can get us. We're walking around with little metal coins in our pockets without any sense of value attached to them. We have no idea if we'll even be able to provide for ourselves, much less your charity case."

"Well, why don't you just worry about providing for yourself, and I'll make sure me and him make it to the next town alright."

I throw my hands into the air. "So just because I don't think we should waste our time and resources on a stranger, you're going to leave me behind for some random person you don't even know? How does that make sense?"

Her frazzled hands shake in the air like she's not sure if she wants to choke me or take me by the shoulders. "Skies, Sean, I'm not planning on leaving you behind! But I'm also not going to leave *him* behind. Why can't you understand that?"

My jaw clenches. "This is irrational, and," I tap against my leg, trying to gather myself, "dangerous, and half-cocked, and—it's just a bad idea, Leavi."

She slumps back onto her seat at the foot of the bed like all the air's gone out of her. "Well, I don't know what else to do, Sean. We can't leave him here. It's not right. That's all I know. It's not right."

"Are all of your decisions based on helping people?" I run a hand through my hair. "Skies." I take a few paces to the side, then turn back to her. "We need to make sure *we're* okay first, Leavi. Don't you see that?"

"We'll make due. We'll figure it out."

I drop my head into my hands. This is useless. Why can't I win arguments with her? "Fine," I murmur into my palm. "But let's actually," I look up, "figure out what we're going to do, rather than stick with some barely thought out idea that we'll decide what to do later."

She looks up, tempered excitement dancing in her eyes. Her words are measured. "We get directions. We hop to the next town, get a tent there. Maybe a job. We figure out our next move from there." She holds my gaze hopefully.

"I meant about somehow also providing for *him*." Sour-faced, I jerk my head toward the bed.

"We'll *make due*, Sean. We'll just have to be careful with our money."

I run a hand through my hair. "Fine. We'll leave as soon as he can travel."

She nods. "Alright. I'll be back in here in the morning." She offers me a tired smile. "Night, Sean."

"Night."

Chapter 41

ASTER

My cloak. I need my cloak. The black door. It's in the black door.
I'm flying, and my arms have weights stuck to them. Moving, flying chains.

* * *

Green and black and white and green and black and white and green green green...

* * *

A room around me. The blazing orange walls roar at me.
"Drink this."
Water trickles down my throat. When my head falls to the side, the liquid puffs from my mouth, and a voice of feathers reprimands, "No, no, no."
A soft hand rights my head, and I drink.
The fire calms, and the orangey-red crawls up my body, strangely liquid in movement and silkier than I had imagined. It doesn't bite or sting. Instead, its caressing flames simply come to rest, holding me.

* * *

Two voices talk, soft, as if trying not to disturb a sleeping child. My heavy eyes lie closed, and I listen for a moment, attempting to decipher what they're saying.

Is that the same girl that spoke to me before?

It suddenly clicks why I can't understand them. They must be talking in whatever tongue the girl had spoken in.

Am I still in the prison?

Light filters through my eyelids. My body rests against something soft, a smooth, heavy comforter atop me.

Doubtfully.

Trying to keep my breathing as even as possible, I slit my eyes open. Glaring orange is the first thing to greet me, and my lids close again. Now knowing what to expect, they peek open. I'm on a flamboyant bed, a large orange quilt over me. Standing across the bright space, the girl from the prison and a boy about my age are quietly talking.

His flat-brown hair is just a little too long, falling slightly into his eyes and ears. Despite the gangliness of his arms and legs, his stance is easy and arrogant. He's wearing some sort of strange leather clothing, chains poking out of pockets throughout, and an ankle-length coat with long, round sleeves rests over it all.

149

I open my eyes the rest of the way and wait for them to notice me. I don't think I'll get any more information about the situation without talking to them. The girl sees me and cuts off the conversation. She moves to the bed. "Hey." Her kind eyes flit over my face. "How do you feel?"

"Where am I?"

She sits on the edge of the bed. "An inn. In Draó," she adds.

A brief chuckle escapes me. "Really? That's specific." I smile at her. *I'm really out.*

She considers. "It's the same town as the manor. We're safe, though," she hurriedly continues. "No one knows you're here."

For now. Surely that can't last long if I'm in an inn.

"Speaking of which," the boy pipes up, "what *are* you doing here? Or more specifically," he takes a step forward, "why were you in that cell?"

"I didn't do anything wrong."

The boy's eyes maintain their suspicious gleam. I wonder why he would assist in my rescue if he thought I was guilty of some crime.

She casts a glare at the boy. "We didn't say you did," she says, turning back to face me. "We're just curious how you ended up there. What did Lady Veradeaux want you for?"

I open my mouth to speak, trying to come up with what to say. Then something occurs to me.

This could be an illusion.

My mouth shuts. This would be such a clever way to get me to give up information.

The girl looks concerned. "Are you okay?"

"Yes, thank you." I don't feel like a walking corpse anymore. If this were an illusion, I would, at the least, still be fuzzy-headed.

Probably.

No, unless the illusionist saw this girl promise to help me, this can't be fake. Besides, they wouldn't create me this strange space—a room splattered in orange—if they wanted me calm and cooperative. Unquestioning.

But I don't think I want to go yelling on the rooftops who I am, either. My identity's already been taken advantage of once.

"Then are you planning on answering anytime soon?" the boy prompts.

The girl shoots him a look, but I nod. "She thought she could get... information. From me. About N'veauvia."

"What's N'veauvia?" the girl asks, curiosity dancing in her eyes.

Mild surprise registers on my face. I thought everyone knew about N'veauvia. "It is the capitol of Morineaux." I trail off, confusion lacing my words.

Her eyes brighten. "You're from Morineaux?"

The boy scowls. "You're off topic, Leavi."

Her name's Leavi. "Yes," I answer her. "I work in the castle." Since I help Agraund and do live in the castle, it's not quite a lie. I'm just not an important part of the corps yet.

"So Veradeaux thought you could give up country secrets or something?" the boy clarifies.

"Something like that, yes."

"What do you mean?" Leavi asks.

"I am not as important as she thinks I am." My lips twitch upward. Also not a lie. She nods.

"Thank you, by the way," I tell her. "For saving me." *For keeping good on your promise.*

Out of the corner of my eye, I see the boy's expression turn annoyed. He likely assumes that I was purposely excluding him. Now, though, if I thank him as well, it'll sound patronizing. Knowing there's nothing I can do, I attempt to push up, but my arms give out. Leavi helps me into a more comfortable position.

I dip my head in thanks. Suddenly, panic shoots through me. "Did you get my cloak?"

"Yes," Leavi assures. Simultaneously, the boy exclaims, "What is with the cloak?"

"It has… important things in it." Considering the Book, powder, and other casting materials essential to me working any kind of magic, I feel that's an understatement. But I shouldn't give away anything more about myself than necessary.

"Here." Leavi slips it off a coat hook and lays it across my lap.

Relief fills me, but worry immediately replaces it. "How long have I been here?"

"Thirty-two hours and seventeen minutes," the boy rattles off. "Which is about thirty hours too long. We need to be leaving soon."

Nerves create jitteriness within me. I've been here too long. I need to get back home. I can't get caught by Amarris again.

There's a knock at the door. "Hello?" a woman calls. "Anyone in here?"

Panic floods across Leavi and the boy's faces. He shoves me down and flicks the blanket up. He slips under it, between me and the door, propped up on one elbow. I pull a pillow down over my face.

The handle turns. "Ah, there you are, Leavi," the woman says. "What is this trouble I heard of from wor—Oh!"

Chapter 42

LEAVI

When about to get caught in the act, there are always many solutions to the problem. Deny it, plead for forgiveness, roll with it… Taking off my shirt never entered my mind. Apparently, however, it's at least in Sean's top ten because that's exactly what he does before Marcí walks in. When she enters, Sean is reclining bare-chested among ruffled blankets and rumpled pillows. A startled exclamation cuts off her flow of words as her wide eyes dart between me and him. Her cheeks speckle scarlet.

My expression is surely similar as I sputter, "Missus Marcí, this-"

Marcí waves her hand, forestalling any explanation. Eyes trained on the ground, she says, "I really, really don't want to know. Really don't. In fact, I so much don't want to know, why don't we just talk about something else entirely? For example, what I came up here to discuss. Miss Leavi, why don't we head downstairs? Mr. Sean can join us in a moment." She nods once and leaves, not allowing us a word.

I turn and glare at Sean, fire blazing in my gaze.

Languidly, he stands. "Well that worked, didn't it?" He's smirking.

I pick up his shirt and pitch it at him, hoping for a satisfying smack. Instead, he ducks, and it knocks over the candlestick on the bedside table. The candlestick clatters to the ground. From the landing, Marcí calls, "Is everything alright in there?"

"Yup," Sean calls back unconcernedly. "Be down in a moment."

"Well, then. Come along, Leavi."

I wait until I can't hear Marcí's steps, then hiss at Sean, "Hide him."

"Where?" he whispers back. "Out the window? He'll be fine as long as he stays quiet and the crazy landlady doesn't come back up here." He turns to the blanket-covered boy. "Stay quiet," he commands in Avadelian, "and don't move." Then he turns back to me. "And *you* need to go before crazy-lady gets suspicious." I press my lips together, giving one last glance to our hidden fugitive.

I go, Sean following a few moments after. Marcí's waiting for us in the dining room. After we enter, she draws the double doors on either side of the room closed. For once, she's unnervingly quiet, looking between the two of us. "Well," she finally says. "Aren't you going to sit? That is what the chairs are for."

Confused, I do. Sean leans against the wall.

A hand comes to rest on Marcí's hip, a frown creasing her lips. "I have been more than generous with the two of you. Letting you come into my house, eat at my table, sleep in my beds. I expect a bit of respect in return. Please," she emphasizes, eyeing Sean, "sit."

He hesitates, then slides into a chair beside me.

She nods, stepping forward. Her hands rest on the back of a chair. "So, I just had two very interesting visitors come to the house. Would you like to guess who they were?"

Above us, a clock ticks in the silence.

"No? I'm surprised! Well, how about I give you a hint? In fact, you might even know them, considering you work together. Or, at least, you used to. They seemed to be under the impression that you'd up and quit, no word, no anything." She raises her brows in a falsely innocent and inquisitive expression. "Do you know why that might have happened? No? Oh, and I haven't even gotten to telling you who they are yet. Silly me."

She moves to sit, leaning forward on the table. "You see, my visitors were two lovely guards from Veradeaux Manor. And I know you two haven't been around here very long, but if you had, you would know this: if the guards of Veradeaux are interested in you, then you've done something wrong. Something very wrong indeed. As in, you might want to think about not living in the area anymore." Her serious eyes, a trait I thought I'd never see in Marcí, regard us. "So what, exactly, have you two done?"

My mouth goes dry. We're had. What idiots were we to bring a wanted man home to a friend of the woman who wants him? Marcí's still watching us, something soft, curious almost, behind the gravity of her gaze.

This is the woman who took in two strays from the rain. The woman who gives treats to a cat who surely can't even mouse. The woman who runs an inn with no paying customers. No matter how close she and Lady Veradeaux may or may not be, she's not going to turn away someone in need.

I hope.

"Missus Marcí." I pause, meeting her level gaze, and realize I'm not going to be able to spin this. If she has the faintest inkling that I might be lying, she'll turn us in. My mind flashes back to the mountainside with the fallen cart and all those condemning fingers pointing my way. We're strangers in a foreign land, and natives don't take strangers' sides.

"I'm waiting, dear."

I can't just tell her the truth; I must tell her the truth and make her believe it's the truth. I take a deep breath and dive in. "What we did, we did to help a man."

Sean's head snaps toward me. In Errelian, he hisses, "What the blazes are you doing, Riveirre?"

I cut him off with a gesture, and Marcí's eyes narrow. "What are you two saying?"

You know what step one of getting someone to trust you is, Eleaviara? my mother lectured.

I turn, angling myself toward Marcí and away from Sean. *Open body language,* she told me.

And step two? "He wanted to know what I am doing," I answer.

Honesty. People can smell a lie like a dead fish.

"Leavi!" Sean exclaims.

Step three?

I ignore him. Marcí regards us curiously, and I meet her gaze evenly, hesitant smile at my lips. *Eye contact. Undivided attention. Make them feel important, whether or not they really are.*

Marcí settles back in her chair.

Because when they feel important, they feel in control. When they feel in control, they relax. And when they're relaxed, they're ready to listen to you.

"Go on, dear," she says. "What did you do at the manor to get the Veradeaux guards after you?"

Step four? I pause. *Slow speech. Liars are nervous, frivolous fast-talkers. But a slow pace adds weight to your words. People will listen when they think you know what you're talking about.* "We helped a man. A man Lady Veradeaux had..." I mime turning a key as I try to think of the right word, "locked in her manor."

"Lady Veradeaux had someone imprisoned?"

I nod.

Her lips twist. "There haven't been any trials lately, though."

I wait, letting her come to her own conclusions.

She shakes her head, suddenly demanding. "How is this possible?"

"I don't know, Missus Marcí," I answer calmly. "All I know is the boy was locked in a room without food, or light, or a blanket."

Shock filters across her features. "Veradeaux wouldn't... Surely. She can be a cold woman, for certain, to servants and the such, but-" She shakes her head again. "No. There's something else going on here. If Veradeaux was holding someone, there had to be a reason." Marcí rises. "You brought him here, I presume?"

I'm losing her. *And the last, most important step?* my mother finished.

"Missus Marcí, please."

The innkeeper pauses.

Passion. Be so passionate they don't just hear it in your voice, they see it in your eyes, in the tilt of your body. Be passionate enough they can't deny that you, *at least, believe what you say. Be passionate enough that they want to believe it too.*

"He needs help. He's been..." Words in my language tumble around in my head faster than they can come out of my mouth in a tongue that she can understand. I almost turn to Sean to have him translate but stop myself.

Open body language. Honesty. Eye contact. *Slow* speech.

Passion.

"The people at that manor have put him through worse than I-" I swallow, thinking of all the fear, the hunger, the bone-aching exhaustion of my journey here, yet honestly say, "Worse than I can even dream about. Locked in a dark room. Hungry. Weak. Helpless."

She breaks eye contact with me.

"I don't think *anyone* deserves that, Missus Marcí. No matter... No matter what they have done."

She wrings her hands, eyes down as if thinking.

"Please don't send him back to that. If-" I pause, weighing the words before committing to them. I forge ahead. "If you think I am bad—wrong," I correct, "for helping him..." I take a deep breath. "Send me to the manor. Send *me* back."

"Are you crazy, Riveirre?" Sean exclaims in Errelian.

I ignore him. "But don't send the boy, and don't send Sean. It was my..." I tap my temple, "idea. Let them leave, and send me."

Marcí's eyes meet mine now, and I feel like she's digging into my soul, weighing my sincerity.

Open body language. Honesty. Eye contact. I have nothing to hide.

Her lips press into a thin, white line. "Fine."

My heart drops into my stomach.

154

"There's no way I'm going to let you send her off to that madhouse!" Sean protests.

Marcí waves her hand, cutting him off. "No one's getting sent back to the manor. That's not what I meant at all. Goodness." She shakes her head exasperatedly. "Take me to him."

Relief floods through me. Grateful, I nod and start off, but Sean says, "What about the guards?"

She waves that away too. "I sent them away a long time ago. Told them you skipped town. Now, the boy?"

I push out of the dining room and lead Marcí upstairs. We open the door. On the bed, the boy's remarkably still. It looks more like an unkempt bed than a hiding place.

"Where is he?" Marcí asks.

Sean nudges past us and flicks the blankets down, disturbing the pillows and exposing the boy's face.

Marcí's eyes widen. "Oh my."

The boy's gaze flicks over all of us distrustfully. "What's going on?"

I step forward. I wonder what this must all seem like to him—in a cell, delusional from hunger one day, and then waking up here, lost and knowing no one. "It's okay." I sit at the foot of the bed. "This is Missus Marcí, the innkeeper. She wants to help you."

The suspicion in his eyes softens some, but his gaze is still keen, searching, like a scientist waiting for the final piece of data before reaching their conclusion.

"She turned away the guards looking for you," I add.

The room is quiet as he considers. After a moment, Marcí says, "Leavi, dear, you only got through half of your introduction. What's *his* name?"

I look at the boy to answer.

He sticks out a trembling hand. "Aster. Pleased to meet you, *Maedame* Marcí." A frustrated look blinks onto his face, but it disappears just as quickly.

"Maedame?" Marcí shakes his hand, blushing. "So very proper. I take it you're from Morineaux?"

He gives a single, curt nod as he lets go. "Yes, maedame."

A somber look passes over Marcí's expression. "I just can't fathom why Veradeaux—you're a young Morineause man, one of her own people. I just, I can't fathom it. The things Leavi told me-" She shakes her head, then stares Aster straight in the eyes. "Did she really imprison you? *Starve* you?" She shakes her head again. "Well, look at you; she must have unless you're some poor, homeless vagrant. So it's true."

Aster swallows, a dark look passing through his eyes. "Yes, maedame. It is true."

Marcí shakes out her hands, as if settling her nerves. "Well, then." She clasps them in front of her. "As long as you're in my house, you'll receive *proper* Morineause hospitality, and first on that list is a good meal. I'll be right back, dear."

After Marcí leaves, the atmosphere of the room goes flat. Sean's contemplating some middle distance, and either Aster is quiet by nature or doesn't know what to say. I consider starting some conversation myself, but figure whatever trivial topic I pick, Sean will shoot down with some snarky comment. So we wait.

Thankfully, it's not too long before Marcí returns. A tinkling arises from an overstuffed tray of cups and saucers as she makes her way into the room. "Here you are, dear," she announces, settling the tray in his lap.

"Oh." His eyes widen at the abundance of snacks and drinks. "Thank you, Maedame Marcí," he manages after a moment.

She waves it away. "I wasn't sure what you would want, so I grabbed a little of everything. But I'm sure you could use it. Go ahead, eat up."

He nods, giving her a thin smile, and picks up his fork. Surprisingly, malnourished as he is, he doesn't scarf the food down. Admittedly, there is some speed to his movements, but they are all precise, polite, dainty almost. Marcí, much out of character, waits to speak until he's finished. Folding his napkin, he says, "Thank you again, Maedame Marcí for your hospitality."

"Of course, my dear, of course. Now, if you're all done-"

A crash shatters the soft noises of the room as the tray Aster was setting aside tumbles to the floor. His open hands hover in the air, eyes closed but flickering, like a man dreaming. Everyone stands there, shocked, as tea slowly seeps into the carpet.

Suddenly, his eyes snap back open. He takes in a steadying breath, eyes flicking to the catastrophe of china on the floor.

"Oh. I apologize, maedame. That must be my fault," he says. He moves to lower himself down, as though to clean up the mess, the only one of us seemingly untouched by the oddity of the situation.

But Marcí recovers, waving him back into bed. "Stop that. You're worried about my dishes, meanwhile you nearly gave me a heart attack with all of that, you dropping things and going still and scaring the wits out of the rest of us. What *was* that anyway? Do you have some sort of infirmity? Here, back in bed now-"

"Infirmity?" Confusion crinkles his eyebrows. "Not that I was aware of. Other than what," he pauses, a sour look twisting his lips, "the Lady Veradeaux did."

"Well, you certainly must have developed one, then, unless you habitually go around throwing people's breakables into the floor."

"No, maedame…" Suddenly, the confusion clears his face. "You mean the, ahm, the vision." He bites the side of his lip in a bothered sort of way. "Maedame, I advise that you avoid your porch for the winter."

"My porch, dear?" she repeats, as though trying to make sure she heard correctly.

He nods, offering no further explanation.

Marcí seems at a loss. "But I have to use that to leave my house."

"I'm not sure what to tell you, maedame."

I cut into their conversation with the question Marcí doesn't seem to know how to ask. "Why?"

Aster glances at me. "What?"

"Why can she not go? On the porch," I add.

"Oh." He seems uncomfortable but continues. "She'll fall."

I look at him askew. "How do you know?"

He hesitates. "My magic. It was a vision, like I said."

Marcí says, "You're a magician? Like you said, that is magic. Seeing the future, I mean."

Aster nods hesitantly, mild discomfort in his eyes.

"Oh, good! Very good! In that case, you *must* do some tricks for us when you are feeling better. It would be such a treat. I've never seen a real magician before." She smiles, chatting with him a second longer before she leaves.

I glance over at Sean and ask in Errelian, "What are they saying? 'Magician'?"

One sardonic brow lifts. "You know. Con-artists in the streets, lifting wallets and dazzling crowds." He waggles his fingers in mockery.

My gaze slides over to the thin boy on the bed, curiously and worriedly trying to follow our conversation. "Him?" He doesn't look like any of the slick charlatans I've ever seen.

Sean shrugs. "That's what he said. Anyway, I'm out. I don't care to get tricked out of what few coins I have. I don't have time for the nonsense anyway. 'Vision,'" he scoffs as he goes, shaking his head.

After a moment, Aster asks, "What was that?"

My attention returns to him. *We were talking about you.* "I asked him to explain a word," I answer instead.

His head tilts. "That was a long conversation for a translation." His voice isn't quite accusatory but instead pointed.

He reminds me of a boy I used to go to academy with. Kind, but quiet. Sat in the back of the class watching everything. Everyone figured he was that solid C student—after all, he never bragged about his grades, and where I went to school, if you're not bragging then you don't have anything to brag about.

At the end of the year, he was on the honor roll list.

I shrug. Neither of us says anything for a second until my curiosity gets the better of me. "Why did Veradeaux want to know things about Morineaux?"

His eyes turn serious, thoughtful. "I don't know. She didn't tell me. But I'm sure it won't be good for Morineaux. They were the kind of questions you ask if you were wanting to attack."

"How did she find you? Morineaux is," I think of the way Jacin talked about the country, "far from here. No?"

"She sent me an invitation to the manor, claiming it was an academy for casters. When I arrived, they grabbed me, took my things, and dragged me to the cell." Bitterness lightly laces his words.

I lean forward, intrigued. "Why would she want to hurt Morineaux?"

He shrugs, looking back up. "She used to be important in the castle. A Lady of the court. I didn't know her that well, but she was known even then for doing whatever it took to get what she wanted."

I shake my head slightly. "I don't understand." I'm missing certain phrases and desperately wishing I wasn't. His words carry a sadness behind them, and I'm lost as to why.

He presses his lips together, then continues his story, perhaps hoping to clarify matters. "She was a liar and a thief, stealing our secrets and selling them to other countries. The queen set a date for her trial, but Veradeaux never showed. She fled the country instead." His gaze has moved away from me onto some point in the past. After a moment, he comes back saying, "This, whatever she's planning for Morineaux, is her *azhiet-friae*." There is bitterness embedded in his words.

I struggle to repeat the strange word, confused.

"Oh." He smiles at me. "Sorry. I suppose that's not Avadelian, is it?" Slightly slower, he repeats, "*Azhiet-friae*. Her, ahm... actually I am not sure how to say it in this language. It is like when someone does something to you, so you do it back, but worse." He shakes his head ruefully. "I am afraid that is not a very good explanation."

"No, no," I assure. "I think I understand." *Revenge*.

His smiles widens. "Good. I'm not completely useless then."

I chuckle, the atmosphere lightening. "So what are you going to do now? Go back to Morineaux?"

"Yes." He murmurs the country's name back to himself, as if thinking of a dear friend far away. His attention returns to me. "Yes, I will go back to Morineaux, as soon as I can make the trip." His lips purse slightly as he considers something. He rummages through his cloak pockets for a minute. Dropping the fabric back in his lap, he runs a hand through his hair. "Of course Amarris would take the money." He shakes his head, dismissing the matter. "It will be fine. At least she left the important things."

"It looked like she was..." *analyzing, inspecting, examining*. Everything was pulled out only partially and carefully. It seemed precise, scientific almost. But I can't think of the words to convey this to him.

He leans forward. "Like she was what?"

I wave it away.

He falls back, disappointed. "Oh."

We sit there awkwardly for a moment until I stand. "It was nice meeting you." I offer him my hand. "Outside of the manor, I mean." I smile.

He returns a sincere smile. "It is nice to *be* outside of the manor. Thank you. Again."

We shake, and I move to leave. Pausing in the doorway, I say, "I'm across the hall. If you need something."

His expression exudes the gentle warmth of a living room hearth. "In that case, I should see you soon. Hopefully," he adds, as if trying not to be presumptuous.

"Hopefully," I repeat, teasing, as I back out of the room. It's not until I close the door that I realize, technically, this is Sean's room.

Oh, well. Sean can move.

Chapter 43

ASTER

Between yesterday's meals and last night's sleep, I feel like an entirely different person than the one that was wasting away in that cell. Beside me at the island sits Leavi, eating one of the muffins Marcí made for breakfast today. On her other side, Sean taps on a strange contraption.

I don't know how to get them to agree to let me cast the anti-scrying spell on them. Yesterday, I tried to explain why it's necessary, but they wouldn't believe me. They don't seem to think magic's real. They don't realize how easily Amarris can find us by scrying.

I can't let her find me again. She'll kill me, she'll kill them, and then she'll wreak whatever havoc she likes on Morineaux. My beautiful country won't have any warning.

I steal another glance at the both of them. Leavi catches my gaze and smiles. A thin smile in return slips onto my face.

I could cast under the table.

It would be harder, but I think I could make it work. Whether they want it or not, they need this spell on them.

I cast.

* * *

"Vîc å rêarre. De viêt, de vaö, de vis."

The setting sunlight bounces off the fallen snow and streams through the living room window. As I speak, entranced by the spell, I slip my casting knife, a blade no bigger than my finger, across my thumb. Then, reaching in front of me, I slide the digit over the bottom of my overturned blackwood bowl.

The soft and terrifyingly irresistible pull of the magic suddenly releases, and I relax back into my chair. I look up at the young blonde in front of me and smile, wiping away the small amount of blood from my nose. Her eyes are wide.

"Why was your nose bleeding? Are you sick?"

I chuckle. "No, I was just casting. Besides, it was not so bad. There was not much blood."

She still looks doubtful, but before she can say anything, I direct her attention back to the bowl. With a flourish, I pull it up, revealing the now Morineause-blue cube beneath. Zena gasps in pleasure. It used to be red.

"Dad! Look!" She hops up, tugging on his sleeve. "Mister Aster really does do magic!"

Markus casts an evaluating eye on me.

I laugh at her antics. "I suppose you don't see a lot of it around here?"

Markus shakes his head.

159

I guess it makes some sense; the materials are expensive, and I've heard of people getting sick and even dying from using poor quality powder. So I can understand it not being a common practice in such a remote place. Especially this close to Kadran, a country of barbarians that detest magic. But at least Markus and his daughter *believe* in it. Leavi and Sean's total dismissal of the practice still confounds me.

I slip the cube back into my cloak as Markus takes Zena off to bed. From the corner of my eye, I notice Leavi standing nearby, watching me.

She approaches, sitting in front of me on the floor. "How did you do that?"

"Magic," I reply simply. "How else would I have?"

"Science?" she says like it's obvious.

I chuckle. "Theories and predictions? While helpful, I'm not sure I could science the block different colors." I smile good-naturedly.

She seems shocked. "I can think of at least three ways to do it right now."

"Really? Are you a scholar?" Out this far in the middle of nowhere, it's surprising that she would have a good enough education to be.

She laughs. "If, ah," she mimes reading a book, "studying my whole life is being a 'scholar,' then yes."

"Where did you study? Bedeveir?"

"No. Draó." Her words are too quick. She's lying.

"That's impressive. I never knew that there was an area of Draó stable enough to focus on education. Where?"

"North."

Smiling, I press, "You can't really get much more north without hitting Kadran."

"Weren't we talking about something else?" She picks the blackwood bowl up, catching my eyes as she holds it in the air.

Curiosity burns inside me at whatever she's hiding—and a little fear. *Why would she hide where she's from? What does that mean?*

But I know I'm not going to get any more information out of her right now, so I nod. "That's a blackwood bowl. It helps with a lot of spells."

She runs her fingers along the wood, tapping different spots as she inspects it. "How does it really work?"

I ignore the disbelief. "Blackwood has strong magic-affecting properties. A spell cast with blackwood is much easier than a spell cast without."

"It is also conveniently," she holds it up over her eyes, "not clear." Beneath the bowl, a smile twitches up.

My eyebrows draw together. "What does that have to do with anything?" My words are thick with confusion.

She moves the bowl away from her face, teasing smile broadening. "Because you can't see the-" She gestures, looking for the right word.

"Cube?"

She nods. "You can't see the cube during the," she pauses, then says with mild distaste, "spell."

I pause, unsure how to reply. "I'm afraid I don't see what difference it makes." My words trail off.

160

She shrugs, still smiling. "All magic is-" she stops, a frustrated expression flashing over her face before she pulls folded-up papers out of her pocket and flips through them.

She seems to find what she's looking for. "Trickery," she pronounces carefully. She looks back up at me, tucking the papers away.

I cock my head, interested. "What are those?"

"These?" She tugs them back out, and I nod. "My notes," she says, passing them to me. "To study Avadelian."

I glance through them. Neat, tiny handwriting covers the papers' surfaces. The left side lists Avadelian words, and short paragraphs in a foreign, swirling script cover the right.

"This is very detailed. What is this language, though? It's not Morineause or Bedeveirian."

"Errelian." She takes them back.

"The language of your hometown?" I guess.

She nods as she folds them away. "You changed the conversation again."

My eyes widen. "I'm sorry. It was not intentional. Habit, I suppose." I smile.

"You... dodge questions by habit?"

I pause. "It sounds strange when you say it like that."

"It sounds normal when you say it another way?"

"Ahm." I rub the back of my neck. "No, I suppose. But it does when you don't really think about it much."

"Maybe you should think about things more, then." There's mischievous glint in her eyes.

I laugh. "Perhaps. But perhaps you think about things too much."

She tilts her head, giving me a sly look. "Never. You never can. Now, then. Stop dodging." She taps my knee with the blackwood bowl. "How did you do the trick?"

I grin. "No tricks."

She rolls her eyes. "How did you do the 'magic?'"

"I spoke the proper phrases of the Old Tongue and followed the proper ritual, using the proper materials, and all with the proper timing." She laughs at me. "But that one's actually a pretty easy spell."

"Easy trick, you mean," she teases.

"I don't understand why you so distrust magic. I've never met someone that doesn't know about it."

"I know about it. I know that it's not real." I laugh, and she smiles. "In my... hometown, everyone knows that 'magician,' like you say, really means *'vihnzeirre.'* A, ah..." she pauses, thinking. "A trickster. That's what Sean called you yesterday when you told us who you are."

Understanding clears in my eyes. "Like the pickpockets on the streets?"

"A pickpocket is a thief, yes?" I nod, and she continues. "Some are. Others, ah, beg."

"I know what you mean. But," I chuckle, "I promise I am not a thief or a beggar. I work for the Morineause castle."

"That *is* a good story for a thief." She winks.

I narrow my eyes, mirth still lurking on my lips. "Magic is real." An idea sparks in my mind. "Let me prove it."

"Oh?" Interest and confidence lights in her eyes at the challenge. "Sure. Let's see you 'prove it.'"

"Alright then." I pick up the bowl. "I need to fill this with water."

"Let me," she offers.

I pass it to her. "Only about half-way."

She can't ruin the spell, if that is her goal. A smile plays at my lips, imagining the shock she's in for. When she returns with the bowl, I motion for her to sit. "Who do you want me to scry?" Her eyebrows come together, confused, and I simplify. "Give me the name of someone you know."

She seems suspicious, but responds, "Tavion Zahir."

I nod, pulling the Book from my cloak and carefully removing the protective cloth. I lay the pages open across my knee, then grab a pinch of arcanum powder and sprinkle it in two clockwise circles over the water. Muttering, I pull my casting knife back out of my cloak and lightly slide it across my palm. Thick red wells up in the line, and the light glints on the emerging ichor. I close my hand into a fist. Three circles counterclockwise of blood-drops fall into the bowl while my incantation crescendos. With my other hand, I barely dip my thumb into the water and swipe the green-red liquid across her forehead.

She jerks back, but as I breathe the name she gave, she leans forward again, attention rapt on the water in the bowl. In the image, a pale-skinned boy around our age lazes on a metal bench at a crowded table, arm draped around a slender blonde. Resting in their hands, cups of twisted blown-glass hold drinks with frothed tops. The busy movement and smoky lighting of the room reminds me of a tavern, but it's looks more like something from the bedtime stories Jeanna used to tell me than the real world.

Now that the initial casting is over, I feel the tug of the magic more acutely, escalating as the spell continues. Blood trickles down my lip.

When I'm sure she's gotten a good look at Tavion, I dash my fingers through the water, disturbing the surface and ending the spell.

An overly silent pause fills the air. Then, eyebrows drawn together as she puzzles over what just happened, Leavi stands. Distractedly, she mutters, "Nice trick."

Before I'm able to reply, she walks away.

Chapter 44
LEAVI

It's midnight, and my eyes are still wide open.

Him. That was really Tavion. Tavion in all his charming, late nights out, drink in hand, girl on arm glory.

I don't know why I gave that name to Aster. I didn't think I'd really see anything. It should have been harder—impossible—for him to show me someone random like Tavi than someone like my father. A hard knot forms in my stomach. I wonder if Tavi's thought about me since he got me kicked out of my own house.

It didn't look like it.

I turn over for the dozenth time tonight. There had to be some trick to it. That couldn't have really been Tavion; it was just how I imagined him to be. There had to be some sort of chemical in that powder, some hallucinogen. There had to be.

"But it didn't *seem* like a hallucinogen," I mutter frustratedly. I pound my pillow, then, still not comfortable, push up.

A hallucinogen would have taken too long to kick in, and there would have been something to tip me off. A haze around the edges, a confusion to my thoughts, something. But no. His trick had all the clarity of a normal day to it.

Which is what unnerves me. There has to be an explanation. "And I'm going to find it," I mutter.

Mind made up, I throw the covers off and slip on a robe Marcí loaned me. Wrapping it tight, I cross the hall to Sean's old room, Aster's now. The knob turns easily; Sean must still have the key. My fingertips press the door open, and it slides gently on its hinges.

Moonlight filters through the window, giving form to Aster's sleeping silhouette. His cloak hangs on the bedpost, gently brushing the floor. I tiptoe toward it, reaching inside the folds. My fingers trip over something solid, and I pull out his bowl, along with the little, cloth-wrapped book and bag of powder.

Aster sighs in his sleep and shifts to face me.

I freeze.

Outside, a nightbird caws, and I cringe. Aster's breaths stay steady though. I relax. He's still asleep.

I slip down the stairs. *Where to do this?* I consider staying in my room, but the last thing I want is to accidentally wake Aster up. And anywhere downstairs, someone could walk in on the experiment, which won't do either. No. All I need is thirty minutes—just enough time to run a few trials—and then all of Aster's things will be back where he left them. I'll have my answer, and he'll have his materials back, no harm done. As long as no one sees me.

My eyes light on the living room window.

Outside. No one should wander in on me there.

The chill winter air nips at my face as I slip out the door, and I tug the robe tighter. The snow *shffs* off the porch as I swipe my foot. After a circle is cleared, I

163

sit, facing the forest. The tops of the trees sway, almost hypnotically. Pale moonbeams glisten against the snow, making the air shimmer with an otherworldly light.

You're being ridiculous, Leavi. Focus. I place the materials on the ground in front of me.

The nightbird caws again, and my eyes snap up. There he sits on the railing, black feathers puffed up slightly, as though sensing some danger. Apparently, he pushes his doubts away because he settles down on the bar. His head cocks, considering me. "*Kaark!*" Still he stares.

I shiver, returning my attention to my experiment, and unwrap the little black book.

"*Hello…*" The whispered sound echoes in the wind, one voice overlaying another and another and continuing on and on over the sea of treetops.

I drop the book, and there's immediate silence, as though someone slammed a door inside my ears. I glance around, but the only other living soul out here is the nightbird, still sitting, still watching. My mind doesn't know how to believe it, but my senses all understand—it's the book. It came from the book.

"Be rational, Leavi," I scold. "Books don't talk." But neither does anything else out here, and my words sound shaky even to me.

I take a deep breath and pick the object back up.

"*Well, that was rude…*" the voices chorus.

This time I manage to keep my grip. "Who are you?" I whisper, my breath frosting in the air.

It's as if the wind-words all turn and confer with one another. The sounds are muffled, whispered. Then they breath, "*We are the Book…*"

I feel as though I've lost my words. Finally, I manage, "How?"

A light, rustling laugh echoes through the tree branches. They're mocking me. "*We just are.*"

"I'm losing my mind. A book. I'm talking to a book."

"*Are you planning on casting? Or are you just going to sit there and lament your sanity?*"

Desperately trying to clear my head, I shake it, black locks tumbling around my face. "No. I'm planning on performing an experiment." I say this more to myself than to the voices in my head, but they still laugh at me.

"*Then we fear you're in the wrong place.*"

"What is that supposed to mean?"

'*We help with casting, not science.*' They still seem derisive, as if they find my attempts childish.

Somewhere in the back of my mind, it suddenly occurs to me that they're speaking my language, not Avadelian. A growing unease fills my stomach. "This can't be real."

"*Believe what you like. But if you're not planning on casting, could you return the Book to its owner? We don't want it to get lost.*"

"I'm not going to *lose* you!" I protest.

Tinkling laughter.

I pull my hair up, trying to gather my wits. "Just do what you came out here to do, Leavi." I stand, scooping water into Aster's bowl from the barrel Jacin keeps filled on the porch for cooking. I return to my spot and open his powder bag.

"What are you trying to cast?"

"I think he said it was 'scry,'" I answer distractedly. Imaginary or not, the voices don't seem to be going away, so I might as well.

"Scrying," they correct.

This time I ignore them, focusing on sprinkling the powder into the water like he had.

"Here..." Suddenly, the book flips page after page, coming to rest on one crowded with foreign words. My jaw drops. That had to be the wind.

"Say this..."

The first word lights with a golden glow, and I gasp.

The voices sound impatient. *"We're waiting, young lady."*

Experiment, I remind myself. *This is just an experiment.*

My lips struggle to find the right sound of the word, and the voices help.

"Ahresåe..." they breathe.

There is something ancient in the tone of the word, something beyond comprehension yet compelling. Almost unconsciously, I repeat it, and the next word lights up. It passes from my lips quicker than the last, the action almost frightening in its ease. From there, the words are drawn out, not of my will, but from somewhere deep inside me. The voices guide me, reminding me of Aster's movements from before, perfecting my pronunciation, lighting up word after word my tongue can't help but speak.

Pressure builds inside me, rising through my body, urging me, pressing me, pushing me, *forcing* me. It swirls inside like a living force, demanding control, ordering submission.

Panicked, I fight back. It cannot have me. I will not give in, I *cannot* give in, I cannot—

The pressure twists into pain, like water in my lungs, like fire in my soul. I am teetering on a precipice, and the force is a wind raging for me to fall, but I refuse.

The pain redoubles, and a scream tears out of me. I curl inside myself, aware of nothing, nothing but the foreign force and my death-grip on my will.

Suddenly, murmured words in my ear break through my field of isolation. "Let go, Leavi. Let go. Give in to it."

But I can't, I can't fall off the ledge, I can't give in to this force, I can't let it take over me...

Suddenly, the pressure is decreasing. I become aware of someone's hand on my shoulder, and then a splash as they dash the water in the bowl. My face is wet, hot and sticky, and my mouth tastes of salt and iron. Slowly, my head rises from its rest on my knees. Aster is there beside me, a handkerchief pressed to his nose. His eyes dart across my face, and he pulls another out from his cloak.

"Here. You might want this."

Dazed, I take it, but it stays fisted in my hand. "What *was* that, Aster?" My voice trembles in the air, giving away exactly how terrified I am.

His answer is simple. "Magic."

My lips move, but no sound comes out.

"Are you alright?" he asks. It seems he suddenly realizes that his hand is still on my shoulder because he moves it to the ground, a few centimeters from my hand.

I manage to close my mouth. I nod once, then immediately shake my head. "No! I mean, what *was* that?" I demand again.

I'm one crack away from shattering. I'm shivering. Blood still seeps out my nose. Distractedly, I wipe at it with the kerchief.

"I told you. But magic can be dangerous. That's why I don't go around handing out the materials." His eyes hold a pointed look.

"I-" My mind is swirling in circles, a spiraling path to nowhere conquering my mind. I'm finally freed from the loop, asking, "How did you know—I mean, why did you come-" I can't manage a full sentence and end up just making a gesture at the surrounding area.

"You screamed."

My words are numb. "I remember that." More coherently, I ask, "So you came *toward* it?"

He pauses. "I… I wanted to see if I could help."

A short laugh bursts from me, more disbelieving than amused.

He considers me, eyes concerned. He sighs lightly, a small, sad smile playing at his lips. "How about I take you back to your room? We can talk about this in the morning," he offers gently.

My eyes flick up to his. "Oh." My fingers tangle themselves in my necklace. "Sure."

He nods, then pulls himself to his feet, offering a hand to me.

I take it, but my knees buckle beneath me, and I stumble.

"Whoa." Aster catches me, steady arms surrounding my shaking body. My dazed gaze takes in his face. His warm amber eyes have flecks of deeper brown close to the iris.

He stands me up.

I feel like I haven't eaten all day.

"You might be weak for a little while," he says. "You'll feel better after you get some sleep."

I nod, and he helps me back to my room. I collapse into bed, and I'm faintly aware of him pulling the covers over my shoulders.

I fall asleep as soon as I manage to close my eyes.

Chapter 45

ASTER

Leavi's not up yet. I'm worried about her; the Book refuses to tell me what it told her, if anything. I don't understand why she stole my materials, especially as opposed to magic as she is. That was dangerous, and reckless, and poorly thought-out, and—

Leavi seemed more careful and logical than that to me.

I finish my breakfast and move from the otherwise empty island to one of the couches around the fireplace. Zena squeals and skips over to me, her father not in sight.

"Mister Aster, do another trick for me! Please?" she tags on.

I smile at her. I should be practicing harder spells than the little cantrips she seems to enjoy, but I can't resist her excitement. She reminds me of the children I'd meet while sneaking out to the marketplace in N'veauvia. A few kind words, a small spell, and suddenly I've made their day. Easy to please and eager to love, they posed innocent requests that I couldn't help but comply with, just like now.

I finish a spell that throws a small shower of sparks into the air. Just like after every spell, Zena gasps and claps. Then her eyes widen further, looking behind me, and she exclaims, "How did you do that?"

I turn, shocked. In the middle of the room stands a blonde girl about my age. She didn't come down the stairs or through the door; she somehow must have simply appeared. Twisted into her many tiny braids is a collection of feathers, beads, and what looks like small bones. Her dress is made of unremarkable cloth, but strips of dyed leather, horsehair, and stones are knotted into it. Bare feet peek out from under thick leggings. One hand, lighter than my own but darker than Leavi's, is clenched around a pearl, the other holding a knapsack. She's looking around, as if surprised at her surroundings.

I stand, facing her. "You're a kra'kaa." Uneasy around a notoriously unstable kind of caster, I step between her and Zena.

Her gaze lands on me, and she bobs into a curtsy, grin spreading across her face. "Why, yes I am! What gave it away?" She giggles at herself.

Presumably, she knows full well that her eccentric attire declares it, so I ignore the pointless question. "Why are you here?" I demand.

"Didn't you poof her, Mister Aster?" Zena pipes up.

"No. I think she 'poofed' herself." My eyes don't stray from the stranger.

She dips her head in affirmative. "That would be correct! And, as for your question," she hesitates for a split second before continuing, "I just thought it would be an interesting place to be!"

Marcí enters from the kitchen. Seeing the kra'kaa, she starts. "Well, hello. I didn't hear the door."

The girl smiles, her eyes twinkling. They're the same color as Leavi's. "Hello. I'm sorry, but could you tell me where I'm at?"

"The Kuddly Kitten, of course. There *is* a sign outside." She eyes the kra'kaa's clothes. "Do you need something to change into, dear?"

Leavi comes downstairs. "What's going on?

The stranger looks at Leavi and smiles. "Hello." She steps forward to shake Leavi's hand. "I'm Idyne."

Leavi looks at her strangely. "You're limping."

Her eyes widen. "No. I just said I was Idyne. What's your name?"

"Leavi. Let me take a look at your leg." She starts to lead the girl over to the couch, but Idyne protests, stopping her. Only now do I notice the slight hitch in her steps.

"I'm fine. I'm *fine*," she insists, waving Leavi away. "I just need a room for the night, and I'll be on my way tomorrow."

"Tomorrow?" Marcí says. "No one's going anywhere tomorrow. Have you not seen the storm outside? Much too dangerous to travel in."

All eyes turn to the window, where heavy, slushy flakes pour from the sky.

"Everyone's staying warm and cozy right here," Marcí says decidedly.

168

Chapter 46

LEAVI

A simple snowfall has never made me nervous before. But the idea of being stuck here a few more days while Veradeaux and her shady companion are still on the hunt for Aster gives life to a fluttery dread in my stomach. I shove it down, though, and smile at Idyne.

Her gaze is light, body language relaxed, weight shifted onto one leg—an almost natural pose. A smile rests on her lips, one hand at ease on her hips. But looking closer, there's cracks in her easy-going facade. Dirt streaked down her face, dark bags under her eyes, tiny twigs strewn among the beaded braids. She reminds me of some of the Dock girls Tavion and I used to go out with. They'd smile and laugh like they didn't have a care in the world. Then they'd drink themselves into oblivion. There was always something in their eyes. A haunted look, like they were running from a past they couldn't quite escape. And Idyne is a runner if I've ever seen one.

I try to keep my expression light. "See?" I say, gesturing to Marcí. "Like she said, you're stuck here. Might as well get that leg fixed before it gets worse." I wink at her. "My room's up the stairs, first on the right. I'll meet you there."

Not giving her time to argue, I go to get some water and cloths. When I go into the room, she's there, sitting on the edge of the bed.

"You know, I don't know a lot of people that go around bossing strangers in weird clothes."

I laugh, sitting the bowl of water on the bedside table. "I don't know a lot of people who don't want their injuries treated."

"I don't know a lot of people that like admitting they're injured."

"That's fair," I smile. "Here, let me see."

"Are you a doctor?"

"Not exactly, no." I dip the cloth in the water. "But I study…" *Vitaliti* is what I want to say. "People. And animals. It doesn't take much," I tap my temple, "knowing to be able to clean an injury."

She cocks her head at me. "What language do you speak?"

A sly smile slips over my face. "Show me your leg, and I'll tell you."

She tips her head at me in playful irritation. Waving her hand, she says, "Fine." She pulls up the bottom of her leggings, revealing a long, jagged cut.

"That doesn't look too deep," I tell her as pat the skin with the wet cloth.

She hisses, then frowns. "You haven't kept your side of the deal yet."

"Errelian," I answer. "Can you turn your leg slightly?"

She does, then says, "Say something."

My smile gains a mischievous tinge. "*Gihseirre.*"

"Just repeating 'something' in the other language is *not* creative, Leavi."

The cloth drops from my hand. "You… you're speaking my tongue," I say, still in Errelian.

"Mhm! I mean, I assume I am."

My mouth moves in silence as I try to process it. Then a rush of questions tumbles out. "Where did you learn it? Do you know how to get back to the High Valleys? When did you-"

"Whoa, whoa, whoa. High Valleys?" A strange expression crosses her face. "You know, that sounds like an oxymoron."

How is she so calm? "How—how can you speak Errelian and not know about the High Valleys?"

From underneath her collar, she draws out a small, corked glass bottle on a tarnished chain. Something colorful swirls within the bottle, giving off a faint light. It must be some sort of neon solution. "I speak whatever language I heard last."

Another trickster, then, like Aster.

But last night was something far beyond a trick.

My eyes study the neon in the bottle.

"Are you done?" Idyne asks.

"Oh." I look back at her leg. "Not quite." I pick the cloth back up, wetting it again, and finish cleaning the wound.

There's something going on here that I don't understand. But I'm determined, I will figure it out. Just because I can't explain last night doesn't necessarily mean that Idyne isn't some sort of con. It's possible she's from the High Valleys or has learned the language from someone who left. Maybe she's a linguist and uses the magic excuse to pull more interest. Whatever the situation though, there's a logical reason behind it.

There always is.

I finish cleaning her leg and do my best to wrap the wound in clean cloths. After offering her a change of clothes, I encourage her to get some rest, and she grudgingly listens.

I wander downstairs, but not finding who I'm looking for, head to the kitchen. Marcí's dicing potatoes.

"Where's Aster?" I ask her.

"Oh, in his room, I think. Said something about needing to practice something or another. Here, chop these for me, would you?" She hands me the knife.

I oblige her. "What are we making?"

"Right now?" She bustles over to a pot on the stove. "Potato soup. But then we'll be busy cooking refreshments for the party tonight, so don't run off."

Panic spikes in my heart. "Party?" I choke.

"Oh, no, don't worry. It won't be like your party. Town's about in a blizzard; who would want to come dance in that? No, sweet little Zena suggested we have one, just our little group here, for Miss... Idyne was her name, right?"

I nod, and she points at my cutting board. "Leavi, dear, I need those potatoes about half as big and twice as quickly. Show a little urgency." She smiles, working herself, and we stay busy cooking, only stopping briefly for lunch.

Hours later, she lets me off a little before she says the party is going to start so I can get ready.

I press open the door to my bedroom. Idyne is curled up on my bed, little blonde braids splayed across my pillow. I gently shake her awake.

Her eyes snap open. The panic visible there drains into recognition, and she relaxes. "Leavi. How long have I been asleep?"

She's still speaking Errelian. It's strangely comforting and unsettling at the same time. "Most of the day, actually. But I came up here to warn you. Marcí, the innkeeper, wants to throw a party for you. You don't have to go, but-"

"A party?" Idyne exclaims. "Why, I *adore* me a good party! Of course I want to go."

"Your leg-"

She waves it away. "It's not that bad."

"Are you sure?"

"Yeah. It's practically just a scratch. Besides, I'm sure I won't be doing anything too crazy to it." She grins at me. "When's it start? How long do we have to get ready?"

"Ah. An hour, maybe?" I'm not sure what kind of 'getting ready' she expects to do. It's not like either of us have a closet of clothes or a caddy of makeup. All my party dresses are in a rotting trash heap somewhere in Erreliah. My mother threw them there after she found out that respectable, high class Eleaviara Riveirre was associating with *Dock* girls rather than studying.

"Great, that should be plenty of time." She grabs her knapsack and pulls out two simple cotton dresses, one grey and one tan. She hums. "Tan's going to wash you out. Here," she tosses the grey dress at me. "Try that on."

I catch it. "There's no reason to dress up," I tell her. "It's just the boarders."

"There is *always* a reason to dress up." She slips hers on. Her gaze flicks up and left. "No, I don't know why she's not dressed yet. Shush." She looks back to me, smiling. "Go on."

Trying to hide my askance look, I change, pulling the dress over my head. The cotton's not as high quality as I'm used to, but the fabric is still soft on my skin, well taken care of. The sleeves flare out, loose, and the skirt bells as it hits my waist. However, what fits Idyne mid-shin only comes down to my knees.

Idyne looks me up and down.

"You know, it's a little short, but I think you pull it off." She claps. "Now, hair and makeup."

Ushering me onto the bed, she starts a flurry of beautifying preparations, shushing me any time I try to speak. She keeps up a steady dialogue with herself, though. Her conversation bounces here and there, high and low, and then to some non-consecutive point in the middle. On top of that, it seems she's alternating with no discernible pattern between doing my makeup and her hair and her makeup and my hair. There's something strangely comforting about the busyness of it, though. Even in a room with just the two of us, it makes me think of large crowds, bright lights, and a night of excitement. Finally, she makes her last sweep of makeup and places her last pin.

"Ready to go? Let's have some fun." She shoots me a mischievous grin, then, before I can answer, saunters out the door. I shake my head, smiling, and follow.

Music fills the living room as Markus plays the strange stringed instrument I heard at the last party. The cat threads through the boarders' feet. In the center of the room, Aster twirls Zena, and she laughs.

171

"They started without us?" Idyne exclaims. She grabs my hand and pulls me to the middle of the floor. We dance, and there is nothing but the music, the movements, and her infectious smile. Eventually, though, we both tire and move to lean against the wall, laughing. Now we watch as everyone else moves to the beat of the music.

"Thank you, Idyne," I breathe, still catching my breath.

"You're welcome!" she enthuses. Then her head tilts, regarding me. "What's it like here? You know," she laughs, "when you're *not* having parties."

I shrug. "Quiet mostly. I haven't been here long, though, so maybe I'm not the best to ask. We're planning to head for Morineaux as soon as the snow clears."

"We?" she echoes, wiggling her brows.

I roll my eyes. "Sean and I."

"Ooh. Which one is he?"

I look at her sideways. "You're being weird. It's not like that. Anyway, he's the gangly one sitting in the corner."

Her gaze follows my vague gesture. She tilts her head. "He's not that bad."

"Wouldn't bother, Idyne. He wouldn't know how to have a normal, friendly conversation if he read a library on the subject."

She giggles. "Sounds like a challenge! I like it."

"Don't say I didn't warn you," I shrug. "I doubt you'll get past the introductions. If he wasn't the only one who could speak Errelian, even I wouldn't talk to him." The lie pops out of my mouth too easily.

"What about him?" She nods her head at Jacin on the other side of the room, sipping out of one of Marcí's cups. His eyes meet mine, and I look away.

"He's trouble." My own words almost surprise me coming out, but immediately settle true inside my mind. Yet I can't put my finger on why.

"Really?" Idyne says. "He doesn't look like it to me."

"Don't get me wrong, he's nice. Really nice." Nothing but nice.

"How nice? He's looking this way right now."

I hit her. "Stop that. Like I said, he's trouble." Then it hits me. "He's nice, but put-on. A," out of the corner of my eye, I can still see him watching me, "a rake, and I'd bet my last coin on it."

Something about him—he's charming, but almost too charming. He reminds me too much of Tavion, and I know better than to make a mistake twice. "We're just friends, and I'd suggest you stay that way as well. Besides," I tap her arm, "why are you looking at boys anyway? You're leaving too as soon as the snow clears, aren't you?"

"Well, yes. But it's a party. What are parties for if not dancing and discussing gentlemen?" She winks.

I shake my head, turning to watch the two pair of dancers. Bukki and Marcí sway to the music alongside Zena and Aster. The little girl is standing on his feet now, and he carries her through the dance. She giggles. He dances straight-backed, arms and head held high—as high as a four-foot partner allows. The candlelight shimmers gold in his short, blond hair. Mirth shines in his eyes, broad smile adding gentleness to his sharp, high-boned features. He looks like some noble fey from my storybooks.

"Who are you gazing at so dreamy-eyed?" Idyne asks.

172

"I was not 'gazing dreamy-eyed' at anyone," I protest.

"Mhm. Sure."

I roll my eyes. "Unlike you it seems, I'm not looking for anything—or any*one*."

"Okay." She grins at me. "Well, I have higher hopes for my social life, so…" She pushes off the wall, heading toward the corner where Sean's sitting. Halfway there, she glances back over her shoulder and twiddles her fingers at me.

My fingers drift to my necklace as a cold anxiety rises in my stomach. For some reason, I suddenly don't want to be here anymore.

The music pauses. In the center of the room, Aster bows to Zena. Her little hand covers her mouth, a blush spreading across her cheeks. As he stands, she runs to her father, chattering excitedly.

"Keep playing, Markus!" Marcí says, and the music starts up again.

Aster walks toward me, offering me his hand. "May I have this dance, *maedimoiselle*?"

I tilt my head and tease, "Was that an insult?"

Startled, he refutes, "Not at all! It means 'miss.'"

I press my lips together. "I don't know. I think you might have said something rude in a," I search for the word, "foreign language."

A knowing glint lights in his eyes. "Ah, yes, you've caught me." He spreads his arms wide. "What can I say?"

"I think an apol—apolo-"

"You have my most sincere apology."

A grin spreads across my face, pleasantly shocked he knew what I was trying to say. "Good."

"You never did say about that dance."

I smooth my dress out. "Are you not tired from dancing with Zena?"

He laughs. "As demanding a partner as she may be, it wouldn't feel right to pass the night by without a dance from the girl that saved my life."

My eyes flick up to his. "I can't say no to that, can I?"

His face lights up, and he sweeps me onto the dance floor.

He's a good leader, confident, poised, and it's easy to follow his steps. His surety seeps into me, and I feel like a princess in a ballroom rather than a poor traveler in a parlor.

"Do you know Idyne from before here?" he asks suddenly.

"No. Why?"

"The two of you just seemed very friendly. I thought you might be acquaintances."

"Not before today, no." He spins me. "She knows my language," I explain as I come back to face him.

A sly smile plays at his lips. "You never did tell me where you were from."

I miss a step, narrowly avoiding stepping on his toes. "No. I didn't, did I?"

Eyes shining, he waits for me to answer.

I open my mouth to change the conversation but pause. What harm could telling him do? After all, he's already told me something I don't believe. What's the worst that could happen? Him think me as strange as I already do him? "I lived in a land called the High Valleys."

Our steps take us only inches away from Bukki and Marcí, but Aster seems unfazed. "I didn't know there were any mountains in Draó." He chuckles. "Especially not any so tall so that even the valleys were high."

My laughter is tinged with nerves. "I'm not from Draó."

His head tilts. "You'd said before…"

"I lied?"

He laughs, head leaned back, eyes closed. "Why?"

Because we're from two entirely different worlds. "It's hard to explain. My home was… different."

"Different how?"

I close my eyes, imagining standing in Erreliah's streets, bustling and brightly lit even at night. The music there would have the scratch of a gramophone and be competing with the steamy whistle of the passing public rail. The scent of perfume, wet rock, street vendors' food, and too many people in one place would press in on us, the awful, wild, exhilarating smell of life——

"Leavi?"

My eyes snap open. "Different… completely." I'm at a loss how else to describe it.

"You miss it." Empathy floods his gaze.

"Is it so obvious?" I ask.

He smiles. "A little. What do you miss? Maybe we can," he casts around for the word, "replicate it."

"Right now?" I glance around the room. "The busyness. Even when we do things here, it feels-" *Empty. Too small. A facade of what real life should be. Going through the motions. Flat.*

"Too quiet somehow? Like there is something, somethings, that's missing?"

My eyes widen. "Exactly! How—how did you-"

He shrugs, somehow still light on his feet. "N'veauvia is much busier than here."

"I hope that is where Sean and I end up, then."

"N'veauvia is beautiful. You should see the castle in the summer."

"I would like to." He spins me again, and I muse, "I wonder where Idyne's headed." Something in his expression hitches. I cock my head at him. "What?"

"I'd just be careful around her."

"Why?"

"Kra'kaas," he pauses, thinking, "aren't exactly known for their stability."

"What do you mean?"

"They're impulsive and unpredictable." He dips me. "And dangerous." Serious eyes hold me in their gaze. He pulls me up.

"Idyne doesn't seem dangerous to me." But hesitation tinges my voice now.

"Kra'kaa magic is powerful. That paired with their erratic decisions can quickly turn situations volatile."

The song ends, and I pause, staring up at him. "But what *is* a kra'kaa?"

"A strong, lone-wolf type caster. Their magic is material based, and they're chronically untrustworthy."

A million questions flash through my mind.

"They offer magical help, but their kind of magic always comes with a price."

Beside me, Bukki coughs, a thick, wracking sound. The cup in his hand slips, clattering to the ground, and his punch drenches the fabric of my dress.

"Miss Leavi," he wheezes, recovering. "I am so, so sorry. I didn't mean to-"

I wave it away. "It's perfectly fine, sir." *With me, at least. I can't speak for Idyne.*

Jacin moves to clean the mess. Marcí sets a hand on Bukki's shoulder. "Are you alright dear?"

"Yes, yes," he assures, pushing the glasses up on his nose. "Just a little coughing spell, nothing more."

"It didn't sound like a little coughing spell…"

Aster looks at me. "Are you okay?"

I nod. "Just wet. Let me go change?"

"Of course."

I smile and head upstairs as Aster goes to help Jacin. Halfway up, the music starts again, and I glance back down.

The mess is cleared, and everyone's happy, continuing the revelry. Aster dances with Marcí, Jacin dances with Zena, and Idyne dances with… Sean. Sean's dancing, steps awkward and stilted, but dancing. He's not even scowling.

Apparently, he doesn't have all that much problem with the activity itself.

Just who asked.

When I change, I don't come back down.

Chapter 47

SEAN

This is the first time I've ever seen her wearing something like that. Something so... simple. Carefree. Easy. It's fitting.

That sounds strange.

The first thing I think of when I think of Leavi is the scientist. The vitalitist. The somewhat arrogant, cocky, sure-of-herself girl that saunters into any situation acting like she knows what's going on. Like she knows what she needs to do. Calm, organized, put-together. Mastera Riveirre.

But I've learned a bit about her too. I've learned that she's not so confident. It's easier than I ever would have imagined to shake her world view. But not necessarily in a bad way.

I suppose it just means that she's not a robot.

Which is a good thing. After all, she's quirky, and she's helpful when you're not injuring her pride. She's kind, funny, witty—at least, when you can get her to actually talk to you. But, like I said, I think that has to do with whether she thinks you're on the offensive. Because she's good to everybody here, except for occasionally an extra-condescending Marcí.

Well, and me. She's made it clear plenty enough times that she has *something* against me.

So maybe I'm wrong. Maybe it doesn't have anything to do with her pride getting injured. Maybe it just matters if she likes you.

It doesn't matter if she doesn't like me, though. We are partners in science. Albeit different branches, but ones that overlap more than I think she realizes. The science is all that matters—whenever she wants to leave the fantastical world that everybody else is living in, she'll come back to her science. And, for some reason, it seems she always comes to the same area I'm working in when she feels the need to do research. And I'm here, with the science. She doesn't need to like me. I don't need her *to* like me. We both just need to not let the illogical people we're around infect us. We need science.

Across the room, Aster twirls her. Her smile and shining eyes right now could light the room on their own.

My eyes study her simple dress, complimenting makeup, pinned back hair. Her free attitude.

Something about it all seems more fitting. I feel like that scientist girl, that cockiness, isn't really her. Instead, it's more who she pretends to be.

It's a mask. Tonight, I think she's letting that mask come down. She's dancing.

Not a part-awkward, part-nervous, *part*-having fun dance like with Jacin. Not a slightly-swaying-to-the-music dance, but an honest-to-goodness *dance*, with her walls down, arms up. She radiates contentment, and somehow, that feels truer. More *real*.

But never around me.

It's fine, obviously. She doesn't need me, like I said, or I her. She doesn't need to come greet me or whatever. That'd be stupid. I suppose I just find it interesting that she doesn't even seem to glance at me.

It doesn't really matter. I'm not sure what I expect would come of it anyway. An awkward 'hello' on both sides, then silence until she walks away, upset with me once more? So it doesn't matter.

But maybe something would come of it.

It won't, though. I'm not the kind of person she would want to spend her carefree, mask-down time with, and I get that. I don't suppose I'm easy to get along with like that.

Except for with Idyne.

She actually seems interested. Actually seems like she wants to pull me out of my presswrite and have a conversation with me, and not in that awkward, 'let's talk because I really just want you to pay attention to me' kind of way, either, that people seem to have. She actually talks to me. For some reason, I let her.

So, when yet another song begins, I also let her pull me into the middle of the room and drag me around.

I don't even hate it.

So maybe it isn't that something's just inherently wrong with me. Maybe it isn't that I'm just an awkward, messed up guy that conversations don't come easily around.

Maybe I was right before, and Leavi just doesn't like me.

And that's fine. We don't need each other. We just need each other to need science.

Chapter 48
ASTER

Sitting in the corner of the living room and practicing the next morning, I watch as Leavi comes down the stairs. I greet her, and as she walks over, I ask, "What happened last night? I never saw you after you went to change."

Unease sparks in her eyes, and she fumbles for an explanation. "I didn't feel much like dancing," she finally answers.

Not wanting to press her, I nod.

"Speaking of things that didn't happen," she says, "we never got a chance to talk about what happened the night-before-last. You said you'd explain."

"I'm sorry. With all the excitement because of Idyne, I suppose I forgot. What would you like to know?"

She sits beside me. "How did any of it happen? How was it possible?"

I look at her helplessly. "I'm not sure what you want me to say, Leavi. I've told you before—it's magic."

"But *how*?"

"'How' what? All of it? That's a bit of a tall order." I give her a small smile, not wanting to sound angry or unwilling to try to answer.

"How does it work?" she bursts.

I run a hand through my hair. "Well, there's a lot of magic theory I could try to explain, but it might take a while. Where do you want me to begin? Then I would be able to do more of a crash-course thing, I figure."

She pauses, eyes wide, as if flummoxed by the infinite number of starting places. "How is it possible?" she stresses.

I drop my hand, thinking. "There are many theories as to how magic is initially able to work. The one I suppose I believe the most is that magic is a fundamental part of how the world works, just like science. But it's different than science, since it operates on certain different rules—I mean, magic has several rules outside of and that go against science."

She pauses, quiet and looking frustrated.

Finally, I ask, "Are you alright?"

She takes a deep breath and nods. "Yes, I am. I just-" She breaks off, and I wait patiently until she eventually continues with, "What were those voices I heard?"

"Ah." I feel my face fall slightly. Not only would telling break the unspoken code of all wizards with a Book, it would completely disregard the instructions of the Voices themselves. "They, ahm. They are just the Voices of the Book."

"That much I figured out myself." She raises her eyebrows. "You promised explanations."

Frustrated, I say, "I'm trying to explain. But that's what they're called. Sometimes it is shortened to the Voices, but that's it. We don't talk about them much."

She presses her lips together, exasperation clearly rising within her. Finally, the dam of her lips break, releasing her vexation as a flood of questions. "So what happened that night? What was that... pressure? Why did it hurt? How did it make my nose bleed? That shouldn't be-"

Outside, Marcí yells for the cat. A noise like sliding snow sounds, followed by a thud and Marcí's cry of alarm.

All eyes turn to the open door. Sean rises and glances outside. "She fell," he announces.

Leavi's eyes flash. Silver. The same color the fire flashes before dying in the hearth.

It's impossible, but I know I saw it—the signs Agraund taught me for a—
But she doesn't even know what magic is! How could she have done that?

I can tell she's upset. Worried, scared; she has the same wild look to her eyes as a doe that suddenly realizes it's cornered. But even a gentle deer's hooves can be hard and fast, striking true when it needs them. When it's spooked.

"Why don't we go somewhere else?" I suggest.

Her eyes dart from the door back to mine. Through them, I can see her mind whirring to rationalize the events. "Where?"

Somewhere away from everyone else. "How about the porch? It'll be more private."

She nods, and I help *Maejuer* Bukki get the maedame of the house to her couch. Leavi brushes past us outside.

When I come out, her arms are wrapped around her to block the cold, and her black hair falls around her shoulders in messy, untouched waves. She hasn't any makeup on and her hair is unstyled, yet her raw appearance is somehow more regal and appealing than the stuffy, 'refined' women of my mother's court. She seems natural, vulnerable almost, as she stares off at the snow-covered trees.

She turns as I come out.

Suddenly unsure of what to do with myself, I cross one foot in front of the other and lean against the wall. "What, ahm, was your question again? Sorry."

She looks down and to the side, lips motionless. There's something lost in her eyes, but searching, like she's been dropped in the middle of an endless maze but refuses to stand still.

I rub the back of my neck. "You must be cold." I nip in and grab a throw. The warmth of the house revitalizes my sense. There's a *reason* I took her outside, and it wasn't to gawk at her like a besotted courtier. Slipping back onto the porch, I hold out the blanket. "Here you go."

She accepts it wordlessly.

"What did you want to ask me?" I prompt again.

Her attention slides back to me. "Oh." Her eyes search the floor as she tries to decide what to say. Finally, as if the desperate flurry of questions earlier left her drained, she says slowly, "How was any of that possible?" She pulls the blanket around her shoulders. "How did you get Tavion's image in the bowl? And—and *how* did you know she would slip?"

My thoughts attempt to twist into something that she might accept, despite never having had to explain it before. Every *child* in Morineaux knows about magic.

179

I bite my lip, turning to my own experiences. To what *I* know of magic. "There's this... deep, raw power within many people. An ability to manipulate the natural world." A ghost feeling of magic's surging sensation sweeps through me at the memory.

But that's not the kind of explanation I can offer Leavi. It's not one she would accept, I know. Pulling on my textbook knowledge, I say, "There are questions about the source of the phenomenon, but many rules are constant—there are things you can't even break in magic. For instance, you can't ever use magic to directly injure somebody. The spell will invariably backfire if you try to. It's almost as if the magic rebukes you for your action."

Confusion clouds her face. "Backfire?"

I nod. *Right. Baby steps.* "When you do a spell incorrectly, it 'backfires.' The spell will terminate, causing physical consequences like," I think, trying to put concrete examples to things I've always known and experienced, "like a bleeding nose, blurred vision, headache... These can happen any time you cast, but the backlash is worse."

The last spell I tried to cast for Agraund slips into mind. "Sometimes, though, it's a good idea to force the spell to backlash, purposefully messing it up, if you realize while casting that the spell is too strong for you." If he hadn't been there, I *would* have needed to make it fail.

"What happens if it's too strong?" Her expression is one of scientific inquiry, her eyes yearning to learn, but her stance is withdrawn, as if she still does not fully believe me. As if she only wants to know what *I* believe.

"If it's strong enough," I say, capturing her unsure gaze with my steady, serious one, "it could kill you."

Her eyes widen, but disbelief clouds them again. "But you just said that backlash is worse than the cost of the spell. So wouldn't the backlash kill you too? You're," she searches for her word, "contradicting yourself."

I shake my head and sit down against the wall. She settles cross-legged in front of me. "Backlash... backlash takes from you differently than casting does. It punishes your body. But casting..." I close my eyes, imagining how drained I feel after mastering a difficult spell, the empty weakness emanating from my very core. "Casting draws from something deep inside you, your energy, your life force almost. If it draws enough from you, you die."

The corners of her mouth turn down, but I keep on. "There are some rare situations in which the spell is so powerful that even the backlash would take your life, but they're few and far between. Plus, it wouldn't be death because of siphoned energy. It would be from blood loss, fever, et cetera, all of which can be counteracted with the help of a good physician."

She pauses, digesting what I've said, and I let her think. Finally, she flattens her hands against the porch. "But you still haven't explained how magic is pos-"

White flashes around me.

An aerial view of a snow-covered roof spreads out below. Sunlight bounces off the white, sending fractals of blinding flashes in every direction. A dark-haired girl stands at the edge of the roof. A cloaked form picks its way through the forest, coming straight toward the house.

The picture changes. I, as if floating in mid-air, now face the girl. She glances back, alarmed. Her foot slips.

She tips forward.

White flashes.

I open my eyes, inhaling deeply as I attempt to regather myself from the vision. As the Second Son in line, I've only had a few of them, and it's still jarring to slip into seeing the future. Normal casters don't have to worry about it at all.

The form of the girl in the vision is almost perfectly replicated in these different surroundings; she's leaned toward me, eyes-wide.

"Are you alright?" she asks.

"Don't go on the roof."

She looks startled. "What?"

"Do you go on the roof very often?"

"Sometimes," she replies slowly, confused.

"Don't. Not until after the thaw."

"Why?"

I look deep into her autumn eyes, flecks of gold and orange swimming in the brown near her pupil. Her dark lashes waver as she waits for my reply, and I take a deep breath, trying to pour as much sincerity into my words as possible.

"Because I saw you fall."

Chapter 49

SEAN

In the kitchen, I wrap the last bit of cloth around the cut in Marcí's hand. Leavi would be better at doing this, but she seems distracted with her delusional friend. Which leaves me to figure out how to clean the gash without any sort of first aid kit.

Marcí thanks me as I step away, then adds, "I should have listened more carefully to that magician's warning, I suppose."

I wave my hand dismissively. "Anyone with a lick of sense could have guessed that, in this weather, you could slip on the snow-covered porch at some point this winter. I don't put too much stock in his 'magic,' and I suggest you don't either."

Marcí frowns, but I turn and walk into the living room. Leavi enters from outside, a troubled expression shrouding her face.

I raise an eyebrow. "What's up?"

She shakes her head, looking at the floor and keeps walking, but then pauses and turns to face me. "Sean?"

"Yeah?" I'm not sure why she felt the need to say my name—did she think I'd stopped paying attention that quickly?

"You're a rational person," she says.

"And?"

Staring off, she taps that necklace of hers, distracted or agitated. Then she walks forward and grabs my wrist. Surprised, I jerk my hand away.

"What was that?" My query comes out much more demanding and angry than I meant it to.

Her lips fall into a shocked circle. "I just-" She doesn't finish the thought. "Come with me." She heads to the dining room, and I follow.

She pulls a chair out to sit down in, pressing her hands against the dining room table, Then, apparently changing her mind, she pushes up to pace.

One, two steps. Turn. One, two, three steps. Turn. One step. Turn.

I lean against the edge of the table and watch her, waiting for her to speak.

She doesn't say anything for several moments, and her erratic steps are putting me on edge. Unable to keep witnessing this perversion of pacing, I grab her shoulders.

"Leavi. What's *wrong*?"

Her eyes widen, and there's something in them that reminds me of the dog my neighbors in Xela had. It was corralled in a too-small cage, unable to do anything about its fate but still able to see an open, comprehensible world beyond.

She takes a shaky breath, then forces out, "Strange things are happening, Sean." The serious tone in her voice lifts the hair on the back of my neck.

Already unsettled as I am, her words make me pause. "What?" I ask.

Something about her expression—a faked strength, concealing something— reminds me of a person who knows that their situation isn't right but doesn't want to admit it.

'It's okay, sugar.' The corner of her bottom lip slipped beneath her top one as she lightly bit it. She was lying.

'Mama...'

'It's all alright. Everything's gonna work out. It always does.' She stroked the back of my head, trying to comfort me. 'It always does,' she repeated softly, more to herself than me.

Three words I never thought I'd hear from Leavi break me out of my memories. "I don't know." She shakes her head. "I really, I just-" She shrugs her shoulders in an unconscious, distressed movement, and my hands slip away.

"I can't help if you can't explain," I say softly.

She closes her eyes. "Have you seen Aster cast?"

"No." For once, I'm not ridiculing her; I'm simply answering her question. Her eyes slide back open. "He... he does impossible things, Sean."

Please don't have fallen for it, Leavi...

"I saw him make a cube change colors, which at first, I just attributed to some sort of chemical reaction or sleight of hand. You know what I'm talking about." Her eyes are eager for confirmation.

I nod.

Affirmed, she continues. "But then he did this thing, just a bowl of water and some green powder, and a book, and some blood-" She's rambling, and she seems to realize it. Shaking her head, she starts again. "He made the water show a picture of someone I knew from Erreliah. It was like a painting, Sean. A moving, perfect painting. A scene played out right in front of my eyes. I've never seen anything like it. And I know what you're going to say, that it was a hallucination, except it *wasn't*. I would have known, I've already gone through it all, and it *couldn't* have been."

"Okay. Okay. Hey. Calm down, alright? I'm sure there's some reasonable explanation." *Everything* has a reasonable explanation. That's why science works. I'm sure there's just something she hasn't thought of yet.

She nods, fingering her necklace. "See that's what I thought too, so I stole his materials. I wanted to see what the trick was. Like an experiment, you know?"

I pause. She's starting to get riled up, and it's worrying me. "On... yourself?" I'm trying really hard not to sound condescending.

"I know that's not proper procedure, but what else was I supposed to do? It's not like I had willing subjects at hand. And, anyway, you're the one who wanted to test unidentified substances with your *tongue*."

"Leavi, no textbook says that performing an on-the-spot experiment on *yourself* is a good idea."

She rakes a hand through her hair. "I needed to know one way or the other. I didn't know any other way to go about it. Besides, that's not the point. The point is what happened when I went through with it."

I sigh, trying not to argue with her. "What, then?"

She pauses now. "He has this book." Her eyes flick up to mine, nervous. "When I held it, I swear to you, Sean, it talked to me."

Involuntarily, my eyebrows shoot up. I manage to reign them back in, and I attempt to say in my least disbelieving voice possible, "It, um. Talked to you?"

"I'm serious, Sean!"

I raise my hands. "Okay. Okay. I wasn't saying you weren't. I just, um, well. What, exactly, did it say?"

She makes a frustrated noise. "You're making fun of me."

"No," I gently assure. I'm walking on eggshells. "No, I'm just trying to understand."

She looks around the room, refusing to meet my eyes, but says, "They helped me cast the spell."

"You cast something?" I can hear the dubiousness in my own voice, but I'm not sure how else to respond.

"Yes! Well, not exactly, because Aster says I didn't let the spell work, but it hurt. It made my nose bleed, Sean," she says, like this is incontrovertible proof of something. "Aster had to come finish it. And there was this weird pressure, like some foreign force was trying to take over my mind."

I'm worried about her. Voices? A foreign force trying to take her over? Magic? Either something is seriously wrong with her, or this Aster guy has done something with her head. I could almost believe that the powder she'd mentioned was some kind of drug.

Calmer now, I say steadily, "Leavi."

Here she looks up at me again, eyes wide, and cuts off her river of words. "What?"

I'm going to hope it's the powder. "Where's the green stuff?"

She seems confused. "With Aster," she says like it's obvious.

I nod. Setting a hand on her shoulder, I say, "Alright. Leavi, can I make a suggestion?"

Her dark eyes watch me.

"Stay away from him. At least when he's 'casting.'" I can't help the tint of doubt that seeps into the last word.

"You don't believe me," she realizes, hurt.

"I… don't disbelieve you. I just want to check all possible avenues."

"No. No, you actually *don't* believe me. You think I'm making it up."

"No," I say definitively.

"Skies, why wouldn't you think I'm making it up? You probably think I'm crazy, don't you?"

"No," I say more forcefully. "I don't think you're crazy. I think that, perhaps, some things have happened whose explanation might not be immediately clear, but I don't think you're crazy. In general, I'm pretty certain you think too clearly to be crazy. But I do agree that something's going on."

She stares at me for a minute. Not sure what conclusion she's going to end up coming to, I preempt the situation. "Can I have a blood sample?"

"What?"

"Can I have a blood sample?" I repeat. "And your hematester. There's a logical explanation to this. I'll find it," I promise.

She seems surprised, and for a moment, I'm not sure she's going to agree. But then she nods. "I'll go get it," she says quietly.

184

Chapter 50

ASTER

The room around me tried to be opulent, I think. Considering all the mismatched oranges and gaudy-but-poorly made decorations, I fear it failed. But at least it tried.

Then again, I'm sure most places even in Morineaux would pale in extravagance to the castle. I suppose, here in the Stelry-forsaken tip of Draó, the establishments are doubly disadvantaged. Done trying to explain magic to Leavi for now, I sit in the corner of the room, cross-legged.

Part of me is glad this isn't the castle. This whole excursion was a waste of time, resources, and energy. It was a complete mistake. I can't even imagine the rebuke I'll be facing from my mother and Agraund. I take out my casting knife and sit it on the floor beside me. It would have been one thing if I had managed to get more schooling, if I had managed to find other ways to improve or accomplish something by all of this, but I have nothing to stand for my absence. And there will be consequences, I know. I put my wood cube a few feet in front of me.

I took a risk, and it won't pay off.

But just because I didn't find what I was looking for here does not mean I cannot still study while I wait for the snow to clear.

That's another thing. I was an idiot for leaving right before winter—to go north.

I need to get better; I need to have something to show for all of this. It's not good enough that I have been re-casting the spell to keep people from scrying us—I need to *improve*, not keep doing what I already can.

The spell Agraund was trying to teach me enters my mind, a spell to keep an item unmovable in space. The holding spell.

A spell you should have learned long ago! he said.

I take out some powder and sprinkle it at the cube, beginning to mutter an incantation. The knife slips deep into the pad of my thumb, and I sling the blood toward the cube.

The pull rises inside me. I can still let go of the spell, end it before I am too far in. *No*, I tell myself. *I need to do this. I need to get better.*

The pull increases, a pressure deep inside me, yearning to escape. It flits across my mind that the spell might be too strong, just like every time before, every time I've tried to cast this with Agraund. But it's too late.

Now—I let go, let the spell take its course, let it take control. No longer making my own movements, I watch my blood-stained thumb smear the liquid red onto my other digits. My arms gesture at the cube, and the incantation crescendos.

Faintly, I feel blood drip from my nose off my lip, and something deep inside me drains. I can't keep this up. I need this spell to end. Soon. But as the pull rises inside me, I know I don't have the strength to complete it.

Again.

I remember what I told Leavi: *Sometimes, it's a good idea to force the spell to backlash.* And Agraund's not here to save me this time.

Come on, come on. I need to muster the strength, the will to take my body back, to control my movements.

I'm numb and distant from myself, though. The magic has filled me, banishing me from my own frame.

I feel like my body is the world outside a well. My consciousness is the water draining down a hole that the magic tore in the bottom, while the sky fades into a pinpoint I can hardly see.

I'm not going to be able to do this. The magic is everything—the magic has me, *is* me, everything I am is the magic.

And I'm numb.

Another flash of resistance darts through my mind. *I die if I don't end this.*

I push at the magic, shove, fight, claw. My fingernails scrape at the stones of my mind's well, grabbing and clutching at the wall, dragging myself up. *I must get out.*

An inkling of feeling twinges in my arm, and I jump on the opportunity.

I make a sharp motion to end the spell, and the power of the magic snaps back into me, away from the almost-spell. As if the magic's force is a physical blow, I fall back into the wall behind me, blood dripping from my nose, eyes closing involuntarily.

My chest aches where the energy sucked away by casting leaves me hollow. My head aches from the backlash. My nose aches from the blood trickling out. At least I'm alive, though.

I want to curl up, sleep this pain off, revive, and not worry about magic for a while. But no. I cannot just give up. I cannot allow myself to become any weaker than I already am.

"If you can't cast properly, the least you can do is not crumple when you fail," I mutter.

I force my leaden arm up with a handkerchief and clean my face. I must continue; I have to try this spell again. Maybe not immediately, maybe I need to build up a little more strength first, but soon. I need to be stronger than this.

For Morineaux.

I take a deep breath, clearing away the black dots dancing around my vision. For Morineaux.

I keep practicing.

Chapter 51
LEAVI

It's always easiest to the think in the quiet dark.

Unfortunately, my current situation doesn't accommodate that. Glasses tinkle, the little chandelier's lights flicker cheerfully, forks scrape their dinner plates, and voices rise and fall in the rhythm of warm, overlapped conversation.

But in my mind—

In my mind, I've gone to an attic and cleared all the clutter to the sides. The shutters are drawn and only skinny slats of the dying sun peek through. The roof is low, the walls close, but in a secret, calming way rather than a claustrophobic one.

In my mind, the voices around are dulled and silenced, and there is nothing before me but a pile of crumpled papers. I pick one up and unfold it, reading the question scrawled therein. *What is magic?*

A subset of science, Sean argues.

Itself, Aster states, confused I even question.

Impossibility, I said. But it's slowly seeming less so.

In my mind, I shake my head and toss the note away, reaching for the next ones. *Why are you here?*

What are you doing?

Who are these people you surround yourself with, these people you listen to, you learn from, you lean on? You are better than this, Leavi. You trust you own wits. You trust your own—

I throw that one away too and reach for the last.

Are you losing it?

No. No, of course I'm not. I'm a scientist. I'm… analytical. I'm smart. I'm methodical. I—

'No textbook says that performing an on-the-spot experiment on yourself is a good idea.'

I push the memory away. I had to do it. It was logical. *I'm* logical. Always—

'How can you be so illogical?' Sean demanded.

No! I know what I'm doing. I've devoted my life to understanding things, understanding the natural world. I—

'I don't know,' I admitted to Sean, *finally breaking down.*

There. Right from my own mouth. I can't ignore that.

But I wasn't thinking straight then. Sure. That's it. I wasn't thinking straight. I am now.

I can figure this out. If Sean thinks he can figure it out, then I can too. I understand science. I understand it at least as well as Sean does. But—

'I mean, magic has several rules outside of and that go against science,' Aster said.

Magic goes against science. Science goes against magic. That means there's only one or the other.

And it has to be science. I know science. Science is in my veins, in my heart, in everything I do. Science makes sense. And magic—

Magic is not so easy to dismiss, though. Things happened, I saw things, I *did* things.

No. Science and magic cannot coexist. If science is real, then magic is not. If magic is not, then nothing Aster has… *seen*, means anything. It's just the mutterings of a mad man. It means nothing.

So nothing will happen.

But if I'm wrong, a quiet voice inside me argues.

Shut up, the rest of me calls.

Everyone is getting up around me, and the scratch of their chairs against the floor drags me out of my attic room and back to reality. I stand up myself, moving to leave. I think I mutter some thanks to Marcí. Her voice buzzes on, and I don't know if she's talking to me or someone else.

I head for the stairs. There's only one way to prove this once and for all.

I push Aster's door open and wade through the sea of orange to throw his window open. The curtains shiver in the evening breeze, and the setting sun paints blood on the fallen snow.

I step onto the window ledge, allowing the wind to toss my hair and bite my skin. The sky is cloudless, and I look out over the dusted forest. Here I stand on the border between worlds—safe and trapped in the confines of the house's ignorance, or reckless and receptive to all the knowledge the open world has to offer me.

I always choose knowledge.

I drag myself onto the roof. Snow crunches under my fingers, setting them to tingling, and I push up, wiping my hands on my shirt.

For a minute, I stay there, frozen as the icy layer I stand upon. Vertigo sweeps over me as the strange notion grips my mind that the ground is pulling me toward it. Irritated with myself, I squeeze my eyes shut and draw in a deep breath. Letting it out, I look around. The roof is flat, nothing is moving, and I'm certainly not falling. My mind was playing tricks on me, paying too much heed to words of a lunatic. I'm completely safe.

"Magic," I scoff, my limbs thawing. I walk across the roof, toward the other half of the forest, a renewed vigor to my steps. A relieved laugh escapes my lips. What an idiot I've been! This proves it, once and for all. There is no such thing as magic, no such talent as seeing the future, no mystical forces playing beyond my reach. Sean was right; everything has to have some sort of rational explanation.

I'm near the edge of the roof now, staring at the ground as though taunting it. *You have no power over me*, I tell it. *You never did.*

A voice behind me calls my name, and I start, head whipping around. My heel slides on the slick snow, and my body topples forward, toward the gaping ground.

I fall.

Chapter 52

SEAN

The clamor that is dinner dies away as people get up to leave their plates in the kitchen. Aster appears surprisingly tired, and Leavi has this far-away look in her eyes as she wanders away from the table, abandoning her plate. As I turn to pick it up and put it with mine, I glimpse Jacin moving to follow her. She doesn't seem to notice.

There's something calculating in his movements, reminding me of a wolf homing in on his prey. Mentally cursing the stupid dishes, I beeline to the kitchen and swish the plates through the water, leaving the cleanish china dripping on the drying towel.

Marcí cocks her head at me. "Sean, those aren't clea-"

I ignore her and hurry after the other two. The creep's about halfway through the living room when I intercept him. "Jakob," I call.

He glances over his shoulder, eyes narrowed. "My name is Jacin."

Heart racing, I affect a casual manner. "Well, you responded to it," I shrug. I open my mouth to continue, but he cuts me off.

"Don't you have some corner to go hole yourself up in?"

I tsk at him, shaking my head. "That was rather aggressive, wasn't it?"

His jaw tightens, but he doesn't answer. Trying to keep him here, I toss out, "Anyway, I was wondering how you came to live here." I'm not sure why that's the question I ask. I honestly don't care. But I do know that I'd rather him be answering it, here with me, than doing whatever else he had planned.

His mouth tightens. "Why?" Obviously impatient, he glances up the stairs, body angled to follow his gaze.

"Just curious," I say, forcing his attention back to me. "You know, just trying to get to know everybody." That came out rather deadpan. I was going for nonchalant.

From the corner of my eye, Aster heads up the stairs, oblivious to Jacin and me.

"I was traveling. I happened upon here. The end." He turns to keep going, but I catch his shoulder.

"That wasn't very specific," I reprimand, attempting to sound playful. I'm pretty sure the tension in the air kills the whole lighthearted thing, though. A stare-off ensues, the real intent behind this conversation thinly veiled. His eyes spark a dark fire, but I hold his gaze, waiting for him to get the point and leave Leavi alone.

Shaking his head, he gives a low snort of frustration, swiping my hand off his shoulder. That strange necklace's chain peeks out from his collar, and he tucks it back underneath. "Mind your own business." With that, he turns to jog up the stairs.

I follow.

Once he reaches the top of the landing, he glances back at me. "What do you want now?" he hisses.

I shrug, leaning casually against the wall. "I have as much right to be anywhere as you do."

He scoffs, an irritated noise, and turns back, beginning to glance in the rooms. He doesn't seem to find what—or who—he's looking for, though, because he finally disappears into his bedroom.

I let out a breath of relief. Then, shaking my head, I tap back down the stairs, picking up my study materials from where I left them earlier and setting up shop in the upstairs hall. I try to work, but someone keeps coughing. Bukki and Marcí are having yet another too-loud conversation I have to tune out, and my thoughts keep circling back to the confrontation on the stairs rather than alkemi.

What have you gotten yourself into, Leavi?

Chapter 53

LEAVI

The air rushes past my ears. My arms windmill as if trying to find traction in the atmosphere. My stomach flops as I drop weightless, hurtling toward the earth.

I scream.

Midfall, I wonder what my dad's doing. He'll never know what happened to me. He'll never know why they couldn't find my body. I hope he doesn't wait for me to come home. I hope he just thinks I'm dead.

I stop moving. But I'm not against the snow.

My breath catches in my throat as I glance around. Heart hammering in my chest, I realize I can't move my head, my arms, my legs. I'm trapped, but I'm breathing. I'm alive. Somehow, I'm still alive.

My gaze flicks everywhere, trying to take everything in. The kitchen window hovers in front of my feet; no, my *feet* hover in front of the kitchen window. I'm suspended, hanging in mid-air, limbs frozen, hair splayed up around my head like I'm still falling.

The world starts moving again, the kitchen window dropping out of sight.

What's happening to me? Steady panic pumps through my mind, pushing out any rational thought. I raise up toward the roof ever so slowly. *Time's rewinding. Time's rewinding, and I died, but now I'm coming back to life, back to the roof, second chances. Time's rewinding.*

My feet meet level with the roof. Aster kneels there at the edge, face contorted and arms outstretched toward me. Sweat rolls down his forehead and blood drips from his nose. He jerks his arms toward him, and I skid onto the roof. He slumps forward. My hair drops around me, suddenly obeying gravity again.

I lay there, snow seeping into my clothes. My mind is frantic, but I'm strangely still. Warm water trails down my face; I'm crying. Somehow, this all feels like it's happening to a different person, like I'm standing a few feet away, watching silent sobs shake through someone else's body.

I almost died, I realize detachedly. *I should have died. But I'm here, safe on this roof.*

"Leavi." Aster's shaking my shoulder. "Leavi, are you okay?"

I look up at him, my face wet with tears and ice crystals. Trails of blood still stain his face.

"Aster, how—how-" I can't even finish the sentence.

"Like I've been telling you, Leavi." His hand shakes as he draws it back. "Magic."

The cold is numbing my brain.

"But we have more problems right now, and I am so sorry, but I am going to have to ask you to do something difficult. Do you trust me?" His words tremble in the air, but his eyes are steady and serious.

"You just saved my life."

"I'm going to take that as a yes. Take this."

He presses the Book into my hands, and a whispering chorus fills my head.

"What? Why? Aster-"

"I'm going to need you to cast a spell."

"You mean-" My mind flashes back the moonlit porch and the force trying to take over my mind. "No! I'm not doing that."

"Leavi, listen to me!" He looks deep into my eyes, bags under his, the intensity of his gaze startling. "I would do it, but in this state, the next spell I cast could very well kill me. Please. I would not ask you to do this if it wasn't important."

Something dark flashes in the corner of my eye, and my head snaps that way. There, just inside the forest, stands a dark-robed nightmare.

"The Man from the East," I murmur.

His robes billow in the wind, the dying sun darkening the forest shadows around him. His hood conceals his face, but I swear he's staring at me. Goosebumps raise on my arms.

"Hello, child." His voice sounds directly in my ear, and I startle. A quiet chuckle echoes from beside me. "I see you didn't learn your lesson last time. I warned you to keep to your own affairs."

"Aster…" I warn, fear and confusion pitching my voice high.

"I know," Aster says. "I see him too. That's why I need you to listen to me. We can stop him; the Book will help you-"

The man keeps talking in my ear. "But I am a forgiving man. Do exactly as I tell you, and you won't die this day. Do you understand me?"

Aster's taken the Book from me and flipped to a certain page. He shoves it back into my hands, along with the powder bag.

"Do you understand me?" the man repeats. "I can see what you're doing, girl. You are in no dimension my equal. Put down that Book. *Now.*"

"Cast, Leavi!" Aster urges. "Focus on that branch right above him; you see it?" My eyes flick to the tree and a branch laden with snow. "Cast on it. The Book will help you."

The first word on the page lights gold.

Five feet to my right, fire ignites, somehow burning despite the snow. "I *will* have my way, child. Put down that Book or face the consequences." The fire leaps toward the sky, and I jerk away.

"Focus, young lady," the Voices of the Book chorus. *"Repeat after us. Exairêt…"*

"Exairêt…" I breathe. The tug of the magic begins, pulling the next word from me.

The fire dances closer, heat radiating off it in waves. "Stop!" the man growls. "Stop or burn."

"Fiärvir…"

"Fiärvir," I repeat, chest shaking.

The fire circles around, hemming me in. Helpless to do anything but follow the Book's instructions, words drip out of my mouth as tears trickle down my face.

"Your puny *magic* cannot save you," the man snarls. "Now I suppose you can choose between death by fire or by fall. The fall would be quicker."

The fire shoots toward me, and I scramble to my feet.

192

"Leavi, no!"

The fire edges closer to us. I turn, wanting to warn Aster, to beg him to get up, to move away from the flames, but my words are not my own.

"Retiræ," the Voices command.

"Retiræ," I choke, tears blurring my vision.

Aster struggles to his feet, and brief relief surges through me before the fire darts forward. I step back.

My foot only hits air.

If I could scream, I would. Instead, the next word of the spell tears from my lips.

Aster's arms slip around my waist. Weak as he is, he stumbles forward with my momentum. Then he yanks me back onto solid ground. The fire roars around us.

"Finish the spell, Leavi!"

"Just focus on your target," the Voices whisper. *"Then let go and say the final word..."*

My target? What target? Dazedly, I remember the branch from earlier. I spin to face it, almost losing my balance again. Aster stands between me and the inferno.

The foreign pressure builds within me, begging—no, *telling*, demanding—me to release it, to let it go, let it have control. My face screws up in fear and concentration. I will *not* let this thing have me. It may have stolen my words, but it will *not* steal my mind.

Suddenly, Aster's voice is in my ear. "It's okay. Everything's okay, Leavi. Just relax."

The fire surges closer, and I startle, but Aster's arms are around me again. "Relax and let go. Let the magic take over. Relax..."

I shake my head, but the pressure's building, tearing at my insides. Aster's calming words buzz in my ear while the magic stabs my heart and needles my skin. "Relax..."

Pain and exhaustion overwhelm me, and I let go. The magic bubbles up and bursts from within me, tearing a final scream from my lips.

"Vinêxte!"

Cracking sounds from across the clearing. The man looks up. We both watch as the branch above him freezes solid in ice. With a noise like thunder, it breaks off from the tree and crashes down. It hits the ground, taking the man with it.

Around us, the fire disappears.

I collapse.

"Leavi?" Aster says worriedly.

The fire's gone. Gone, just like that. Gone, like it never was. The snow doesn't even look affected.

"Leavi?"

My insides are hollow. I feel like I'm shaking even though I'm laying still.

"Leavi." Aster sets his hand on my shoulder, turning me to face him.

"Never again," I say, voice trembling.

He pulls back, confusion clouding his eyes. "What?"

"Never again," I repeat, slowly sitting up. "I'm not doing that. Ever. No matter what." I meet his eyes, driving in my point.

He swallows and nods. "I won't ask you to. Are you alright?"

I feel sick—hungry, empty, shaky. I had a fever of a hundred and four once, when I was really little. This reminds me of that.

"No." I hug my arms around myself. "But I suppose you aren't either."

"I'll be okay." His eyes sweep over my face. "It'll all be okay. You'll get some rest; you'll feel better. I'll go figure out what to do with him." He cocks his head at the fallen branch and stands.

I catch his wrist. "He's dangerous, Aster."

He looks down at me. "I know." He gently disentangles himself. "But I'll be okay." He offers a small but comforting smile.

"Aster?"

He pauses. "Yes?"

My fingers fiddle with my necklace. *He's going to think I'm crazy.* "Where-" I bite my lip. "Where did the fire *go*?"

He glances around. "What fire?"

"The fire that was surrounding us? The one that almost killed us?"

"Leavi, there wasn't any-" Understanding lights in his eyes. He crouches back down. "It was an illusion."

"A what?"

"A… magical trick, to make you see or feel or hear something that isn't real." He considers me. "He was trying to get you to jump, wasn't he?"

"The fire wasn't real?"

Aster shakes his head.

I think back over everything that happened, the fire that wasn't a fire, how I reacted to it, what the man said to me. *The fall would be quicker…*

Anger spikes in my chest. "He tricked me. He was trying to kill me, and he—he couldn't even do anything to me! That lying, manipulative piece of-"

"Leavi." Aster catches my gaze. "I can't understand you."

I suddenly realize I switched to Errelian. My hand tightens into a fist around my necklace. "Oh," I say in Avadelian. Then, "How did you know he wanted me to jump?"

He taps his temple. "He was casting on me too. Just enough so I could hear him talk. Told me if I didn't come down with him, he'd kill you. I put it together when you almost slipped off the edge." He stands again. "I need to go, though. I'll come check on you later."

"You're not going by yourself!" I stand. My limbs feel hollow, but I'm no longer shaking. I'm not sure how much of the sickness was due to magic or shock. Either way, I feel a little steadier now. "Blazes if I'm going to let you face him alone."

I march toward the window to go down. I glance behind me where Aster's watching, a pleasantly surprised expression filling his eyes.

"Well, come on," I say, trying to overcome my numbed mind. "We're in a hurry, aren't we?"

He nods, and we climb down.

Chapter 54

ASTER

That was too close.

I swing on my cloak before leaving the room. Jittery from the man's mind games and the magic, I make my way through the house as nonchalantly as possible. Leavi's close behind.

I can't believe she went to the roof, not even a day after I warned her—actually, no, I can believe it. She's scared. She's confused. I don't fully understand yet why she can't accept magic, but I feel like they didn't have it where she grew up. She's a little reckless, clearly. She stole my materials, she went on the roof. I think it all stems from the same reason.

She doesn't want to believe in magic. But now she has no choice, surely. There's been too much proof, too many instances where the scientifically unexplainable has happened.

In the living room now, I turn the handle of the door. My feet whisper across the porch, and Leavi crunches behind me.

As we turn the corner of the house, she softly says, "What are you going to do with him?"

"The first thing to do when detaining a caster is eliminate their ability—tie them up and take their materials."

"And then what? We can't let him go back to Lady Veradeaux."

"No," I gravely agree. "No, he won't get back to Am—Veradeaux."

She shoots me an alarmed look. "You're not going to-" She doesn't finish the sentence, either too startled to or unsure of the word.

I glance at her. "No." Her almost-accusation stirs unease within me, but I continue. "We'll keep him tied up until I can leave for Morineaux. I'll take him with me."

"So then you're not coming with us? Sean's not going to let someone else come, and," she searches for the word, "certainly not someone dangerous like that man. And I don't... disagree with him."

"He can't do anything if restrained." It's easier and safer to travel in a group, especially on foot. I don't want to go by myself once again, but I will if I have to.

Leavi shivers, a thin blanket she grabbed as we left her only protection from the cold. "I'm more worried about what he can do when he's not restrained."

"He won't be."

Her lips press into a thin line, but she doesn't say anything else. We've made it to the forest.

I gesture for her to stay here. Then I move through the trees, cat-footing behind where the illusionist should be. Tense, I watch for his form beneath the branch. Despite my exhaustion, my heart beats fast as I worry if he's recovered and left already.

There. I steady. He's still unconscious, pinned face-down by the wood. I hesitantly heave the branch off and kneel beside him, pulling twine from my cloak.

"You're going to tie him up with string?"

I glance up at Leavi. "You were supposed to stay back there," I whisper, turning back to my work.

"I can't help if I'm back there." She crouches beside me.

Not needing assistance, I say nothing and pinch the man's fingers together. I wrap the twine around them and do the same with the other hand.

"What's that for?" Leavi asks.

"So he can't cast. No fingers, no spell." I bind his wrists together.

The man moans.

Leavi shoots up, and I speed my work. As I move to his ankles, Leavi goes to stand at his head, a small but thick branch in hand.

"I don't think that's necessary, Leavi." I tie the last knot. "He can't do anything to us now." I start searching his robe for casting materials.

"I'd prefer to be too ready than not ready enough. I'm fine here."

A slight smile slips onto my face, and I turn back to my search. It's strange that he's in a robe rather than a cloak. I've never seen a wizard wear a garment like this. It doesn't even have enough pockets in it to hold half the materials a decent magician would want on their person.

Confused, I stare at the man. My search turned up empty. He doesn't have any materials, yet casts like an experienced magician.

My mind flips through the books and lessons I've taken in.

The Man from the East, Leavi called him.

My eyes widen in shock and disturbance. *He's a shaman.* A Kadranian wielder of dark power, unbound by materials and phrases, and self-proclaimed 'anti-magicians.' No one in Morineaux knows where they get their ability from, all only theorizing with myths and legends—they sell their sanity for skill, they kill people to absorb their power, or they draw on the souls of the dead.

"What's wrong?" Leavi asks, tightening her grip on the branch.

I look up, pausing for a moment too long. I attempt to sound unconcerned. "Nothing. I just realized what kind of caster he is, that's all."

Her eyes study me. I haven't fooled her. Voice tight, she asks, "And what kind of caster is he?"

I shrug. "They're called shamans." At least she believes me when I say something about magic now. "They're powerful but not indestructible."

"Obviously." She gestures at the frozen branch.

I chuckle grimly and roll him over. The back of my hand pats his cheek. "Wake up."

"What are you doing?" Leavi exclaims, still in a whisper.

"Talking to him." My hand moves from his cheek to shake his shoulder. "Wake up," I repeat, harsher.

He moans. His eyes snap open.

I stare at him, unflinching. "Who are you?"

He spits at me.

I straighten, wiping the spittle from my cheek. "Alright." I set my foot on his shoulder. "Let's try this again. Who *are* you?"

196

His gaze moves up to Leavi. "Hello, child." A sly smile slips across his face. Against his bright teeth, his pink lips create an effect like blood on snow.

My boot nudges his cheek, pushing his head to the side. "Wrong answer."

He turns his smug smile on me, now pressing his lips tightly closed.

I tsk. "If that's how you want it." I move my foot and drag him propped against a tree. Using more twine, I tie his wrist bindings to the tree. With his hands bound behind him as they are, his arms will lose circulation in minutes. Plus, the snow and freezing temperatures can drive a man mad. Three feet away, I light a fire so he won't die of the cold, but the night will be a miserable one. "We'll talk in the morning."

Leavi catches up to me as I stalk away. "You're just going to leave him there?"

I glance at her. "What would you have me do?" It's not like there's much other choice.

"He could freeze to death!"

I shake my head. "He's got the fire. He'll be fine, just very uncomfortable come morning."

Her footsteps pause. Then she starts back toward the forest.

I catch her shoulder. "What are you doing?"

She shrugs me off and keeps walking. "I'll be right back."

"Leavi." She glances back, and I repeat, "He'll be fine."

"Okay." She slips into the forest.

There's no need to mess with him further. I need him to want to talk in the morning. It's like she still thinks I'm going to kill him.

I head toward the forest after her. The sun's finished setting, leaving us in the dark. We really don't need to be out here this time of night. I break through the treeline and see her in the gloom, heading back toward me.

Her blanket's gone. I run a hand through my hair.

"Let's go," she says. "It's getting dark."

I drop my hand. "Yeah. Come on." We head back to the house.

Amarris must have been fairly certain we're here to send the shaman. Now that he won't return, she'll know.

And everyone knows that Amarris Veradeaux does whatever she can to get what she wants.

Stepping onto the porch, I say, "Leavi."

She pauses, looking up at me.

"We need to do something about Veradeaux."

"Do something? What do you mean?"

"We need to stop her. She's going to track us down." The first stars of the night reflect off the snow, and the darkness makes her skin look like it's glowing. "She'll almost certainly kill us."

Fear spreads across her face, but she keeps it out of her voice. "What are we going to do then?"

I look out over the winterswept clearing, thinking. "She's wanted in Morineaux. I can take her back with me, too." But to transport two prisoners, I would *need* to be traveling with the others. There are too many ways that could go wrong otherwise.

If Sean would ever agree.

She presses her lips together. "Let's go upstairs. It's cold out here."

I nod. She opens the door. The house is quiet, everyone likely in their rooms, even if awake. She pads upstairs to hers, and I follow. As I enter, she closes and locks the door. She settles onto her bed, and I sit on her foot chest.

"If you want to," she fingers her necklace, "take Veradeaux with you-" She breaks off, looking away. "What exactly are you suggesting we do, Aster?"

"What do you mean?"

Now she looks at me. "Veradeaux's not going to simply follow you to Morineaux. What are you suggesting we do?" she repeats.

I take a deep breath. "I'm suggesting we kidnap her."

Chapter 55

SEAN

I set my presswrite on the bed, finally having some information to bring Leavi. She's probably in the living room.

As I turn to head that way, someone knocks on my door. "Sean, are you in here?"

"Leavi. I was wanting to talk to you." I let her in. "I finished analyzing some things." Waving her to follow me, I sit on my bed with my test results.

"Sean, there's something else going on-"

"Can't it wait? You'll want to see this. Here." I pull the paper from my presswrite and hand it to her. "The data's there."

She glances at it but hands it back. "Sean, I can't look through all this right now. There's important things going-"

"Didn't you say this was important too? I found some... things."

She stops, appearing to finally listen to me. "What do you mean? What did you find?"

I consider. The marker in her blood, for one. The trace amounts of radion-poison in the powder. Aster acting shady when I asked for his book.

I decide to start with the simple stuff. "There's an element to your blood that I've never seen before. I checked mine, and it wasn't there. Took Aster's, and it was. So, there's that. Plus... well, I'd be careful with that powder."

Her eyes widen, fear shooting across her expression. She steps closer, voice lowered. "There wasn't a hallucinogen in it after all, was there?"

Ignoring her oddly intense reaction, I forge on. This is too interesting to get sidetracked from. "Not that I could find, but multiple prolonged exposures could significantly shorten your life."

She looks startled. "What?"

"There's trace amounts of radion-poison in it."

"When you say trace amounts-"

"I mean enough that if you're consistently exposed to this stuff, it could definitely take a decade or so off your life. Not enough to give you radion poisoning, but still."

"How many parts per thousand?"

"Less than a tenth. But you're not getting my point, Leavi. It's radious."

"I understand that, Sean!" She pushes her hair back from her eyes, then sits on my bed. Calmer now, she says, "I'm done with the stuff anyway."

I pause, flummoxed. "Okay, hold on. I would normally just let you go on and not question it, but-" I'm so baffled that I don't think of the words falling from my mouth. "You're telling me that Leavi Riveirre is just 'done with' something that she hasn't figured out and conquered?"

She gives a short laugh, but it's confusingly mirthless. "Done using it at least. We can figure out the science behind it later. Right now-"

"But I have figured it out. The beginning, at least. Like I said earlier, there's a marker in your and Aster's blood that's not in mine. I'm not sure what it means, exactly; I've never seen it before."

"A genetic marker?"

I nod, and she cocks her head at me. "How did you get all this with just some magni-crystals and my hematester?"

"I took your blood, separated it—like you do-"

"I figured that much, Sean."

Annoyed at her interruption, I continue, "Removed each net, then scraped the cell-layers into a glass of water. Held a collector-string in the liquid after stirring the mixture around. Once the genetic material had gathered on the string, I removed it and examined it with the crystals."

She's nodding as if she figured out where I was going with that. "Of course." She taps her fingers on her leg. "Any hypotheses as to what it signifies?"

"I've not figured it out yet. But if I had the ability to test it and the willing subjects, I'd want to see if it was connected to whatever allows you to do the," I search for something to call it other than 'magic,' "currently unexplained things."

"It's not a hoax, Sean." She rubs the bridge of her nose.

My brow furrows. "I didn't say it was. If I thought it was a hoax, then I wouldn't think that it was somehow linked to your genes."

A weary grin ghosts to her lips. "There are things going on here that we are wildly out of our element trying to understand."

"Nothing is unexplainable, and thinking that you can't be the one to explain it only increases the odds that your assessment is true."

The smile widens a little, still tinged with tiredness. "You're right."

I consider. "I haven't figured everything out, and Aster wouldn't let me examine his book. But I'm certain it's all explainable. I hypothesize that what he's calling 'magic' is a subset of science that we haven't run across yet. People might have figured out how to use it to their advantage, but that doesn't mean they know how it works. Science has always been like that."

She nods but stands up. "That's not priority number one right now, though. We have another problem."

I sigh, letting her talk now that she's humored me.

"Lady Veradeaux may have found us."

My eyes go wide, and I stand as well. "Leavi, that's the kind of thing that you talk over me to bring up. What *happened*?"

"The Man from the East showed up. And tried to kill me," she adds.

For once, shock and panic overwhelm me to the point that I can't even think of something to say. My mouth gapes, moving without sound.

"I'm okay. Obviously. Just tired. But Aster has a plan."

I manage to reel in the net of words that I cast out a moment ago. "Okay. Which is?" Startled incredulity fills my voice.

"We're going to kidnap Veradeaux."

"What?" The shock packed into the one word pitches it about two octaves higher than normal.

"But we need your help."

"I already helped you steal someone from that manor! And we almost died doing it. I would rather brave the not-plotting-against-us snow and high-tail it out of here than go back there."

"Aster says she can find us if we leave and that she won't let up. She's going to hunt us down."

"Are you *sure* you trust him? I'm still not convinced he's not a lunatic."

"He saved my life twice tonight, Sean."

"Why are you trying to die?" I demand. "Considering all the really bad situations I've seen you in, I'm almost sure you have a thing for trying to cheat death."

"That's hardly fair!"

"I think it's very fair. And you always drag me along with you, and for some reason, I don't know how to stop you!" My jaw manages to shut. I didn't mean to say that much.

"Well if you're so tired of me 'dragging' you around-"

"I—skies." Frustrated, my hands raise in front of me like I'm grasping at air. "Leavi, I'm not yelling because I'm mad!"

"Then why are you yelling!"

"I don't know! I just-" My arms drop, and I start pacing. My voice calms. "I just don't want either of us dying."

She puts a hand on my shoulder, stopping me. "Sean. I don't want us to die either. But that's why we have to do this. Okay?"

Her face is closer to me, I think, than it's ever been before. I swallow, pulling in a shaky breath. "Um." My fingers tap. "Not really, but fine."

She nods, dropping her hand. "Let's go talk to Aster. We'll catch you up."

Chapter 56

LEAVI

Startling reality is settling into my stomach.

We're really doing this. We're really kidnapping the head of the local government. She really wants us dead. Aster's really telling the truth about magic. Sean and I are really stumbling into yet another dangerous situation.

We're doing this.

I sit down on the foot chest.

"Leavi says she knows the way to Veradeaux's room," Aster says, standing against the wall.

Sean stands, arms crossed, on the other side of the room. "And?"

"I think I can subdue her. So all we need is some way into the room. Leavi said you might be able to help with that."

Sean turns to me. "You know I can't make a copy unless I have the original. I don't think you want to sneak in and steal another one." He raises an eyebrow.

"Surely there's another way to do it," I say.

"Why can't your friend over there just magic the lock open?"

Aster rubs the back of his neck. "I can't pick the lock with magic unless I can see into it. That means there has to be good light on at least one side of the door, and most locks are too small to see into anyway. So, no. I can't 'magic' the lock."

I turn to Sean and say in Errelian, "If you can off-the-cuff create a bomb in a closet, surely you can come up with some way to get past a single door."

"That was different. I had access to all kinds of lovely chemicals in that closet and was *trying* to make noise," Sean replies.

"I don't believe you're really out of options. The great Doktor Sean Rahkifellar surely has some kind of ace up his sleeve." I watch him, hoping my words prove true.

He reaches into a pocket, pops open a device, and puts it away. Exasperatedly, he says, "I guess I have to figure out something. It'll work." He gives me a thin smile that looks like it took more effort than it should.

Aster says, "So are you two going to translate, or do I just have to guess?" He smiles, taking the sting from the words, but leaving their point.

"Sorry." I smile back. "Sean says he can do it."

Aster nods. "Good."

"Hold on," Sean says. "I think you've got a bit of a hole in your plan—well, a few, but this one's really glaring. You said you 'think you can subdue' Veradeaux? So what, you planning to waltz in there and carry her out over your shoulder? Without her warning the guards?"

"We would gag her, obviously," Aster says.

"And you think she's going to welcome you with open arms when you walk into her room and let you cart her out?"

"You wanted me to solve *your* task with magic, so how do you guess I'm going to accomplish mine?"

"So you've got some kind of magic-presto knock-out spell? Or can you wave your fingers and make her follow your every command?"

Aster raises an eyebrow. "Exactly what are you implying?"

"I'm *saying* that your 'magic' isn't exactly reliable."

"Really? Only moments ago, you were trying to get out of this by relying on my magic."

"I wasn't trying to get out of anything. I was using sarcasm. Obviously you're not familiar with it."

Aster's eyes spark. "Oh, of course not, because I'm some crazed con-man, right?"

"Well, I'm certainly not convinced you're everything you claim to be."

Aster pushes off the wall. "Then what do you think I am?"

"Lunatic's usually the word I use, but crazed con-man works."

Something goes frighteningly calm in Aster's face. His hand makes a motion in the air, and the dictionary on my bedside table flies into the air. It spins to face Sean, only a foot from his head.

"Does that look like a con?" Aster asks coolly.

I stand and snatch it out of the air. "This has gone far enough!"

Something snaps flat in the atmosphere. Aster calls out, hand coming to his nose. He takes a deep breath, wiping away the blood. Sean looks disturbed but like he's trying to hide it.

Regret sweeps through me at the idea that I might have caused Aster's reaction, but I don't show it. "We have more important things to deal with than you two's bickering." I set the dictionary down on the foot chest. In Errelian, I say, "If you're worried about her being awake when we sneak in, I think I can concoct some sort of soporific from what Marcí has in the kitchen. We could sneak it into her dinner."

He nods. "I think that sounds like a good idea."

"Pardon?" Aster asks.

I turn to him, trying to translate. "The night we kidnap her, I'm going to put something in Veradeaux's food to make her sleep."

"That sounds dangerous. How would you get in there?"

"I-" I swallow. "I still have a maid's uniform."

"They won't recognize you?"

"I won't stay there all day. Just long enough to put the," I wave my hand, not knowing the word in Avadelian, "thing in her food."

"I don't know," Aster hedges.

The door flies open. "So, Leavi, I was think-" Idyne stops talking, taking in the three of us. "Oh. Hello."

Panic flashes through my mind. Idyne's not the type to just wander off when she runs into a group. I don't know how we're going to get rid of her without coming off more suspicious than we already look. She's going to ask too many questions, and we're going to be caught before we've even started.

"What's going on?" Idyne asks.

I open my mouth to dodge, already knowing she's going to see through it. *Blazes.*

Idyne watches me, her winged eyeliner making her eyes seem even wider than they are.

"Nothing," Sean answers bluntly.

Idyne frowns.

She's not going to leave. Something occurs to me. *Maybe we don't need her to.* In my language, I ask Idyne, "How much makeup do you have left?"

The frown disappears. "Plenty?" She cocks her head. "Why?"

"We might need your help."

"For skies' sake, Riveirre, do you not know how to keep a secret?" Sean bursts.

"Secrets? I'm good at secrets. Tell me." Idyne grins.

"See?" I gesture toward her. "She's trustworthy." *And better here, working with us, than standing outside the door, listening in.*

"A self-claim to trustworthiness does not win my confidence," Sean retorts.

Idyne sets a hand to her chest. "I'm hurt."

"Does anyone want to tell me what's happening?" Aster interrupts.

"I'm going to tell Idyne what we're doing," I say in Avadelian.

Alarmed, he asks, "Why?"

"Because I think she can help me get in the manor. Besides, she is a caster too, no?

"She-" he cuts himself off, glancing at her.

Her head's tilted, as if waiting to see what he wants to say. "No, please, go on." She sweeps her hand, smiling, though a sharp light glints in her eyes.

For the first time, Idyne almost scares me.

He ignores her, looking back to me. "Do you disregard every warning someone gives you?" His face is lighthearted, as if his comment is a joke, though I know it's anything but.

My eyes flash. "I do what I have to to get results. Idyne can help us. And she's willing to. Right, Idyne?"

"Of course!" She grins at Aster, as if his discomfort amuses her.

"So then we tell her." At this point, I'm not sure there's much getting around it if we wanted to.

"So," Idyne says definitively. She shuts the door. "What's the plot?"

Might as well get it all out there. "We're kidnapping a woman who wants us dead."

Her eyes widen. "Oh."

"I need you to make me look as little like me as possible. Can you do that?"

A wicked excitement slips onto her face. "Absolutely."

Her smile ignites my own. "Perfect."

"Look, this is all nice and good," Sean says, "but none of that solves the dozens of other problems. For instance, what the blazes do we do with her once we've got her? Or, a more pressing question, don't we need to go somewhere else since she expects us to be here? It's only a matter of time before she realizes that you—wait a second, what *did* you do with the guy that tried to kill Leavi?"

Idyne gasps angrily. "*Who* tried to kill you?" she demands. There's an unsettling darkness to her gaze.

"It doesn't matter." I glance at Sean. "We tied him up. He's in the forest, with a blanket and a fire."

"You still haven't answered my other questions."

My gaze roves to the ceiling, the weight of the night suddenly crashing down on me. "I don't kno-" But wait. I do know. "Hold on." I head for the door.

"Where are you going?" Aster calls.

"And can I come?" Idyne says.

I glance back at everyone. "Stay here. I'm finding us a place to go." I leave, closing the door behind me. Outside, I lean against its frame, weariness slowly adding weight to my limbs. The excitement and adrenaline from before are wearing off, and all I want is to find somewhere to lie down and sleep.

But not here.

I walk down the hall and knock on Jacin's door. It occurs to me that I have no idea what time it is. The encounter with the Man from the East feels like it happened yesterday. In reality, it must be—what, thirty minutes? An hour or two ago?

Jacin might be asleep.

He doesn't answer the door, and I quietly knock again. Markus' room is just next door, and I don't want to wake him up.

Jacin doesn't say anything.

Pressing my lips together, I try the handle. Surprisingly, it's unlocked. Then again, he has been here for a few months. Perhaps he's not in the paranoid habit of locking himself away from the people he lives with the same way I am.

I push his door open. He's sprawled out on his bed, covers pulled halfway up. His hair's tousled with sleep, and as I move closer, I realize he's bare-chested. His necklace catches the faint moonlight.

"Jacin," I call.

He stirs, eyes blinking open. "Leavi." He sits, peering at me in the darkness. His gaze grows concerned. "Are you okay?"

"Yeah, I just-" I swallow, nervous for some reason. "I had a question. Sorry for waking you."

"It's fine," he assures. He rises, standing to face me. "What's wrong?" His voice is soft.

I'm suddenly very aware I'm standing in his bedroom in the middle of the night, just a couple feet away from his shirtless form. My fingers twine themselves in my necklace. "Nothing," I answer. "I was just… curious about that farmhouse you told me about before. The one with the book of words?"

"Yeah?" He steps closer.

"Yes." The darkness seems heavy. "Is it still empty?"

"As far as I know." He steps forward again, and only inches separate us. "Why?" Blue eyes search my face.

My tongue fumbles for a lie. Not landing on one, I dodge instead. "Can you give me directions?"

"Of course." He tucks a lock of hair behind my ear, and I flinch. "Sorry," he murmurs, eyes meeting mine. His hand drops.

"It's okay." I lean back slightly, heart pounding too quickly. "Where did you say it was?"

"South end of the village, just outside the forest." His words are slow, barely above a whisper. "About a five-minute walk from town."

I nod, releasing the death grip on my necklace. "Thanks." I turn to go.

He catches my wrist and steps in. "You didn't just come here to ask about a farm," he says softly.

"I didn't?" My voice is treasonously high.

"I don't think so." His hand comes to rest on my cheek, and I freeze. Eyes closed, he leans forward, close, closer, too close. His lips pause in the dark, just a millimeter from my own.

I jerk from his grip, stepping back. My heart pounds.

His eyes flick open, hurt flashing across his face.

"Goodnight, Jacin," I say, breathless. I hurry out of his room and duck into my own before he can follow me.

All three pairs of eyes in my room snap to me as I lean against the door.

"What happened?" Sean asks, brow furrowed.

I push off the door and brush my hair away from my face. "Nothing. Found us a place." I hope my cheeks aren't as flushed as they feel. Trying to affect nonchalance, I walk across the room and pull my satchel from underneath my bed. I glance back at them. "Well, what are you all waiting for? Let's pack and leave." I open the foot chest to grab my clothes.

I can feel people watching me, but I ignore them and shove my things into my bag. After a moment, the boys file out of the room.

I glance up at Idyne. "Are you coming with us? We could use you tomorrow. I doubt we come back here until we have Veradeaux." A shirt goes in my satchel.

"I already said I was, silly." She looks up and to the left. "No, I didn't forget. Shush." She turns back to me before I can ask her about it. "I have a gift for you. It's why I came in here in the first place actually." With a flourish, she produces a bracelet of wooden beads. The center bead is hollow glass, glowing the same swirling, neon way the charm of her necklace does. "Well, aren't you going to take it?" She jingles it at me.

I accept the gift. "Thank you." My finger runs over the cold beads. "It's beautiful."

I move to slip it on, and she calls, "You might not want to do that!"

Startled, I look up at her. "Why not?"

"Because you'll be speaking gibberish for anywhere from about an hour," she clucks her tongue, "to maybe a few days."

I tilt my head. "It's magic?"

"I'm pretty sure normal bracelets don't make you speak gibberish."

"Why would you give me a magic bracelet?"

"Oh." Her face lights up. "Because it's helpful. Once you get past the gibberish stage, I mean."

The neon substance swirls inside the bead. I press my lips together. "Thank you, but I'm afraid I'll have to return it. I don't want to use any more magic."

"Oh, but you won't be using it. It's a charm. I already cast the spell on it, no energy required from you." She beams, eyes dancing with excitement. "I think you'll find it more useful than you expect. I charmed it to let you speak Morineause. Since we're planning on going there and all."

"So I just put this on, and presto, I'm a native speaker?" I raise an eyebrow at her.

"Well, no. I already told you it makes you speak gibberish for a while—you can't use *any* sort of intelligible language. And the charm needs exposed to the language for a bit, but then, sure. You'll be more or less fluent. Oh, and look at this!" She taps the center bead three times, and the glow dies. "If you want to stop speaking Morineause, just do that. You'll still understand it, but the charm will stop making you speak its language." She taps the bead three more times, and it flares back to life. "It's not as handy or complicated as mine," she points to her necklace underneath her shirt, "but it gives you a little more choice. And it's easier to make." She flashes a smile and stands. "Well, I'm off to pack, I suppose. Meet you in the living room."

I nod, and she flounces off. Not sure what to make of her gift, I tuck it into my pocket and continue packing.

When I'm done, I hurry downstairs and scribble a note to Marcí, laying a few of the copper coins I earned on top of it. I start rifling through cabinets, putting food inside my purple throw to carry what we need to the farmhouse. That done, I open the doors to her tea and spice cabinet.

In the back of the second shelf rest two jars. I twist them open and smell the contents to be sure. A smile creeps to my face. Valerian root and chamomile. Just like I thought.

Lady Veradeaux's about to have the best night of sleep in her life.

Chapter 57

SEAN

It's strange to be here. This farmhouse is so similar to some of the buildings in Xela. Wooden, but with a good build, humbly decorated, and terribly behind the science of the caves.

'Mama, why's their house so big?' I asked, staring at the two-story home Mama's uncle lived in.

'Well, sugar,' she hedged, 'They're just a bit better off than us.'

'What do you mean? You've always said we weren't poor.'

'We ain't,' she emphasized. 'But, you see... well, just because we got more than some don't mean we don't still got less than others. Do you understand?'

'Yeah. It's like the food chain. We're better and more capable than some, and -'

'No.' Her eyes gripped mine.

My mouth shut, shocked that she interrupted. Mama didn't do that.

'We ain't no better than anyone else, and ain't no one better than us. People got different skills and resources and luck, but no one should think themselves "better." Okay?'

Mama was always right, so I didn't want to argue. I blinked and nodded, unconvinced and confused.

Working by the light of a candle, I finish pouring the hissing liquid into the bedroom door lock in front of me. I'd forgotten about going to her uncle's house. It was nice there. No one yelled.

This house is two stories too, with a quaint window seat on one end of the top floor. The resemblance is eerie. There's hardly any furniture, though, and the whole place has a thin layer of dust.

The liquid in the lock starts to solidify and expand, the hiss fading.

"Hi!" Idyne chirps, suddenly beside me. I start.

Settling down, I give her a distracted *hmm* and return to the lock.

"Whatcha doing?" she whispers, head beside my own.

I jerk away. "What the blazes?" My startled gaze meets her innocent one. I shove my hands into my pockets. "Sorry."

She perks back up, smiling. "It's fine. So, whatcha doing?"

I turn back to the lock. Great. The substance has leaked out the front, done solidifying. I pull out my pocket knife to dig it out. "I'm trying to formulate a solution that, when mixed with this catalyst," I point at a tube filled with liquid, "will solidify quickly and abruptly enough to bust a lock."

"So," she pauses, "you're trying to break locks with science. Got it."

I scowl, and she giggles. "You know, there was this girl at the academy I attended. You remind me a lot of her." I turn back to the lock and finish scraping out the gunk.

"Oh, yeah?"

"Mhm. Yeah, she was eccentric, hilarious. Considered the life of the party, really."

She nods at each item, ticking off the list with her fingers. "What else?"

"She flunked out of all her classes." I barely restrain a smile.

She whacks my shoulder. "I'm not dumb!"

I glance at her innocently, prepping the materials for my next test. Thankfully, the only thing I couldn't get at Marcí's was the catalyst, which I don't need much of. "I never called you dumb. I didn't even call the other girl dumb. I think maybe you're feeling defensive."

She gapes at me. "You're such a mess!"

"Resorting to ad hominem now, I see."

She glares, a smile lingering at her lips. "Is it really resorting to insults if I'm just stating facts?"

"I'm not a mess," I protest. "I think I'm very well in order."

She laughs.

"Now, stop distracting me. I've work to do."

She sticks her tongue out and flounces away. I shake my head at her antics. I get the feeling she'll keep us on our toes.

Although, I'm not sure what to think of her claiming to be a caster as well. When I get a chance, I want to take her blood too, to see if she has the marker in it that Leavi and Aster do.

If only I can get this blasted liquid to work. Finished prepping for the next test, I pour it into the lock.

Chapter 58
LEAVI

The wooden living room floor is hard against my back. I tug my blankets tighter, trying to ward off the chill. Aster suggested we not light a fire, which makes sense. It's cold, though.

Everyone's breathing is soft and steady in the dark room. Even Sean, who was up fiddling with locks earlier, came and laid down about half an hour ago. But for some reason, even as exhausted as I am, I can't get my mind to shut off. It keeps playing back scenes from earlier in an endless, twisted loop.

The fire, darting toward me.

Aster's warm arms around my waist, keeping me from falling.

The tree branch freezing and snapping off.

The Man from the East, miserable, leaned up against the tree. The shocked expression he quickly struck from his face as I covered him with the throw.

My dictionary flying through the air.

Jacin trying to kiss me.

I shift, struggling to get comfortable. I'm tense, and the memories cycling through my mind make it impossible to relax. I feel like yesterday was a lifetime ago. The Eleaviara Riveirre of yesterday didn't believe in magic, and yet today, that same girl has used it. Magic has coursed through her body and stolen energy from her and made the impossible happen. The Eleaviara of today has a magic charm tucked in her pocket, just in case she might need it. Tomorrow, she'll walk side-by-side with a 'wizard' and a 'kra'kaa'—with magic *users*—and trust in their skill to keep her from winding up dead.

Sean says their 'magic' is just science we don't understand yet, and the researcher in me agrees wholeheartedly.

But the little girl who read fairy-tales in her father's study?

She knows that there's something more to it than that. Something that's powerful and frightening, deeply visceral and wholly *real*. Something that can't be reduced to just facts and figures, any more than art can be separated from emotion. Something that can't be simply studied and torn apart and replicated. Something that just *is*.

The researcher shakes her head at the superstition, nonsense, and willful ignorance.

But little girls trust their instincts.

So if Sean produces more evidence about the logistics of magic, I'll listen to him, of course. I'll probably even believe him.

But, I think, no matter what happens, I'll always know that there's something more to all of this than the human mind will ever be able to explain.

My brain clicks off as dawn greys the sky.

* * *

I can't focus.

In one of the bedrooms, Idyne swipes makeup onto my face as she talks to herself. A rickety and splintering foot chest, one of the few items left in the house, functions as my seat. The slanting, afternoon light spills in through a dirty window.

I should be reviewing my plan, making sure that all the kinks are worked out, that I know what I'm doing, but I can't. Nerves block my mind, rendering all the details too hazy to grab hold of and manipulate.

We're really going to do this. We're going to kidnap a woman, take her from her own bed in the middle of the night, and cart her to a country where she's a wanted criminal. Last night, everything was abstract, and the steps we laid out to kidnapping her seemed no different than the steps of a research plan.

Now, though, as the sun readies itself to close the day and Idyne perfects my disguise, reality sinks in. Despite what Veradeaux did to Aster, despite what he says she'll do to Sean and me, this somehow feels wrong, but I don't know any way to make it right.

"Idyne."

She glances up at me. Earlier when I spoke, she shushed me, saying I'd mess up her lines. Something in my voice must catch her off guard, though, because now she sits down beside me and puts her brush away.

I meet her gaze. "Have you ever done something bad because you were too scared to do something good?"

"Yes." Her simple sincerity is frightening.

My fingers creep to my necklace. "What happened?"

"In what respect?"

I look out the window to the snow-covered field. "Did it turn out for the better or the worse?"

"You can't exactly know once you've taken the other path, can you?"

My mind wanders back to Karsix. What if I'd stayed? Maybe I'd still be there, going to work every day, hoping I don't contract the Death. Maybe the disease would have died out, and I'd be back home in Erreliah.

Or maybe I'd be dead.

Idyne catches my attention as she stands. "But I'm still alive. That's what counts in the end, right?" She flashes a smile. "Come on. Let's get your makeup finished. You've got a manor to infiltrate."

When she gets done, she pulls a long shard of silverglass from her bag. "Not exactly a mirror, but it'll work. Tell me what you think."

When I catch a glance of myself, I almost drop the glass. My paper skin has darkened to a warm peach color. Some sort of chalk makes my hair look more brown than black. A mole rests below my eye, and the curvature of my face even looks different. My hand drifts up to touch my skin.

Idyne swats it away. "Don't. You'll smudge it. But you think that will work?"

"Work? Idyne, I don't even recognize myself." I can't take my eyes off my reflection. I'm in another person's skin. "It'll be a miracle if anyone else does."

"Just don't talk. Your accent's awful."

I glance up at her, frowning. "Is Avadelian even your native language?"

211

"It doesn't have to be." She pats the charm beneath her collar. "Come on. Let's go see what the boys think." She steals back the piece of silverglass and leaves the room.

Sean's pacing when I enter the living room. His head snaps up. "Riveirre?"

A smile tugs at my lips.

Across the room, Aster turns away from the window. Shock ripples across his face. I'm glad to see he's back. Idyne whisked me off shortly after he went to check on the Man from the East. I've not seen him since.

Sean's eyes follow me as I cross the room to stand beside Aster. "What did you find out?" I ask.

His jaw clenches. "Nothing. He won't talk."

"He's in the barn now?"

He shakes his head. "We don't want him to know where we are any longer than we have to. Once we have Veradeaux, we can collect him and start out in the morning."

"You said before he can't hurt us." My arms cross.

"He can't, but a plan never failed from overcaution."

"Is it overcaution, Aster, or-" My tongue fumbles for a word I've not learned in Avadelian. "*Azhiet-friae*," I settle on pointedly. *Revenge.*

Hurt flashes across his face. "No, Leavi, it is not. I'm trying to protect all of us. Hopefully even learn something from him. But I'm not trying to kill him, and I'm not trying to hurt him like or worse than he did me." He leans forward, voice dropping. "If I were, then he'd be cold, alone, and *starving*."

I step back, stung and embarrassed. "I didn't mean-"

He waves it away. "It's okay. We're all a little off right now." He offers me a less than confident smile.

"Hey, Riveirre," Sean calls.

I look back.

"You're going to miss shift change if you stand around here much longer."

My lips press together. "Yeah." I head for the door but pause when I reach the handle. I glance back.

Sean's already pacing again. Aster watches me, pensive expression clouding his face.

Idyne's hands are clasped in front of her. "Good luck!"

A nervous smile finds its way to my lips. "Thanks."

I leave.

* * *

The kitchen is hot and busy when I walk in. Maids wipe down counters, scrub dishes, drench fires, and sweep floors. Over the cacophony of hard work and clanging pots and pans, the head cook shouts, "Move those feet, girls! Show some urgency! Or do you want to be here until midnight?"

The cook bustles over to a counter where a lidded platter sits. "Who's taking the Lady's supper to her tonight?"

212

Everyone keeps their eyes on their task. Across the room, a girl's head hesitantly lifts and glances around the room. Scowling, she dusts her hands off and starts toward the cook.

I weave through the busy maids. Someone shoves a broom into my hand.

The girl, oblivious to me, is halfway to the tray.

I drop the broom against a counter and hurry to cut the girl off. She's five feet from the cook when I slide in front and pick up the platter.

From behind, I feel a pair of eyes study me.

The cook seems not to notice the race. "Well, what are you doing just standing there? Get on with it!"

As I turn, I see the other girl move forward and snag a towel off a nearby counter, as if that had been her goal the entire time. She slinks back to where she came from and continues cleaning.

Maids glance at the tray and avoid me as I make my way out. I'm to the door when the cook calls, "Hey, you!"

I freeze.

"Be sure you take that to her quarters and not the dining hall. And hurry up with it! It'll be your hide if her supper's cold, not mine."

Her quarters? Cold fear settles like ice in my stomach. I'd hoped to set her tray on the table and leave, or better yet, pass it off to some serving maid when I neared the dining hall. My head dips a nod, and I push through the door.

I walk head-down through the halls as servants trickle out of the building, leaving while the smaller night staff comes in. Chatter rings all around me, and I pray no one stops me. *Your accent's terrible*, Idyne said. Which means one word from me, and this whole thing could come crashing down.

My steps are quick, though, and purposeful. *No one stops a person who looks like they know where they're going*, my mother used to quip, *unless it's to ask for directions.* Slightly comforted by that, I keep walking until I clear the crowd.

As I slip onto an empty hallway, I cast a glance behind me. No one's there. All the servant's voices ring distant.

Setting the tray down, I dig a vial out of my pocket. The dried valerian root and crushed chamomile are perfectly invisible inside the concentrated solution.

Hopefully the good Lady will appreciate the change in flavor. Or, even better, not notice.

I lift the lid off the tray, careful sitting the metal down so it doesn't clatter. Steam rises from a bowl of soup. Popping the cork on my vial, I pour its contents into the broth. I hurry to set the lid back and pick up the tray. My steps echo down the hall, and wavering torches chase me.

I knock on Lady Veradeaux's door. The platter trembles slightly, and I shove my nerves down, forcing my hand to still.

"Enter," her high voice calls.

Head down, I do.

A giant, four-poster bed rests against the far back wall, surrounded by a wardrobe and dressing screen. A basin of water is in one corner. Throughout the space, silver candlesticks sit in low alcoves. Burgundy rugs and tapestries drape the floor and walls.

In the front of the room, Veradeaux lounges in an armchair before a roaring fire. A satin robe covers her, and her blonde hair falls in loose, messy waves as she stares sullenly into the flames. She waves her hand distractedly. "Just sit it there."

Slowly moving forward, I place the tray on the coffee table she indicated. Nerves make my skin tingle in spite of the fact that she hasn't even looked at me.

I turn to go. Halfway to the door, I think I'm home free. By the time I can almost reach the handle, my heart's beating three times too fast, celebrating before I'm even out.

My hand is on the cool metal when she calls, "Have you always lived in the village, child?"

I force myself to let go of the knob and turn to face her. She still stares at the fire. Thinking it easiest to agree, I nod. I might be able to get out of this without talking. *Please let that be true...*

"I can't hear the rocks inside your head rattling, girl," Veradeaux snaps. "You will speak when spoken to."

My stomach jumps into my throat. Struggling to keep as much of my accent from my voice as possible, I say, "Yes."

"Yes what?"

I swallow. "Yes... my lady."

Veradeaux settles further into her chair, seemingly appeased. "So I suppose you don't know what it's like to miss home, do you?"

"No, my lady." The lie tastes like bitter ashes.

"I do," she murmurs.

As she stares into the hearth, thin robe wrapped around her shoulders, this commanding, put-together woman suddenly looks sad and weary.

For the first time tonight, she makes eye contact with me. There's something metal-cold in her gaze. "And no one's going to stop me from getting back." She leans into the chair, ignoring me again. A dainty hand flicks toward the door. "You're dismissed."

Gratefully, I slip outside. She didn't recognize me. The profound relief weighs almost as heavy in my chest as the fear did. I hurry down the quiet halls.

Now to hide and wait.

Chapter 59
ASTER

In the darkness, the manor rises in front of us like a foreboding master I've only just escaped. Glaring down, it seems to mock me. *Coming back, are you? Did you not learn the first time, imbecile?*

I set my jaw. We'll accomplish what we came to, and we will not be tossed aside.

Idyne and Sean walk beside me. Idyne is relatively quiet, but unfortunately, Sean's steps are like thunder in my ears. Idyne tries to shush him, but he doesn't seem to understand how to be quieter.

The iron-bar gate stands before us. Metal decorations stretch from bar to bar, making it impossible to reach through and lift the crosspiece that locks the gate. We stop.

"What do we do now?" Idyne whispers.

I adjust my angle so I can see the bar better.

"We can't lift it from this side," Sean says.

"Clearly," I reply. "Leavi and I planned everything out, though. Remember?"

His nostrils flare, but he stays quiet.

Satisfied with the amount of the crosspiece that I can see, I take a pinch of powder from its pouch and cast. "Et væ." My outstretched hands direct the bar up and off the notch supporting it.

This spell is my favorite. Relatively simple for even a beginner to cast, it has many applications. All I have to do is practice them.

The bar is in the air now, and my fingers guide it to the snow beside the gate. I end the spell with a sharp gesture, and the bar drops into the drift. Idyne claps her hands together soundlessly.

"Thanks!" she breathes, pushing the gate open. We slip through.

I lead the way, sneaking from shadow to shadow across the snow. The bare trees standing just outside the wall throw reaching darkness, as if they're previous victims of Amarris, begging us to turn back and escape the danger ahead.

Sean points the way to the servants' entrance we're going to use, and we ghost up to it. We cram into the shadows surrounding the door, hopefully invisible to anyone that might be around.

We wait.

Idyne whispers, "When's Leavi going to get here?"

"When she knows it's safe," I reply.

"If that's the case, she'll never come," Sean snarks.

I ignore him, returning my attention to the door. A few minutes more pass, then the lock clicks. The door swings open, revealing Leavi behind it.

Tension I didn't realize I had drains away. She didn't get caught.

She ushers us up the lightless staircase and into the halls beyond. Silence pervades the empty halls and seeps into every crack and alcove. The only

215

interruption of the soundlessness is the soft slap of Sean's boots against the floor and the faint shuffle of Leavi and Idyne's footsteps.

Minutes later, Leavi stops in front of a door, gesturing.

This is it.

Sean steps forward, uncorking a vial filled with cloudy liquid. He squeezes a few clear drops from an eyedropper into the vial. The mixture begins to grey and expand, and he hastily pours it into the lock.

Tense, we watch as the liquid transforms into a dark, hard material, larger than the lock allows. A sharp crack rings as a split runs from the opening of the lock outward.

It worked.

Sean gently pulls the door open, and everyone slips into the silent room. All is still except a dying fire clinging to what life it has left. Ignoring the sitting area and room decor, I sneak toward the back of the room. As I near it, though, I realize something.

Amarris isn't in her bed.

Panicked, I scan the room. My eyes come to rest on a faint form in a high-backed chair turned away from the fire. Amarris grins, and suddenly, the fire doesn't look so pathetic. Rather, it appears to be hurling menacing tendrils of snapping light, chasing my companions and the shadows away from the traitor in the chair.

"Thank you for coming to see me, and for sending little Miss… Riveirre, is it?" The grin spreads wider as she glances at Leavi. On the coffee table, I notice a tray of food, untouched. "To warn me."

From the shadows on either side of the entrance, two guards step forward and swing the door shut. Dismay grips me. We're trapped.

"Drop your weapons and your powder," Amarris commands.

Tension charges the silence. With two guards in the room and her somehow awake, our odds of making it out of here by fighting are less than slim. If we wait, if we just bide our time, maybe the opportunity to escape will arise.

Everyone is paused, like some sort of strange statue collection, watching, waiting. Amarris smiles.

If they take us, I know they'll kill us.

"Et væ!" I spray powder. A heavy candle flies from the wall at Amarris.

She copies my call. Her hand flicks, and the candle flies to the side. Blood courses from my nose as my spell backlashes, and terrifying realization sinks in my stomach. *She's a caster.*

Near the door, Sean, Idyne, and Leavi attempt to fend off the guards. Idyne whirls toward a one, drawing out a long shard of silverglass. Sean flips out a folding knife, and Leavi snatches a silver candleholder from an alcove. That leaves me to face Amarris alone.

She casts again, and the water in the basin streams into the air. Cold fear surges inside me. I'm not going to be able to face a caster with this much experience.

The water splits into two masses, the larger one hovering in the air and the other splashing across the floor.

I can't let this traitorous snake capture me, refuse to let her kill my companions, and will not let her have her way with Morineaux.

I cast, yanking a candlestick from behind her toward her head.

216

She mutters, and the water on the floor begins to freeze.

I release my spell, and the candlestick's momentum carries. Concentrated on her own casting, Amarris doesn't notice my attack. The stick connects. Her hand shoots to the wound, disrupting her incantation, and she calls out. Blood drips from her nose.

The thrill of success fills me. Immediately, it drains as she gestures and some of the water in the air breaks off, freezing as it flies toward my gut. I dart out of the way. My feet fly out from under me, and I sprawl onto thin ice.

Amarris casts again to catch her ice-shard before it crashes into the floor. It changes direction and charges for me.

I roll to the side, off the ice, and scramble up. "Et væ!" The rug beneath her feet shoots to the side. She tumbles to the ground, yelling, and her water globe falls in time with her.

Maybe I can do this.

She gathers the water back into the air, and my confidence disappears. All I managed was to stall her. I need her to stop fighting. There's got to be some way to knock her out or paralyze her.

Paralyze—that's it. When I saved Leavi from falling, she couldn't move. "Et v-"

Leavi screams. My head whips around, words cut short, and my spell backlashes. Her arm is bleeding. One of the guards moves to attack her again, and Idyne darts forward.

On chance, Leavi glances toward me. We lock gazes. Her eyes dart to the side, behind me. "Aster!" she shouts.

I spin. Ice is streaking toward me from all around, an army of inch-long frozen daggers. Behind them, Amarris is preparing a second attack.

Time slows as distant realization numbs me. *This is it.* I can't jump out of the way this time, and though those might not kill me straight off, whatever she hits me with next surely will.

She's going to murder me.

Fear invigorates my instinct—my mind scrambles for a spell to stop her for good and turns up one, single, dangerous possibility. My hands raise, making the motions as quickly as the spell allows, lips forming the words I know now by heart.

The time is now. If I'm not strong enough, it's all over anyway.

I cast.

The terrifying pull of the magic rages within me as my will succumbs to the spell. Agraund's words ring in my ears. *A spell you should have mastered long ago!*

My veins are acid as the magic burns throughout me. Black dances through my vision as I fight to stay conscious to the end of the spell. Awareness is slipping from my mind like water from cupped hands. I fight to finish the spell, dropping to my knees.

If the ice makes it any closer, it won't matter if I don't end the spell. The momentum will carry the shards into me anyway.

The magic explodes from me, channeling into Amarris. My scope of vision shrinks as a black tunnel closes around it.

Exhausted triumph fills me as Amarris goes still, blood trickling down her lip. The shards dip as they lose momentum. I'm falling too.

My spell should stop her long enough for the others to deal with her. *But at what cost?*

Everything goes black.

Chapter 60
SEAN

Aster calls out a strange word, sounding simultaneously triumphant and choked. I spin. Ice-shards fall toward him through the air, but clatter to the ground before touching him. He falls, and across the room, Veradeaux stands, arms mid-air, mouth open.

One of the guards lets out a gurgling sound, and I snap back. He falls, an open gash across his throat. Idyne stands over him, blood dripping from her silverglass. The other guard is already on the ground, clutching his bleeding gut. Their lives seep from their eyes like the blood from their wounds.

Fear and disgust flood my mind.

Leavi stands back, horror set in her features. "You didn't have to kill them," she chokes out.

"They would have killed us," Idyne says. She turns to Leavi, sympathy in her eyes. "Besides, they already hurt you. We were all fighting for our lives."

Leavi's gaze is still fixed on the dead-eyed stares of the guards. Looking for some way to ignore them, I turn her to face the rest of the room. "Look what he did to Veradeaux."

Instead, her gaze fixes on the floor, eyes going even wider as she rushes to Aster's side, fingers flying to his pulse. Blood on Leavi's arm catches my eye. We'll need to tend to that cut when we get to the farmhouse.

She relaxes. "He's alive."

I pick my way through the ice to Veradeaux. Closer now, I can see that her chest is rising and falling slightly. Her eyes narrow, watching me. Otherwise, though, she's unmoving. It's almost as if an immobile case surrounds her, just enough room between her and it for her to breath and blink.

Her finger twitches, and I start.

"Hey," I call, backing up. "Whatever Aster did, I think it's wearing off."

Idyne hurries over, snagging a candleholder along the way. "I can fix that." She smashes it over the woman's head. Veradeaux's eyes shut, unconscious, but the strange force keeps her erect. I glance back to see if Leavi noticed, but she's preoccupied with Aster.

"We should leave as soon as the spell's worn off," Idyne pipes up.

"Yeah." Uneasy with her, I glance at the bodies. Remorse for their families fills me. I force myself to look at their faces, to commit them to memory. They deserve that much at least. One's a blond fellow with a crooked nose and thinned-out cheeks. He holds the ceiling in an unending stare, never to close his eyes again.

One of them is the man who forgot his truncheon. The one who talked about drinking every night.

The remorse for him drains. His family's probably better off without him.

219

Behind us, there's a thud. I turn. Veradeaux's limp, sprawled on the ground. Idyne picks up the woman's arms and starts dragging her to the door. I help Leavi carry Aster.

We've accomplished what we came for. We're safe.

In the halls, we hear a few guards hurrying toward us—they must have heard the fight—but Leavi leads us around them, back out the side entrance, and we speed off the grounds.

We keep off the path, staying at the edge of the woods, as we walk to the farm. When we make it to the farmhouse door, I push it open. Tired and coming off the adrenaline high, we don't notice anything unusual as we straggle in.

The door closes, and Jacin peels from the shadows.

Idyne yelps. "What're you doing here?" Smoothly, she slides between Jacin and Veradeaux. Hopefully that cuts off his view of the woman.

He eyes the slumped form of Aster between Leavi and me. "I was curious why you all disappeared from the inn." His gaze locks with Leavi's, and her free hand comes up to her necklace. "I had a feeling you might be here."

"Yeah, well, everything's fine." I say. "None of your business anyway, so…" I gesture at the door.

He takes a suspicious step toward it. Now at a different angle, his gaze snaps to the unconscious and defenseless form of Lady Veradeaux. Trepidation flashes onto his face.

Blazes.

"What have you done?" he accuses.

Leavi's head turns to him, and she hurries to set Aster down. "It's not what it looks like."

He raises an eyebrow. "It's not? Because from where I'm standing, it looks like that's the most powerful woman in Niv. And it seems like you've kidnapped her."

She steps closer to him. "She wanted to kill Aster, to kill all of us."

"Leavi," I hiss. The creep doesn't need to be hearing this. She ignores me, though, as always.

"If you've done something like this before, I'm not shocked."

"Jacin, *please*." She steps forward and sets a hand on his shoulder. Her voice lowers. "We were just trying to protect ourselves. She," she stares into his eyes, the home of a darkness I'm shocked she's not noticed yet, "is not a good woman. Please don't turn us in."

His gaze moves down to Leavi's arm, where blood trails down her skin. "You're hurt," he murmurs. His fingers brush her shoulder. My skin crawls at how quickly he turned from accusatory to concerned.

"It's shallow. It'll be fine." I heard the way she called out when the knife slashed her skin, but I understand her not wanting his interest any more than necessary. Then again, I doubt that's her actual reasoning.

"You have to come back to the inn. Get a good night's rest; recover. Marci's worried about you." His voice is disconcertingly soft, giving me the uncomfortable feeling that he's forgotten there's others in the room.

"I left a note," Leavi says.

He chuckles softly. "She thinks you're dead in a snowdrift somewhere."

Leavi offers a thin smile. "We're leaving in the morning."

"Still. A warm house and a soft bed will be better than a night here." He looks over Leavi's shoulder at Veradeaux. "What are you going to do with her?"

Leavi drops her hand. "Keep her here. We take her with us when we leave."

He raises his eyebrow again, appearing doubtful. He looks like he wants to say something, but Leavi glances back at me before he can. "Are there any locks you didn't break?"

"A few. I suggest the last room."

"On it," Idyne says, pulling Veradeaux that way.

Leavi fully faces me. "I don't see anything wrong with staying there tonight. There's no danger anymore. And," she glances at Aster, "he needs to recuperate before we go."

I watch her. Jacin clearly has ulterior motives in coming here, in convincing her to go back, yet she's going along with it anyway. She doesn't heed my warnings from the past about him, and among illogical, nonscientific-minded people, she chooses to trust them more than me.

I'm not even sure at this point why she feels the need to try to justify the idea to me. Especially since, even if I objected, she'd argue with me until I gave in.

I shrug. "Sure."

As we gather everything to head back to the Kuddly Kitten, painful resignation settles in my chest. She doesn't want me. She's said to my face that she only wants to be around me if she needs me. For her—just like for everyone else alive in this world—I'm more of a snarky burden than a companion. I'm definitely not a friend, and here, she seems to have made plenty of those.

Numb, I head with everyone else out the door.

She doesn't want me, and she doesn't need me. I'm just going to have to learn to accept that and act accordingly.

Because, even though I've known her longer than any of these people, lived through struggle after struggle and the eventual successes with her, even though I'm the only one that understands where she's from and how leaving there has hurt her, one fact somehow remains.

She doesn't need me.

When we reach the Kitten, I go straight to the room dubbed mine after Leavi gave mine away.

Chapter 61

LEAVI

I'm numb.

I'm alive, I'm responding, acting normal even, taking charge, making sure we don't get caught. On the outside, I probably look normal as I talk Jacin down, pick Aster back up, trudge through piled drifts all the way to the inn. It's snowing yet again, and the flakes pelt my face, but I don't feel them.

I'm numb.

Heat washes over us as we open the Kitten's door, and I dully appreciate the release from winter's embrace. We drag Aster upstairs to his room and lay him on the bed. Idyne asks me about my arm, but I have other things to do, and she's the last person I want to talk to right now. I walk down the hall. Glassy-eyed faces pop into my mind. My steps pause.

Idyne lays a hand on my shoulder. I shrug her off and stride to the bathroom, trying to banish the images.

I scoop up a washcloth and plunge it in the basin's water. For some reason, I expect it to swirl red, but it doesn't. It stays clear, clear as crystals, clear as glass, clear and reflective as that silvered shard that thrust into the guard's—

I wring the washcloth out. I'm numb.

I'm numb, and I'm happy to stay that way.

I brush past Idyne and go into Aster's room. He's still unconscious. I dab the damp cloth beneath his nose, wiping the blood away. My hand slips against his cheek. His skin is ice.

"Help me get him under the blankets," I say to no one in particular.

My hands work at pulling the covers out from under him, and then up again. I'm surprised to see it's Jacin's hands who join me, not Sean's. Where is Sean? I don't know, and I don't raise my head to look.

Jacin sets his hand on my shoulder, little finger brushing my neck. My skin crawls. I don't want to be alone with him, but he's here, and he's helping me, and he's not turning us in. Maybe we're not alone after all, either. Maybe Sean is here.

Now I glance up to look for him. Jacin's hand slips off. The room is dark but for the moonlight. Sean's nowhere to be seen.

Idyne's nagging me about my arm again. Aster's face is clean. I wave Idyne away and attend to my own injury. I don't need her hands on me any more than I need Jacin's.

I wish Sean were in here.

I ignore Idyne's worried gaze. The cut isn't that deep. It just stings. I lay the washcloth over it to help the blood coagulate. Yes, I'm fine, I tell them. They ask more than once. Yes, I'm fine. I just want you to go away. I don't tell them that part.

They seem to figure it out, though. They leave, shutting the door behind them.

I should go too. Get some sleep in my own bed. Rest. I didn't do much of that last night.

But Aster's sleeping face looks troubled. I'd hate for him to wake up alone, not knowing how he got there.

And I don't want to be by myself when I close my eyes. I steal a blanket and pillow from my room and curl up on the floor for the second night in a row.

I pray I don't dream.

* * *

I jerk awake from a dead sleep. My blanket tangles around me, and panic shoots through me as I struggle to recognize my surroundings. I'm on the floor, legs of a bed frame at eye level, orange quilt hanging down.

Orange quilt.

I'm in Aster's room.

A shaky breath of relief pushes from my lungs, and I sit up. The grey dawn sky shines weak light into the room. Tousled blankets cover a still-sleeping Aster. He looks more at ease now, the morning light taking most of the pallor from his face.

Untangling the blanket from my legs, I stand up. I'm too unsettled to go back to sleep. Might as well do something useful with myself.

I ease Aster's door closed and pad down to the kitchen. Catching a sound, I pause outside the closed door. Inside, soft sniffling is punctuated by a sob.

I gently press the door open.

Marcí slumps on a barstool at the counter, forehead resting against her palm as tears splash against the wood. Her shoulders shake as another sob escapes her.

I cross the room to lay a hand on her shoulder. "Missus Marcí, what's wrong?"

She looks up, wide eyes rimmed in red. "Leavi. Leavi, dear." She stands, hugging me. "Thank Lady Jacqueline and every star in the sky that you came back." Her voice is hoarse, and her tear-soaked face dampens my shirt. She clings to me, and I don't pull away.

"Missus Marcí, I'm okay. We're all okay." There's a growing dread in my stomach, though, that it's not us she's worried about.

She pulls back, searching my face. "You're a doctor, aren't you? Or an apothecary, a nurse, something? You fixed Idyne's leg," she offers hurriedly as though solidifying her claim.

"I-" *I just cleaned and wrapped it, Marcí.* The hope in her eyes freezes the words in my mouth. "I know a little bit. What's wrong, Missus Marcí?"

"It's-" She can hardly get it out. "It's Bukki," she finally manages.

She grabs my hand and pulls me toward her bedroom. "The cough has been going on for a while now, and he said that was all it was. Wasn't much I could do but hope it'd go away. Winter makes people sick, sometimes, you know?" She glances back at me. "I'd hoped it was just that, and he'd get better when spring rolled around. But yesterday, he was worse, and-" She breaks off, pressing a hand to her lips as she pauses in front of her door. "Last night, fever set in." Her grip on my hand tightens. "I don't know if he's going to make it through this, Leavi."

Her eyes hold a wild fear. I meet their trembling gaze as steadily as I can manage. "I will do my absolute best for him, Missus Marcí."

She gives a shaky nod and releases my hand. We go in.

Bukki lays in bed, straight as a corpse in a coffin, skin the color of ash. Wet cloths drape over his forehead. His breath barely shakes his chest. It's no wonder Marcí's so worried about him. I couldn't be more convinced he's on death's door if the specter himself showed up knocking.

"Let's take the cloths off," I say.

Marcí looks at me alarmedly. "But the fever-"

I wave my hand. "The fever will," *help neutralize the virus or bacteria, letting his immune system fend it off.* Not knowing how to explain that in her language, I say, "help. It's natural," I explain when her startled doubt doesn't disappear. "Trust me. Your body knows how to take care of itself." *Most of the time.*

I move forward, examining him. He's asleep, a light sweat shining his face. He mumbles softly but unintelligibly, then is silent once more. I lay my hand on his clammy skin and feel the fever beneath my fingertips.

As she takes the cloths off, I press my ear to his chest. His breaths are thick and labored, a low wheeze followed by a faint rattle. There's fluid in his lungs.

Pneumonia, then, more than likely.

I straighten, trying to keep my expression as neutral as possible.

Marcí's eyes search my face. "Do you know what's wrong? Can you fix it?"

I don't know what they call it here, if they even know what it is. I'm not sure that's what he has, but I don't have a better guess either.

I really hope I'm wrong.

"Leavi."

I refocus on Marcí. "I will try my best, Missus Marcí."

Her shoulders sag. "Oh."

I press my lips together, trying to think of something concrete we can do to help him. "He needs water—as much as he's willing to drink. Rest. Other than that," I resist the urge to fiddle with my necklace, "we will just have to watch him." *Watch him, hope, and make him comfortable.*

Tears well in her eyes, but she nods, blinking them away. My heart aches that there's not anything else I know to do.

I reach over and squeeze her hand. Together, we sit and wait at his bedside.

* * *

Three hours later, the only change is steady decline. His breaths are slow, rasping things that speak of death. It'd take either an extraordinary doctor or a miracle to save him now. It's late morning, and the other inhabitants of the inn move through the house. Aster and Sean are probably waiting for me to show up in the living room with my things so we can get on the road.

I can't leave Marcí like this, though.

We sit, Bukki's breaths becoming shallower and shallower, until Marcí shoots to her feet. My head snaps up, alarmed.

Her jaw is set, tears shining in her eyes. "I'm not going to just let this happen. I'm just not. He can't die. I—I won't allow it!" Picking up her skirts, she sweeps from the room.

"What? Marcí!" I hurry after her. "Marcí, where are you going?"

"To someone who can help." She passes through the living room, head sweeping back and forth. Not seeming to find what she's looking for, she hurries up the stairs.

"Who?" I ask.

She reaches the top of the flight, and I manage to catch up. Just outside his room, Aster closes his door, cloak already swung on like he's ready to leave. He stops short when he sees us, worry clouding his gaze. Heavy bags still rest under his eyes. "What's wrong?"

Marcí strides up to him. "I need your help."

"With what?" Confusion and concern are clear in his face.

"My husband. He's sick. You're a caster. You can fix him." Her voice cracks. "Please."

His eyes widen, and his hand comes up to rub the back of his neck. "I-" He takes a deep breath. "I'll try."

Marcí throws her arms around his neck, and surprise fills his face. She pulls away just as quickly and tugs him downstairs before I can say anything to either of them. I follow them down, but unease tugs at the back of my mind.

We enter the room. Aster steps closer to the bed, examining Bukki with the confidence and compassion of a doctor to a sick man. He turns to Marcí. "Do you know what he is suffering from?"

Her tear-stained face pinches together, head shaking silently.

Aster nods as if he already assumed as much, returning his attention to Bukki. He considers the man, then pulls out his spell book, flipping through the pages as he thinks.

After a few minutes, he nods once and turns to Marcí. "Can you remove his shirt, maedame?"

Confusion momentarily flits across her features, but she bustles to her husband's bedside and gently tugs his tunic off. Aster nods at her in thanks and begins preparing his materials.

He lays his wooden bowl on the bedside table, sprinkling powder and dashing a bit of oil into it. He removes a tiny knife from his cloak and slices the palm of his hand open. Marcí hisses in sympathy, and I wince, but Aster doesn't flinch. He leans forward, concentrating on getting the trickle of blood into the bowl. He begins to massage the mixture with his fingers, turning it into a thick red paste. He continues to mix the ingredients until he nods, satisfied. He wipes his fingers off on the inside of the bowl.

Beginning his incantation, he dips the tip of his pointer finger into the bloody sludge, swirling it around in steady circles. His motions are measured with his words, almost like a dancer swaying to a song. He turns back to Bukki, dripping one single dot over the center of the sick man's heart.

From there, Aster's finger moves out, painting lines and curves that radiate from the center-point, the meter of his words ever so steady though the volume increases.

I glance up from his work, surprised to see the strain already starting to show on his face. His movements are seamless, but his features are hard, forehead crinkled in concentration and effort. As he moves to collect more of the mixture onto his fingers, a telltale drop of blood gathers under his nose. He completes the drawing on Bukki's chest with a final spray of the mixture and sharp rise in volume. Slathering the remaining contents of the bowl onto his finger, Aster moves up to Bukki's head.

The caster's breaths come harder now, the blood dripping freely from his nose, but he pays it no heed. His movements stay measured and precise.

The spell finishes with two wide swipes across Bukki's face. Aster's incantation reaches a shout, his voice clear and commanding despite the pain evident in his eyes. A heavy, charged moment hangs in the air like an echo.

The bowl clatters to the ground, and Aster follows it.

I rush to his side as Marcí crosses to Bukki's. Aster is sprawled on the floor, no breath shaking his chest, no random impulse twitching his finger, nothing to give evidence that life still inhabits his body. I drop to the floor beside him, frantic fingers searching for a pulse. Their shaky tips flit over his neck unsuccessfully, and I curse. *Calm down, stupid girl! You're never going to find anything unless you get still.*

Frustrated, I lean over his chest, ear pressed against the soft material of his cloak, trying, hoping, praying to hear anything. A breath, a beat, no matter how soft, just *something.* As I wait, panic seeping through my mind, I still can't hear—

No. Wait. There it is. A heartbeat, a single quiet heartbeat, and then there again, like a determined little drummer in a marching band alone.

I breathe a sigh of relief, straightening. He's going to be okay. He just needs some rest. The spell took more out of him than he was expecting. That's all.

It's going to be okay.

Who exactly are you trying to convince, Leavi? The voices in your head?

I call out for Jacin. He'll help me get Aster somewhere he can rest.

Because that's all he needs. Some rest.

Chapter 62
ASTER

Every slow breath my lungs drag in burns like a million suture needles digging their way out of me. My head pounds in time to my intermittent heartbeat. My bones ache, a weary, chilling pain that makes me want to fade into unconsciousness once more.

Slowly, the sounds and sensations that surround me filter into my awareness. Nearby, someone breathes softly, and clothes rustle against wood. It's probably the same someone shifting in their seat. Something soft and heavy is pulled up around me. A blanket.

Another wave of pain hits me, sending blood coursing from my nose. I moan.

I hear the person stand, sense them lean over me, feel them press cloth beneath my nose.

"Aster?" Leavi's soft, hopeful voice murmurs.

I force my eyes open. Behind Leavi's concerned face, orange greets me. I'm in my room.

"Hey," she says quietly, sitting down beside me. "How do you feel?"

I swallow a thick lump. "I'll be fine," I manage. My eyes attempt to close, but I push them open again.

"Is there something I can get for you?"

I start to shake my head, but pain and dizziness wash across my mind. My eyes squeeze shut, regardless of my will this time.

Leavi lays a hand on my shoulder. "Aster?"

A wordless hum escapes me. The cloth presses at my nose, soaking up the blood trickling down my lip. A burning, shooting sensation wracks my body again, and I groan.

This has never happened to me before.

"Aster, what's wrong?" Leavi's voice pitches high with worry. "What do I need to do?"

Fog swells in my mind, slowing my thoughts. I don't know what to tell her. The pain infects my body.

"Leavi," I breathe.

Her hand brushes my cheek, soft fingers sending comforting chills through me. "I'm here." Her voice struggles to be level and fails. "What do you need?"

Ricocheting needles storm through me, and I suck in a sharp breath. "Leavi," I murmur again, voice weak and wobbling. Dark dread and fear sweep my mind.

"Yes?" The word is soft.

"I-" I don't know how to say this, don't know how to face this, don't know what to do if it's true.

I draw in a rasping breath. "I think the spell was too strong."

My awareness tries to fade, but Leavi's speaking, saying something, asking something. Her voice, words, are insistent, worried, breathless.

227

Now she's yelling, but I don't know, can't tell what she's saying. I can't tell what I'm thinking; everything's blurry, everything's fading.

"Don't-" she chokes. "Don't-"

Everything's gone.

Chapter 63
Leavi

He goes limp.

Panic shoots through me, and I press my ear against his chest. *Please, please, please...*

The soft, unsteady thump of his heartbeat allows me to relax. I blow out a shaky breath. "You're okay," I murmur. "You're still okay."

I lay there for a minute, letting my head move with the rhythm of his breaths. It's comforting, this tangible reassurance of life. I could almost fall asleep here and dream up a world where everything is okay again.

Blood dribbles from his nose, and I pull back, wiping it away with his handkerchief. My hand shakes as I set the cloth aside.

I think the spell was too strong. His last words to me echo in my head like the bell for a funeral service. I refuse to let that mean what it sounds so very much like.

That he's dying.

"No," I say. Despite myself, my voice shakes.

Trembling fingers pull my hair into a loose bun. He's going to be fine. He can't die, not from this, not from some stupid spell, not after everything we went through to get him away from Veradeaux. He's not dying.

I straighten the already even covers. He'll be fine.

All he needs is some rest.

* * *

His nose is pouring again. It's been five hours, and he has yet to wake up. Not a word, not a flutter of his eyes or a restless toss. No. It's been five hours, and except for the frail rise and fall of his chest, he looks like nothing more than the cadavers I dissected in lab.

I hold the handkerchief to his nose until the blood stops trickling, then gently wipe it away. His skin is cold under my fingers, and I tuck the blankets up higher around his shoulders.

A tear drops, dampening a spot on the quilt. Surprised, I dash my eyes.

"He's fine, stupid girl," I mutter to myself. "He'll be fine. He said so himself."

I think the spell was too strong. He said that too. An honest admission from a frightened boy, not a pretense to keep someone else from worrying.

I think the spell was too strong.

"Then why did you cast it, you-" My voice breaks. "You-" My throat tightens, closing off the words. *Hero*, my mind finishes. *He's a hero, a dumb, compassionate, reckless hero who put his life on the line to save someone else's.* "Don't do that again," I order, my voice thick.

But I'm not sure he'll get a chance to listen.

"Shut up," I tell myself. "When did you become such a pessimist?"

229

I swallow my tears. All he needs is some rest.

* * *

A candle on his bedside table holds back the darkness coating the room.

We all tell ourselves lies every now and then. We have to so we can keep our sanity.

But sometimes lies are dangerous. Sometimes they hide what we desperately need to know, no matter how much we don't want to. Sometimes they have to die.

Sometimes we have to kill them.

My hand hesitates above his neck, not wanting to take his pulse. Because I know what I'm going to find. I know that rest has done nothing for him, no matter how much I want to believe it should, can, will. The reality is, it hasn't.

My descending fingers confirm my strongest fears.

Chapter 64

SEAN

Leavi doesn't come down for dinner. Aster's not present either. Bukki looks like he just woke up, and Marcí is fretting over him as if he's all but dead. Zena is as much the seven-year-old little kid as ever, Marcus is as silent as ever, and Jacin is, if possible, looking creepier and more brooding than ever. Idyne acts, as always, as if she hasn't a care in the world.

Sitting at the dining table, I feel like everything is disconcertingly normal, uncomfortably *usual* after kidnapping the most important person in the area, after us almost dying, after Idyne killing those people. After me realizing Leavi has no interest in my companionship.

In a moment of uncommon honesty with myself, I acknowledge it hurts. I've been with her through so much more than anyone else here, and she wants to blow me off.

But then I shove the useless emotion back down because I also acknowledge that I brought it on myself. It was foolish of me to expect her to want any more to do with me than anyone else ever has. It was idiotic of me to set myself up for this kind of letdown by assuming, for some reason, that I would be someone she'd want to be around.

I ask Marcí what's wrong.

She turns to me, surprised. "Did Leavi not tell you?"

I raise an eyebrow. "I haven't seen her all day."

"Oh. Bukki was," she lays a hand on one of his, smiling at him, then turns back to me, "ill, and dear Leavi didn't know how to help him. But that blessed wizard came and saved him, gave Bukki more time." She blinks away the grateful tears that are trying to form. Her face falls as she continues to speak. "But now the boy's paying the price for the spell. I don't know much about it, but he's been in bed ever since. I think Leavi's with him."

My distracted mind pauses before supplying me a response. "Thanks. For the explanation."

Marcí gives me a curious look, and Idyne confusedly tilts her head at me. I offer a thin smile to the first and ignore the latter.

As much as Aster gets on my nerves, I hope he's okay. I think there's been too many things going wrong recently as is, and for both his and Leavi's sakes, I want everything to turn out alright.

I finish eating a minute or so after Marcí and go into the kitchen to wash my plate. She's standing at the counter, putting a full plate and a bowl of broth on a tray.

Marcí looks over at me. "I'm going to take this up to Leavi and Aster." She hesitates. "If you're wanting to go check on her, you can take it instead," she offers.

I pause, watching the ripples in the broth. Do I want to go check on Leavi?

Yes.

Would it be a good idea or serve any sort of productive purpose?

"No." I turn away from Marcí and finish washing my plate. "Thanks."

231

Chapter 65

LEAVI

I never liked being told what to do.

No, that's not quite it. I never liked not being given a choice. I can follow instructions just fine, but I refuse to allow myself to be consigned to the inevitable. There is *always* a way out. There is *always* another option.

Aster's pulse has declined. Again.

A knock sounds at the door, startling me out of my careful watch. I rise to open it.

Marcí stands there, holding a tray with a plate of food and a bowl of broth. "I brought you some dinner."

Wordlessly, I nod my thanks and take the tray, laying it on the bedside table.

Marcí inches in. "How is he?"

Back turned to her, I fiddle with the placement of the dishes on the table.

"Leavi?"

My lips press together. "Not good, Missus Marcí."

"Oh." Her voice is quiet. "Is he...?" *Dying.* I know that's what she means, but she doesn't quite say it.

"I don't know," I lie. "We'll just have to wait and see." *Wait and see how long he clings to the slip of life left in him.*

"I see."

I'm quiet, watching Aster breathe.

"Well, if there's anything I can do-"

She's backing out of the door as I turn around, an idea occurring to me. "Marcí?"

She pauses. "Yes?"

"Is Idyne here?"

"Oh." She considers. "No, I don't think so. She said something about going for a walk when we finished dinner."

My hopes deflate some, but I nod.

"Do you want me to send her up if she comes back? It can't be too much longer, dark as it is."

Unless she left in the dark so no one would see her go to the farm house. She's probably feeding Veradeaux. Or maybe she got tired of waiting around and decided to get a head start on the journey south.

Besides, I'm not sure I trust her anymore. Aster told me not to a long time ago. Maybe her being gone is a sign, a blessing in disguise. I doubt Aster would want her casting on him anyway. If she would even be able to help. "No."

"Okay, then." Marcí seems confused. "Well, like I was saying, let me know if you need anything."

I nod, and she slips out. I sit back down at the edge of the bed. The loss of blood has drained the color from his almond skin, and his face is scarily still but strangely peaceful. He reminds me of the enchanted princes of fairy-tales, waiting to be awakened by an act of heroism or true love.

A strangled laugh escapes my lips. Perhaps he is, or something like it. After all, I do live in a fairy-tale now, don't I? A fairy-tale where black-robed villains taunt maidens off roofs, heroes capture the evil witch, and magic slowly curses men to death.

Aster's cloak catches my attention. If magic can create a curse… maybe it can also break one.

I shake my head. "No." I already told Aster I wasn't doing any more casting. Never again.

But if I don't try something, he'll die.

I push to my feet and tug his cloak off its hook. No more waiting. No more sitting idly by. No more letting fate, or nature, or whatever outside force wants to control me and those I care about, take its course.

If Aster dies, it will not be because I simply let him.

I slip his Book out of his cloak and pull its cloth off. As soon as my fingers touch the leather skin, the Voices start rustling in my head.

"Look who's back…"

"I'm not here for pleasantries."

"How rude," they drawl. *"That was rather uncalled for…"*

I press my lips together, trying to reign in my swirling emotions. Aster needs a clear head right now, not one that's alienating the only people who can help.

If they are people.

I shudder, and I swear they snicker at me. "I need your help," I say.

"Well, we assumed. Why else would you have come to us?"

Repressing the urge to bicker with them, I draw in a steadying breath. "Aster's sick," I explain.

"Mhm… Continue."

Their nonchalance evaporates my shallow reserve of patience. "So I need you to tell me how to fix him!"

"Oh?" Dread slinks into a pit in my stomach. The Voices draw away, seeming to whisper among themselves excitedly. They sound like they're plotting something.

The sound snaps toward me again. *"We have a spell for you…"*

The pages of the book flip, flying faster than my eyes can keep up with. Startlingly sudden, they settle, resting on one still, open page.

My eyes roam over the words, searching for the promised answer, but finding none. Everything is written in the same foreign tongue I saw the first time I used the book. Frustrated desperation fills me.

The silence in my head is full, as if the Voices are just waiting for me to have to turn to them yet again. Resentfully, but having no other choice, I give into their game. "What do I have to do?"

It feels as if they smile at me like open-mouthed eels—sharp, spiny teeth gaping and sinuous, sinister body twisting. They give their first direction. *"Get some powder."*

Doubt floods my veins like poison. The first time I listened to them, I wound up in a situation beyond my control, in pain and incapacitated. The second, I almost died.

But it's either do as they say and take the risk or do nothing. I refuse to let Aster's life slip away like sand through fingers too lazy to close.

I push the doubt away and retrieve Aster's bag of powder. I can feel the warm glow of their satisfaction; it's like sitting slightly too close to a fire. *"Now, repeat after us…"*

Just like last time, the letters in the Book light up for me to follow along with, and I do, words tumbling out of my mouth ever so carefully, fingers making the motions I'm instructed to, slightly beyond my conscious control. I feel like a living marionette, captured by the power of the Voices, the power of the spell, unable to accomplish anything beyond mechanical, rhythmic obedience. Having learned it does no good, I don't even try to fight it.

As the spell keeps going, though, and going, and *going*, panic begins to taint my numb submission. *I'm not going to be able to finish it*, I realize with a confident horror. My energy is draining like water in a tub, being sucked away faster and faster, to disappear with a twist and a sudden finality.

Aster warned me magic would be dangerous.

You stupid, conceited girl. You thought you were untouchable. I've learned too late just how wrong I was.

My world disappears in a flash of light.

* * *

I'm not sure what I thought the afterlife would look like. Actually, I never thought there was an afterlife at all, so I never spent much time considering what mine might be. I never believed in ghosts or any of the supernatural claptrap that doomsdayers cook up to guilt a stone-mark or two out of passers-by. A body is organic matter, nothing more. No invisible, all-powerful force holds it together. Simply alkemitic reactions and neural stimuli.

I suppose I owe all those people I scorned an apology.

In front of me lays an open field, bright vibrant grass swaying in the wind. The sun hangs in a tranquil, pale yellow sky, no cloud to somber its brilliance. A pretty place to spend eternity, but not very interesting. I figure I'll probably go crazy at some point with no one to talk to.

My eyes widen as I hear a faint rustle in the grass behind me, and I spin around to see Aster, just a foot away. Sorrow floods my mind as I realize what his presence here means. "Aster," I start, heart heavy. "I am so sorry I couldn't-"

He cuts me off. "Leavi, what have you *done*?" The reprimands of a million childhood failures could never add up to a voice so accusatory and horrified.

My mouth gapes, hurt and lost, not sure how to even begin explaining.

Regret immediately washes over his face. "It—it will be okay," he assures. Taking a breath, he runs his hand through his hair. "I'll get you out of here," he promises. His attention is on something else, though, eyes somewhere on the horizon.

"What are you talking about?"

His gaze finds me again, and he sighs, taking in my bewildered expression. "We are in the *Laeazi*," he explains. "'Meadow,' I think, in Avadelian."

So we're not dead. At least, not yet. Relief fills me at the place's innocuous name, but some sort of inevitability hangs in his manner. "What's wrong with a meadow?"

His lips lift wryly. "Nothing, in most cases, but this isn't any meadow. The *Laeazi*, it is… I do not know how to say it. A pocket of space in a different… reality. Different realm. Our world is sort of like a house with many locked rooms. Most people wander through the house without ever knowing that there *are* other rooms because they cannot get into them. But if you have a key—like the spell you cast—you can open the door, and then you're somewhere you have never seen before. The *Laeazi* is one of those locked rooms." He pauses. "The problem is, whenever people go into it, one less comes out. Someone has to stay behind to send the others back to their bodies."

I stare at him for a shocked moment. My mind is still processing when I spot something on the horizon. "Aster, what is that?"

He squints, then opens his eyes wide. "Not what. Who." Without answering the question, he hurries that way.

I rush after him. "Hold on. What's going on?"

He doesn't respond, though, and we hurry forward to meet two people arguing. As we get close, they look up from each other, eyes fixed on Aster.

The first of the pair, a young woman in a silver circlet and a gossamer dress, gasps. Her features are remarkably similar to Aster's; they have the same refined cheekbones and high brows, despite their small, slightly rounded noses. The main differences arise from their hair and eyes—hers is a styled ash-blonde, whereas Aster's is sandier, and her irises are a piercing blue instead of his warm brown.

"Aster," she greets.

Her companion, a middle-aged man appareled in finery and a cloak like Aster's, simply nods at him. The man's composed face now conceals his initial shock. He and Aster also resemble, even sharing the same brown eyes, but the man's face is more hawk-like and worn.

"Sela. Agraund," Aster says, voice shocked. He asks them something—in his language, it sounds like—and the woman rattles off an explanation. A sorrowed shadow gathers in Aster's eyes as he listens. I wonder if they told him someone he knows died.

Agraund steps forward, interrupting the other two. His words are logical and measured, and at the end of his brief speech, he gestures to me.

Aster shakes his head adamantly, tone respectful but decisive. Agraund appears troubled and continues speaking.

I desperately wish I knew what was being said. There's a gravitas to the conversation that cautions against not paying it heed.

Whatever Aster has decided, though, he's uncompromising. He makes some assertion again.

A soft frown creases Sela's face. "Aster," she says regretfully. It doesn't seem like the kind of address meant to persuade, but simply to lament.

He smiles gently at her and inclines his head, comforting words passing his lips. She nods back at him. To the man, he simply repeats, "Agraund."

The man seems rueful, but there's something slippery about it, like he's glad whatever it is isn't happening to him.

I grab Aster's arm. "What's going on?" Part of me already knows the answer, but I need to hear him say it, if nothing more than so I can argue him out of it.

He turns to me, and I let go of him. "We were trying to decide who would have to stay." I can almost see gears turning in his head as an idea begins to form.

I tip my head slightly, considering him, words heavy in my mouth. "And what decision did you make?"

He pauses. Suddenly, he asks, "Do you trust me, Leavi?"

Shocked at the turn in the conversation, I can only answer, "What?"

Words more insistent, more desperate, he repeats his question. "Do you trust me?"

"I-" Do I trust the boy who helped me when I stole from him? Who saved me when I slipped and caught me when I fell? Despite the uncertainty of the situation spiking fear in my heart, I can't help *but* trust him. He's earned that much from me, at least. "Yes, Aster. I trust you."

He smiles at me, but something about it seems bittersweet. He nods once, decisively, expression clearing. "I have a plan," he tells me confidently, voice lowered so the others can't hear.

"A plan." I repeat, the words almost a question.

He nods. "A plan." He pauses for a second, then reaches forward and squeezes my hand once, quickly, before stepping a few feet away.

There's something off about this situation, something dangerous, like watching a performer balance an upright plate on the tip of his finger. Any second the china could crash to the ground and shatter, but right now all you can do is stand there, breath trapped in your throat, watching. Believing in the skill of the performer.

Trusting.

Aster calls out in the magic tongue. His raw, commanding voice appeals to the sky, head tilted back, palms turned up. My stomach drops, but I remind myself of his promise. *He's not sacrificing himself. He's not going to be the one to stay here. There's some trick to it. There must be.*

The peaceful sky begins to swirl, a widening whirlwind forming above Aster's head out of firmament itself. The maelstrom glows from within, its light source hidden by the churning clouds and static electricity coursing down its surface. Still Aster shouts to the sky, hair whipped by the winds reaching for him, yet body still.

It's against my every instinct to hold my ground, to let this storm extend its fingers toward the boy in front of me, to not try to drag him to some modicum of safety. *There must be some trick to it,* I repeat to myself.

Almost as if the winds themselves heard me, the eye of the storm shifts course, drifting toward where I stand with Sela and Agraund. I look to them, panicked, but neither of them seem shaken. Sela looks pale, but stands confidently, and Agraund, despite the slight remorse in his eyes, simply looks calm.

As the winds reach us, they soften, brushing my skin almost like a mother caressing her child. Now directly above, I can see the center light, a warm, peaceful thing, expanding as if to come cradle us.

I manage to tear my eyes away from it to find Aster, now done casting, just standing, staring at us. The emotions on his face reflect the storm he called, his eyes pained but resolute. He catches my gaze, and something in his expression breaks. His lips move, but I can't hear it through the wind's roar.

I'm sorry, he mouths.

Then I'm bathed in a blinding pulse of light.

He lied, I realize, hollow. He lied. There was no plan. There was no mastermind idea. Just a simple choice, a simple sacrifice. His life for ours.

He lied.

As quickly as the light washed over me, it retracts, hesitating.

Agraund calls out to Aster, accusatory almost, but Aster seems as confused as the rest of us. Before he can respond, a chorus of voices whisper over the winds. Their volume is level, yet despite that, I can hear them clearly, and in Errelian even.

It's the Voices from the Book. A chill runs down my spine.

"We cannot allow you to remain here, young caster. This is no longer your decision to make."

The eye of the storm contorts and expands, winds buffeting Agraund out of its umbrella and dragging Aster in. He looks aghast and tries to protest, but the Voices pay him no heed.

"You are more useful to us than your uncle." With that simple, cold explanation, my world coalesces once more into light and nothingness.

Chapter 66

ASTER

It's an eerie feeling to know someone will be dead soon. I can't help but think of the person as such, even if the killing blow hasn't hit yet, or the condemning spell hasn't finished yet, or their body hasn't given up life yet. Because, either way, there might as well be no time left for them.

My uncle is dead.

His body is alive for now, but his mind will never return to it.

My uncle is dead, my country needs me, and instead of being there, I'm off on some fool's quest for power that, really, I knew I'd never obtain.

My country and my family need me, and I've abandoned it.

I'm a traitor.

"Aster?" The worried word cuts into my thoughts.

My eyes crack open. The debilitating weakness I felt before the Meadow has been washed away with the return of my consciousness—the solitary benefit of that horrendous spell.

Leavi's concerned face hovers over mine. As soon as she registers my open eyes, though, her concern transforms to anger. "You *lied* to me," she accuses, her accent growing thicker in her vexation.

In my grief, the meaning of her words escapes me. *Lie? Lie about what?*

It clicks.

"Leavi, I was saving your life." My tone is sharper than I meant it, and she draws back.

"Perhaps I didn't want you to!"

I sit up. "So you cast that spell with the full intention of sacrificing yourself?" The barely thought through words are full of doubt and derision. My thoughts hang heavy on what Agraund told me—how N'veauvia is under siege, how Sela's body was lying, bleeding out, in a castle hall.

She reddens. "I cast that spell to save your life! Not to have you throw it away."

"Leavi, there are more things involved than just my life." I shove my fingers into my hair, leaving them there.

"Like what?" she demands.

I bite my lip hard and look away. I can't tell her I was sacrificing myself so the actually useful Second Son, the second most important person in Morineaux, could stay and help with the catastrophe that's begun in my absence. I can't tell her that I'm a traitorous, runaway prince, full of foolish ideas and stupid decisions.

I can't tell her what's really going on.

I drop my hand. "It doesn't matter."

"Well, you almost died over it, so I think it does." Her eyes are hard.

"I don't understand why you're so angry that I didn't want you to die!"

Shock softens her face as she takes a half-step back. "I-" She gathers herself. Voice quiet and slow, she says, "I'm not angry you wanted to save me. I'm angry you lied to me. That you didn't give me a choice."

"Well, Leavi, there wasn't exactly a lot of time." If we didn't decide quickly, the enemy soldiers in the castle could have killed Sela and Agraund before the spell finished, or Sela would have just finished bleeding out and died despite the spell.

But Agraund is dead.

Hurt flashes on her face. "You had long enough to tell me you had a plan." She looks down, avoiding my gaze. "To make me think you were going to come back safe."

My irrational anger drains, leaving me cold and hollow. I close my eyes, head falling back to rest against the wall. "I did what I thought I needed to." My eyes open. "And I'm alive after all, right?" *At Agraund's expense.* A lump rises in my throat, and I try to ignore it. "It's done."

After a silent moment, Leavi sits on the edge of the bed. "Aster?"

"Yes?" I feel drained, and the weight of the word reflects that. I meet her gaze, though.

"When you cast that spell on Bukki..." Her hand comes to rest against her necklace. "Did you know it would kill you?" Her eyes search my face.

"No." She cocks her head, and I correct myself. "Not quite. I knew there was the chance, and I knew I was still suffering effects from the night before, but... I thought I could do it."

Her brows draw together. "Why-" She shakes her head, as if she can't quite comprehend it. "Why would you risk that?"

I pause. "Why did you rescue me?"

Chapter 67

SEAN

I hope we're leaving today. I'm done sitting idly around, waiting for the next opportunity of something interesting to arise. I'm done letting life, and Leavi, drag me around without my consent.

It's time for me to forge my own path, and I can do that once we get to Morineaux.

The rising sun tries to use the snow to blind me as I trudge to the farmhouse with Veradeaux's breakfast wrapped in a cloth. I don't like the idea of Aster carting along two dangerous prisoners on our trek. There are too many things that could go wrong. But I also don't want them able to roam freely—frustratingly, them coming is better than nothing.

I push open the door to the farmhouse and make my way to the last room. Unlocking it, I step inside. It's empty except for Veradeaux. Twine binds her wrists in front of her and pinches her fingers together. I set the open cloth down within her reach.

"You expect me to eat with my hands tied this way?" she demands.

"Have fun." I turn away. "I'm not untying you."

"Leaving so soon?" A hint of desperation tinges her otherwise smooth voice. "I have some information you might find interesting."

"That's nice." I reach the door.

"Aster's not who he says he is!"

I pause. What's she talking about? I laugh, glancing back at her. "How would you know who he's told us he is?"

"I don't. But I know him well enough to know he didn't tell you the truth." There's a calculating gleam in her eyes, the look of a person making a gamble.

I turn back to her, considering. She could easily lie to me here. In fact, she's probably going to.

But what harm is there in letting her speak?

"Then what's the truth?" I prompt.

"He's not just any caster."

"What is he?"

A smile slips onto her lips. "A runaway. From what, where, and why, I'll tell you when you unbind me."

"Is he dangerous?"

"His lies could be."

"Why?"

"Because he's using you." She leans forward. "I'd imagine he has been since the moment you met him."

"How so?"

She glances around the room. "I'm here, aren't I?"

Unease courses through my veins as if pumped by my accelerating heart.

240

"You want to find out the truth about him? Untie me."

I hesitate, and all my old worries flash through my mind. What has she really done against us? Who *is* Aster? We have nothing to go off of other than his own word, and that's the only thing that 'proves' he's not guilty of anything. Yes, Veradeaux attacked us night before last, but we were there to *kidnap* her. We stole her prisoner, who we, really, know nothing about, are holding captive her associate from the east, and snuck into her home in the dead of night to abduct her.

Who really are the bad guys here?

My focus returns to her. She sits there, watching me.

I don't know anything about her, either, though. Plus, Aster was delirious from hunger when we found him. Starving your prisoners to death isn't exactly the habit of a quality leader. She was intentionally unnerving when we came to her room, and for no good reason—she was playing with us.

And the Man from the East did try to kill Leavi.

I shake my head at Veradeaux. "Look, we both know you can still eat like that. Thanks for what you told me. I'll see you later." I leave, locking the door behind me.

I know I don't trust Veradeaux. I can't afford to take that chance. But I'm not so sure I can trust Aster either.

* * *

After breakfast, I catch Leavi in the living room. "You going up to pack?"

Confusion flits across her face. "No."

I cock my head. "Why?"

"Aster's afraid the roads are still too hard to travel. We're going to wait a few days and see if the snow clears up any."

I pause. Aster decided. So, of course, she didn't feel the need to talk to me. "Well, Leavi," I shove my hands into my pockets, "you sure we shouldn't just go anyway? We've been here for long enough, don't you think?"

"It's not like we've been staying here without reason. Like Jacin said the other night, I don't want to end up dead in a snowdrift, and with Veradeaux out of the way, there shouldn't be too much danger. The guards think we've moved on, right?"

"Sure, but they're also going to be looking for Veradeaux."

"And how likely do you think it is they're going to find her? I think we're better off waiting here than braving the weather."

"I'm not really sure that we should be traveling with her and the eastern guy at all."

"We can't just leave them here."

I glance away. I know what I want to say, but I also know that she's not going to respond well. I look back at her. "There's another way where we don't have to travel with them."

She narrows her eyes. "What do you mean?"

"We don't go with Aster."

"Sean." She shakes her head. "I thought we already went over this."

"Leavi, that was when he couldn't fend for himself. I'm pretty sure he can now."

"Where is all this coming from?"

241

My hands come out of my pockets. Stalling, I flick open a timepiece, but don't bother interpreting the numbers on its face. I close it and look back up. "Leavi, how much do we really know about this guy?"

"What do you mean?"

"I mean all we have to go off of is his word about what's happened. What if he's lied? What if he's just been pulling our strings this entire time?"

"Why would he lie to us, Sean?"

"If he had something to hide." My tone implies it's obvious.

"Yes," she says sharply, "but what would he want to hide? He's got nothing to lie to us about; we don't even know him."

"Exactly! We *don't* know him. He could be anyone. He's not confined to telling us the truth about who he is."

"He's saved my life, Sean. I don't think he's looking for our imminent demise."

I ignore her sarcasm. "Maybe not, but it also certainly helped him to keep you alive—we turned around and abducted the woman that was after him!" I raise a hand to cut off her protest. "My point is just this, Leavi: we don't know him, so we have no reason to trust him. I do not think he's who he says he is."

"Why? What reason has he given you to doubt him?"

I look away. "Think of it like this—we broke a prisoner out of jail, are holding against his will the man that came to reclaim the prisoner, and abducted the most important person in the area."

"Because they wanted to kill us?" she says pointedly.

"And where did we get that information? Aster."

"Aster didn't have to tell me the Man from the East wanted to kill me. I figured that much out myself when he tried to get me to jump off the roof!"

"I'm not saying that we necessarily did the wrong thing. I'm just saying that there's two sides to every stone-mark, and we don't know what angle Aster's working."

"You realize he almost killed himself trying to heal Bukki? Tell me what angle that is."

"I don't know! Leavi-"

I'm done. The thought suddenly pops into my head, and I realize it's true. I'm done trying to carefully explain myself, trying to make her listen by playing nice. "Leavi, I'm just trying to point out that we have no reason to trust everything he says is true. Now," I hold up a hand again, "I know that you don't like heeding other people's warnings, but I'm trying to bring up a legitimate point that can impact a lot from here on. I don't think we need to stay here, and I don't think we should travel with him and his prisoners." My sharp gaze pins her.

"Well, then, why don't you leave without me?"

"Skies, Leavi, I'm trying to help! I don't understand why you so readily trust this stranger's word over a friendly warning from someone that understands where you come from! Someone you *know*!" Marcí pokes her head into the living room, then withdraws it. I lower my voice. "Leavi…" My frustrated words trail off. I'm never going to convince her, and she's never going to listen to me. "You know, whatever. I'm done. I'm done trying to help you see sense in the cases where you clearly don't want to listen. I'm done trying to be here when you fall."

I shoulder past her, ready to pack my bags.

"What? Sean, wait." She catches my arm. "What are you talking about?"

Drained, I turn to her. "What do you mean?"

"You—you really are just going to leave?"

"It's not like my presence here changes much, Leavi. You don't listen to me, and you don't need me." I gently push her arm off mine. "Maybe I'll see you again someday."

She stares at me, features frozen.

I release a deep breath and start up the stairs.

Chapter 68

LEAVI

He's out the door and trekking through the snow in less than ten minutes.

He's going to come back. That's all my shocked brain can muster. *He's not really leaving. Any second, he's going to turn around and come back.*

I watch him through the window. His backpack rests on his shoulders, trench coat flaring behind him in the wind. Within seconds, he disappears into the treeline.

Then he's gone.

Go after him! my heart screams. I stay, though, leaning on the windowsill, like if I stare long enough, he'll reappear.

Besides, even if I did go after him, what would I say? *I know I told you to leave, but I didn't mean it?*

Or maybe, *Just kidding, I really am willing to leave Aster here and trek south through the snow with you.*

He has his reasons for leaving; I have mine for staying. But that piece of logic doesn't numb the ache inside me.

He's really gone, and I'm the one who pushed him out the door.

"What kind of idiot are you, Leavi?" I mutter. "'Leave without me'? Why the blazes would you say that?"

He's going to come back.

But he won't. Why would he? He has no reason to.

Why couldn't I, for once in my stupid life, ditch my stubborn pride and admit that he was right? I *don't* listen to him!

I don't listen to anyone.

Sean told me it'd be dangerous to break Aster out, and we've almost died more than once because of it. He told me Jacin was a creep, and I'm not entirely sure he's wrong. On top of that, Aster told me not to go on the roof, but I did anyway. He told me Idyne was trouble, that we shouldn't bring her, and now the blood of those guards is just as much on my hands as hers.

Even though Sean's wrong about this one—that we can't trust Aster—I didn't have to attack him when he brought it up. I could have countered his points logically, with evidence I have that Sean doesn't have access to. Maybe if I had, he'd still be here.

Maybe I still can.

I shove away from the windowsill. Someone's boots lay discarded by the door, and I tug one on. My other foot is only halfway in as I throw the door open and rush into the blistering wind. "Sean!"

I run toward the forest, too-large shoes slapping my heels with each step. "Sean!" Reaching the treeline, I cup my hands around my mouth and call his name again. My eyes search for any flicker of his form through the branches and undergrowth. "Sean!"

I wait, praying he calls back. Any second, he'll emerge from the foliage, collar popped, smug smirk glued on his face like he expected this to happen.

The only noise is the morning chatter of the birds.

The woods close around me as I take a few steps forward. Hands still cupped, I shout his name into the quiet forest. "Sean!" My hand slaps flat against the bark of a tree. "Sean, you idiot, would you please just come back? Please! Sean!"

Returning silence echoes, and its import settles heavy inside me. "I'm sorry," I whisper. "I really am sorry."

Birdsong and wind fill the air around me, the sun shining high above. The normality of it all sends a pang through my heart.

Because it's too late. He's gone, and he's not coming back.

I stand there for minutes, waiting, until the cold turns my skin pink. Then I turn and trudge back home.

Chapter 69

SEAN

I embrace the cold. There's always been something about winter snow that entrances me—it's numbing. Whatever pain I want to quiet, whatever memories I want to forget, in the cold, I can.

The snow covers the forest in a peaceful, uninterrupted blanket. The frosty bite in the air calms my breaths. Chill bumps rise on my skin, and my thoughts turn from the aching inside me to the simplicity around.

The cold is numbing. My mind sinks into a comforting rhythm of nothing but my steps in the snow.

"Sean!" The call shatters my carefully composed distance from the world.

"Sean!" Leavi's voice rings out once more. It feels like a knife to my chest.

My feet stutter to a stop. She's yelling for me.

"Why?" An incredulous laugh escapes me, and I mutter, "Leavi, what could you want from me?"

"Sean!"

I look to the side. A tree stands tall beside me, its dark bark frosted. It's not going anywhere any time soon. It knows its place in the world.

I know where I need to be, too. I also know where I'm not going to be of any use. I take a step forward.

"Sean!" she yells. She's packed more desperation, more emotion into my name with the one call than she has in the culmination of every other time she's said it, it feels like.

I swallow and take another step.

"Sean!"

Something inside me cracks, and I set a hand against the tree, head down.

"Why do you torture me like this?" I murmur. "You don't want me. You have other people, and I'm clearly not one of them."

"Sean, you idiot, would you please just come back? Please! Sean!"

My head tips to the sky. Through the leaves, pale grey clouds stare back at me.

"I'm sorry," I whisper. "I really am sorry." I pause. "But I know nothing's going to change."

I stand there for minutes, the wind whistling a mournful tune through the trees. My shaky breaths cloud the air.

Finally, I drag my hand down my face. "You've made your choice," I mutter. "Now go through with it."

I push off the tree and pull out an old compass. Morineaux's south.

Chapter 70
LEAVI

I just lost my best friend.

The thought echoes through my head as I wash the dinner dishes. I've been in Marcí's kitchen all day, trying to keep my hands busy and my mind shut off. It hasn't worked.

I just lost my best friend.

I can imagine what my mother would say if she was here. *Stop being so dramatic, Eleaviara! He was hardly your friend, let alone your best one. All you two did was argue.*

But he was also always there. Even when he didn't agree with me, even when I led us into danger, he was there. I suppose I assumed it'd always be like that.

Which is dumb. People don't spend their lives together unless they're married, and even then, they often wish they didn't have to. My mother certainly never counted anyone as her friend. Acquaintance, annoyance, assistant, or a tool to manipulate favors out of. Those were about the only categories she had for people.

"I, however, am not my mother," I tell the dishes, "and I don't aspire to be."

I scrub at a particularly stubborn piece of food, then dunk the plate into the water. It bothers me more than it should that there's one less plate to wash tonight.

The window over the sink reveals the falling snow. I wonder if he's safe. Did he manage to start a fire? I think he still has coal and his flicker, but out in the open, with the winter wind, that won't do him much good. He'd have to find some deadwood to build a decent blaze, but I'm sure everything's wet.

And what about shelter? He doesn't have a tent. Maybe he'll sleep in some convenient tree hollow, like lost children do in story books. Or maybe he made it to the next town, and he's in a different inn where the rooms aren't orange, or flowery, or—

What decoration did Sean's new room have? It suddenly occurs to me I never went in after Aster took his old one.

My hands fall still in the water-filled sink.

The door swings open, and I go back to scrubbing. My focus stays down on the dishes. A piece of hair escapes my bun and hangs down beside my eye, concealing whoever entered the room. Maybe if I ignore them, they'll go away. I really hope it's not Jacin, but I don't want to look to find out.

I bring the plate out of the water to inspect it.

"Here." Aster's soft voice shocks me into looking at him. The dish towel rests on his hand. "Let me."

"Oh." I pass the plate to him and tuck the piece of hair behind my ear. "Thanks." If anyone in the house had to come help me, I'm glad it was Aster.

He's just as quiet as I am, the swish of the water and the soft clink of the dishes taking the place of conversation.

It's strange to see thoughts swirling in someone's head. It's like trying to read a tome in a foreign language—knowing something weighty and important is going on but having no idea what it is. Right now, Aster's face is a maelstrom of troubling ideas, but I don't bother him about it.

That would leave it open for him to turn the question back on me.

I watch him dry dishes out of my peripheral vision. His lips are in a soft, contemplative line, eyes focused on his task. It staggers me that right now, instead of being solid and real in this kitchen, he could be stuck in some hazy half-world, body wasting away.

His life for mine. His life for *mine*. Whatever would have possessed him to make that decision? He's a nice person, sure, but that kind of sacrifice goes above and beyond a simple nice. That ignores survival instinct and defies the most integral instructions our bodies are programmed to obey.

His life for mine. It's such a contrast to the backbiting world of academia that I'm used to, where the only way to get ahead is to shove the others behind. Perhaps that's just the way he is, though. After all, he didn't offer his sacrifice for me alone. He was trying to save Sela, and if the Voices are to be believed, his uncle. Even before that, the event that started it all, he healed Bukki. He told me himself that he knew the devastating outcome it could have.

He tried to give his life for mine, though, and I can't help but feel a pull toward him, a companionship, a trust. Though his gesture might have been meaningless, though he might not have any special preference toward me—it's still there.

We finish our task and leave the kitchen. In the living room, everyone else is playing some sort of acting game. Zena is in the middle, gesturing wildly while the others toss out guesses. Marcí waves me over, but I give her a weak smile and shake my head. It feels wrong to take part in any sort of joviality tonight, and the cacophony of household leaves no space for thinking.

Aster slips out to the front porch, nothing but his cloak to ward off the cold.

Acting on impulse, I snag a couple of throws and follow him. He sits on the steps, framed by the dark of the treeline. I settle beside him, passing him one of the blankets. He looks up, surprised.

"I thought you might be cold," I explain.

Distractedly, he takes it, setting it on his knees as I wrap mine around my shoulders. Safe under the eaves, we watch the snowfall set a muted hush to the world. We sit like that together for who knows how long, each lost in our own thoughts.

Softly, he says, "My uncle is dead."

I glance over at him, trying to read the emotion in his face. The night masks it.

"He was practically my father." He fists the fabric of the blanket. "The girl that was there, Sela—that's my sister."

The woman in a fairy queen's dress was his sister? I study him, as if I can discover his history by staring hard enough.

He continues. "She'd been attacked. She," he looks down at his hands, "she was going to die, and Agraund saved her. And he *knew* how the Laeazí works."

"What do you mean?" I ask softly.

He glances over to me. "He knew he was dying for her."

Emotion tightens my throat.

He bites his lip, looking down. "I need to get home," he murmurs.

Sorrow weighs his words, and I wish I could lift some of their burden. "We can head south as soon as it's safe to travel," I offer. Worry for Sean darts into my brain again, and I shove it away. Nothing I can do about it now.

His head straightens, and a sardonic smile twitches on his lips. "I needed to be home a long time ago. There's-" He runs a hand through his hair. "There's things happening, and I need to be there, but instead I'm relaxing half the continent away-" He cuts off, fists clenching.

I set my hand on his. "Aster?"

He looks at me.

Gently, I say, "Why would someone hurt your sister?" I don't know why, but for some reason, I feel like that question holds the key to all the others buzzing in my mind.

He pauses as a million thoughts appear to flit behind his eyes. A pent breath escapes him, and he deflates. His fingers move in his lap, slowly twisting around each other as he thinks.

Finally, he says, "You've saved my life more than once, risking yourself in the process." His hands still, tightening together. "I have no reason not to trust you."

My heartbeat rises, scared what he's about to say, and I struggle to keep suspicion off my face. Hoping he'll continue, I nod.

He stares off at the snow as he speaks. "As you know, I'm from Morineaux and work at the castle."

Uncertainty rises in me.

"But I didn't tell you the whole truth."

My stomach drops. Sean was right.

"I'm not just a random worker." He pauses, mouth closed, and then forges ahead. "I'm the upcoming Second Son. A prince."

My mouth creeps open as a million emotions whirl through my mind—anger, amazement, confusion, betrayal, regret.

He turns to me again, uncertainty wavering in his eyes.

"Sean was right." I don't know why that's what slips out of my mouth, but for some reason, I can't stop it. "Sean was so right."

Confusion clouds his face. "What do you mean?"

I push to my feet, blanket falling to the porch. "He told me you were lying. And I stood up for you!" Now he's gone.

Hurt flickers across his expression. "I was just trying to protect myself," he says gently.

"How does lying protect you?" I demand, but I know the answer even as I ask it. I know I'm being unfair. I know I'm making a bigger deal out of this than it is, but Sean left, and it's my fault, and I don't know what to do with that.

He draws back. "I had no way of knowing that I could trust you. And it's not like I hurt anything by what I said."

"Sean left!" Aster's shocked eyes follow me as I sink back down beside him. "Sean left," I say more softly, "because I wouldn't listen to him. And he was right." My gaze drifts to the forest.

He watches me, expression just as somber as mine. I pick my blanket back up and pull it around me again. It's cold now.

"I'm sorry," I say after a long moment. My words feel flat. "I didn't mean to yell at you."

He shakes his head, the moment dragging out. "No matter. I'm sorry too. I never wanted to deceive you, but I felt it was necessary since one person had already tried to use my identity against me."

The snowfall grows heavier, and the clouds above are thick and dark, concealing the stars. "What do we do now?" I ask.

He leans against the stair railing. "I need to get home. Quickly. A different country has attacked Morineaux. N'veauvia is under siege." He scoops up a handful of snow and tosses it off the porch. "But I don't know how to *get* there. Some of the Draón lordships let the attackers, the Kadranians, through, and now both sides— Morineaux and Draó—are guarding the border. And no one guarding is going just let me through because I claim to be the prince. It's not like I look it, do I?" His words are pointed, but their frustration is directed more to himself than me.

I wish I could do something to help him. I wish I could change that frustration to success, the doubt and worry to contentment.

If I could choose right now between sending him to N'veauvia or me to Erreliah—

Though it would hurt, though my soul would ache for missed chance home, I'd send him. I'd have to send him. I can't bear the idea of him being like this, me being able to fix it but not. I'd never forgive myself.

I'll never forgive myself now if I don't find some way to make this better.

"I'll help you," I promise.

He stares at me, as if trying to puzzle out a complex equation. "How?"

My mother once told me that if I actually wanted something, then I had to do whatever it took to make it happen, no matter what, no excuses. "I'll figure it out," I assure.

He looks doubtful. I catch his incredulous eyes and hold them with my soft, steady ones. "I'll figure it out," I repeat. I offer him a small smile and stand up.

Time to keep good on a promise.

* * *

Magical help. Aster's words from the night of the party echo in my head. That's what he needs, after all. A way to make possible what isn't. I've yet to find a better definition for magic than that.

My hand hesitates at Idyne's door. *Magical help.* Powerful magical help. That's what Aster said people like her provided. He also said they were impulsive and dangerous. *Chronically untrustworthy.*

I didn't listen to him before, and two men died. I'd be a fool to disregard his warnings now.

Besides, I've never even seen her cast. For all I know, she's every bit the con I thought her to be originally.

Aster said she was a kra'kaa, though. He'd know better than I would. He also said she was powerful, though he'll never ask her for help himself.

Right now, we need the impossible. Whatever its cost.

I knock.

"Who is it?" she calls from inside. Before I can answer, though, the door swings open. "Leavi! What are you doing here this time of night? You're usually in bed. Not that I mind. I don't sleep much anyway. Come in!" She grabs my wrist and drags me over to her bed.

I sit straight-backed on the edge.

"What's up?" she asks. "And where's Sean? I haven't seen him since this morning."

My breath catches, and I try to compose myself. "He left."

"Oh. Oh, no. Why? Is he-"

I wave a hand, cutting her off. "It's complicated."

"Oh. Okay." She settles cross-legged on the bed. An easy smile still rests on her lips, setting ablaze an uneasy fear in my stomach. How is she so calm, so normal, just two days after soaking her hands in blood?

It's like she has no conscience.

"What's up?" she asks again.

I try to quench my anxiety. Offering her a small smile, I say, "I need a favor, actually."

"A favor? What kind? No, don't tell me, silly. I'd rather guess." While she's considering, she lays down in front of me, hands propping her chin up, feet kicking lightly in the air above her. "Hmm... A love potion," she teases.

Seeing my flash of irritation, she laughs. "No, I knew that wasn't it. You don't need one, and I don't make them anyway. Too messy." She waves a hand, dismissing the subject. She glances up, and as if speaking to someone else in the room, says, "See? I told you so."

My forehead crinkles, but before I can ask her about it, she waves it away as well. "So, not a love potion. Not fashion advice either, though I *am* remarkably good at that." She grins broadly. "No. Hmm..."

I stop her before she can make any more guesses. "I need a way to get to Morineaux. As quickly as possible, and without going through the border. Aster's family contacted him. He needs to get home." That's not even a lie.

"Oh. Well, why didn't you just say so?"

I glare, seeing right through her games, and she giggles, pleased at being called out. Her childishness is unsettling. I try to refocus her. "I really do need your help, Idyne. I promised I'd find him a way home."

I expect her to ask why, or what's keeping him from just going, but she simply nods. "Okay. I think," she bounces up and starts digging through her bag, "that I have just the thing." Flashes of strange objects catch my eye as she tosses them to the side. Finally, she pulls a pearl out and holds it above her head, triumphant.

She scrambles back onto the bed, giving me a glimpse of the sphere. Its shimmery surface is covered in etched runes. The letters remind me of the ones in Aster's book. "This can get him there. Well, anywhere, really. But it will take a week to be ready, and it tends to be shifty on location. I'll get it to put him close enough, though. Oh, and," she stresses, "it only works for two people. Him and Veradeaux, I suppose, right? Once he gets there, he won't be able to come back through. The pearl will stay with me, on my side of the portal, so I can use it again. Got it?" She grins. "Great."

She moves to stand again, but I lay a hand on her knee to stop her. I don't want to agree to some hidden contract without knowing what the cost is. "What's the catch?"

She seems slightly taken aback, affronted almost. "No catch."

I press my lips together, not wanting to offend her, but also not wanting to get caught up in something beyond my understanding. "Aster said casters like you asked for a price. In return for your help."

Her eyes narrow, hurt, and for a split second, the flighty, over-the-top Idyne I'm familiar with is replaced by a girl collapsing in on herself. Her eyes transform into wells of stories too deep and troubled to ever fathom. Loneliness radiates from her like cold fire.

Then it passes, and I'm struck with the sense it was all some fanciful hallucination. She pouts playfully. "Why, Aster just doesn't understand me at all. I mean, after all, Leavi, you're my friend. You don't charge friends for things, now do you?"

I'm struck for a moment. This object she's offering to use for me is obviously valuable. Something that lets a person cross any amount of distance. All for free.

No, not quite for free. In order to keep my friendship.

That's frightening.

She doesn't give me any more time to consider, though. She flounces off, heading downstairs.

"Where are you going?" I call after her.

"The farmhouse," she answers back, not stalling her pace. "There's not enough space in my room, now is there?"

How am I supposed to know?

I pull on my boots, grab a blanket and follow her out the back door. We twist through the forest as the snow falls around us. Crossing the dead, white field, we enter the main room of the farmhouse. It's just as quiet and empty as when we left it.

A shudder runs through me as I remember it's not quite empty. Veradeaux is tied up in the last room.

Idyne paces forward and puts the pearl in the middle of the floor. She begins casting, using a longer ritual than I've ever seen Aster use. Powder floats through the air, sprinkled at intervals as her voice rises and falls. She withdraws a white feather from her hair, crumpling it in her hand. She opens her fist, and dust falls over the pearl. As the spell draws to a close, she sticks the pad of her thumb between her teeth, biting it. When she brings it back out, she sinks to the floor, allowing a single drop of blood from her thumb to fall onto the shining surface of the sphere. It slides off one side, forming a tiny red puddle on the floor.

An ethereal light suddenly comes to life inside of pearl, darting and swirling like fish in a pond. Idyne sits back heavily. "There we go." She smiles at me weakly. "It should be all but ready seven nights from now. He can go through the following morning."

There we go, I echo. The beginning to the end of Aster's stay here.

When he leaves, I can't go with him. Only two. That's what Idyne said. Obviously it has to be him and Veradeaux. Or perhaps the Man from the East. I'm not sure how he'll work that out, but either way, I'm not on the ticket.

252

For a second, the irrational urge to tell Idyne to end the spell sweeps over me. I've already lost Sean; I don't want to lose Aster too. Even though he lied to me, I still can't help but trust him. There's something about him—a warmness, goodness, protectiveness—that makes me feel safe. I don't want to lose that.

I don't want to be alone.

But he misses his Morineaux, and his Morineaux needs him.

Skies above know that if I had the cure to the plague in my hand right now and a way to get back home, nothing could stop me from tearing back to the High Valleys. No person could either, and no person worth caring about would ask me to. No. If the situation were reversed, and I was telling Aster what state my homeland were in, and how they would be better off if I was just *there*, I know exactly what he would do. And he wouldn't hesitate.

So I can't either.

I leave the farmhouse with Idyne.

Chapter 71

ASTER

She said she would help me.

An impossible task, even if Draó and Morineaux weren't guarding their borders; during wartime on her own land, Morineaux enacts a strict policy about people coming into the country. In the travel-disheveled state I would be in, I have the feeling I might have a hard time convincing guards that I am, in all actuality, the Second Son and *not* some random person badly lying about my identity.

But she said she would help me.

The sun is low in the sky as I walk to the forest, toward where the shaman is hidden.

What purpose would saying something like that serve? What does she think she can do to change this stupid situation I have gotten myself into?

This really is all my fault. If I had stayed, I could have helped defend the castle. I could have defended Sela so that she wouldn't have to have been taken to the Meadow. I could have been the one to take her if it was unavoidable.

Instead, Agraund is dead, and it's my fault. Instead, I'm stuck in this inn, wasting away the days.

What is wrong with me? That I would forsake my country, my duty, for such a foolish quest?

What was I even thinking?

Leavi said she'll help me get home, though. She'll help me figure it out. Even though I lied to her, even though she has her own problems to worry about, even though she's upset that Sean left. She said she'll help.

The wavering moonlight is scattered by the barren branches of the trees, but there's still light enough for me to see by. Food in hand, I slip through the forest.

Amarris's questions make sense now. An ache rings through me that my uncooperativeness didn't stop the attack. Disgust fills me that she would help the Kadranians try to conquer Morineaux. Then again, she always has been a self-serving snake.

Part of me doesn't even want to give this food to the Kadranian worm. Part of me thinks it's the least he deserves after helping with this attack on my homeland.

I don't want to stoop to his immoral, cruel techniques, though. I will not allow myself to be comparable to a Kadranian.

I step into the clearing he's in.

Completely limp against the tree, he's covered in mostly-dry blood. His head lolls back, revealing a jagged gash so deep in his neck he's nearly decapitated.

I recoil. I've seen bodies before, but never one so gruesomely murdered. His dark eyes stare into the branches, pain and shock eternally etched into his bloodless face. Strands of lank red hair stick in the gore of his neck.

A small, disturbed voice whispers in the back of my head. *Who would do this?*

I run a hand through my hair to shake off the shock. I'll figure it out later. Right now, I can't just leave this body sitting here. I don't want someone else to run across him—no one needs his image in their head, and I don't want people to start poking around.

Besides, no matter how much I detest him, no one deserves to sit out as carrion.

In the center of the small clearing, I clear away the snow as best I can and gather brush in roughly the same dimensions as the shaman. I grab his wrists and drag him onto the pile. I cover him in more brush.

Despite his homeland's customs, I refuse to barbarically bury him as they do.

I light the sticks above and beneath him. It takes multiple efforts to get it to catch into a proper funeral blaze.

My disgust for him burns like the flames, but as I watch them, I can't help but wonder.

Who was he? Did he have family? Children? None of them will ever truly know what happened to him.

What drove him to serve the attack on Morineaux? To be a caster?

Staring through the flames at his face, pity rises within me. I don't condone his practice, but he was a powerful man and was reduced to solitarily living his last days a snowy prisoner. A man that should easily have been able to fend off his killer was reduced to idly watching as they came closer until he was unable to watch anything again.

"Life is so fleeting," I murmur.

I watch the fire, making sure it doesn't die, until the body of the man is gone. Somber, I break up the ashes and charred wood, then spread the snow back across the site as best I can.

The moon is peaked in the sky as I walk back to the inn. Once again, the thought enters my mind: *Who would have done this?*

I suppose it's always possible that someone completely unconnected to the matter ran across him and, for whatever reason, saw fit to kill him, but I find that unlikely. That cut wasn't the clean kill of someone just trying to rid the world of their victim; it was angry, violent. It was revenge.

Leavi wouldn't do that. Considering she reprimanded me for keeping him outside in the first place, I can't see her murdering the man, despite his attempts to do just that to her. She's too kind, too non-violent.

There's Sean. Though he's gone now, looking at the state of the shaman, I don't have a hard time believing that he could have been killed yesterday. I can't picture Sean killing someone, though, much less a man he hardly had any dealings with. As helpful as he was in detaining Amarris, I still don't think he could stomach it. At least he has a cutting weapon, though, unlike Leavi, unless she stole something from the kitchen.

Jacin and Idyne don't even know he's here, unless Leavi or Sean asked one of them to go feed him while I was sick. As far as I know, Jacin also doesn't have a weapon.

Idyne, though… The image of her whipping out that shard of silverglass flashes into my mind. She held it like she knew what she was doing, her stance ready for a fight, rather than the awkward and hesitant ones of Leavi and Sean.

She's a kra'kaa, where practically the only predictable thing about her is that she'll do the unexpected.

"But so unexpected as to murder a man for no reason?"

Then again, we don't know anything about her—where she's from, who she is. Maybe she does have a reason to hate him enough to murder him. Maybe she's unbalanced enough to do it too.

I want to approach her and demand an answer, but I realize I have nothing, really, to say. What good would it do, anyway? She'd either deny it or not, and then what would happen?

Nothing.

There's no reason to tell Leavi, either. She already didn't accept my warning from before that she shouldn't trust Idyne; talking to her won't change anything, and if it does, probably not for the better.

Resolved to keep my silence, I push into the house and up to my room. Leavi paces in the middle of the orange.

I stop short but then finish coming in, drawing the door mostly shut behind me. She looks up.

"What's wrong?" I ask.

"Nothing. I was waiting for you." Her eyes sweep over me, brows drawing together slightly. "Where were you?"

I pause. "The Man from the East died while I was sick." I scan her face for her reaction.

Her jaw drops, confusion mingling with shock. "How?" Guilt creeps into the mixture.

The thought flits through my mind to tell her that it was just animals. I don't want her to blame herself, though. "Someone killed him." I'll let her come to her own conclusions about who.

Her mouth moves but no sound comes out.

Not sure what else to say, I ask, "Why were you waiting for me?"

She sinks onto my bed, eyes not quite focused. "How—why…" She can't seem to finish a thought.

I sit beside her. "I don't know."

Her gaze is still on some middle space. Numbly, she says, "Why didn't we move him? To the farmhouse, with Veradeaux. It wouldn't have been that hard."

"We can't blame ourselves. It wasn't anything we did or didn't do."

Her gaze snaps to mine. "Yes, it was! You can't say we didn't have a hand in it. *We* tied him up, *we* left him there. Helpless. Don't tell me that wasn't our fault."

I set my hand beside me on the bed. "We didn't do anything we didn't need to."

"We needed to tie him up and leave him in the cold?"

"Even if we'd moved him to the farmhouse, this could have happened, Leavi."

"How? A stranger's not going to run across him in the farmhouse. Veradeaux's still alive, isn't she?"

I run my other hand through my hair. After a long pause of her staring at me expectantly, I say, "It probably wasn't a stranger."

She blinks at me. "You just said you didn't kill him."

"I didn't."

She draws back. "You don't think I did it."

My gaze meets hers, and I pour as much sincerity as possible into it. "Of course not."

"Well, Sean didn't do it either!"

"I don't think he did."

She draws herself up. "Then who do you think did?" she explodes.

My hands come up, placating. "I don't know, Leavi." I hold her gaze. "I'm sorry."

She deflates, as if suddenly tired. I set my hands back down, one accidentally closer to hers than I meant it to be.

"Why does death keep following us, Aster?"

"I-" My brow draws together. I'm not sure what all she's referencing. "I don't know. But it's going to be alright."

She gives a mirthless laugh. "Not for the people who have died the last few days."

I look away. I can't imagine what the castle will be like without Agraund.

Her eyes turn sympathetic. "I'm an idiot," she mutters, shaking her head. She sets a hand on my shoulder. "I'm sorry, Aster."

"It's fine," I reply softly, turning back to her. The flecks in her eyes catch the candlelight. My shoulder buzzes beneath her hand, and my thoughts have slowed to a strange stop. I feel like I should be saying something, but I don't know what.

"I found a way for you to go home, though," she offers quietly. "If that helps."

Suddenly, panic burns in my chest, and I drop my gaze. I want to help, I want to right what I've done wrong, but—

I don't want to go. I certainly don't want to walk into a war, leading men I'm not prepared to lead, making decisions that alter the lives of thousands.

I swallow. They're depending on me. The dread numbs my tongue. Even if I can't do much, they're depending on me.

Which means I need to be there.

I force down the fear as I meet her eyes again. "How?" My lips offer a smile. It's fake and practiced, but she doesn't know that.

"Idyne. She set up a… portal, is what she called it, that will take two people to Morineaux. You and Veradeaux." Her lips twitch a small smile, but I get the feeling it's just as fake as mine. "It'll be ready in a week."

Despite the fear and dread, gratitude fills me. "Thank you, Leavi." I know what I have to do, an impossible task, but she's somehow made it slightly more conquerable.

Then it sinks in who she said offered the portal. "Are you sure that's a good idea, though? What did she make you do?"

She shrugs, dropping her hand. "Nothing. Said she didn't charge for friends." Something wavers in her eyes, uncertainty or fear or maybe something else. Whatever it is, though, it's not confident.

I rest my hand near hers, fingertips barely touching. I want to comfort her, but I don't know what about or how. I want to fix things for her, but I don't know what, if anything, is broken.

I want to tell her I'm here, but I'm leaving soon.

"Like you said," she smiles weakly, "it'll be alright. You'll get home and hopefully the rest of us won't be far behind you. Maybe we'll meet again someday."

Something in me plummets. It didn't occur to me that this next week will likely be the last time we'll ever see each other. It's hard to believe that someone that has been such a constant in my life for the past week will probably never be in it again. It feels like so much longer than that.

"Yeah," I finally manage. "Maybe."

She nods, looking away. "I should let you get some sleep, shouldn't I?"

I chuckle dryly. "It's fine. I don't mind." I probably won't get to sleep soon anyway. The image of the dead shaman forces itself back into mind.

She glances back at me, hopeful surprise flickering on her face. "Oh?" Turning her gaze to her hands, she says, "I could make us some tea and bring it up. We could talk. If you wanted."

The lightness of the idea lifts my spirits slightly, leaving me pleasantly surprised. I nod. "I think I'd like that." A smile lifts my lips.

She looks back up at me, smiling in return, and goes.

* * *

I'm dancing. Sleepy firelight illuminates the party around me. Leavi dances with me, an easy grin lighting her face.

She's beautiful.

I admire her—her intelligence, determination. Her integrity. I've never met someone like her, someone so foreign, yet so kind and unselfish. Someone so good.

Her mouth moves, talking, but I can't hear her. The sounds around me are clear—laughter, conversation, music—but Leavi's words don't reach my ear.

I strain to listen, and she keeps talking like everything's normal, but I can't hear her, something's off, something's wrong...

The scene fades into us sitting on the porch, facing the flurry of falling flakes. The air is weighty with our worries, yet she's here for some reason, trying to comfort me. I turn to her. She's silent, and I rest a hand on her shoulder.

The porch shows through her lightly translucent skin.

Fear and concern burn in me. She looks at me and tells me something important, impassioned, but I can't hear her.

Around us, everything shifts until we're standing on the snowy roof at sunset. Leavi, looking behind me at nothing, fearfully steps back, and her foot connects only with air.

My arms snatch out and hold her close to me. I stumble forward. I won't let her fall. My feet steady. I won't let her fall.

Her terrified eyes search my own as the spell tears words from her silent lips. I can hardly feel her, and through her head I see the forest.

In her ear, I whisper assurances, because even though I'm scared and don't know what's happening to her—why is she fading?—I know she's scared, too, and I want to help.

She's fading in my arms, disappearing, and I don't know why, and I don't want her to go, but she's disappearing.

She meets my gaze, pained tears coming to her eyes. Her fading lips form one word, and this time, though I can't hear it, I know what she says. My own lips echo the message.

'Goodbye.'

Heart aching, I slip into wakefulness. Cold sweat dampens my forehead, and I sit up, trying to steady my shaky breath.

"Calm down," I murmur. "It was just a dream. I've dealt with them before."

At the same time, though, I know this one was different. It wasn't a nightmare of past sights or a torture by my guilt—it was simply an expression of my pain, sorrow, and fear.

I don't want to go. I don't want to go lead men that disapprove of me, to rule beside family who think me useless, to make decisions where the outcome can decide who lives and dies. I don't want to spend my life a pawn of the queen, a tool that no one cares for but everyone needs though I don't even work properly.

I rake a hand down my face, sunlight working its way through the curtains.

I don't want to leave Leavi.

I shake my head violently. "That's absurd. I've known her for less than a month. I hardly even know anything about her."

Which is true. I don't know any of the little things that a person should about a friend. Her favorite color, favorite food, her pet peeves—these are all still mysteries to me.

"But I know the important things." I know she's kind and self-sacrificing for what she knows is right. I know she's witty and sarcastic, that she's far more intelligent than I, that she's trustworthy.

"I know that after I leave, I'll never see her again."

That shouldn't matter, though. I've been foolish to allow myself to form whatever level of attachment to her that I have.

I'm only going to end up having hurt both of us.

Which is why I'm not going to bother her anymore. I won't bother any of the people at this strange, cozy little inn. I can't afford to want to stay any more than I already do, and I don't want to hurt them by going.

Instead, I'll practice. There's no reason to be downstairs for more than meals. I can stay in here and cast.

Because when I get home, I'll be thrown into the middle of a lake of responsibilities and be expected to already know how to swim.

Chapter 72

LEAVI

Everything feels dead. Outside, the wind won't blow. The clouds stay full but refuse to snow, like they're frozen in the sky. One day blends into the next, their similarity stretching time into an eternity.

Somehow the week still passes too fast.

After the night we have tea, Aster and I don't talk much. I don't know what to say, and he spends most of his time in his room. The few times I try to coax him downstairs, he doesn't even bother opening his door, telling me he's busy. When he does make an appearance, he's drawn, face a silent storm. It's like he shut off.

I wish I could open his brain and find all the heavy secrets weighing him down. I'd take them out and give them wings and watch them fly away. His wide, easy smile would replace his pensive brood. Everything would be okay again, easy as that.

It doesn't matter, though. He leaves in the morning.

The sun falls tonight like the blade of a guillotine. I watch from my window, hands pressed against the glass, as the sky flashes blood red and then cuts away, dead and fixed in its finality. The stars appear one by one, hopeless rebels against the ever-expanding darkness. They'll fade and disappear from the heavens one day, and they know it. Still, they wave their shining banners, hoping they can overcome their fate, hoping it's not so, that they can avoid the inevitable. But endings come for everything.

Even stars.

He's in his room right now. After dinner, I didn't hear the door shut or his feet creak on the stairs; I never do. All the same, I know he's in his room. He never stays up very late anymore.

I'm sure he probably wants to get good rest, even though, as far as I understand, his journey won't tax him any tomorrow. I imagine he'll have a full day ahead of him, though, attending to whatever it is his country needs him so badly for.

I shouldn't bother him. I certainly shouldn't knock on his door and risk waking him up. Besides, what would I say? I had countless opportunities for meaningful conversation and allowed them all to flit away, too scared to reach out and grab one. Tonight won't be any different.

Tomorrow, he leaves and walks into a war zone. The last war in the High Valleys was centuries and centuries ago, back when our people were all topsiders. All I can imagine of war is storybook depictions. Skies know what's waiting for him.

My fingers rub the shield charm of my necklace. Will he get hurt? Do princes in Morineaux lead their people to the battlefield? Perhaps, there's not a battlefield, though. That word he used—siege—I looked it up. It's different than the scene my mind conjures up of warriors fighting in sweeping valleys, two sides charging toward each other. Either way, there will be fighting, and he could be in the midst of it.

Tomorrow, he leaves. After that—

After that, I never see him again. After that, he's a prince a world away, and I'm a little foreign girl, scrubbing floors to get by. After that, I lose the last person that I'm close to, that I can rely on.

After that, I'm alone.

Well, not entirely alone; I'm sure Idyne will come with me, whether I like it or not. I'm scared to do anything else than pretend I do. I'm also developing a sinking feeling Jacin will tag along too. I should be grateful—I'm sure I'll need them, navigating a strange land with no weapons but improvisation and intelligence. Even so, dread hangs in my bones.

Tomorrow, he leaves, and I'll never see him again. Which means I can't let him slip away without at least saying goodbye. After all, this could be my last chance to talk to him. No matter if I'm waking him up, no matter if it won't change anything, I just can't.

I cross the hall and rap on his door.

There's a pause, and I wonder if I should knock again. I really don't want him to tell me to go away. Maybe he won't. Maybe he's asleep. Maybe I should say something—

Aster opens the door, tucking away a handkerchief. "Leavi." He seems surprised to see me, like I'm an apparition that showed up instead of the girl who lives just across the hall.

"Aster." More words mean to follow but get stuck in my throat, and we're left staring at each other in the hazy moonlight streaming in from his window. There's something in his eyes, an encrypted message swirling in the depths, but I have no key.

He clears his throat self-consciously. "What do you need?"

"I-" *Skies, I don't know how to start. Why didn't you come up with that before you knocked, stupid girl?* "I just came to wish you luck. For tomorrow," I clarify, internally cringing as soon as the words leave my mouth.

"Ah." He doesn't seem to know what to say for a moment. "Thanks," he adds a second later.

"You're welcome." I offer a stiff nod. *You're welcome? Leavi, just talk to him!* "Do you," I start nervously, "look forward to it? Getting home, I mean?" The question hangs between us in the quiet half-light.

"Of course." His words hold no excitement, just a cold sincerity. "I'll be glad to fulfil my duty."

My head tips to the side. "That's all there is to it? Duty?" He hesitates, and I say, "You don't miss your home?"

"Yes. Of course I do." For the first time, a little bit of passion bleeds into his speech. "N'veauvia is beautiful, and the people are wonderful."

Despite the praise, he still seems like he's holding something back, hiding something. My brows draw together. "You sound more like an unsure tour guide than a homesick native."

He chuckles, but it sounds forced. "It is hard to describe the city."

"I didn't ask you to describe it." My eyes search his. "I asked if you missed it."

"I do. I was just trying, and failing apparently, to express what I missed." His feet shift.

261

I should go, let him get to sleep, but for some reason, I can't leave. There's something off here, a mystery, and it bothers me that I can't put it together. "I see."

I know he's hiding something, but I can't bring myself to ask about it directly. It's not my place to press even if it sounds like he's trying to convince himself more than me.

I change tack, trying to keep our teetering conversation from falling. "Whatever will you do without the, ah… wonderful decorations the Kitten has to offer?" I chuckle awkwardly, gesturing to his room.

He smiles thinly. "I guess I'll figure something out."

"I doubt your castle can provide such interesting scenery," I say as straight-faced as I can manage.

He nods solemnly. "The reaching views and ornate architecture will never compare." He seems to think of something, and his barely concealed smile falls.

"What?" I ask softly, setting my hand on his doorframe

He doesn't look me in the eyes. "I'm not sure what you're asking about."

I study his face, the slight downturn to his lips, the heaviness to his shoulders. No one has that kind of weight on them without an idea of how it got there. "I think you do."

His eyes shoot to meet my gaze, one eyebrow tipping up. "Pardon?"

"I think you do know what I'm talking about." The pieces of the mystery—his hesitation, shaky denials, thin facade—all click together, and before my brain can override my mouth, I blurt, "You don't really want to go back, do you?"

"Of course I do," he stutters. "It's my home."

I step into his doorway. "Some people don't want to go home."

I expect him to back up, but he holds his ground, us just inches apart. His eyes close, the first crack in his facade appearing. "It's not that I don't want to go home."

My fingers come to rest lightly on his shoulder. "Then what is it?"

His eyes open, and his lips fumble for a response. "Nothing," he finally manages, slipping his shoulder out from under my hand. "Nothing's wrong."

Letting my hand drop, I insist, "Then why don't you want to go back?"

"Leavi, I-" He takes a deep breath. "I do."

"Really? Then tell me one thing you're looking forward to—*actually* looking forward to."

His hands explode outwards. "You want me to name something good about the war in my homeland, the war that I'm not prepared to lead, that I-" He runs a hand through his hair. "What do you want, Leavi?" He pins me with his gaze, pain haunting it.

My heart aches for him. In that moment, if I could take all his pains and fears and put them on myself, I swear I would. "I just want you to be happy, Aster."

He turns away. "That's not what matters."

I catch his wrist, and his troubled eyes meet mine. "How can it not matter?" I exclaim.

He shakes me off, turning toward the window again. "Because there are more important things than just me."

I circle around in front of him. "Like what?" I demand.

"Like the welfare of my country! I have a job to do, duties to fulfil. People depend on me, and I'm not there!"

262

"Let someone else do it!"

"It doesn't work like that."

"If you don't want to go back, you shouldn't have to!"

"What do you expect me to do, Leavi?"

"Stay here, if that's what you want!"

"And abandon my people?"

"And live your life," I challenge.

"My country is my life. I've always known that."

"And I always knew I was going to be a scientist that never stepped foot out of the High Valleys!" I gesture to the room. "Things change, Aster. Sometimes the world intervenes, but sometimes we have to change them. This is your chance. This is your choice. Please don't let anybody else choose for you."

His eyes study my face, frustration trapped within their wells. His voice dissolves into a pained whisper. "What do you want me to tell you, Leavi?"

He's going to go back. I know, deep inside me, that I'm not going to change his mind, I'm not going to convince him to choose for himself. The boy in front of my is far too selfless for that. But I don't want him to be. Just this one time, I wish he wouldn't do the right thing.

Tell me that you don't have to go, I want to say. Tell me you want to travel with me, to find somewhere big and busy and interesting like we both like and live there for a little while. Tell me if we get bored there, that we can leave together. Tell me we can stay friends, and that you don't have to leave. Tell me I can save you from your prisons and find you ways to the impossible places you want to go. Tell me you'll always watch out for me when I get in over my head and catch me when I fall off roofs.

My stomach wrenches, and a strange electricity prickles in my veins. An orb of silver light materializes in between us. It expands and spirals up, giving form to a long-haired girl no larger than my thumb. She extends her arm, and a boy appears beside her. He takes her hand, and they stride forward, his cloak billowing behind him.

Then the lights break apart into dozens of separate streams, swirling around each other to reform the two figures, foreheads pressed together, hands clasped between them. Behind them, smaller lights form a city skyline. They wisp apart again and come back together, this time showing the girl falling backward. The boy catches her waist and pulls her close against him. He holds her there, safe.

My mouth gapes. That couldn't have been me. I didn't even say anything, don't even have his Book or powder or instructions—

Aster's eyes are wide. Before either of us can say a word, the images fade out of view, almost as if they were never there at all, and the odd energy I felt disappears with them.

My head is spinning, heart hammering, mind looking from some sort of answer, and my eyes turn up to find his.

He pauses, seemingly as shocked by the display as I. He replies slowly. "I'm so sorry. I—I'm sorry. I didn't mean to-" He shakes his head. "I can't do this. I can't say goodbye to you." He leaves. Pushes around me and, as silent as ever, hurries down the stairs.

I stare after him in open-mouthed shock. *I can't say goodbye to you.* What is that supposed to mean?

A horrible thought occurs to me. He's going to disable the portal.

I may want him to stay, but I want *him* to want it, to fully, completely, rationally want it. Not to fly off and do something he'll regret by morning.

He's too good-hearted to be happy serving his own desires.

"Stupid, stupid boy," I curse. I fly down the stairs, but by the time I reach the bottom, he's already gone. I rush outside, the door banging behind me. Crisp air nips at my face, but I ignore its sting. My feet carry me through the woods, across the dead farmer's field, into the husk of a house.

In the living room, the portal floats around the pearl suspended in its center, untouched. Wispy blue lights swirl around it like a living thing. *So he hasn't tampered with it.*

Maybe he doesn't know how to. Idyne does, though. To my knowledge, she's at the inn.

I run back the way I came and burst into the Kitten. Searching, I sweep through the house, but there's no sign of her or Aster. My frenzied mind forces me back outside, but the empty clearing and treeline are all that greet me. "Aster!" I call, looking around. *Where could he have gone?* "Aster!" I yell again.

Against the snow, my voice sounds dead in my own ears, and I earn no response. I circle the house, then venture as far as the edge of the woods, peering against the dark for any sign of him. My search reveals nothing. Frustrated, I shout, "Where are you, you stupid boy?" Stupid, kind, sweet, loyal boy.

Receiving no answer, I kick at the snow, its flakes spraying up in the air, further drenching my already soaked socks. Vaguely, I realize that I never put on shoes.

He has to be out here somewhere. All he has is that stupid cloak to keep him warm, and he doesn't have any food, and if he gets lost…

"Stupid, *stupid* boy," I mutter, making my way back to the porch steps. I wait.

Snow falls from the sky like sticky popped corn, speckling my hair and gathering on my skin. I pull my arms around me.

"I didn't mean to do this, Aster," I whisper to the empty air. "I'll learn to keep my mouth shut one day, I promise." A bitter laugh escapes my lips. "One day."

Eternity could pass by in this snowstorm, and I would miss it. There's just the cold, my tingling skin, and my eyes, searching. Waiting.

At some point, someone appears at the treeline, and I brush the flakes out of my face, trying to get a closer look. It's not Aster, though.

Idyne hurries over to me, concern filling her features. "Leavi, what are you doing out here?" Her hands move up and down my arms, trying to warm me up.

"Just waiting." My voice sounds oddly flat in my own ears, but I can't work up the will to inject any energy into it. Then my eyes light, thinking. "You haven't seen Aster, have you?"

"Um… no."

"Oh." I hunch in on myself again, disappointed. After a second, realizing I probably owe Idyne some modicum of conversation, I use my head to gesture toward the door. "You should probably go inside. It's late."

"I could say the same to you!"

I shake my head. "I'm waiting up for Aster."

"Well, you can wait inside."

"No," I explain quietly. "I should-"

"Where you won't freeze to death," she finishes. "Now come on." She pulls me to my feet despite my protests. "You can just as easily stare at the treeline from the window inside."

She drags me to the hearth, stripping off my wet socks and bringing me blankets. A mug of something warm is placed into my hands. My body sets to tingling, that burning, spiking sensation you only get after being in the cold too long and coming back to the heat.

Honestly, I think I preferred the numbness of outside. My thoughts are gearing back to life, but I don't want them to.

Because there's another explanation to his statement from earlier, other than that he decided he wasn't going to leave.

He simply doesn't want to see me, doesn't want to say the word 'goodbye.'

And that's okay. I'll honor his wishes. After all, maybe it's better this way. Easier.

After I'm warmed up, I go to my room. It's been a long night. I don't think I'll make it up in time to see him off tomorrow.

Chapter 73

ASTER

The moonlight reflects off the snow, tinting the world with an ethereal silver glow.

It's too peaceful compared to the turmoil inside me. My mind rages against itself, and my emotions war each other. Above it all, anger at myself reigns.

I shouldn't be so reluctant to go home, to serve my country, to lead the people I love. I shouldn't have allowed myself to become so attached to the people here.

In the darkness, the forest trees around me look like skeletal dancers outfitted in shining ice. I clear the snow away in a large enough circle for me to sit and cast the temperature adjustment spell. My fingers drag the chalk against the frozen ground, scraping out a circle inch by inch. I raise the temperature within my little circle just enough so that the cold stops biting my skin and numbing my bones. That's all I can manage.

I don't want to say goodbye to Leavi. It's stupid, but I can't. I can't acknowledge to her that we will never see each other again, that even if we somehow do, I would never be allowed to have anything to do with her.

Agraund's oft-repeated words echo in my head: *princes of Morineaux do not associate with lowly serving girls.*

I'm never going to see him again, either. My uncle, my master, the man who all but raised me—is dead. I set my jaw against the emotion trying to rise within me. Now I'm the one Morineaux expects to lead their wizards, and I'm not even there. Despair and frustration threaten to overtake me.

"Why can't I do anything right?" I yell at the trees. "Why does each decision I make only make things worse? Why-" My voice cracks, and I fold in on myself.

My country is in danger.

My uncle is dead.

My people need me.

Instead of being there, doing what I need to, I'm moping in a freezing forest like the dimwit I am.

I straighten.

Yes, my situation is bad. Yes, I'm going to have to spend the rest of my life as nothing but a pawn for Morineaux's well-being. Yes, I'm going to be eternally surrounded by sickly sweet courtiers trying to carve their way up the political ladder.

Despite that, I *have* a place. I might not be good enough, but I'm the best they have; I'm more acquainted with the laws of our land, with magic theory, with strategy than almost anyone in the corps.

I can lead them. I *will* lead them. My magic might not be as strong as it should be, but I will be the Second Son they need—and I will lead them well.

Tomorrow, I cross half the continent in one step.

Tomorrow, I take on the role of the Second Son of the Court.

Tomorrow, I forget the mistakes I've made here.

Tomorrow, I take care of my land and my people. I do whatever I need to. I become whoever I need to.

Tomorrow, I make my country all that matters to me.

Chapter 74

LEAVI

The voices downstairs are hard to ignore. I can't tell what they're saying, but I can imagine. *Good luck. Have a safe trip.* Marcí probably says that bit. She doesn't know that he's not really traveling after all. *We'll miss you. Best wishes.* He'll look around because everyone's down there but me, or maybe he won't; I suppose it really doesn't matter. Life will resume as normal.

Except I'm not sure what normal is supposed to be. After all, we've been stuck in a sort of limbo for a while, waiting to see when Aster would get better, when the snow would clear up, when the portal would finish. I suppose he's been fine for a while now, though. Besides, Sean braved it through the snow; I guess we might have been able to as well.

I just didn't want anything to change. Which is ridiculous.

Get your head out of the clouds, Eleaviara! My mother's voice echoes in my head. *Nothing worth pursuing is up there. You need to focus on the real world. That's the only place you're going to find purpose. Stop daydreaming, stop playing pretend and chasing after boys, and start getting serious. It's high time you acted like an adult.*

It was only three days after that lecture I found out I had miraculously earned a job I hadn't applied for in a city where I didn't want to be.

Maybe that's what I needed, though—*need*, now. A change of scenery. A purpose. A place in the real world. It's time I stop mooching off Marcí, stop hiding in the inn, and start acting like an adult. It's time to move on. Since Morineaux's at war now, I'm not sure where we'll go, but wherever it is, it's waiting for us. I'm done standing still.

For some reason, though, my newfound resolve fails to pull me out of bed.

Downstairs, the door shuts, and my heart drops. He's gone. Headed to the farmhouse, feet crunching across the snow, cowl surely pulled against the cold. In a few minutes, he'll be halfway across the world.

I'll never see him again.

Stupid girl, why didn't you swallow your pride and just go say goodbye? My feet long to jump up and chase him down, but if he doesn't want to say goodbye, I'm not going to force him to. I'll regret it by tonight, but by then, it'll be too late. And that's okay. That's the way he wants it.

I try to tell myself it doesn't matter, because honestly, it really, really doesn't. That's what my mother would say if she were here. She had a way of cutting to the reality of a situation. Maybe that's what I need—a little more reality, a little less feeling, a lot less imagining what could have been.

Because what I want—wanted—doesn't matter now. My feelings have no bearing on reality, and it is contemptuously absurd to expect them to. My mother spent sixteen years trying to drill that into my head, and I was too hard-headed to believe her until now. He's gone, or about to be. Last night was the last time I'll ever see him. These are the facts, this is reality, and reality must be accepted. Anything else is pointless.

My heart still aches.

I bury into my pillows and blankets, finding comfort in their cozy warmth. I feel like a little kid, ignoring the outside world in favor of a few more minutes of sleep and dreams. Any second, I imagine my father coming in to shake me awake, gently pulling me out of bed to keep my mother from shouting up the stairs again. But I'm a million miles away from that bed, that home, that city, and I'm not getting back.

I'm a foreigner in a foreign land, and the person I hoped would be my guide is gone. Now I don't know where to go, *can't* go anywhere, for fear of taking a misstep. *How pathetic are you, Leavi? Get a grip. Get up.* But I have yet to move.

Feet tap up the stairs. Figuring it's just Zena, I don't bother rising. I could still do with a couple more hours of sleep. Last night's rest was fitful at best.

My door opens. Idyne calls, "Leavi?"

I glance up, startled. Idyne runs over to me, grabbing my hand and tugging me out of bed. In one breath, she says, "I have a way to get you through the portal, and I changed it last night after you went to bed, and then I passed out and just woke up, but you have to leave *now*."

She's trying to drag me out of the room, but I stop. "Wait, wait, wait. I don't know what you're saying, Idyne. Slow down."

She huffs. "I can't. Not if you want to get to Morineaux! I passed Aster on the way here; once he's through, the portal will close in minutes. For good. And then I'll have wasted my charm for nothing. Come *on*."

Letting go of my hand, she snatches up my bag and heads out the door.

Bewildered, I hurry after her. "Hold up. Are you saying I can go with him?"

"Are you just now catching on?" She quick-steps down the stairs, and I follow.

"I thought you said only two people could go through!"

"I *changed* the spell. Okay?" She hits the landing and shoves my bag into my arms. "I have to get my things. And Jacin. Now *go*. Hopefully we'll see you on the other side."

She nudges me forward, and I stumble. Numbed realization is clicking in my mind. I can go with Aster. That's what she's telling me. We don't have to say goodbye.

I run.

I snag my boots from the door, but don't waste time putting them on. I'm barefoot in the snow, but I don't care. I'm running as fast as I can, branches whipping past my face, twigs tugging at my hair. I stumble over a rock and go flying. Face-first in the snow, the cold tingles through my body. I shove back to my feet and am off again.

I break through the treeline. The farmhouse appears before me, and I dash through its field. The door slams against the wall as I burst in. "Aster!" I call.

No one answers.

The flat, blue disk of the portal faces me. Its surface no longer calmly swirls, but instead ripples in angry, chaotic waves. In the center of the portal, flecks of Idyne's pearl break off to be carried along by the waves. Half the pearl is already gone, with more dissolving by the second.

The turbulent waters give me pause. I don't really know what lies on the other side of this strange pool of angry, gravity-defying water. The best-case scenario is Aster, and Morineaux, and war. The worst-case scenario?

Maybe the portal breaks me apart, just like that pearl, and swirls me around its waters. Maybe I go through and wind up in one of those 'locked rooms' Aster talked about, like the Meadow. Maybe I go in but never come back out.

Maybe I die.

Rationally, I know the most reasonable, logical option is to stay here, to play by the rules of reality and avoid this perversion of the natural world's laws. To play it safe.

But I know just as much that I want more than that. Despite knowing nothing of what will happen next, what might become of me, or if Aster, being as important as he is, will even give me a second glance, I want to step through. I want to chase him down and tell him we don't have to say goodbye, not unless he wants to. I want to see Morineaux, see N'veauvia, and hope it's something like my old home. I know it will be strange, I know it will be foreign, but I want to learn. I'm ready to move on; I'm done being stuck.

The pearl is rapidly disappearing. Eyes closed, I dive into the blue.

End of
Book One

Glossary and Pronunciation Guide

Note: "zh" refers to a sound most people don't make in native English words. It's somewhere between a "j" and a "sh" sound. For an example, consider the "g" in the word "menagerie."

Character Names

Agraund – *[Uh - **grawnd**]*

Amarris Veradeaux – *[Uh - **mair** - is **Vair** - uh - doh]*

Aster Jacques – *[As - ter Zhawks]*

Bukki Dae – *[Buh - **kee** Day]*

Eleaviara "Leavi" Riveirre – *[Uh - **lee** - vee - ar - ah "**Lee** - vee" Ri - **vair**]*

Idyne – *[Uh - **deen**]*

Jacin Jazere – *[**Jay** - sin Juh - **zeer**]*

Jeanna – [**Zhee** - nuh]

Marcí Dae – *[Mar - **see** Day]*

Markus Delroy – *[**Mar** - kiss **Del** - roy]*

Ren – *[Rin]*

Sean Rahkifellar – *[Shawn **Rawk** - i - fel - er]*

Sela – *[**See** - luh]*

Tavion Zahir – *[**Taw** - vee - on Za - heer]*

Ufir – *[Oo - **feer**]*

Zena Delroy – *[Zee - nuh Del - roy]*

Places and Peoples

Avadel *[A - vuh - del]* – the land that contains the five countries (Morineaux, Bedeveir, Kadran, Draó, and Retra). Those that live there consider it all the known world, while those who live in the High Valleys only know Avadel as "the Outerlands."

Bedeveir *[Bed - uh - vair]* – a country in southern Avadel. Borders Morineaux and Draó.

Draó *[Dray - oh]* – a region in the middle of Avadel, bordering all the countries [except the High Valleys, which is not considered one of the "countries" of Avadel]. Draó is a collection of small states called "lordships" typically at war with each other. The Kuddly Kitten is located in a more stable part of northern Draó.

Erreliah *[Er - rel - ee - ah]* – the capitol of the High Valley's underground peoples. A hub of scientific research and intellect, as well as Leavi's home city.

Kadran *[Kuh - drawn]* – a barbarian country in northern Avadel. Borders Retra and Draó.

Karsix *[Kar - six]* – a medium-sized underground city in the High Valleys. Ground zero for the Blistering Death. Home to Trifexer's Institute for Research and the Sciences, Leavi and Sean's workplace at the start of the story.

Morineaux *[Mor - i - noh]* – "the home of magic." Morineaux is the largest and most powerful country in Avadel, as well as Aster's home country. It lays in southern Avadel, bordering Bedeveir and Draó.

Niv *[Niv]* – a small village in northernmost Draó. Home of the Veradeaux Manor and The Kuddly Kitten.

N'veauvia *[Nuh - voh - vee - uh]* – the capitol of Morineaux, as well as Aster's home city. It is constructed with three walls, the first circling the bulk of the city, the second encompassing the rich district, and the third surrounding the castle itself.

Retra *[Ray - truh]* – a country in eastern Avadel. Borders Kadran and Draó.

The Docks – a less reputable part of the city of Erreliah, home to cheap inns, sleazy taverns, gambling, and parties.

The High Valleys – a massive and remote mountain range (including the caves) that Leavi and Sean hail from. They are geographically and culturally isolated from Avadel. The people that live there believe the world is entirely covered in mountain. The range lays in the northernmost part of Avadel.

The Kuddly Kitten – a small, eccentric inn in northern Draó. Run by Marcí Dae and her husband, Bukki.

The Outerlands – the land outside of the High Valleys. Considered mythical by most of those who live in the Valleys, it actually is the home to five different countries (Avadel).

The Traders – a group of nomadic peoples who serve as traveling merchants in the High Valleys.

Topsiders – the people that live above ground in the High Valleys. Poor and simple people (mostly farmers) who are technologically behind the underground science.

Undergrounders – the people that live below ground in the High Valleys. Very technologically advanced compared to the rest of the world.

Veradeaux Manor *[Vair - uh - doh]* – the center of all activity in the village near the Kuddly Kitten. Owned by Amarris Veradeaux, a former lady of the Morineause court.

Xela *[Zee - luh]* – a topside village in the High Valleys. Sean's hometown.

Errelian Words
the language of the High Valley undergrounders

aehrixi *[aw - er - ix - ee]* – the group of animals that fly (birds, flying insects, bat, etc.)

alkemi *[al - kuh - mee]* – the study of alkemetic substances, also known as chemicals, and how they combine

amura *[ah - moor - ah]* – an feeling that occurs when one experiences two conflicting emotions at the same time so that the brain registers them as pain

doktor *[dawk - toor]* — a title given to a person with several (typically eight) years of specialized study in a scientific field. The second highest level of academic distinction possible, topped only by 'professor' (a person with a doktorate who teaches and has released more than one academic paper).

gihseirre *[gis - sair]* — something

mastera *[Ma - stair - uh]* – a title given to a woman with several (typically six) years of specialized study in a scientific field. Compare "Master" for males.

mentaliti *[men - tal - i - tee]* – the study of the mind

vihnzeirre *[vin - zair]* – trickster

vitaliti *[vi - tal - i - tee]* – the study of living things

Common Words
the language of the High Valley topsiders, including the Traders

Ach escherisch *[osh esh - er - ish]* — Who are you?

Ufir *[Oo - feer]* — leader

Morineause Words
the official language of Morineaux

azhiet-friae *[ah - zhee - ay free - ay]* — Revenge, specifically long-planned and strong revenge; lit. 'cold plate'.

Laeazí *[lay - ah - zee]* — Meadow

mae *[may]* — my. It may be connected to a word in front of it.

maedame *[may - dahm]* — honorific title for a married or wealthy woman who is not nobility; lit. 'my dame'.

maedimoiselle *[may - dee - moh - sehl]* — polite title for a young, unmarried woman; lit. 'my little dame'.

maejuer *[may - zhoor]* – polite title for a man who is not nobility; lit. 'my sir'.

Old Tongue Words
the dead language that magicians use to cast spells

Note: As no living wizard currently understands the literal meaning of the Old Tongue words, these have been translated for what spells they are related to instead of their meanings.

ahresåe *[aw - ray - saw - ay]* – the first word to the scrying spell

Airesë asjault erræ *[Air - ays - e ahs - jolt air - ra]* – the command to release the hidden door in the castle wall

Et væ *[Et va]* – the command for the telekinesis spell

exairêt *[ayx - air - ay]* – part of the freezing spell

fiärvir *[fee - awr - veer]* – part of the freezing spell

retiræ *[ret - eer - ra]* – part of the freezing spell

Vîc å rêarre. De viêt, de vaö, de vis *[veek aw ray - ar. Day vee - ay, day va - ay, day vihs]* – the command for the color change spell

Acknowledgments

First, thanks be to God because outside of Him, we can't do anything. He made this book possible and watched out for us every step of the way. Even through the struggles, so many things perfectly fell into place that we never could have planned (and occasionally, that we were actively trying to avoid. Funny how that works). He is so much wiser than we could ever hope to be, and we owe everything to Him.

Secondly, a huge thank you to our parents, who not only encouraged us, but also toned down our workaholic tendencies and put up with our constant planning, in-book talk, and requests for them to weigh in their opinion. A special thanks to Dad, who helped us hammer out Aster's first chapter, and to Mom, who gave us the spelling for Leavi's name. You two are the best!

To our Wattpad friends:
Kellie Bowe, who heavily edited several chapters for a couple of random strangers. She gave us our first (and much needed) real dose of constructive criticism and changed our writing forever.

B. M. Hurst, our first and most enthusiastic beta reader. She encouraged us when we weren't sure anything we were saying made sense and kept us writing when we didn't feel like posting a new chapter. We love you, 'Rowan.'

Phoebe Lynch (@lionobsession) with the eagle-eye for unnecessary 'And's; Ethan DyTioco (@DeltaTangoEthan) for the helpful—and hilarious—reader response; K. E. Smith, who lent us her attention to detail; I. W. J. Keller for showing us what to cut; and everyone else who read, commented, and voted. You were our first audience, and we appreciate you more than you can know.

Also, thanks to everyone who let us pitch this book to them and talk about it more than we probably should have. Your excitement kept us excited.

Lastly, thank *you*, our readers. Thank you for making it all the way through this mess and sticking with Leavi, Sean, and Aster through their journey. You all mean the world to us.

May your skies stay bright.
   - *Laine and Aria Nichols*

About the Authors

Laine and Aria Nichols are a pair of fantasy geeks who spend far more time with their heads in the clouds than with their feet on the ground. They live somewhere in the United States but are more often found on the internet reading, writing, and Googling funny cat memes.

Find out more at https://www.wattpad.com/user/avadel, email them at avadelauthors@gmail.com, or follow "Of Caverns and Casters" on Facebook.

51693534R00171

Made in the USA
Columbia, SC
23 February 2019